The Last MacKlenna

The Celtic Brooch Series, Book 2

Katherine Lowry Logan

Print Edition

This book is a work of fiction. The characters and names are entirely the product of the author's imagination and there are no references to real people. Actual establishments, locations, public and business organizations are used solely for the intention of providing an authentic setting, and are used fictitiously. Any resemblance to actual events, locales, or persons, living or dead, is entirely coincidental.

Cover art by Damonza
Interior design by BB eBooks

Website: www.katherinellogan.com

Dedicated To

My sisters-in-law who battled breast cancer during the writing of this book,

Donna Conley Lowry & Rhonda Jean McMillin Lowry

~*~

In Memory Of

My sister-in-law

Sarah Manning Lowry

who lost her valiant twelve-year battle with breast cancer on October 29, 2012

and

My mother,

Anne Lyle Poe Lowry Brown

October 1, 1926-June 30, 2013

Part I

Chapter One

Montgomery Winery, Napa Valley, California – December 21

MEREDITH MONTGOMERY FLOATED above the ground as she ran. She didn't bounce. She glided with perfect form, using her energy to propel herself forward, watching the horizon like a rock-steady pan-cam in a movie.

The worn path snaked through ten thousand acres of Montgomery Winery's dormant vines. She tried to push her stress and fear aside to enjoy the sense of well-being that came with running. Today it wasn't working for her. There were too many items on her to-do list. Number one had her stomach tied into triple knots. As soon as she got home, she'd check off the item, not because she wanted to, but because she had no choice.

It was a matter of life or death.

That sounded divaesque. The Lord knew she wasn't a diva, but she *was* a breast cancer survivor. To most women like her, monthly breast self-exam day was a big deal, and she performed it religiously. She raced forward, trying to suppress her fear. Unfortunately, that didn't work for her either.

The Italian-style villa where she'd lived for most of her life came into view. She sprinted the last quarter mile toward the residence that had perched on top of a private knoll for more than a century. The sun glinted off the copper gutters and the gold streaks in the Portuguese limestone walls. The estate vineyards that surrounded the villa showed rows of bare trellising. Wild mustard flowers wouldn't bloom among the vineyards for another couple of months. By March, they would awaken and begin to bud. The new growing season filled her with hope and renewal every year. This year even more so.

When she hit the driveway, she slowed to a walk and checked the time. The unplanned nine-miler put her behind schedule on a day packed with appointments. If her assistant couldn't rearrange her commitments, Meredith's afternoon flight to Scotland looked dicey.

She entered the house through the kitchen, grabbed her iPhone off the counter, and snatched a bottle of chocolate milk from the refrigerator. The phone's home screen listed several text messages marked urgent.

"So what's new?"

The master winemaker needed to meet with her. She wiped sweat from her forehead and neck, thinking. The results of the field trials were in, and he wanted to start a vineyard on the south-facing slope. He had yet to get his one-track mind around the fact that launching *Cailean,* the winery's new chardonnay, was too important to be sidetracked by a new project. What would an expansion mean for the winery? If he could develop a new vineyard without draining resources, she might agree. But that was a huge *might.*

The breast exam needed to wait five more minutes while she forced herself to stretch. She hated stretching. Instead, she took two yoga classes a week. The odds of finding a class in Edinburgh over the holidays seemed unlikely. So she stretched, hating every minute. She didn't have time to waste. Not today.

In the bathroom, soaked clothes fell into a pile at her feet. She kicked them aside and stepped into streams of hot water pulsating from top and side-mounted jets. Her schedule for the next few hours came into focus. *Ask Cate to confirm the reservations at the B&B in Edinburgh and the National Archives.*

Meredith lifted her left arm and placed her hand behind her head. The soapy pads of three fingers rotated up and down her breast, using overlapping dime-sized circular motions, feeling for lumps in the soft tissue. *Get the agenda for the meeting with the web designer.* Her fingers traced the same path they had followed every month since cancer took her other breast. *Call Hank to find an exercise rider for Quiet Dancer while I'm—*

Her hand froze. Fear, bitter and fire-hot, coated her tongue.

Do it again.

She retraced the edges of a lump. An irregular-shaped one she would never have discovered without being extra sensitive to the feel of her small breast. Dizzy and tingling, she gulped in lungfuls of air and clutched her chest with a trembling hand.

Do it again.

The lump remained—hard and rooted in the breast. The floor buckled beneath her feet. Her vision blurred. Shampoo and soap bottles became little more than blotches of white and pink and yellow. The clammy wall slapped her back, and she slumped against the marble. *Snap* went the tether to her anchor, sending her sliding down the wall and into despair.

Not again. Please, not again.

Time stopped. Nothing existed but heart-racing fear. The water turned lukewarm, yet she remained in a stupor. When the water turned cold and she still hadn't moved, a voice tunneled through the haze. *Move your ass. Now.* The internal voice had pushed her through endless training miles, five marathons, and cancer surgery. It had also kept her company during the bleak days at her late husband's bedside and the final hours with her father. She never ignored it, and she never, ever quit.

The voice cranked her up the wall, vertebra by vertebra, until she came to her feet, grabbing the lever handles as if they were lifelines. She turned off the tepid water.

The phone rang, shrill and intruding. Meredith stumbled out of the shower stall, cupping her breasts. God made one; man made the other. While it wasn't a bad imitation, it had scars and a fake nipple.

The answering machine picked up, and her executive assistant left a message. "You're probably in the shower. I was tracking you on MapMyRun. Why'd you do a long run today? That'll put you behind schedule. Let me know if you want to postpone the ten o'clock media call. That newspaper reporter is still stomping through the vineyard hoping to be the first to write a review of *Cailean.* Call me."

Meredith lifted a heated towel from the warmer and dried off, patting her breast, nice and easy. "The winery is all that matters," her father had said. "Put it first and everything else will fall into place."

Will it, Daddy?

When the flow of tears slowed, she squared her shoulders and called her assistant.

"Hey, why'd you run this morning?" Cate asked. "It's a rest day."

"Jet lag messes with my schedule." An icy finger traced Meredith's spine as she debated whether to tell Cate about the lump. *Not this time.* It was more important to keep her assistant focused on the launch than to confide in a friend.

Meredith snugged the warm towel around her, comforted by the heat. "I'll get there before the conference call, but I might need to delay my departure a few hours, maybe forty-eight." She grimaced, waiting for a barrage of questions.

In her trademark clipped voice, Cate asked, "Why? What happened? Are you hurt? You fell, didn't you? You reinjured your knee."

Meredith massaged the lump buried deep in her breast. "No, I didn't fall, and it's nothing that can't be fixed."

"Are you sure?" Cate asked.

Meredith took a shaky breath. A lie, no matter how small, was still a lie even if it was meant to protect someone. Her hand went to her face, close to her mouth. "Yes," she said with a muddled voice. She could be fixed, couldn't she? The doctors fixed her last time. Surgery and reconstruction, no chemo or radiation. If she had cancer again, treatment would go just as smoothly.

Chapter Two

Napa Valley Medical Clinic – December 22

MEREDITH SLAMMED THE outer door of the Napa Valley Medical Clinic with one hand and slipped on her sunglasses with the other. She didn't need glasses on the overcast day, but the shades hid her sunken, bruised-looking eyes caused by a crying jag and a sleepless night.

The fine needle aspiration was suspicious but not conclusive. The uncertainty created tension in her neck and an explosive headache. She had expected to get results before she left the doctor's office like she had five years earlier, but this time she had to wait on pathology to issue a report.

"You can stay home and fret over the holidays, Meredith, or you can go to Scotland," her doctor had said.

That's what she intended to do. Get the hell out of town. It didn't matter where in the world she was when the call came. The news would be the same, and odds were good she'd be alone regardless.

Her cell phone rang, flashing Cate's name. Meredith pasted a smile on her face, hoping it'd come through in her voice. "Hello."

"What'd you decide? Are you going or not?"

Meredith opened the car door and tossed her purse to the passenger's seat. "Heading to the airport now. Will you contact the B&B and let them know I won't be there until late?"

"I'll call before I leave," Cate said.

"I'm not even out of town and you're taking the day off?"

Cate huffed. "Yeah, right. I'm looking at the stack of work in my in-basket. You cleaned off your desk last night and put everything on mine."

Meredith climbed into the driver's seat and fastened her seat belt. "Not everything."

"Could have fooled me." Cate shuffled papers. "Oh crap. I spilled coffee." More papers shuffled and something hit the floor with a thud. "Okay, I've got your itinerary now. Yep. You're confirmed for a late arrival. Anything else you need before I go to the meeting?"

Meredith swallowed her second Aleve of the day with a swig from a bottle of water. The pinched nerve in her neck decided to act up and irritate her. She grabbed an instant cold pack from her purse, squeezed the sides together, shook it up, and the pack instantly turned cold. She tucked it into the collar of her sweater, pressing it against her neck. "I hope there aren't coffee stains on the letters I signed."

Cate chuckled. "If there are, I'll white out the stains."

Meredith started the engine and put the car in gear. "I should be going to that meeting. The latest slicks for the gala and the new website pages are ready for review. Chances are they've screwed them up."

Cate hissed, shuffling more papers. "That gorgeous picture of you that's on the cover of *Wine Digest* will be on the home page."

Meredith hit the brakes, stopping inches from a car backing up behind her. "Damn."

"Don't you want to use that picture?" Cate's tone fell squarely between disappointment and confusion.

Meredith said, "I'm sorry," but the driver only glared at her with beady eyes and flicked his middle finger against the window.

"Well, screw you, too," she said.

"*What?*" Cate snorted what sounded like a mouthful of coffee.

Meredith forced her fingers into a fist so she'd refrain from returning the driver's obscene gesture. "Whose idea was it to use that picture?" she asked.

"Are you mad at me?"

"I was talking to another driver. Tell me about the picture."

"Your marketing VP says you're beautiful and your face sells wine."

"Pshaw. You know what Daddy would say if he was still president."

"Oh, I can hear him now," Cate said. "'A skinny forty-two-year-old childless widow isn't the right image for my winery.' But he's dead, and your name is on the door to the president's office."

The memory of her father's thunderous voice and sharp-edged words sent a shiver in a death spiral down her spine. "I'll make the decision after I see the web pages. Email copies as soon as you get them."

"I will, but only if you relax. Take a few days off. Work twenty-two/six instead of twenty-four/seven. And quit worrying about what's happening here."

"I might as well stop breathing."

"At least then you'd rest. Your stomach is in more knots now than that Chinese butterfly knot work hanging on your wall."

"As soon as the launch is over, I promise to take a vacation."

"I'm marking out the last two weeks in February as we speak," Cate said.

"Well, I'm not on vacation yet." *And I'll probably spend those two weeks in the hospital.* Meredith pulled out of the parking lot and headed toward the highway. "Call Hank and tell him I'll be gone a few days. If I call him now, he'll be between lessons and will keep me on the phone. Ask him to find someone to ride Quiet Dancer. Also, call the florist. I ordered flowers for Daddy and Jonathan's graves. I want to be sure they're delivered to the cemetery before Christmas."

"Did that. Now, go to Edinburgh. And while you're there find a handsome, smooth-talking Scotsman and have fun."

"I haven't had time for fun in two years. Besides, there's an event to plan." *And a lump in my breast.*

Meredith dropped the phone into the console. Maybe after she completed the genealogy research at the archives in Edinburgh and drafted the Montgomery family history, she'd relax for a few hours and drive up to the Highlands. If she didn't get the material to the printer by deadline, the brochure would print without the winery's history. The 160th celebration deserved the best from her, even if she did have cancer.

She fished a rumpled to-do list from her pocket. The Springsteen contract and addendum were numbers one through five. As soon as she boarded the plane, she'd send the agent an email reminder to return the original signed documents. Panic could easily top her tension if she thought about all that could go wrong. The event had to be perfect in every detail.

Cailean wouldn't have a second chance to make a great first impression.

Chapter Three

Teterboro Airport, New Jersey – December 22

THE CHAUFFEUR DROVE the Lincoln Town Car onto the tarmac at Teterboro Airport in New Jersey and parked alongside MacKlenna Farm's Gulfstream. The driver stepped from the vehicle and opened the rear passenger door just as a cell phone beeped. Elliott connected the Bluetooth and answered, "Fraser."

"Galahad's still not on the ground," Harrison Roberts, the Thoroughbred farm's chief financial officer, declared in the nasal voice of one mired in the throes of a winter cold.

Elliott checked the time. "Where the hell's the plane? That stallion's been in the air over eighteen hours."

"I talked to the equine transportation manager at Prestige International. Air traffic control rerouted the plane due to weather."

Elliott's heart rate shot up as if he'd been sprinting. "To where? The South Pole? If the horse stays on that plane much longer, he'll get dehydrated."

"Galahad's made the trip before without side effects," Harrison said.

"New South Wales is too far to shuttle him." The harder Elliott's heart pumped the louder he spoke. "I don't give a damn if those bastards at Hazy Mountain Stud have Galahad covering a full book of mares. This is the last trip."

"There will be a battle over that." Harrison sneezed into the phone before continuing. "If you want the horse to be commercial, the stallion has to ship to the southern hemisphere."

The limo driver handed Elliott a pair of crutches. With a grimace, he put his left foot down on the rain-soaked tarmac and stood, bringing the right leg around slowly. Six narrow steps leading to the cabin door presented a challenge. The rain had stopped, thank God. Negotiating the stairs on crutches was difficult. The slippery surface made it even more so.

"We'll deal with the travel issue at the next shareholders' meeting. For now, keep heat on the people at Prestige. They're agents for both the Breeders' Cup and the Dubai World Cup. If anything happens to Galahad, I'll see that the company loses both contracts. If the pilot doesn't land that plane, we'll own shares in a sick horse or a dead one."

Elliott climbed the first step with his left foot, held the injured leg steady, and gave more than a little groan when pain lanced through his right side from toe to hip.

"You okay?" Another sneeze punctuated Harrison's question. "Sounds like those New York doctors are cutting you open without anesthesia." He laughed. "Should have stayed in Kentucky."

"Hell no, I'm not okay. I'm trying to get up the stairs. And I would have stayed if my doctor hadn't refused to operate again."

"Maybe you'll listen to your medical team this time."

"Shush." Elliott halted on the third step to readjust the crutches. The release instructions from New York-Presbyterian Hospital, folded up in his pocket, said to keep the leg immobile for four weeks. He hadn't lasted forty minutes. "Call Jim Manning. Tell him what's happening. I haven't reviewed Prestige's contract in a year. Get his opinion. I want to be clear on liability."

Harrison blew his nose. "Get on the plane. I'll call back after I talk to him."

Elliott ended the call, wondering if he should spray the device with a disinfectant.

His personal assistant/paramedic/flight attendant stood poised at the cabin door. "You need help, Boss?"

Elliott reached the last step. "Move aside." Kevin Allen made room in the passageway but still hovered. "Tell the captain I'm ready to depart." Elliott negotiated the narrow aisle toward the sofa where he sat back and elevated his leg.

The limo driver handed up a laptop case that Kevin stowed before giving a wave to the ground crew. He then secured the cabin door. "Want coffee?"

Elliott nodded, powered down the Bluetooth, and slipped the device into his shirt pocket. "What's the flight time?"

"We'll be in Edinburgh in eight hours." Kevin set a cup on the table next to the sofa. "This is the good stuff. Not like that weak hospital brew you've been drinking."

Elliott slipped his fingers around a mug sporting the new MacKlenna logo that incorporated Galahad's features. "Ye've made the last five days bearable."

"After four surgeries, I know the routine."

"Five." Elliott sipped the coffee. "If ye think I'm a bastard now, ye should've been around for the first one."

Kevin laughed. "I heard about the catheter incident."

"Whatever ye heard was not true."

"The story I got was that you woke up to find a twenty-year-old nurse about to insert a tube into your dick and you pissed yourself."

Elliott groaned. "That bloody hospital is an incubator for rumors."

Kevin headed toward the front of the plane to secure the aircraft for takeoff. "My source is reliable, Boss."

To be twenty-eight again. Although at fifty, Elliott kept a very active social life, but the stress of running a multimillion-dollar Thoroughbred breeding operation was hell on his blood pressure. His satellite phone rang, yanking him from his reverie. "Fraser."

"Manning's in court," Harrison said. "I left a message with his paralegal."

"If I need to return to Lexington, tell me now." Elliott didn't want to be in town for the holidays and the first anniversary of the deaths of Sean and Mary MacKlenna. They were not only the owners of the Thoroughbred farm, but Sean had been a lifelong friend.

"No reason to come back. There's nothing you can do to get your horse on the ground any sooner," Harrison said.

"What's the weather doing there?"

"They're predicting ice storms from Texas to Maine. If Kentucky's in the bull's-eye, our airport could close."

"Damn." Elliott glanced out the window. The plane was pushing back from the gate. "Call me as soon as ye learn anything." His gut told him to go home. The CFO was a jerk and overly critical with the staff. He'd made two costly mistakes recently. Leaving him in charge inspired Elliott with little to no confidence. Unfortunately, Harrison still had the support of the board of directors. Until that changed he'd keep the position.

Elliott tapped his fist on the sofa arm. If anything happened to his twenty-five-million-dollar Thoroughbred that insurance didn't cover, the farm could end up on the auction block.

Kevin picked up the half-empty coffee cup. "We're next in line. You'll need to buckle up." Elliott pulled the belt tight across his lap, and ten minutes after boarding, the plane lifted off. When the aircraft reached cruising altitude, Kevin returned with another cup of hot coffee and Elliott's briefcase. "Do you want to finish the syndication agreement we were working on in the hospital?"

"Why don't ye finish it? Ye know as much about it as I do," Elliott said. The lad was an equestrian and the son of an equine lawyer. He had an aptitude for grasping legal issues that on occasion surpassed Elliott's.

"The lawyers added stipulations that weren't in the last draft. I've marked them for your review."

Elliott blew out a long breath. There weren't enough hours in his day to get the work done even with a top-notch staff working their asses off. He opened the briefcase. Beneath the agreement was his goddaughter's journal. His fingertips brushed the smooth, brown leather binding. She had left it for him to read, but he hadn't and wasn't sure he ever would.

"You know, Boss, you should spend more time in the ICU. You get a break from work."

"But the work doesn't go away, and I detest hospitals." The ICU smells permeated his skin, and he couldn't rid himself of the fear of a tube stuck in his dick. He withdrew the agreement then snapped the briefcase closed and handed it back to Kevin. "Stash this in a closet." Elliott turned to page four of the contract.

Now, where was I?

Chapter Four

En Route to Louise's B&B, Edinburgh, Scotland – December 22

HOURS LATER, as the aircraft neared Edinburgh, Kevin interrupted Elliott. "We're forty-five minutes from landing. You want a drink?"

"No. Pain meds," Elliott said.

"Pull down your pants." A needle filled with pain medication appeared in Kevin's hand.

Elliott hissed as the needle punctured the skin. "Ye always know what's needed."

Kevin shrugged. "You pay me to know." He disposed of the needle. "You've got just enough time to wash up. A shaving kit and a change of clothes are in the lavatory, and a shower sleeve for your leg is hanging on a hook by the door."

Elliott scratched his whiskers. "Definitely need a wee shave."

"Buzz if you need help."

He hobbled to the lavatory at the rear of the plane for a hot shower and shave. Thirty minutes later, he dressed in a kilt and a navy cashmere V-neck sweater. There were pressed khakis hanging in the closet. Several had the right leg cut off to accommodate his post-surgery boot. But when he was home, like other Highlanders, he preferred to wear a kilt, regardless of the occasion.

As he clipped the iPhone on the waistband, he noticed an addition to the photomontage hanging on the wall—a glossy eight-by-ten of Wynonna Judd and his goddaughter, Kit MacKlenna. The photographer had snapped the picture during last year's Kentucky Derby breakfast held at the mansion. The day had been stellar, especially the eleventh race when the farm's three-year-old, Regal Now, won the first jewel of the Triple Crown.

God, he missed them—Kit, her parents Sean and Mary, and his da. Elliott's shoulders sagged a wee bit, then he stiffened. *Seasons of grief don't conform to expectations and automatically end after a certain length of time.* How many times had he heard his father say something similar? Too many to count.

"Want a whisky?" Kevin asked as Elliott exited the lavatory.

He shook his head. "Will ye get a bottle of the Bussiador from the cabinet? I want to give the wine to Louise."

Kevin lifted his eyebrow, slow and easy, shaking his head. "She loves that chardonnay. If she ever decides to branch out, I'd recommend a Montgomery wine from Napa or a Barolo wine from Northern Italy."

Elliott ran his tongue across his bottom lip in anticipation of opening the 1951 bottle of Macallan waiting for him in Louise's library. His father had paid an exorbitant amount for the bottle in 2010. Earlier in the year, he had given the whisky to Louise and asked her to save it for Elliott's fiftieth birthday. With Christmas three days away, it seemed appropriate to break the seal now.

"Louise will never accept that single malt, not wine, is created by God's kiss," he said.

"That's an argument you'll never win with her," Kevin agreed.

"I've never won that argument with any woman. If I ever find one who loves Scotland, horses, and a wee half when she's thirsty, I'll rearrange a corner of my life and squeeze her in." Elliott's phone rang, wiping the anticipated taste of whisky from his lips. "Fraser."

"It's Allie."

He heard a smile in his executive assistant's voice, and he breathed easy.

"Galahad's at the quarantine facility at LAX. Doc talked to the groom who traveled with him. He said Galahad passed manure and drank plenty of water during the flight. And he appeared fine when he got off the plane."

Relief welled inside Elliott. "Good. I'll send Doc an email." Elliott blew out a long thankful breath. "Call Tex's Charters to transport Galahad to Kentucky when he's released."

"That's the next call. I'll send a text as soon as he's home."

Elliott disconnected and stared out into the clear night sky. The flight path took the plane low over the Firth of Forth. Edinburgh stretched out from the northwest coast at Leith all the way to the castle in the city center and south of the city beyond. Scattered lights twinkled on the ground. The familiar punch of excitement hit low and deep and warmed his heart. Home and the offer of sweet refreshment lay ahead. Over the years, he'd flown into capital cities all around the world, but none compared to the beauty of the small capital of Scotland. Now that Galahad was safe, Elliott could put the stress of high-stakes Thoroughbred breeding and racing aside for a few days and relax. *Aye, I'm home.*

The aircraft shuddered as the pilot extended the landing gear and it locked in place.

"When are ye driving up to Fraser House?" Elliott asked Kevin.

"Since you don't need me tonight, I'll stay at the hotel with the rest of the crew and drive up tomorrow. But I'd like to return for the Hogmanay events."

"That's a New Year's celebration not to be missed. We'll work it out."

Wheels bumped against the runway. The engines roared as the captain reversed thrust and applied the brakes, slowing the plane. Then the pilot taxied the aircraft to a private hangar.

Kevin gazed out the window. "There's David's limo. He's got someone with him."

"His sister?"

"I've never met his sisters." Kevin's voice carried a note of disappointment. "I heard what David did in Afghanistan. He's a hero."

"Aye, but don't tell him." Elliott unbuckled the seat belt and glanced out the window. "That's the customs officer in the car." Elliott stuck his head into the flight deck. "Merry Christmas, lads."

"Merry Christmas, Dr. Fraser," the captain said. "The crew is staying in Edinburgh. We can leave within an hour or two if you need to change plans."

"Let's hope there's no emergency. See ye on the first."

Elliott cleared customs and thirty minutes later, David McBain drove the limo under the porte cochere of Louise's B&B. Elliott smiled when he spotted her at the door. "Did ye call Lou? She's usually not up this late."

"She wanted to know when the plane landed," David said.

Elliott crossed the cobbled drive, gritting his teeth with each swing of the crutches. He tightened his grip as he approached the three steps leading to the door. Thank God, the house had a lift or he'd never make it to his second-floor suite.

Louise welcomed him with a big smile and a kiss on the cheek. "Ye're a handsome devil, Elliott Fraser." She held him at arm's length and gave him a once-over. "The boot looks fetching with a kilt. Maybe yer tailor will make a cover using the Fraser tartan."

David entered the house with luggage under each arm. "Ye got him in the same room, Louise?"

"Aye, and the door's unlatched." She glanced outside. "Where's Kevin?"

"Staying at the hotel with the crew," Elliott said.

David disappeared up the wide, sweeping stairs instead of taking the elevator and returned a couple of minutes later. "If ye need me, send a text. I'm staying at my sister's."

Elliott patted his mate on the shoulder. "Ye've got one in every city in Scotland."

David slipped his phone out of his jacket pocket and glanced at his messages. "My *sister* in Edinburgh is wondering where I am." He put away his phone and donned his cap. "What time do ye want to leave for Inverness tomorrow?"

"I'll let ye know in the morning. I think Kevin is renting a car. He's going sightseeing. Ye'd think he'd never been across the pond before."

David's square-jawed face tightened; a telling gesture from a man who rarely telegraphed feelings through body language. "While ye were meeting with the customs inspector, the lad told me he was going for a pint with the university lassie he met last time he was on holiday."

Elliott shook his head, sighing. "Watch over him."

"If ye dinna," Louise said, poking David in the arm with her finger, "he'll get lifted by the police again."

David kissed Louise's cheek. "I'll go to the pub from here, m'lovely. But don't be surprised if I have to box his ears."

Her pinched brow showed concern. "Dinna hurt his face."

David opened the door and stepped out, saying over his shoulder, "It'd take more than a boxing to hurt Kevin."

Louise closed the door, but left it unlocked. "Come with me. The fire's blazing, yer malt is waiting, and Handel is playing on our new home theater system."

"What? Ye weren't supposed to open my present until after I arrived."

If she had a smidgeon of remorse, she hid it behind a bulging grin. "Have ye ever known me to wait?"

"No, but I was hoping the *Do Not Open Until Christmas* label on the box might act as a deterrent."

"Ye're joking."

Elliott grimaced. She'd ruined his one and only Christmas surprise. "Do I look like I am?"

She patted his arm. "Suck it up. Ye're not a wee laddie."

They entered the library, a room lined with bookshelves and crammed with leather-bound classics. "Ye painted the shelves," Elliott said.

"Evelyn insisted on painting them white." Louise's tone held self-doubt. "She has an eye for color, but I wasna sure I'd care for it."

He noticed the placement of the speakers: center, right, and left. Each produced sharp, clear sounds. "Yer installer has a good ear."

Elliott's disappointment eased. At least he wouldn't have to spend several hours installing the system, and if he were honest, he wouldn't have placed the speakers in the same positions, which could have reduced the sound quality.

"Look." She patted her hand against the tufted detail on the back of a brown bonded-leather chair. "I got it just for ye."

"Shite, Louise. Have ye changed everything? Ye know I liked the old one."

She shoved him into the chair. "Sit."

The pitch of the chair put him in a comfortable position, and he sank into the supple leather cushions. Louise helped arrange his injured leg on the matching ottoman. "Not bad," he said. He closed his eyes and let his breath go in a long, heavy sigh. The music and memories of his da and Sean MacKlenna ensnared him.

In this room, he would always hear the echo of their voices rising to a clamor over the merits of beautiful horses and fast women—bloodlines and lovers. Although as volatile as the other two, Elliott rarely joined the ruffle. He much preferred to toss kindling onto their disagreements, which continued until they drained a bottle or two of whisky and their cigars died in peace.

Louise gave him a drink along with a pointed look. "Dinna get maudlin on me."

Elliott took the glass and stared at the golden-hued liquid, praying it would placate the pain. "Is this the Macallan?"

She slapped her hand against her chest, emitting a sharp gasp. "Ye told me that's what ye wanted. Dinna ye trust me to give it to ye?"

He covered the top of the glass with his hand and swirled the liquid. "With the changes ye've made, I thought ye might forget." The swirling agitated the dark amber with a golden hue and released more of the honey and caramel scent. Slowly, he brought the crystal to his lips and kissed the whisky. "Ah." His tongue picked up the honey with a hint of peat taste, and he sighed again. "*Slainte.*"

The rocking chair creaked as Louise nestled into the seat and raised her glass. "*Slainte.*" She sipped her wine. "Speaking of health, what'd yer doctor say about yer surgery? Is this the last one?"

"Possibly,"

"If ye'd listen to yer medical team *and* go to counseling, ye might heal this time."

He pointed his glass at her. "Damn, Lou. Don't start in on me."

She narrowed her eyes and tapped her fingers against the crystal goblet. "It's been six years since that bastard butchered your leg."

"*Stop.*" He gulped his drink. After a moment, he said, "Tell me about Evelyn."

Her eyes widened, and the same girlish smile he'd first noticed so many years earlier inched across her face. "We just celebrated twenty-five years together."

He raised his glass. "Congratulations. And ye thought it wouldn't last."

"I wish ye'd find someone ye could be happy with for longer than six weeks. Ye're not a young man now."

"That's yer second reference to my age, and I've only been here"—he glanced at the clock on the chimneypiece—"fifteen minutes."

"I worry about ye, especially now that the MacKlennas and your da are gone. I dinna want ye growing old alone."

Elliott sipped the whisky. The liquid slid down his throat, warming him like a twill-weave plaid of fire. "I've got a hundred people on the farm. I'm never alone."

"There's a difference between being alone and lonely. And, at the end of the day, those people go back to their safe, wee houses—to their families." She cocked her head and studied him with troubled eyes. "Who's at MacKlenna Mansion waiting for ye?"

He gave a tight shrug, or was it a flinch? "Tate and Tabor."

She set her glass on the table, folded her arms across her chest, and settled them comfortably beneath her large breasts. "They're wonderful pets. Very devoted. But I'm talking about a companion ye can have a conversation with, not a golden retriever or a long-haired, tabby Maine Coon cat."

Her concerned gaze spilled over him, and he glanced away.

"Sean married a lass who understood the farm and its demands. So can ye."

"He was a young lad when he met Mary," Elliott said.

"Ye need to be open to love. I'm not sure ye are. Ye're too strong-willed and private. Ye rarely let anyone see yer sensitive side."

"*Shush.*"

She pointed her finger at him. "Ye can shush yer mates, but don't ye dare shush me."

As if on cue, a log snapped in the fireplace. Louise irritated the hell out of him. She could be bitchy and possessive where his well-being was concerned, but he loved her as a sister and had for thirty years. She had stood by him when he'd screwed up with that married woman during college. So, he tolerated her idiosyncrasies. Elliott had plenty of his own. Even Jesus would have a hard time loving him.

Louise cupped her cheek in her hand. "I dinna ken what I'm going to do with ye. I'm talking about love, not sex, and not one of yer Thursday or Saturday night dates either. Those women come with six-week expirations tattooed on their arses. Ye need a woman who's a priority in yer life, not just an option."

"Ye're being a wee crabbit tonight. Go to bed."

"The truth hurts, doesna it? Ye're too self-oriented, but I love ye in spite of it."

"What the hell are ye talking about?" Elliott said. "Are ye taking a psychology course now? Shite. Go back to astrology."

The stereo remote sat on the table between them. He pushed the volume up arrow. The room filled with sounds of a string quartet playing a Haydn composition. He didn't know which one and didn't really care.

Louise turned the volume down and moved the remote out of his reach. "Turning the music up a bit, eh? Trying to tune me out?"

"Don't know why I thought I'd find any peace here."

She handed over the remote. "Ye can be such an arsehole. How does yer staff tolerate yer moods? Oh, pish." She held out her hand as if that would stop him from answering. "I'm the only beneficiary of yer black moods, aren't I? Ye save up your shitey attitude just for me."

She stepped over to the cupboard, poured another glass of wine, then busied herself at the bar. He rested his head against the cool leather and closed his eyes again.

"It's going to be a quiet holiday. I have one guest staying through the Hogmanay—a woman from America."

He chuckled at the nonsequitur. Louise had long ago perfected the conversational device to redirect uncomfortable discussions. "She must have family here."

"The travel agent who booked the room said she was coming to do genealogy research."

He opened his eyes to finish his drink, but instead frowned at the empty glass. Louise refilled his glass. "I bet she wears granny shoes, has gray helmet-hair, and a bit of wobbly skin below her chin."

"Ye're incorrigible. Please be civil to my guest."

He had tolerated more than one noisy, obnoxious guest while visiting Louise. The way he felt right now, he'd be a jerk to the granny-shoe woman. "Thank God I'll be gone by the time she gets here."

Louise glanced at her watch as she headed back to her chair. "Not unless ye're leaving within the hour."

"*C'est la vie.*"

"Ye could go to the archives with her and solve that eighteenth-century family mystery about the lad born on the wrong side of the sheets."

"I always thought Grandda Fraser knew more than he let on when he told that story."

Louise settled once again into the rocker. "Ye're leaving tomorrow. Ye dinna have time to do research on this trip. Maybe when ye come back after the February sales."

"The mystery's likely buried so far under old dusty books it'll never see the blinding light of a winter afternoon." A sharp pain shot down his leg. He squirmed in discomfort. The whisky wasn't working for him tonight. He slipped his thumb and forefinger into his shirt pocket and snatched two pills he'd squirreled away, popping the painkillers into his mouth.

"I wonder why she's traveling alone," Louise said.

He chased the pills with a swig of whisky. "Holidays are a time for family."

Louise leaned forward, choking on her drink.

Elliott patted her back as she coughed. He watched until the high color faded from her face. "Ye okay?"

"Did ye hear what ye just said?"

The rhetorical question lingered in the air where it could stay for all he cared. He withdrew his hand from her back.

"That's why ye're going to Fraser House, so ye can celebrate by yerself?" She puffed up, looking rather put out. "Ye'll be wallowing in whisky all alone in that ancestral castle of yers."

"I wasn't talking about me."

"So what? Ye dinna deserve to be with people ye love and who love ye."

"It's too late for me. I'm an old—"

She slapped her hand over his mouth. "Stop talking about age."

"Then get me another drink. I'll need it"—her hand muffled his voice—"if I'm going to be nice to yer granny-shoe-wearing guest."

Chapter Five

Louise's B&B, Edinburgh, Scotland – December 22

MEREDITH'S PLANE PREPARED to land at Edinburgh airport close to midnight. An easy smile came to her face when the wheels touched down. No matter what else was going on in her life, when she stepped onto Scottish soil, she experienced the same *welcome home* sensation. Scottish blood flowed in her veins and Scotland filled her heart.

Shortly before one o'clock, her driver pulled under the porte cochere at Louise's B&B on Great King Street in the city's New Town section. She stifled a yawn as she crossed the cobbled drive, hoping for a well-kept establishment, a quick welcome, and the key to her room. That plan changed when she entered through the front door and draped her coat across the arm of a Chippendale claw-and-ball settee.

A crystal chandelier hung above a family crest medallion set in the middle of the marble floor. The fixture showered the room with golden light. *Gorgeous.* The restoration photographs she'd seen on the website hadn't reflected the true elegance of the eighteenth-century Georgian home. Her discerning eye perused the oversized foyer's woodwork, flocked wallpaper, and antique furniture that had convinced her to book the room. *At least I'll be comfortable while I pace and wait for the pathology report.*

The chauffeur entered behind her. "I'll leave your bags next to the lift, Ms. Montgomery." On his way out, he handed her a business card. "If ye need a driver during yer stay, here's my number."

She examined the card before slipping it into her pocket.

Laughter spilled from a room at the end of a narrow hallway. She applied lip balm before crossing the threshold into a library painted a dark brick red. Dozens of votive candles made lonely pools of light in shadowed corners.

"Excuse me," she said to a woman. "Are you Louise?"

A younger version of *Golden Girl* Betty White welcomed Meredith with endearing blue eyes and a dimpled smile. Her toes pointed inward when she walked, giving a bounce to each step. A multicolored sweater hung loose across her shoulders. When she waved, inviting Meredith into the room, the empty sleeves danced like fluttering butterflies, and a half dozen rings in different colors and styles jingled on her fingers.

"Yes. And you must be Meredith Montgomery?"

The proprietress appeared too fun and flighty to live in a stately room where soft white woodwork splashed against deep, red walls lined with bookshelves filled with books by classic poets and Scottish artifacts.

In Meredith's periphery, she saw a man dressed in a kilt and wearing a black walking boot push aside an ottoman and stand with the aid of crutches.

"I'm sorry to arrive so late. I hope I'm not interrupting," she said.

"Not at all. Come in, dearie." Louise's lyrical brogue blended with the quartet playing on the audio system. "Would ye like wine or tea?"

Meredith wasn't in the mood for a cup of tea or the B&B's house wine. She stepped to the hearth, to the brightly burning blaze, noticing three things. The man had the most pleasing fragrance—fresh, spicy, woodsy, and reminiscent of a hike through a Christmas tree farm. He held a crystal glass that contained neither wine nor tea. Also, a bottle of Macallan sat on the bar. She nodded in his direction. "I'll have what he's having."

He smiled as if she'd picked the right door on *Let's Make a Deal.* "I'll be yer barman, Lou."

The man's melodic and hypnotizing voice radiated sensuality and fluttered over her like a soft breeze of pure silk. Meredith inhaled with her eyes. The tall, graying haired Scotsman with a runner's lean body had fine lines on his clean-shaven face. There was an irresistible and handsome quality about him. When he offered her a cut crystal glass, his fingertips brushed her palm.

"Louise forgot her manners," he said. "I'm Elliott Fraser." He tilted his head a bit and glanced at the side of her head. "Ye picked up a wee leaf." He put his fingers in her hair and, after a couple of soft swipes, the strands released the dried leaf. The two brief touches seemed unintentional, but a whetting of interest shimmered in his rich-as-Belgian-chocolate eyes. She dropped her gaze, surprised that she'd lost her infamous 'cold and hardy' grapevine composure. As a result, she found herself staring at an enticing patch of dark brown chest hair in the triangle of his open-collared shirt instead of his eyes.

"Thank you," she said, hoping she didn't sound as breathy to him as she did to herself.

"Ye're welcome to join us," Louise said. "Or maybe ye'd rather take yer wee draft to yer room? Elliott arrived a bit ago. We've been having a good blether."

A bit flustered, Meredith's brain flipped through the memorized dog-eared pages of her childhood English-Scottish dictionary until she came to the definition of the word *blether.* "I don't want to interrupt your *chat,*" she said.

"Ye're a welcome distraction. I was starting to bore him," Louise said, her eyes twinkling.

"Well, if you're sure." A few minutes earlier, Meredith had only wanted to find her bed, but the warm, cozy room wrapped her in a toasty blanket, and she didn't want to leave.

"Ye should stay," Elliott said. "It's warmer here than in yer guest room."

Louise propped her hands on her hips. "Elliott Fraser."

He sent an air kiss in her direction. "I'm teasing, hen." He turned toward Meredith. "Since the renovations—"

She waved away his explanation. "I've been in my share of old houses with drafty rooms. That's part of their charm." She lowered herself to the overstuffed sofa, and after sipping her drink asked, "How far did you travel, Mr. Fraser?"

"I flew in from New York City." He braced the crutches against the table, turned his back to the chair, and gripped the arms. His face neither tightened nor turned red as he held himself aloft and resettled his leg onto the ottoman. When he sat, the kilt fell neatly over his thighs.

"Those rolling *R*s don't sound like Manhattan," she said, pulling her gaze from the long leg stretched across the stool.

"I was in New York for a few days. I'm originally from the Highlands. What about ye? Have ye spent much time here?"

She traced the deep etching of the monogram on the tumbler with her fingertips. "Annual trips since I was five, but I never picked up the accent."

"Ye don't sound like a New Yorker either," he said.

"San Francisco," she said.

He lifted his eyebrow in a curious arch, as if he were trying to grasp a memory hanging out of reach.

A text message beeped. Meredith reached for her phone but came up with a blank screen. Elliott unclipped his phone. "Pardon me. I need to answer this."

Louise picked at the doily-covered chair arm. The fire crackled, and a log snapped as it gave way and turned to ash. Meredith sank into the deep cushions, curious about the man texting on his cell phone with ringless fingers. She turned up her glass and chugged her drink.

Elliott finished his message and reclipped his phone to the kilt's waistband just as Louise nodded off, wineglass in hand. He snatched the glass. "Careful."

Her eyes shot open, and she straightened. "What? Why'd ye take my drink?"

"Ye were going to spill it."

"Oh." She yawned her way to her feet. "It's time to find my bed, then. Come along, Meredith. I'll show ye to yer room. Elliott, please bank the fire? I'll blow out the candles."

He stood, chuckling. "Good night, Lou."

Although he reached for Meredith's empty glass, she dodged him with an easy sidestep and set the crystal on the mantel. "Thank you for playing barman, Mr. Fraser."

"Elliott," he said, nodding for emphasis. "My pleasure."

SEVERAL MINUTES LATER, Meredith closed the door to the Robertson Clan Room and glanced around the suite decorated in green and red clan colors. *Nice.* The rooms in the B&B were named after clans. Louise didn't have a Montgomery suite so Meredith settled on Robertson for no particular reason other than she liked the colors in the picture on the website.

She leaned her shoulder against the door, thinking. For once, her thoughts didn't zero in on her wine or the lump in her breast. The bull's-eye was Elliott's gaze—a slow once-over filled with male appreciation. Normally, she found that sort of *male appreciation* annoying, but she saw something behind his brown-eyed gaze that spoke of a kindred spirit. That, she couldn't ignore.

Find a smooth-talking Scotsman.

"Oh, Cate. This isn't the time or place."

Meredith kicked off her shoes and dug her toes into the thick, wool carpet, grounding herself in something tangible.

Even though she had to confess Elliott was *hot*, she knew a confirmed bachelor when she saw one. Handsome, sexy, emotionally unavailable. A trail of broken hearts probably extended from Scotland to New York and beyond. She didn't intend to add her heart to a trail of tears. Not even if a distraction was what she needed.

FROM THE MOMENT Meredith had entered the library, Elliott's eyes stayed fixed on her, and he had to touch her. First her hand, then her hair. He had lied about the leaf. With horses, he could touch and pat and rub when he met them, but with women, he had to be more casual, nonthreatening. And she had responded with a breathy voice.

The skinny black jeans stretched over slim, toned legs and ass had turned him on. *Bet she's a runner.* The contours of sculpted arms and shoulders were visible beneath a white fitted sweater. She was a classical beauty with a ring on her left hand that spoke in a blurry whisper, "Married." It didn't stop him from looking, though.

Small breasts didn't appeal to him, but her other assets—he whistled—particularly her full, glossy lips, held him spellbound. His hands twitched, feeling an urge to run his fingers deeper into the silky strands of black hair that fell in waves to just below her collarbone. He was a sucker for long, silky hair and shapely legs.

Elliott leaned on his crutches and swallowed the last of his drink. *Silky hair, shapely legs.*

He set the crystal on the mantel next to Meredith's glass. With his index finger, he rubbed the rim where her glossy mouth had touched. Lip balm was a staple carried with runner's gear to keep lips soft and moist. *Kissable lips.* The taste of honey was his favorite.

Now that his heart rate resumed its normal rhythm, he reflected on Doc's text message.

"If Galahad's blood work comes back negative," the vet had said, "he'll be released from quarantine and allowed to go home."

Home was where the horse belonged. Elliott couldn't relax until the Thoroughbred stood in his stall on the farm.

He grabbed the shovel from the fireside tools and buried the flame beneath a heavy layer of ashes. A shovelful of the fire's residue dampened the flames, but left a sexual spark for a leggy Californian with eyes the color of Scotland's deep blue water at sunrise. It might be worth delaying his departure from Edinburgh a day or two to squeeze in a bit of romance.

"Aye, a bit of romance." He turned out the lights and hobbled down the hallway, quoting Robbie as he shuffled, "*O my Luve's like a red, red rose that's newly sprung in June…*"

Chapter Six

Edinburgh, Scotland – December 23

ELLIOTT'S CELL PHONE RANG, sending the god-awful *Brady Bunch* ringtone throughout the darkened guest room. He knew every inch of the Fraser Clan Room. Louise had decorated the suite to resemble his red, blue, and green tartan, and he had never slept in any of the other B&B guest rooms. When she remodeled, she had updated the furniture but kept the same color scheme; otherwise, he wouldn't have come back. He didn't like change.

On the second ring, he shook the damn phone as if that would restore its original programming, but the nauseating sound couldn't be blamed on the device. The fault fell solely on his goddaughter's dry sense of humor.

The illuminated hands on his wristwatch pointed to seven o'clock. When he rolled over, he put pressure on his wound. A rush of air hissed through his front teeth. "Damn." He jabbed the answer button on the phone. "Fraser."

A gasp, and then: "This is Alice."

Elliott scratched his head, hoping that would peel away the confusion and pain. *Why the hell is she calling me now?* The Highlands housekeeper never called unless there was a bloody problem. He sat straight up in the king-sized bed. Another hot stream of pain surged through his leg.

"I'm sorry to bother you. Yer email didna tell me what time ye planned to leave for Fraser House. The water pipe we fixed in the fall sprung another leak," she said without pausing for a breath. "The plumber's on his way. I wanted ye to know before ye left Edinburgh."

The throbbing in his leg jumped to his head with the vigor of a damn flea. "What kind of damage are ye talking about?"

"Ye might need a new floor in the kitchen."

He puffed up his cheeks then let his breath out in a burst of frustration.

"That's all I can tell ye until the workmen get here."

"Ye didn't mention the wine cellar." The value of the priceless wine collection could exceed the cost of repairing the entire six-hundred-year-old estate. He shuddered, feeling his da rolling over in his urn.

"We found the leak before it damaged those old dusty bottles."

The din of money slipping through his fingers quieted. A chain of unrelated events crept along the edges of his foul mood, threatening to destroy his holiday. First Galahad. Now the castle. "Do what has to be done." He grumbled as if he were a Scrooge-like, miserly hoarder who hated to spend a pence to save a pound. The grumbling sounded like his father. The pain in his leg inched up into his chest, sharp and heavy. "I'll drive up later."

Exasperated, he slumped against the headboard, considering his options. How in hell could he have a peaceful holiday with a rattling jackhammer digging up the floor? Visions of horses, construction workers, and leggy researchers jogged around the track in his brain. A wee bit of romance might be more conducive to healing than dealing with those bastard contractors Alice usually hired at a rate more than they were worth for the services they performed.

Decision made, he called Kevin. "We're staying."

"What? Where?" Kevin asked, groggy with sleep.

"Bring my bags to the B&B. I'll explain."

A muffled female voice said, "You don't have to leave?"

Elliott held the phone away from his ear and glared at the instrument—the enemy, the bearer of bad news. He tossed it across the bed.

AFTER CHECKING EMAIL and showering, Elliott went in search of Louise. He entered the Sinclair Clan Dining Room, calling her name, "Louise, where are ye? *Louise.*"

Meredith poked her head up over the end of a long table dominating the green and light blue room. "She's in the kitchen."

He stretched his neck, glancing beyond the tabletop and the tacky orange and white chairs. "Do ye need help?"

"I dropped my notebook and the clips came undone." Her voice held a steely thread of tension. "I'm trying to pick up the pages so they stay in order." Dozens of documents in plastic sleeves spread across the Oriental rug like fully extended accordion bellows. "*Shoot.*" She swept the loose pages into the notebook and slammed it shut. "*He's* changed the slicks anyway."

Her cell phone rang, and she yanked the phone off the table. With the notebook in one hand and the phone in the other, she hurried into the front sitting room. Her voice trailed behind her. "I want to review them now, Gregory, not in a half hour. I don't care that they're not the final slicks. I want to see the artistic direction. Email them now."

Elliott eavesdropped as he poured a cup of coffee from the silver service on the buffet. Although he still drank tea, Lou always had coffee ready. While Meredith's call continued, he glanced at the front page of *The Edinburgh Evening News* spread open on the table. Hogmanay tickets? Attending the Concert in the Gardens would be a nice diversion, and maybe even The Keilidh events. He'd see what plans Louise had made.

Meredith returned to the dining room with her cheeks wearing a lovely shade of pink. "I'm sorry. That was rude." She glanced at her phone as if considering whether she needed to make another apology. "I'm usually onsite when there's a big project in the development stage."

"I hope the problem's resolved."

"Not yet." She returned to her seat and took a sip of coffee.

"What do you do, Elliott?"

He placed the coffee cup on the table and sat across from her. "Manage a Thoroughbred operation in Lexington, Kentucky."

She tilted her head, scrunched her eyebrows. "I thought you were from New York."

"No, I flew in from New York."

She lined up the phone, pen, ChapStick, and highlighter in height order on top of the binder.

Elliott pinched his lips together, intrigued by her idiosyncrasies.

"Lexington claims to be the horse capital of the world. The city must have more horses than people," she said.

"The claim's based on economic impact of the industry, not on horse population."

She regarded him while she fiddled with a spoon. Something glimmered behind her carefully veiled eyes. "Do you race your horses?"

"Yes."

"Do you win?"

He threw her a crooked grin. "I always intend to. Occasionally I don't, but that doesn't happen often. What about ye?" He nodded toward her binder. "Do ye usually win?"

"Like you, I always intend to."

Charlie's Welcome blared from his phone. He pulled the device from his shirt pocket. "My goddaughter and I accidentally switched phones a few months ago. She downloaded ringtones for several of my contacts. The music is always a surprise."

"Teenagers love those, don't they?"

"Teenagers, yes, but Kit's twenty-five. Excuse me. I need to take this call." He pushed the answer button, "Fraser." After telling the caller to hold, he tucked the crutches under his arm and hobbled into the front sitting room where he closed the door behind him. Experience told him that having a short conversation with his father's solicitor was impossible.

Thirty minutes later, sitting in front of the narrow window overlooking Great King Street, he stared off into the distance, seeing nothing in particular. He circled his finger in the air. The lawyer couldn't see Elliott give the wrap-up signal and, even if he had, he'd continue to drone on. That was the kind of man he was, and he flunked Elliott's patience test.

Since his father's heart attack a few months earlier, Elliott had learned all he needed to know about probate in Scotland. He was his father's only child, only heir. Bottom line: at its end, a man's life should amount to more than a catalog of assets.

He barged in on the man's soliloquy. "I'll be there at two o'clock to review the documents." He disconnected before the long-winded solicitor had a chance to take a breath. With that stomach-churning business disposed of, Elliott returned to the dining room to find Meredith gone.

"Damn."

Louise's familiar clogs clomped across the hallway's marble floor. "I heard that." She kissed his cheek. "So what's put ye in such a dreadful mood?"

"Da's solicitor."

"Egads. If that's how yer morning started, ye better go back to bed. The day willna get any better."

"It had a god-awful start, then a delightful reprieve."

She patted his belly. "Ye need breakfast. An empty stomach makes ye grumpy."

"If anything can improve my day, breakfast carries the best odds."

"Sit. I'll get yer plate." She hurried into the kitchen. "Did ye talk to Meredith earlier?"

He braced the crutches against the wall and returned to the chair he'd vacated. "Did ye see her go out?"

"Which time? When she went for a run before dawn, or when she left to go to the National Archives?"

He grimaced, rubbing his thigh. "I figured her for a runner." He'd run several marathons, and he'd even done an Ironman while in his thirties. Now he only competed in his dreams, or—more appropriately—nightmares. He gave his thigh a final squeeze, then reached for the coffee cup.

"What'd ye say?" Louise asked.

"Nothing," he said in a voice that had lost its power. After a few sips of coffee, he asked, "Why do ye think a beautiful woman would spend the holidays alone in a foreign country?"

Louise set a fresh pot of coffee and a plate loaded with bacon, sausages, mushrooms, tomatoes, fried eggs, homemade scones, and haggis on the table. "Ask her."

He shook his head. "I might not like the answer."

Louise sat and poured a cup of tea. "What's the matter? Ye're distracted."

He pushed food around the plate. "It's just the holidays."

Her discerning eyes studied him over the rim of her cup. "Ye want to escape. That's not easy for ye. Ye'd have to find a way through those impenetrable walls ye constructed. Ye sure as hell canna go over them. Ye're stuck, old boy. Ye canna get out any easier than ye can let someone in."

He rubbed his chest, pretending to nurse his wounds. "If ye weren't a lesbian, I'd ask ye to marry me. Then I wouldn't have to worry about any damn walls."

She stuck a fork into his eggs and snatched a bite from his plate. "If I didna love ye, I wouldna put up with yer black moods."

"Ye have to. Ye're sleeping with my sister."

"Evelyn's not yer sister."

He gave a slight shrug. "Stepsister, sort of. And where the hell is she? I thought she was coming in from London this morning."

"She's delayed until late afternoon. She'll be sick she missed ye."

He drilled into the sausage. "I decided to stay through Christmas."

Louise pointed toward Meredith's empty plate.

He wiggled his left-hand ring finger. "Didn't ye notice what she was wearing?"

Louise waved him off. "She's not yer type."

"This should be good. What's my type? I want to hear this."

"Petite, blue-eyed, blond-haired women with larger bust measurements than IQs." She elbowed him in the arm. "Tall, skinny, small-busted women have never turned ye on, and ye know it."

He stopped eating and considered her observation before announcing, "Ye don't know what ye're talking about. I've dated tall brunettes, even a couple of redheads."

Louse stuck out her chest and shimmied. "And they've all had big boobs."

He rolled his eyes then tucked into his breakfast again. "I'm not going to apologize for enjoying well-endowed women."

Louise's schoolgirl laughter twittered through the room. "Why aren't ye leaving today?"

"Last night ye told me to spend the holidays with family."

"I didna think you were listening." Her eyes brightened. "That means ye'll be here for the Hogmanay? Kevin will be here, too. He can have the room on the other side of ye. If I'd known, he could have had the adjoining room instead of Meredith."

Elliott wagged his brow. Louise swatted his hand with the backs of her fingers. "The door's double bolted."

"I'm bogged down with misfortune, and ye don't care."

"Care?" she squeaked. "Here's a dose of reality. Meredith is married. That makes her off limits. And ye canna even talk to yer father's solicitor without tearing up. How the hell do ye think ye can stay at Fraser House over the holidays?"

"Kevin's with me."

"He's yer mini-me. He'll be crying in his whisky right along with ye."

Elliott took the last bite of haggis and pushed the plate away. "The lad's gone back to wine."

She threw up her hands. "Finish yer breakfast and go to work."

"What time does Evelyn get back? Do ye want to go to Number One for dinner?"

"How can ye think of dinner after eating enough calories for an entire week?"

He tossed his napkin onto the table. "I was in the hospital for five days. I don't eat that food."

"Because Kevin brings ye gourmet meals. If ye're buying, I'd love to go to dinner."

He scowled. "Don't I always?"

Louise pulled her phone out of her pocket. "I'll text Evelyn and call Gary at the restaurant. What time? Seven?"

"Whenever he can seat us."

"I'll make a reservation for four. Meredith might join us."

"Oh, I'm sure she'd find two lesbians and a broken down old Highlander very entertaining."

Louise shot to her feet, grabbing a dirty dish in each hand. "The next time ye refer to yer age, I'm going to smack ye. Now get out of here so I can clean up."

Elliott pushed away from the table. "I'll be working in the library."

She clopped into the kitchen. "Whatever makes ye happy."

Chapter Seven

Solicitor's Office, Edinburgh, Scotland – December 23

ELLIOTT MET WITH the solicitor in his law office on Dublin Street. The fixtures and furnishings in the stuffy, dark office dated back to the beginning of the twentieth century. Stacks of books and legal documents covered every dusty surface in the cluttered two-room office suite. The dust made Elliott sneeze. The obtuse lawyer continued his earlier probate recitation and never once inquired about Elliott's health. Not that Elliott cared, but the lack of social graces confirmed for Elliott that his father had hired the solicitor because of a low hourly rate and not for legal competence or social skills.

During the two-hour conference, Elliott missed a dose of pain medication that soured an already bitter mood.

He had loved his tight-fisted father, but after reading through the estate documents, years of built-up resentment settled in Elliott's gut. He had known the extensive wine collection that dated back two hundred years was worth a few million, but he hadn't known the extent of his father's stock portfolio. The man had been a multimillionaire several times over yet had lived a pauper's life. Elliott had had dozens of arguments with the old man trying to convince him to sell a few bottles of wine to pay for the annual upkeep on the castle, but his father always refused, saying it wasn't his wine to sell. He had inherited and added to the collection, and the cellar would remain intact for the next generation. Now that Elliott owned the wine, he'd sell off every last bottle.

The lawyer regaled Elliott with stories of his father that he had heard dozens of time. So he tuned out the solicitor. Instead of listening, he mentally drafted an outline of conditions for an estate sale at Christie's. The collection had caused too much dissention in the family. He'd call the auction house in London to start working out the details.

With a plan in place and an opening in the conversation, Elliott escaped, leaving behind the solicitor with his ill-fitting toupee and droning voice.

Elliott's leg burned with the heat of an iron poker sizzling in the fire. At his urging, David sped through town, rushing back to the B&B. As soon as they entered the library, Elliott grabbed a small medical kit from his briefcase and withdrew a syringe.

David snatched the syringe from Elliott's hand. "Give that to me."

He set his teeth. "I can do it."

"Ye'll stick the needle in yer dick."

He didn't have the energy to argue, so he lifted his kilt. When the needle punctured his skin, he flinched. There was nothing gentle about David's touch.

David took a measure of the amount of medication left in the bottle. He nodded as if putting the demarcation line to memory. "Do not do this yerself."

Elliott knew how many syringes the remaining medication would fill. If he took the drug as prescribed, the bottle could last a few days.

David put the medical kit away. "Where's Kevin? The lad said he'd be here when we got back."

"He had lunch plans."

"He needs to get his sorry ass back here."

Elliott snarled. "I don't need a damn babysitter. Louise's hovering is enough to send me to the whisky bottle."

"So that's yer excuse now?"

Elliott rounded on his friend. "Don't ye have a crime to solve?"

"No."

"Then go visit yer sister."

"She's working."

"Then go write yer memoir."

David clamped his jaw and gave Elliott a steely-eyed glare.

Elliott's lips twisted into a sly smile. "Alice told me."

David's chest rose as he took a deep breath. "If a lad can't trust his mother—"

"She's proud of what ye did in battle. Not many have earned the Victoria Cross. That's an honor unlike any other."

"Pride can get a man killed." David's voice went from brusque to edgy.

"Ye're not on the battlefield now," Elliott said.

"Life's a battlefield. Those who forget get hurt." David walked toward the door, saying over his shoulder, "I'll be back to take ye to dinner. Get some sleep. It'd be good for yer blood pressure."

Elliott waved David away. "Get out of here." He eased into the desk chair, booted up his laptop, and started through a long list of emails. In the middle of a reply to one of the shareholders, his cell phone rang. "Fraser."

"You need to sit down," Doc said in a shaky voice.

Stomach acid gathered at the back of Elliott's throat. "What the hell's going on there?"

"No easy way to say this." Doc cleared his throat. "Galahad's dead."

Sean and Mary MacKlenna are dead. Your father's dead. Galahad's dead. A tsunami-like wall of shock roared through his body, and his fist hit the desk. "We're fooked. What the hell happened?"

"I don't know yet."

"Maybe ye don't, but somebody does. I want a conference call with everyone who saw Galahad from the moment he got off the plane. Include the management staff. Work with Allie to set up the call. Ye've got fifteen minutes."

He punched the end-call button and stared at the phone gripped in his callused hand with its protruding blue veins. Hands like his father. When had that happened? He dropped the phone, hating what he saw, but his hands itched to lob his pain into the stratosphere.

A Churchill Downs snow globe sat in the center of the desktop, a visual reminder that he had lost his beloved Kentucky Derby winner.

It's my fault. I shouldn't have let Galahad leave the farm. He picked up the globe and tossed the glass ball back and forth between his hands. *Strike three. Ye're out, laddie.* Elliott drew back his arm and hurled the globe toward the fireplace.

The sound of shattering glass brought Louise rushing into the room. "What the hell?" First, she glared at Elliott, then she glared at the fireplace where glycerin water sizzled in the flame. Twin spires lay broken on the hearth.

"Ye broke my globe? How could ye?" Tears welled in her eyes. "I've had that snow globe for twenty-five years." She picked up the twin spires and silver-plated label, and clutched the pieces to her breasts. "*Never,*" she said, her voice quivering, "have I known ye to throw a damn thing. Why this? Why now?"

He set his elbows on the desk and rested his forehead in the heels of his hands.

She sniffed back her tears. "The way ye've acted today is so unlike ye. What in God's name has happened?"

Silence lengthened as he lowered the flame heating his temper until only a fine blue light remained. It wouldn't take much to turn up the heat again. He grabbed his crutches and joined her at the fireplace. Using the broom hanging with the fireside tools, he began to sweep up the glass. "Galahad died in his stall."

"What?"

"My horse is dead. And I don't know why."

She snatched the broom out of his hand. "I'll do that."

He took the spires and label from her, rolled the pieces over in his palm, checked for damage, then slipped them into his shirt pocket. "I need a drink." He splashed whisky into a glass and tossed the drink back in a single swallow. "I've got a conference call in a few minutes." He hobbled back to the desk with a powerful swell of grief expanding inside his chest, building pressure that wasn't healthy for his heart or his stomach. "Galahad's dead. I smashed one of yer treasures. What else can happen?"

His phone beeped with an incoming text message. With heightened intuition, he knew he was about to find out.

Doc sent a text message with an attached picture of the horse lying flat out in his stall. Elliott gripped the phone in his hand, afraid he'd throw it across the room, too. Later, after the call, he'd smash the messenger against the wall. But what good would that do? A branding iron had seared the image of his dead horse into his brain. Short of a lobotomy, the haunting picture would remain embedded in his memory.

Why'd Doc send this? I didn't need to see a picture to believe Galahad's dead.

The phone rang. Elliott glowered with distaste. The device had become evil incarnate, and he didn't want to touch it.

Louise headed toward the door. "Take yer call, but *please* dinna break anything else."

He picked up the phone with the tips of two fingers and stepped away from the other breakables on the desk. "Fraser."

"It's Doc. I've got Harrison, Peter, Jake, Allie, and Sandy here with me. We're on speakerphone."

Elliott had no time for niceties. "Were ye in the van with him from the airport, Peter?"

"Yes, sir," the groom said. "I wouldn't let nobody else go pick him up. He's my horse."

"Tell me what happened from the moment he got off the plane—" Elliott paused, scratching his forehead. "Where'd he fly into? Lexington or Cincinnati?"

"Lexington," Peter said. "He was just like always. Ears up, frisky. The groom on the plane said he cleaned up his feed. Didn't see nothing to be concerned about. Once he got home, he settled in just fine. I went in and out of the barn, but I watched him real good. I was gone fifteen minutes. When I came back, he was down. I sounded the alarm. Doc got there and said he's dead."

"I was there when they put him in the stall," Doc said. "Drew some blood. But I told you that in my text."

"Where's he now?" Elliott asked.

"In his stall. We're waiting on the horse hearse to take him to the diagnostic lab for the autopsy," Doc said.

"The shareholders will want to know what happened, and ye're telling me he showed no signs of being sick. He just up and died."

"That's what we're telling you," Doc said. "They'll run more tests at the diagnostic center. We'll get something more definitive."

A pause infiltrated the conversation. Elliott pictured his team sitting around the conference room table with downcast eyes. They'd been through worse. The last time he'd been at the table with them, grieving the loss of Sean and Mary MacKlenna. Elliott took a deep breath. His staff needed direction. They needed him focused on the farm, not on the burn in his leg, the ache in his heart, or the weight of frustration.

"I want a complete toxicology workup, Doc. And Harrison, notify the insurance company. Sandy, I need a press release. Short and sweet. But don't let it out until I've notified the ten shareholders that their horse is dead. I'll send an email and copy ye on it."

The marketing director's nails clicked against a keyboard as she typed.

"Officially," Elliott continued, "the statement will read that Galahad arrived in good order from standing his second southern hemisphere season in New South Wales. The morning of his death, he showed no signs of illness or injury. He died in his stall at ten o'clock a.m. Necropsy results are unavailable at this time.

"Then, Sandy, say something about the brilliance of his best offspring ranking him as one of the most important contemporary stallions. Close with we're very saddened to lose him and that he'll be buried at MacKlenna Farm."

The clicking nails stopped. "Got it."

"Allie, send me a list of the shareholders' email addresses."

"It's on its way," his executive assistant said.

"Peter, bulldoze a trail from the barn to the center. We've got to get those test results."

"I'll do what I can."

"I want *more* than what ye can do."

"Yes, sir."

"Jake, I want a twenty-four-hour security guard posted at all the barns. If that means we hire more guards, do it."

"Are you thinking—"

"We'll take that off-call. Anything else?" When no one spoke up, Elliott disconnected.

It took Jake, director of MacKlenna Farm security, thirty seconds to call him back. "What's on your mind?"

"If someone wanted to hurt the farm, killing Galahad would accomplish that."

"You think someone *killed* him?" The normally unflappable security officer's voice leapt half an octave.

"Galahad was a sound horse. I'm paranoid—"

"And cynical—"

"—enough to believe a wee bastard could have killed him," Elliott continued, ignoring Jake's comment. "We'll wait for the lab results, but prepare for the possibility there'll be another attack."

"Do you have somebody in mind?"

"Yes—"

"Not Gates. He's been dead for years."

"Maybe a family member or a cellmate. The police never recovered the fifty thousand dollars he stole." Elliott fell silent, his heart pounding. He'd never wanted to hurt anyone in his life until Wayne Gates butchered his leg and came close to killing him and Kit. Elliott picked up the letter opener sitting on the desk blotter but dropped it, afraid of the damage it could do if he lost control again.

"I'll double the guards," Jake said.

"We should have a preliminary report in a couple of days. If they find a genetic problem…" Elliott grew quiet as worry catapulted through him, leaving him too shaken to stand. He collapsed in the chair. "If Galahad passed a defect to his offspring, we might have a bigger problem."

"I'll stay in contact with Doc and call you if I get any news," Jake said.

Elliott tossed his phone on the desk and stared out the window. The last flicker of sunlight retired beyond the horizon, leaving the holiday lights twinkling behind the falling snow. Staying in Scotland seemed pointless. He removed the spires and the label from his pocket. The crash had blunted the tips, but there were no cracks or breaks. The silver label engraved with the *104th Run for the Roses* had a few scratches. A jeweler could buff them out. He slipped them back into the pocket. For now, the pieces would remain there—a physical reminder of his temper.

The tapping of heels against the hallway's marble floor yanked him from wallowing in a muddy puddle of self-recrimination. He turned toward the sound, and his mood lifted. Meredith stood in the doorway, one foot in the room, one foot out, frozen in place by an internal pause button.

"I'm sorry. I didn't know anyone was in here."

He hobbled to the other side of the desk. "Come in. I've monopolized the room all day."

She dropped her coat and computer bag on the chair. A bottle of wine materialized from beneath her coat. "How about a drink? I'll play barman this time."

"Only if it's whisky, and I need a double." He joined her at the bar. "Let me open that." He read the label. "A Barolo?"

"I like to try new wines. Have you tried this before?"

"No, I'm just familiar with the name." His eyes settled on her glossy, kissable lips. Nothing would do more for his spirit than to make love with her. He was racked by shameful lust. *Elliott, ye're a wee bastard. Open the wine.*

Louise rushed back into the room and threw a quick tight glance at him with eyes that still held on to the hurt he'd caused. She turned her attention to Meredith. "We're booked in for dinner at Number One at seven o'clock. Would ye like to join Elliott, my partner

Evelyn, and me tonight?"

Meredith shook her head. "I don't want to intrude."

"I made the reservation for four," Louise added with a tone of expectation.

Elliott handed Meredith a glass of wine. "The girls haven't seen each other in a week. They'll ignore me."

She sniffed the Barolo, then swirled the wine and studied the brick-hued liquid. "Do you need rescuing?"

He didn't, but he sure as hell needed a distraction. "Ye won't let me down, will ye?"

After taking a sip, her tongue darted across her lower lip. "Blueberries, plum pudding, milk chocolate. You sure you don't want a taste?"

The smooth, debonair Elliott would be kissing her, tasting the damn blueberries on her tongue, but on crutches, he'd only embarrass himself with a klutzy move. "So what's it to be? Are ye abandoning me to my fate?"

"How could I refuse, especially at Christmas?"

"Wonderful." Louise darted from the room just as she had entered—in hurried-rabbit mode.

Meredith glanced at her watch. "I'll take my wine upstairs and relax for a while. After reading nineteenth-century handwriting all afternoon, my head's killing me."

"Louise has a stash of over-the-counter medications."

"I always carry ibuprofen."

"A runner's go-to drug," Elliott said.

"Is that from experience, or did you tag me for a runner?"

"Both." He tried to keep regret out of his voice. "But in the interest of full disclosure, Louise told me ye went for a run this morning. Only serious runners go out in weather like this."

Meredith snatched a handful of nuts from a container on the bar. "I have a Boston qualifying race in late February. I can't afford to miss a training day, but I did cut the run short." She nibbled on the nuts. "What time are we leaving for the restaurant?"

"The car will be here at six thirty."

"That gives me two hours. Just enough time to return some emails." She grabbed her coat and computer bag, then saluted him with her glass.

Elliott watched her go before returning to his spot in front of the window. The snow fell harder now, creating large snowflakes perfect for making snowballs. Flashbacks to the last snowball fight he'd had with Kit. For someone so agile, she never could dodge a snowball. A tear formed at the corner of his eye.

If only he didn't have a bum leg. If only the calendar could flip back a year—before everyone left him. If only Galahad hadn't died.

How had so much happened in twelve months? His horse's death would change everything at the farm—again. It might ultimately cost Elliott his job. He didn't work for the money. He worked because he had loved the MacKlennas and he loved the farm. He was inexplicably tied to the land. A decade earlier, he had tried to leave, but a siren's call pulled him back. A shot of burning pain slithered down his leg, reminding him that he almost died answering that call.

He exhaled a deep, audible breath. He didn't like waiting games, but that's what he'd be doing until he received the necropsy report. He scrolled through the pictures on his cell phone until he found the one Doc had sent. "Son of a bitch. If someone killed my horse, I swear I'll kill the asshole."

Chapter Eight

Louise's B&B – December 23

MEREDITH UNLOCKED THE guest room door, tossed her keys, and unloaded her computer and handbag. "Ah," she said, easing onto the bed. She'd be mortified if she spilled a drop of wine on the red comforter, although red wine wouldn't show. Neither would blood. Not that she planned to bleed, but she was nursing a blister on her toe caused by a new style of running shoes. She knew better than to try a different brand while training for a race.

Relaxing, she sipped wine. Her thoughts went to Elliott, a handsome man with a soft, full mouth. A gnawing in her gut reminded her that anything more than an evening out with him was impossible. Her complicated life didn't need more entanglements. Instead of the man, she tried to focus on the gorgeous, sexy wine that turned into an aphrodisiac on her tongue.

The Barola held an almost seamless mouth feel with some nice notes of salty nuts, a much different taste than her labels. *What would Cullen Montgomery think of Cailean?* Would the winery's founder have approved of this expansion of their portfolio, taking a financial risk? It had been her father's vision, but that had been before the financial crisis and slump in sales. In her gut, she believed it was the right thing to do. The wine would be her legacy.

TWO HOURS LATER, after a nap, a few stretching exercises, and a hot shower, she stood in front of the floor-length mirror and slipped on a burgundy peplum jacket that fit snugly across her chest and waist.

Should I wear my hair up or down?

She twisted and fiddled, trying to decide. The black wool gabardine pants, suede lace-up, three-inch heels, and matching jacket demanded a fashionable up-do. More twisting, a clip, and a few spritzes of hairspray were followed by a quick turn of her head this way and that. The sides might fall after a couple of hours, but for now, the style looked perfect.

Her wedding band glinted in the firelight. How odd. She hadn't thought of herself as married for two years. Yet the ring sent a clear I'm-not-available signal. She didn't want complications, explanations, or disappointments. Her focus had to be on her wine and her health.

The alarm on her phone beeped. Time to go.

Elliott's rumbling voice met her when the elevator door opened in the brightly lit foyer. She followed the sound. Before entering the room, she snugged her ring-clad hand into the folds of her coat.

"That's not true," Louise said to a woman standing beside her.

The woman hugged her. "Selective memory, my dear Lou."

With his crutches propped under his arm, Elliott double-thumbed his phone. Cream cashmere sweater and gray flannel trousers hugged his body tonight instead of a kilt. A short right pant leg overlapped the top of the walking boot. If he had an ounce of body fat, Meredith didn't know where he hid it.

"There's Meredith," Louise said. "Come. I want ye to meet Evelyn."

Elliott glanced up and met her eyes. His recognition of her made his eyes change from dark chocolate to an even darker, more disturbing color. A flush heated her neck. She lowered her chin, hoping to hide her blushing skin. She breathed in, then out, summoned up a smile, and flashed him a five-finger toodle-oo wave.

Evelyn stepped toward her, extending her hand and introduced herself. "Evelyn Graham." Her handshake held the same warmth as her voice. "Louise said ye're from San Francisco. I was there last year, and I'm dying to go back. I even took a taxi down a crooked street."

Meredith laughed. "Lombard Street. How fun. I haven't been there since I was a kid."

Louise's fisted hands hugged her hips. "That's one of the reasons she's not going again without me."

Evelyn chuckled, and her wispy, frosted bangs shook like fringe above her eyes. "It was a last-minute symposium. Lou had a house full of guests and couldna get away. She's yet to let me forget."

"What kind of symposium?" Meredith asked.

"Finance and economics."

"And don't listen to what she says about the economy or ye'll cry." Elliott pocketed his phone and poured a glass of wine.

"Ev is an incredible teacher," Louise said.

He handed the glass to Meredith. "Mean, too."

"Oh, Elliott." Louise gave his face a gentle cuff.

"Take her class and see for yerself," he grumbled. "I bet there's not an *A* in her grade book."

"Do you teach economics?" Meredith asked.

"Dr. Graham is a full professor at the University of Edinburgh," Louise said with a distinct note of pride in her voice. She pointed at Elliott. "Dinna let this one fool ye either. He probably told ye he worked on a little horse farm in Kentucky. Well, *Dr.* Fraser happens to run one of the top three Thoroughbred operations in the world."

He rotated his neck as if his collar were too tight. "Enough with the *curricula vitae.* Let's go eat. Take yer drinks with ye. Lou, carry mine?" He nodded toward the door. "Ladies…"

Evelyn took Meredith's arm and ushered her out of the library and into the hallway. "Elliott and I have known each other since we were children. He's a charming man, but he's misguided."

Meredith quirked her brow at him. "How so?"

Louise grabbed her coat from the hall closet. "Don't tell her, Ev. Let her find out for herself."

Meredith had the distinct impression there was nothing misguided about Dr. Elliott Fraser. If anything, he appeared as subtle as a high-powered laser beam, and there was already a red dot on his current target. She brushed at the front of her jacket, feeling the heat.

Chapter Nine

Number One, Edinburgh – December 23

A FIFTEEN-MINUTE DRIVE through Edinburgh put them at Number One exactly at seven o'clock. The Michelin-starred restaurant had a reputation for world class cuisine, and Meredith drooled at the thought of eating their Barbary duck, which she had read about in *Wine Digest.*

While the host seated the foursome at one of the onyx, red lacquer and velvet booths, Evelyn and Louise continued the story they'd started in the car.

Meredith picked up the wine menu. "I can't believe he invited both of you to the Kentucky Derby."

"And didna tell either of us," Louise said. "We were stargazing. Who were ye watching, Ev?"

"Ye were watching Princess Margaret and Lord Snowden. I was watching Bob Hope and the races."

Elliott's jaw dropped, looking comically surprised. "Watching the races? Are ye serious? Ye've never watched a race in yer life."

"Ye know horses scare me," Evelyn shot back.

His expression turned sour. "Second biggest mistake yer father made was not putting ye back on that horse after ye fell off."

Evelyn gave him a *whatever* shrug.

"Ye know—" The waiter approached the table, and Elliott swallowed the rest of his sentence.

"Good evening, Dr. Graham, Dr. Fraser, Miss Louise, and pretty lady in red. What can I get for ye this evening? The usual?"

"Hello, Harvey," Elliott said. "We'll branch out tonight and take the Nonino Grappa chardonnay, two Balvenie PortWoods, and, Meredith, what would you like?"

"Planeta La Segreta Rosso, please."

"And a dark fruity wine for the pretty lady in red," Elliott said.

Meredith cocked her head, picking up the mingling aromas in the room. None of them enticed her sense of smell as much as the woodsy scent of the handsome Scotsman sitting beside her. "You know your wines."

He pointed to the wine list. She read the description underneath her selection that he'd repeated to the waiter. "I can read upside down," he said.

"But you never looked—"

Louise patted Elliott's arm to draw his attention. "Back to Derby Day, love. We were watching ye, not the races, because ye looked so bored. But ye werena bored for long, were ye?"

Meredith closed the wine list, more curious than confused. "He was around the horses. How could he be bored?"

Evelyn tucked a strand of hair behind her ear, but the short curl fell into her face again. "It wasna the horses that kept him occupied. He found a Swedish model who spoke only a wee bit of English."

"But our Elliott," Louise continued, "found a way to communicate with her for ten days." She twiddled ten ring-clad fingers to make her point. "And would ye believe, as soon as the model...what was her name, Ev?"

"Adrian or Brigetta or..." Evelyn put her finger to her cheek and focused on the black-framed pictures grouped on the wall to her right. Then she snapped her fingers. "Dagmar. That was her name. Right?"

"Eva," Elliott said. "And she could speak English, just not fluently."

"As soon as Dagmar"—Louise waved her hand as if brushing away something of little significance—"or whoever"—she rolled her eyes—"left town, Elliott went to the farm's condo in Naples, Florida, for a week to recuperate."

Meredith covered her mouth with her hand in a losing effort to catch the laugh bubbling out. She'd never met a man who could sit at a table with three women and subject himself to such harassment. He timed every grimace, growl, grin, or glittery-eyed glance to elicit a touch of the arm, a pat on the cheek, or a smile. He appeared in complete control, the consummate actor in a theater-in-the-round production. The audience loved him, and he loved the audience.

Throughout dinner and after-dinner drinks, *the girls*—as Elliott called them—continued to tell stories, teasing him about his starched khakis and weekly barber appointments. Once, when Louise returned from the restroom, she came up behind him and ran her fingers through his hair.

He gave her a lopsided grin. "Don't stop."

Every strand dropped back into place when she removed her hand. "Honey, that's as far as I go." She winked at Meredith who fidgeted in her seat, wishing she could feel the rich texture of his graying hair glide through her fingers.

Elliott gave her an amused chuckle. "See what I have to put up with."

Meredith lowered her chin and tilted her head, inviting Louise into a conspiratorial conversation all the while gazing at Elliott. "From what I can see, he adores the attention."

"Elliott loves women, and he craves them all to himself. If there were another man at the table, he'd pout. He hates to share. I think that's why he enjoys spending so much time with Ev and me. No men to compete with."

"If I have this figured out correctly, Elliott, you and Louise met while you were undergraduate students at Edinburgh, right?"

"In a medieval literature class," he said.

"Then how did you meet Evelyn? Did you go to grammar school together or were your parents' friends?"

A hush fell over the group, and Evelyn's face tightened.

Elliott's hand twitched, sloshing the whisky in the glass he held.

His face shut down as if a door had slammed.

"Both," Evelyn said under her breath but loud enough for Meredith to hear. Then she mouthed the words, "We dinna talk about the parents."

Meredith lifted her feet, having stepped into a mess no one wanted to talk about; a mess that most likely defined her dinner companions. *I doubt I'll ever get that story.*

Chapter Ten

Louise's B&B – December 23

THE FOURSOME ENTERED the B&B with Elliott reciting a poem.

"*Fare-thee-weel thou first and fairest! Fare-thee-weel, thou best and dearest! Thine be ilka joy and treasure, Peace, Enjoyment, Love and Pleasure! Ae fond kiss, and then we sever!*" His thick and creamy baritone voice hugged Meredith in a sensual embrace. The timbre sent vibrations throughout the foyer, causing a gentle clinking of the chandelier's crystals.

"Oh, no," Evelyn groaned.

Louise put her arm around Meredith's shoulder. "All it takes is a wee dram and he starts quoting Rabbie. He can go on for hours."

"*Ae fareweeli alas, forever! Deep in heart-wrung tears I'll pledge thee.*"

"I've heard his entire collection hundreds of times. I'm going to bed before he starts singing off-key. Good night," Evelyn said.

Louise locked the front door and followed Evelyn to their first-floor owners' suite, calling over her shoulder, "Dinna bore Meredith. She's my guest."

He winked at Meredith. "I've never intentionally bored a woman, and I don't sing off-key." Elliott quieted. When the sound of a closing door filtered down the hallway, he continued in a lowered voice, "I have been known to annoy the girls enough to send them off to bed early."

"Intentionally?" Meredith teased.

He put his hand across his chest. "Nay, hen. But now that we're alone, how about a nightcap? I know where Lou hides a bottle of Richard Hennessy. I'll even stoke the fire."

The double entendre was as pointed as a fireplace poker.

Meredith took a calming yoga breath and said on an exhale, "I can't pass up a glass of cognac." Even to her ears, she sounded embarrassingly breathy. If possible, her goose bumps created their own goose bumps. She slipped off her coat, and for a brief couple of seconds looked at the walls, ceiling, floor, anywhere and everywhere but at him.

"Come. I'll show ye the secret stash." His crutches thumped against the marble floor.

They entered the library, and for the first time, Meredith noticed the name plate on the door. "Macfarlane Clan Library. Are the rooms named after Louise's family and friends, or did she randomly pick names?"

Elliott flipped a switch that turned on the recessed lighting, creating a soft, romantic glow around the edges of the room. "Macfarlane was her mother's name. What room are ye in?"

"Robertson."

"Evelyn's mother is a Robertson. The other rooms"—he shrugged—"I don't know."

"I like it. It's clever marketing," Meredith said. "Makes me want to research the clans' histories."

He laughed. "Do ye have time?"

"Not this trip," she said.

"How long will it take to complete the project ye're working on?"

"I've scheduled three days at the archives, but my life will be hectic for the next several weeks."

"Ye must have a slave driver for a boss."

"Oh, she's a real whip-cracker."

He opened the cabinet above the bar, pulled out one bottle, and pointed to another. "Lou hides the Macallan in here, too."

Meredith stepped over to his side, getting a whiff of grapevine flowers, freshly crushed grapes, and dry vines. A warming smile started from within and spread outward. The pleasing scent was a combination of the cognac and the man. "Do you know all of Lou's secrets?"

He took down two tulip-shaped glasses from a rack suspended beneath the top cabinet. "Most of them. How do ye want yers? Neat? On the rocks? Ginger ale?"

"Neat, please."

He poured a generous portion into each glass then handed one to her. She held the foot of the long, elegant stemmed glass and swirled slowly and gently. "My daddy always said when you tilt the glass just so—" She tilted the glass and examined the intensity of the spirit. "—it makes the cognac cry. See." She pointed. "The tears run down the side of the glass." Her gaze drifted from watching the tears to watching Elliott. The laugh lines around his eyes deepened. His enjoyment of her telling him something he probably already knew caused her face to flush.

She babbled on unable to stop, and her face grew hotter. "Hennessy's PR says, 'All cognac is brandy, but not all brandy is cognac.' I believe that's true, don't you?"

The laugh lines around his mouth deepened now. "Ye won't find another label in Louise's cupboard for that very reason."

The cognac didn't overwhelm Meredith, but Elliott certainly did. "Does Louise know your secrets, too?"

His long fingers wrapped around the foot of the glass and twirled the contents, much as she had done. His hand didn't shake, though. "I don't think I have any."

"Then you must be an open book."

"One page isn't much of a tome."

She savored the cognac and concentrated on all aspects of the spirit's personality, or rather, she tried to. *Is it round, mellow, smooth?* She asked the question but was unable to separate the ambient heat from the cognac from that emanating from Elliott. She stepped back and picked up the conversation. "Makes me curious about what's written on that one page."

"Not much. I have large handwriting." He demonstrated by drawing an oversized letter *E* in the air.

"So you're easy to read?"

He nodded "Most of the time—"

The banked fire suddenly roared to life, startling them.

Meredith watched the glowing embers shoot sparks up the chimney. "A magic fireplace or maybe there's a ghost in the house."

"In this room"—Elliott glanced around and lowered his voice—"probably ghosts."

"A ghost that doesn't believe you're easy to read," she said, giving him a teasing smile.

"I doubt Louise's ghosts care about me," he said in a flat voice. He tilted his head slightly, giving the impression of carefully weighing his words.

"There've been so many ghost stories in my family, see-through people don't scare me." She shrugged, lifting her hand loosely. "I guess that's why they never show up when I'm in the room. What's the fun in being a ghost if the person it's haunting isn't scared?"

Elliott gave her a watery smile that seemed forced into place. "Their purpose might not be to scare people, but they sure as hell scare me." He nodded toward the leather chair. "I need to put my leg up." He held out his glass. "Do ye mind?"

She followed him, carrying both their drinks. "Did you fall off one of your horses?"

He eased into the chair. "I had surgery to repair an old injury." He took his drink from her. "I saw the slicks for the marketing campaign this morning. Do ye own the company?"

Obviously, he's not going to say anything else about his leg. "I own the wine."

He let out a soft whistle of appreciation. "Ye're a vintner? Where?"

"Napa." Excitement pushed into her voice. "We're launching a new chardonnay in February." The flush returned, hotter than before. "I'm a shameful hussy when it comes to the winery. I've been taught never to miss a marketing opportunity."

Elliott sprawled back in his chair. "The teacher must be the same person who taught ye about cognac."

She laughed, partly to release the nervous tension and partly because he nailed her father. "His exuberance was contagious."

"Ye'll have to tell Louise about yer new wine."

"I noticed tonight that she likes her chardonnay."

Elliott raised a hand in mock surrender. "I've given up hope that she'll branch out and enjoy the nectar of the gods."

Meredith crossed one leg neatly over the other and gave him a challenging smile. "We'll have to agree to disagree on exactly what that nectar is. I own a winery." And she had been out of contact for more than three hours. What if someone needed her? Losing track of time was out of character and made her a bit antsy.

He gazed at her, and a curious expression crossed his face. "Is yer husband joining ye over the holiday?"

Her thumb fiddled with her wedding band. "I lost him two years ago."

Elliott looked deep into his cognac as if trying to extract a thought. "Did he die or did ye misplace him?"

Her jaw dropped. She tilted her head, staring at him. At first blush, the comment was offensive. As the words seeped into her brain, she recognized the pain that laced the words together and knew he spoke from his own reality.

"I don't mean to be cavalier," he continued. "Holidays are not an easy time for those who have lost loved ones." After a moment, he said softly, "I'm sorry for yer loss."

When he didn't ask additional questions about her husband, she swallowed relief. "Thank you. Holidays *are* hell. I try to stay busy. Right now, that's not hard to do."

Elliott nodded.

Silence had a language of its own and often spoke in a way that tensed her neck and shoulders. She rolled them slightly but didn't get any relief. The subtle undercurrent in the room even carried its own scent. Musky. Natural. Erotic. She swallowed the rest of her drink in a long gulp. Then she stood, saying, "It's been a wonderful evening, but I have a busy day tomorrow and need to turn in."

In spite of his injury, he rose from the chair with remarkable strength and agility. She guessed him to be close to fifty, and she appreciated his obvious commitment to staying physically fit. He had the physique of an endurance athlete. Sexy and, if she had to guess, ripped.

"Does that include another trip to the archives?" he asked.

She quit visualizing him shirtless, wearing either biker or running shorts, and collected their drinking glasses. "Day two starts early." She set the glasses in the sink at the bar and tidied up.

"How far back are ye researching?"

She grabbed her coat and purse off the chair. "Mid-seventeen-hundreds. Why?"

Elliott flipped off the lights. The room went dark, leaving them standing in the shadow of the hall's yellow light. "There's a Fraser family mystery dating back to that time."

"So you have an interest in genealogy, too?"

He followed her toward the elevator. "I wouldn't put it on my top-ten list, but I'm interested in this particular story." The door opened as soon as Elliott pressed the up arrow. When they stepped inside, his hand hovered over the control panel. "Two, right?"

She did a double take. "Yes."

He gave her a mischievous yet endearing grin. In that grin, she caught a glimpse of the young man he had been before stress and age etched character lines around his mouth and eyes.

"We're the only holiday guests. We're neighbors," he said.

"You really do know all Louise's secrets."

"Lou's very trusting, loyal, and extremely protective." With a nod, he added, "Occasionally bitchy."

A pang of sadness spread through Meredith's heart. Other than Cate, she didn't have anyone else she could say that about. "You're lucky to have her." The elevator began its slow ascent. "What do you know about your family mystery?"

"Only that a Fraser was born on the wrong side of the sheets around 1750. No one in the family has been curious enough to find out what happened."

"Except you."

"Except me." The elevator stopped on their floor. "Seems more important now."

She held the door while he hobbled out into the hallway. "You're more than welcome to join me. I could show you where to start your research."

"What time are ye going?"

"I have a nine o'clock reservation in one of the research rooms." They strolled down the hall. The rubber-tipped crutches made soft thuds against the carpeted floor. "It's a large building. A wheelchair might be easier to use than crutches."

He stiffened. "I get along fine with these sticks."

Stubborn. Just like her late father, Elliott would rather suffer blisters and inconvenience than show any sign of weakness. The thought stung a bit because maybe, just maybe, she would, too.

When they reached her guest room door, Meredith gazed into his warm eyes. A fuzzy sensation trickled down to her belly. *Find a good-looking Scotsman and have fun.*

"Have dinner with me tomorrow night," he said.

Wisps of hair had escaped her butterfly clip and hung freely around her temples. She finger-combed the strands, stalling, not to think of an answer to his question but just to think at all. Finally, she said, "Are you inviting Evelyn and Louise?"

"Ye don't want to be alone on Christmas Eve, do ye?"

No, she didn't, but the thought of spending an entire evening alone with him twisted her belly into a bushel of single knots. "They're your friends."

"And they'll enjoy a quiet evening alone. But if it's important, I'll invite them."

Meredith unlocked her door. "I hope they'll go." She pushed the door ajar yet lingered in the hallway for a moment. "Well, good night."

He leaned in with a slight tilt of his head. She brought her left hand to her face and fiddled with a loose curl. He gave her a wry smile and straightened. "I'll call for the car to be here at eight thirty. Are ye going for a run before breakfast?"

"A short one—five miles."

He tugged on the loose curl she'd abandoned. "Best way I know to clear yer head and focus on what's important." He tugged again on the curl. "Be careful. The sidewalks can get slick. We don't want *ye* needing a wheelchair."

"I'm always careful," she said, brushing her fingers against his as she reclaimed the curl.

Before she could change her mind and accept the kiss she sensed he wanted to give, she slipped into her room and closed the door.

If he had kissed me, would I have kissed him back?

Chapter Eleven

Louise's B&B – December 24

THE ALARM ON Elliott's cell phone beeped, waking him from a night of unsettling dreams. The images and emotions were beyond his grasp, yet he felt weighted down by them. He lifted the covers and searched for the phone. *What a sorry-ass bedmate.* When was the last time he had something in his bed that didn't bark, meow, beep, or ring?

He found the device then scrolled through two dozen new messages that had queued up overnight: An update from Doc letting him know the hearse still hadn't arrived; another one from Harrison telling him the insurance company sent a claims adjuster to the farm; and several others from shareholders expressing sorrow and disappointment. Their anger would come later, while his continued to gallop down the track. The last email was from Sandy. She attached a copy of the press release written exactly as he had dictated.

He eased his naked body out of bed, picked up the crutches, and hobbled to the window. Fixed shutters covered the lower portion, providing privacy. The sun wouldn't rise for at least an hour, but street lamps provided enough light to see that a layer of snow already blanketed Edinburgh. There was a trail of footprints from the B&B to the private park across the street. Only one set heading out. That meant Meredith hadn't returned from a snowy morning run in a strange city. He'd question her sanity if he hadn't done the same thing in places all around the world. Runners were a hardy lot. If he could turn back the clock, he'd be out running with her. But he would never run again. The pain in his leg provided constant reminders of that fact.

I wonder if she's Live Tracking on MapMyRUN.

As OCD as she appeared to be, he doubted she went anywhere she couldn't be found. He hobbled over to the desk where he booted up his laptop, logged onto the MapMyRUN website, and plugged in her name. Sure enough, GPS tracking showed her on her way down Great King Street. A slow smile of satisfaction eased onto his face.

He returned to the window and waited. A couple of minutes later, she jogged across the street toward the B&B dressed in skin-tight reflective running gear. The jacket's neon yellow color provided a stark contrast to the cold, gray stone buildings lining the street. Her warm breath appeared as a stream as it hit the cold Midlothian air. When she reached the sidewalk, she removed her gloves then pulled her phone from a pouch strapped on her waist. After tapping on the device, the live tracking session ended.

He stood at the window long after she'd entered the house, lost in holiday memories.

Chapter Twelve

The National Archives – December 24

ELLIOTT SAT NEXT to Meredith in the backseat of the limo, sending text messages while she replied to a series of emails on her iPad. On the other side of the tinted windows, snowflakes meandered from the sky, swirling about the imposing façade of the National Archives like dandelion seeds blowing in the wind. If only it were summer. The New Year's anniversary of Sean and Mary's deaths would be behind him. His leg would have healed from surgery, and the fallout surrounding Galahad's death would have settled. *Will I even have a job?* Situations like the one he faced typically needed a scapegoat.

No need to go there. Yet.

Getting through the next few days would be a start toward surviving the next six months, and enjoying Meredith's company was the best way to get through today.

He pocketed his phone and refocused on her. The corner of his mouth turned upward as he studied the look of concentration on her face. Her pursed lips held an air of familiarity. Had he grown accustomed to her facial expressions or was he just bewitched by her lips—a damnable temptation he'd resisted, barely. He would have to dance his way around her, one artful step at a time.

"Done." She flipped over the iPad's cover and slipped the device into her purse. A small line formed between her brows. "The catering company I hired had a dozen questions. Most of them I can't answer until I decide on the food and wine pairings. That's at the top of my list for next week." She slipped on a pair of leather gloves, snugging them around her fingers. "Are Louise and Evelyn joining us for dinner?"

Captivated by her long fingers encased in kid leather, he didn't respond to her question, thinking instead of how erotic it was to feel the heat of a woman's hand through her glove. He blew breath out through his teeth and rerouted his thoughts. Yes, ditching the girls had been his plan, but pleasing Meredith won out over pleasing himself. It was Christmas after all. "I made reservations for four at the Rhubarb."

Her mouth formed a perfect *O*. "They have an award-winning wine cellar. I've always wanted to go there. And the girls are going, too." She leaned in and kissed his cheek. "Thank you for working it out."

The touch of her soft, moist lips lingered long after she drew away. Her response was well worth his sacrifice. *One artful step at a time.* "The owner's a friend. I'm sure he'll give ye a tour."

"Those are magical words to a vintner," she said.

Elliott reached for the door handle, thinking he had something much more magical to entertain her with than an old wine cellar. "Shall we go?"

David exited the vehicle, hiding his crew cut beneath a driving cap. He handed Elliott his crutches. The Aviator glasses David wore even on overcast days hid the disapproval Elliott knew he'd see in the former army captain's eyes.

"Stay close in case I need ye."

With a magician's finesse, David slipped pills into Elliott's jacket pocket. "Eleven o'clock meds. Don't let the pain get ahead of ye."

Elliott snapped his pocket closed, securing the tiny envelope containing the pills. He'd taken his eleven o'clock meds at eight thirty, but David didn't need to know that. He settled a good hold on the crutches then stepped aside to make room for Meredith to join him on the sidewalk. "Let's take this slow and easy."

Meredith slung her bag over her shoulder. "There's a lift on the other side of the building if you'd rather not take the stairs."

He judged the distance across the icy sidewalk to the lift, comparing it to the difficulty of negotiating two dozen wide steps, and made a quick decision. "Let's take the stairs."

At the bottom step, he blew out dread on a long breath. Making it to the first landing would be worse than pulling fingernails. He could get through it, but hiding his agony from Meredith might take an Oscar performance. If he rattled her, maybe she wouldn't hover and notice his distress. He hobbled to the first step covered with fresh snow.

"Why do ye still wear yer wedding ring?"

She stumbled, barely grabbing the stone railing in time to remain upright. "That's twice today I've almost fallen."

He managed a grin. "Hope to hell ye don't get yerself killed."

She gripped the railing, too wide to wrap her hand around. "That'd put a damper on your dinner plans."

"Aye." *And much more.*

They reached the first landing without Meredith answering the ring question. Elliott stopped, readjusted his grip, and fixed his eyes on a bronze statue of Wellington mounted on a rearing horse. His thoughts went to Galahad—

"I took it off once," she said, "but I felt like I was running naked."

Running naked? Her comment jolted him back to his question. "So ye're one of those OCD runners who check their Garmin every five minutes?" He'd never worn one, enjoying the freedom of running without being tethered to a watch or smart phone. But he'd always mapped his run afterward to check the mileage and log the run in his notebook.

"I know it's good training to run without a Garmin, trusting your instincts and listening to your body, but not wearing a watch drives me nuts. That's the way I felt without the ring. I put it back on my finger."

"If ye're wearing a wedding ring so ye won't feel naked, won't any ring work?"

"Another ring wouldn't stop men from hitting on me." She chewed on her bottom lip and averted her eyes.

Her obvious embarrassment at exposing herself gave him smug satisfaction. "How's that working for ye, m'lovely?" He placed his finger under her chin and turned her head toward him.

She tempered her glare with a slight smile. "Not so good."

To him, women were unfinished jigsaw puzzles without a picture to use as a guide. His only hope of figuring out complicated creatures was to find the corner pieces first, then pray for inspiration. He had one section identified: obsessive-compulsive.

"Then why?" he asked.

While no longer chomping on her lip, a flicker of tension appeared around her mouth. He let go of her chin. "I don't see myself as a widow," she said. "Society placed a label on me that I can't accept. I'm not old, or a grandmother, or short and dumpy."

"Nay, yer none of those." At that moment, he spotted another corner piece: insecurity. "Reality often doesn't match perception." The cripple he'd become didn't jibe with the image of the man he carried in his mind. He nodded toward the entrance. "Let's get out of the cold."

Meredith flashed her reader's ticket at the door, and Elliott purchased a temporary pass to access the research rooms. With their search passes in order, they maneuvered through the shop area. Meredith appeared subdued, chewing on her bottom lip again. He wanted to snatch the plump, glossy tissue from her incisors. At the rate she was gnawing, she wouldn't have any lip left for him to kiss.

"Loss is forever. Acute grief isn't. Although I'm not in the acute stage now, loss"—she sighed—"*is* forever."

Meredith wasn't telling him a new story. He had a collection of *forevers* arranged in straight lines on a memory shelf. "What happened to yer husband?"

"He died two years ago from a stroke. In hindsight, I should've made him take better care of himself."

Elliott wiped sweat from his brow. "Guilt's like wearing an old pair of boots. Too familiar to throw out but too worn to do any good."

"Is that an Elliott-ism?"

"No. It was one of my grandfather's." Elliott swept his hand toward a chair. "Do ye mind if we sit?"

"You sure you don't want a wheelchair?"

If she thought of him as an invalid, she'd never see him as a lover. Crutches presented enough of a challenge to his masculinity. "No. Just give me a minute." He sat, but he got little relief from the pain. Thankfully, he had more medication. The current dosage was too low. He swallowed the pills David had given him. "Tell me about the rest of yer family."

She sat in the chair next to him. "There isn't much to tell. My parents are dead, and I don't have any aunts, uncles, or cousins."

The way she spoke, the way she gazed at him, touched him in a familiar way. He wanted to pull her into his arms and protect her as he'd never protected anyone, except Kit. But he couldn't stand and hold Meredith, and any attempt while sitting would be awkward and clumsy at best.

"I'm the last Montgomery," she continued, "and that's a perfect segue into why I'm here—to find my ancestors."

He shot a quick glance toward the top-lit domed rotunda. "Ye think they're in this room?"

"I doubt it, but it's beautiful in here, isn't it? They call this the Adam Dome Room."

He glanced around, smirking. "Where the hell are the old musty books?"

"The documents in this building are computerized."

"I'm disappointed. I wanted to blow dust off books that haven't been read in centuries."

"We can find those in another building." She pointed toward a doorway. "When you're ready, the Reid Room is that way."

He stood, gritting his teeth, and looking everywhere but into her eyes. He didn't want her to see his pain. Kevin and David didn't have to look into his eyes. They could hear it in his voice and see it in the slope of his shoulders—subtle signs that were noticed only by those close to him.

"When I get into those old dusty books, I'll have to hire someone to transcribe the documents I need," Meredith said.

He hobbled along beside her. "I'll do what I can to help ye. My grandda taught me how to read that old handwriting. He insisted the skill would teach me patience."

"Did it?"

"I couldn't have made it through veterinary school without it."

"This way." She led him through the Adam Dome Room to the Reid Room where the supervisor welcomed them. The man took Elliott's identification card, gave him a password, and showed him to his assigned seat on the last of four rows. Elliott told the man that if a seat opened up next to Meredith on the front row, he'd prefer to move.

Meredith came back to see him. "Here's a notepad and pen. You might want to take notes."

He rolled the pen between his fingers, reading the Montgomery Winery imprint and putting the phone number and website to memory.

The instruction sheet on the table offered easy-to-follow directions. His Grandda Fraser enjoyed this sort of thing but never mentioned researching at the archives. Whatever the reason, Elliott sensed a stronger-than-usual connection with the passionate old Scot who died the year before Elliott emigrated.

Step one, he entered his father's name and birthday: Elliott Blane Fraser, born July 17, 1936. The first record he found listed his father's date of death. He reviewed it then moved on to the record listing his father's marriage to Aileen McGregor, born October 1, 1946. If he clicked on his mother's name, the trail would lead to her date of death, two days after his tenth birthday.

He didn't want to read the entry, nor did he want to dwell on that long ago phone call from the hospital informing his father that his wife and Roger Graham had been killed in a car accident. Elliott had no memory of what drove his mother to leave home or of her funeral days later. His father never mentioned her or his good friend Roger again. Evelyn came to his mother's funeral, and he went to her father's, but even the two of them never discussed their parents or why they were together that fateful day.

Elliott sucked back the deep pain growing in his chest and forced himself to continue.

It didn't take long to locate his grandfather, born in 1898. Then he clicked the link to his great-grandfather, born in 1876. He followed the Fraser line, taking repeated detours to research a great-great aunt or uncle, or a descendant whose name sounded familiar. Several times he reached for his phone to call his father to ask a question about so-and-so. Twice he went to the men's room and splashed water on his face. When he reached the mid-1700s, he found mention of the session records. The instruction sheet said those documents were available for viewing at West Register House in Charlotte Square.

He sat back in his chair and reviewed his notes and the family tree he'd drawn. There were a few missing branches that he'd have to fill in later, but he had a good start. He checked his watch, surprised to find three hours had passed. Meredith might be ready for lunch. Afterward, he'd decide whether to search the records at West Register House now or wait until after Christmas. He logged out of the computer system and collected his notes.

A few people remained in the room. He stood behind Meredith's chair and watched her finger track the words on the monitor.

"Has anyone ever told you what a delicious scent you have? And it's never the same," Meredith said.

He leaned over her shoulder. "Delicious? Guess that means I don't smell like a horse."

She swiveled in her chair to face him. "I have an acute suite of senses. You left the room twice."

He straightened, surprised that she'd noticed. "Ye should have said something."

"I didn't want to intrude. I know this can be a difficult process." Her cheeks took on a pink, kissable hue. "You can escape my line of vision, but you can't escape my nose."

"So, what does yer nose say about me?"

She tucked her chin between her thumb and index finger, and stroked as she considered the question. "Outdoors. A pine forest. The sea. Christmas."

He stepped back and leaned on his crutches. *Aha. Another corner piece of the Meredith Montgomery puzzle.* Not only was she obsessive-compulsive, she was sensual. Now he wished he'd worn a kilt instead of trousers. The kilt was more forgiving when blood rushed to his dick.

"How about I take ye and yer trained nose to lunch?" *And we'll explore your sensual side.*

She closed her iPad and gathered her notes. "I thought you'd never ask. Let's get out of here. I've had enough for today." She slipped on her coat. "Did you find what you were looking for?"

"I traced the line back to 1760, but the information I need is at the West Register House. I'll go there after Christmas."

"So you found surprises."

"No, but surprises exist."

She stuffed his notepad into her bag but slipped the pen into his shirt pocket. "Keep this. I have dozens."

Before they left the room, he received a text from David. "Good news," Elliott said. "David parked in the disabled visitors' lot at the side of the building. We can take the lift instead of the stairs." Relief punctuated the announcement.

"How'd he do that?" Meredith asked. "I thought you needed a permit."

"He's a resourceful lad." Now Elliott could focus on where to take her to lunch instead of how to navigate the stairs without falling on his ass. "Is there a place ye want to eat?"

"A sandwich or salad is fine. I don't eat much for lunch if I'm having dinner out."

"I've got just the place. A classic bistro, busy and buzzy."

David pulled up as they exited the lift. "Take us to Fishers in Leith for lunch," Elliott said. A short time later, they arrived at the restaurant set in a seventeenth century watchtower located in the heart of Leith, a short walk from the waterfront.

"I haven't been to this restaurant either," Meredith said. "Dining with you is like winning a ticket to a culinary adventure tour."

"I've eaten in most of the restaurants in the city and have a handful of favorites. Fishers serves delicious fishcakes."

"Fish always tastes better when you eat it by the water."

"Then let's go eat fish," he said.

The waiter seated them in a cozy corner and left a wine list on the table.

"I bet," Meredith said with eyes and lips dancing a flirtatious tango, "that I can find a wine you'll like."

The mesmerizing dance held Elliott enthralled. "Impossible."

"Oh." Her voice was now part of the sultry dance. "Are you up for a six-bottle challenge?"

He leaned forward in his chair and placed his hand over hers. "Ah, hen, if we drink six bottles of wine, I'm not sure we'll make it to dinner. In fact, I'm sure we won't."

A blush crept up her neck. She glanced at the wine list again, clearing her throat. "We'll drink parts of six bottles. After the trouble you've gone to, I wouldn't dare miss dinner." She tapped her finger against the plastic-covered list, still not looking up at him. "I'll select six labels—"

"And bet that I'll like one of them?" he asked.

"Yep," she said.

He leaned in closer, close enough to smell the shampoo she'd used that morning, clean as fresh Highland snow. "And if ye don't?"

She cocked her head and gazed at him from hooded eyes. "I've never lost a six-bottle challenge."

His body responded to the finer nuances of sexual tension evident in her forward-leaning body language. He eased back into his seat, afraid of what he might do if he lingered so close. "I've interviewed a few apprentice jockeys with that attitude."

"Did you hire them?"

"Nope. Too cocky for me." He glanced at the wine list, wondering if the restaurant had a rare label he could appreciate. *Doubt it.* Since the odds were in his favor that he wouldn't like any of the wines she selected, what did he want if he won the wager? Sex. And the best location for seduction? Fraser House. A visit to the castle guaranteed they'd end up in bed. "I'll play. If I win, ye have to accompany me on a Christmas Day trip to Fraser House."

"I suppose you do want to see your family."

A chill went through him, cold and biting. "They're all dead." Then he thought of Galahad and the chill turned colder. "The house had water damage the other night, and I want to check on the repairs."

"But I'm going to win," she said.

"What's yer bet?"

A soft smile spread across her face. "That you take me to Fraser House."

In his mind, he had her stripped naked. "Well, let's drink some wine."

TWO HOURS LATER, Elliott and Meredith walked out of the restaurant and into the sunlight, laughing. "Ye made me drink six bottles of wine," he said.

Meredith wrapped a scarf around her neck for protection against the cold winds blowing across the harbor. "We didn't drink six bottles. We drank *from* six bottles. Probably no more than two or three glasses total."

"Ye've opened my palate to a new adventure."

She twisted her finger in her ear. "Wait. Wait. Am I hearing right?"

He chuckled, feeling the dizzying effects of painkillers mixed with a wee bit of alcohol. "Ye've done something no one else has ever been able to do, including na Faither."

"I know my wines." Her face flushed a deep rose color. Sexy as hell. "It was a safe bet that I could turn you on to a bold, striking one."

A bold, striking *woman* had turned him on already.

"You really liked the French wine that had been interred in an old scotch barrel, didn't you?"

He reached for her hand and kissed her palm. "I like to see ye smile. If enjoying a glass of wine will do that, then I'll drink any wine ye put in front of me."

She pulled gloves from her coat pocket and reclaimed her other hand. "Would David mind driving around the port for a little sightseeing?"

"He'll do whatever pleases m'lady."

They climbed into the limo, and David drove down Constitution Street and past Leith Links. "The birthplace of golf, right? Do you play?" Meredith asked.

"It comes with citizenship."

"I don't see you wasting time hitting a little white ball into a cup."

"Didn't we have a discussion about how I developed patience? Well, I can tell ye it didn't happen on the golf course."

David finished the tour of Leith and returned to the B&B. As the car pulled under the porte cochere, Elliott asked, "Are ye still going to the Highlands with me tomorrow?"

"Of course."

David opened Elliott's door, and he slid out first. "I'd like to leave by eight, if ye can be ready."

Meredith followed. "I won't run tomorrow, so I'll be ready on time."

As they entered the B&B, Elliott said, "Ye haven't checked messages for at least two hours. Did ye give yer staff time off?"

"You haven't checked yours either," she replied, laughing.

Guilt tugged at his conscience. While she'd gone to the restroom, he'd returned six emails. "So what do we do now? Dart off for a quickie?"

Her eyes flashed with something unreadable. "I have to work. But I promise tonight I'll leave my phone in the room."

He replied with a simple eyebrow arch. If she intended to leave her phone, he'd have her full attention again. Could he do the same?

No, not even for Meredith could he ignore the farm.

He peeked into the front room and dining room as they made their way through the foyer toward the lift. Louise wasn't there, probably at the market, which reminded him that he wanted to shop before dinner.

The elevator opened as soon as he pushed the call button, but before the door closed behind them, Louise yelled, "Elliott, wait. Cameron called and changed our reservation to seven thirty."

Elliott stuck his head out of the lift. "Why'd he call ye?'

Louise stood in the hallway with an armload of wrapped presents. "He didn't have your mobile number."

"Okay. Meet in the library at seven o'clock." He released the hold button, and the door closed.

"I've heard it's a very eclectic restaurant," Meredith said.

"Ye'll enjoy it." The lift stopped on their floor. Meredith stepped aside to give him room to exit first while she held the door. "Get that event menu sorted out. If it's on yer mind, ye won't be able to enjoy dinner."

She removed her hat and shook out her hair. "You've got me figured out."

Bloody crutches. In five years, they'd never hindered him, until now. He wanted her up against the wall, on the floor. It didn't matter. "Not at all," he managed to say. "Women are a mystery to me. A present to unwrap slowly, without cutting the ribbon or ripping the paper."

What was it about her that intrigued him? Familiarity? He sensed he'd known her longer than forty-eight hours, yet he didn't know her at all, not intimately. And for him, that was the only part that mattered.

They reached her guest room door. "Thank you for lunch and for being a good sport."

"Aw, shucks," he mumbled, feigning embarrassment.

She leaned against the door and moistened her lips with a flick of her tongue.

He slid his thumb over the curve of her cheek, the line of her jaw. Then he lowered his mouth, pausing for an instant to inhale the sweet yet erotic scents of her perfume and shampoo. Before his lips touched hers, he almost moaned, overcome by desire. The first contact—warm and compelling, innocent yet provocative—startled him. He drew away for a breath, and she gazed at him, vulnerability flashing in her eyes.

"I shouldn't have done that." *But I'm damn glad I did.*

"It just took me by surprise," she said.

"Then, let me surprise ye a second time." They had four hours before their reservation. If they weren't interrupted by phone calls, she'd go to dinner wearing the look of a well-loved woman. He lowered his head to kiss her, but she opened her door and slipped out of his reach.

"I'm going to work now."

"Ye sure ye don't want to relax a bit?" He looked past her toward the fireplace. "Maybe stretch out in front of the fire."

She gave him a sultry laugh. "I'm not sure we have the same definition for the word relax."

"Och! D'ye like mine to be the same as yers then?" he asked in his teasing brogue.

Her eyes were laughing now. "You wouldn't like mine."

"Ah, hen, don't ever doubt a Scotsman."

She pressed her hands against his chest and kissed him. "As tempting as you are, I do have to work. I'll see you at seven." She closed the door, leaving him standing in the hallway.

Bloody damn crutches.

Chapter Thirteen

Louise's B&B – December 24

MEREDITH PLOPPED IN a straight-backed chair next to an antique desk situated in front of a window that overlooked Great King Street. The sun appeared to be striking a pose between two dark clouds in the overcast sky. A simple ray of sunlight matched the warmth of Elliott's breath lingering on her skin. She had just spent two hours drinking wine with a man who made her tingle with anticipation. Her eyes closed, and she allowed herself a moment to fall into a dream world where she was both young and healthy. Would he notice the fine scars from surgery and reconstruction? Would they turn him off?

Why in the world was she wondering such a thing? He had only kissed her, for God's sake. A kiss didn't automatically lead to stripping off her clothes.

Stop worrying and get to work. Whatever happens…happens.

She turned on the laptop. The marketing slick she'd worked on that morning opened on the screen. It was time to focus on a narrow stream of thought that didn't include Elliott Fraser.

The rest of the afternoon slipped by, and before she knew it, the cocktail hour arrived. Unfortunately, the B&B didn't have room service, and she couldn't traipse into the library wearing pajamas. *Either throw on some clothes or forget about a glass of wine until dinner.*

While considering what to do, someone knocked on the door.

"Room service."

The voice of a roguish Scotsman made her smile. She rushed to open the door, feeling slightly light-headed. The scent of holly and cedar wafted over her.

"Would you like another glass of wine?" Elliott asked.

Somehow, he had rolled a serving cart covered with a white lace tablecloth, a vase with a single red rose, a glass of wine, and a plate of brie and crackers to her door. A quick glance up and down the hallway didn't reveal a co-conspirator, but she heard a door close on the other side of Elliott's room. She stood on tiptoes and kissed his mouth—warm and soft and delicious. A flirtatious invitation.

He licked his lips. "Cherry lip balm? Let's do that again so I can have another taste."

She ran her tongue along the seam of her lips, tasting the flavored balm. "Come in. I'll share my loaves and fishes." She rolled the cart into her room, gripping the handles with shaking hands. "I need to sit." She fanned herself. "Head rush. I must have gotten up too fast."

He dragged a chair away from the table and pushed it directly in front of her. Then he sat and took her pulse, pressing gentle fingers against her skin.

"Are you really a doctor?"

He raised his watch arm and checked the time, pointing a wait-just-a-moment finger at her. Finally, he released her wrist. "Yes, but my patients are of the four-legged variety and don't make a habit of fainting."

"I didn't faint." She took a deep, shaky breath and let it out in a whoosh. "I'm fine now."

He stroked the side of her face and stole a kiss. "Ye sure?"

She nodded. Although fears and inhibitions tried to tug her away, she pressed into him and spread her hands on his shoulders. He threaded his fingers through her hair, cradling her head. His tongue held the taste of whisky, his skin the woodsy oriental fragrance of aftershave. A different scent for him. The delightful combination tickled her senses and scared her, too.

"We've moved from a drinking game to kissing. How'd that happen?" she asked, breathing unevenly.

"I wanted to kiss ye at the bar, but I didn't want to be rejected in public. That would have shattered my ego." He pushed up his sleeve. "Would ye like to see scars from prior shatterings?"

She laughed.

"I've had half stitches, quarter stitches, and even a couple of French knots," he said.

She laughed again, and then she quieted. "I've got scars, too. Lots of them."

He shrugged, straightening his sleeve. "We all have them. Some are more visible than others."

"Mine aren't pretty," she said.

"Hell, I wouldn't want to get into a pissing contest with anyone over scars."

The sound of his voice, the touch of his fingers and lips, made falling into the swirling depths of his eyes too easy. Where would she fall next? Into his bed? Was that what she wanted? She knew what he wanted, but what was best for her? She pushed her wedding band up to her knuckle, moved it back down, then did it again.

He watched her play with her ring, and silence sizzled between them. After a moment, he kissed her cheek. "I'll see ye downstairs at seven. Enjoy the wine." He left, letting the door close softly behind him.

Chapter Fourteen

In the library at Louise's B&B – December 24

AT SEVEN O'CLOCK sharp, Meredith walked down the hall toward the library, following Elliott's raspy singing voice. "*There was a lass, and she was fair, at kirk and market to be seen, when a' the fairest maids were met, the fairest maid was bonnie Jean.*"

The heartwarming sound put a smile on her face as she entered the brick-red room. When she saw him, she stopped and her heart did, too. Standing before her, singing to an empty room, was a breathtakingly handsome man with the relaxed charm of one comfortable in his own skin. And tonight traditional Scottish dress from bow tie to ghillie brogues covered his skin. The blacks, whites, and grays were the same three colors in his slightly graying hair. A Prince Charlie jacket hugged his shoulders as if the tailor had stitched it together while the garment hung on his frame.

When her heart restarted, it fell into an awkward rhythm.

Elliott took a slow sip from the glass he held, then he gave a cheeky smile—part grin, part serious. Wide, appreciative eyes spoke before words came from his mouth. "Ye look—"

"You look—" she said, butting against his words.

They both laughed, but her throat held tight, nervous tension. Instinctively, her fingers splayed across her cleavage, visible above the scoop neck of a teal knit, body-hugging dress.

"Amazing," he said.

"Stunning," she said.

Elliott held up an empty wineglass. "Or whisky?"

"With a dash of—"

"Spring water," he said.

He turned toward the bar, and while he mixed cocktails, she ogled him, doing what she'd criticized men for doing. But in her own defense, she decided there was nothing degrading in the way she looked him over, appreciating his hot and rugged physique, not lusting. Who was she kidding? Hell yes, she *was* lusting. And what surprised her even more was that she had those feelings while being petrified that she had breast cancer. Were her hormones screwed up or what?

Now that his back was to her, she noticed that the portion of his right leg showing above his walking boot appeared thinner than his muscular left leg. A jagged scar was visible between the kilt's hem and the top of the walking boot. She cringed.

The sound of Louise's distinctive footsteps announced her arrival moments before she entered the room. Meredith drew her attention away from Elliott's leg and proffered a smile for her hostess.

When Louise's eyes settled on Elliott, she shrieked. "Ye look divine and worthy of yer scallywag reputation."

He raised his glass as if offering a toast.

Evelyn stopped in the doorway. "Why didna ye warn us? I havena seen ye in full Highland dress since that bastard chopped up yer leg and tried to kill ye."

Louise straightened his tie. "And if he wasna dead, I'd shoot him then cut his bloody dick off and shove it in his mouth."

Elliott's face tightened, and a warning sparked in his eyes. "Not tonight, Lou."

"That bastard died too easy," she said, patting the tie in place.

He tossed back the remaining whisky. "Let's not talk about it."

"Ye know how I feel about what he did."

A vein stood out on Elliott's temple. "Ye remind me often enough."

"It's hard for me to watch those I love live in pain," Louise said.

Elliott tossed a splash of whisky into his empty glass. "*Enough.* Let's go eat."

Evelyn threaded herself between the furniture until she reached Louise. "Come on, dearie. Let's get our coats." Evelyn looped her arm with Louise's and together they walked toward the door.

"It upsets me to think what that horrible man did," Louise said.

Evelyn patted Louise's arm. "Let's not think about it. Tonight, is Christmas Eve. Time to celebrate, not dwell on what canna be changed."

Elliott rubbed his brow as he moved his head side to side, murmuring something unintelligible.

"We'll meet ye at the door," Evelyn said before leaving the room with her arm still laced with Louise's.

"I'll help Meredith with her coat." Before he took a step, he blew out a long breath. Then, with each swing of the crutches, his face appeared to relax. He tugged the mink coat from her hands. "Ye could make this easy for me and turn around."

The lush fur settled on her shoulders. He swept her hair out of the way and placed a kiss on the nape of her neck.

"Don't pay attention to Lou," he said. "She's never learned to back off."

"The way I saw it, there were two people butting heads and sparks were flying." Meredith brushed her arm. "I think one landed on me."

Using the tips of his fingers, he skimmed the side of her neck. Her breath stopped as she tilted her head, leaned into him, and gave him access to the curve of her shoulder. His mouth covered the spot she offered with a warm wet kiss that left her tingly.

"It's Christmas Eve. Let's talk about us," he said.

She turned to face him, breathing in his musky scent and gazing into his eyes. "I don't think there is an *us*."

"We need to work on definitions. When I kiss a woman and she faints—"

Meredith smiled. "I was light-headed. I didn't faint."

He chuckled as he pulled her coat collar up and tucked it under her chin. "My kiss turned ye weak-kneed. Admit it."

"*Never*," she teased.

"Ah, my wee sweetheart." He lowered his head just enough to sink into her mouth. She rose up on tiptoes to meet his soft lips. "Ye're not going to change yer mind about tomorrow, are ye?" he asked, kissing the corners of her mouth.

"Hmm. I might be too *weak-kneed* to go anywhere."

"If that means I get to keep kissing ye, I'll risk having to change plans." He stole one more kiss. "If ye're ready, we need to go. A wine cellar tour awaits."

"*Oh*. I forgot. I didn't even check the restaurant's website to see what wines they stocked."

His teeth closed over her bottom lip. "That sounds like someone on holiday surrendering control. How does it feel?"

There was a sudden uptick in her heartbeat. She leaned back to gaze into his eyes. The dark irises were indistinguishable from the pupils, making his eyes difficult to read. "Scary as hell."

He wiggled his brow and twiddled an imaginary cigar. "Ye have nothing to fear."

Tickled by his antics, she gave him a smile that radiated from within. *I'm in way over my head here.* For someone always in control, always with a plan, she found letting go a bit like holding up her hands while riding a rollercoaster—exciting yet terrifying and not something she'd likely do again. The fare for the ride was too expensive.

Evelyn stepped in the room and grabbed her purse off the table. "That sounds like the Big Bad Wolf crooning to Little Red Riding Hood. Hurry, Meredith, before he has his way with ye."

"Evelyn calls you a wolf. You say I'm safe. I think I'm in danger either way."

His jaw tightened. "In my condition, I'm not a danger to anyone. Now, can we go before Cameron gives away our reservation?"

Maybe dangerous. Maybe not. But he had the word *heartbreaker* tattooed on his forehead. For all the common sense, she had nurtured during her life, when it came to him, she suited up in a common-sense deflector.

Chapter Fifteen

Christmas Eve Dinner at Prestonfield House

A CHILLED BOTTLE of champagne awaited them inside the car. Elliott popped the cork and poured the bubbly while David drove down Princes Street. They passed last-minute shoppers hustling across the snow-covered streets, bundled against the cold. Meredith arched into Elliott and not just for warmth. He laced his fingers with hers and drew her hand to his lips.

"If the Edinburgh Wheel is still operating after dinner, we'll take a ride," he said.

She had never been on Edinburgh's Ferris wheel but had heard the view of Edinburgh Castle from the top of the wheel was spectacular. "I'm a California girl. We don't do cold."

A small line formed between his brows. "Ye're bundled up like ye're in Iceland. It was colder this morning when ye went for a run."

"Running's different. My gear is made for cold weather."

He tugged on her coat. "The creatures who gave their lives for this coat lived in the cold. Ye'll be plenty warm." He smiled, slow and hot. "If ye're still cold, I'll warm ye up."

Even in the car's dark interior, she couldn't miss the blazing intensity in his gaze. He'd had her in his clutches the moment he said, "I'll be the barman, Lou." A brief touch, a sizzling look, an erotic scent covered her like a whisper-soft cashmere blanket that had been heated in the dryer.

"Wear the coat tomorrow," he said, breaking into her reverie. "I have a surprise for ye."

"Hmm. A heavy coat." She tapped her nail against her tooth. "Are we going to a parade?"

A soft smile spread across his face. "No, it's a surprise. Ye'll have to wait and see."

The vehicle stopped in front of the entrance to Prestonfield House. The door opened and closed as new diners arrived.

"Is there anything I should know before I go in?" Meredith asked.

"It's flamboyant," Elliott said.

"That's an understatement," Evelyn said.

Meredith walked into the lobby of the boutique hotel and gasped. "I've just stepped out of black-and-white Kansas into Oz." Brocade and velvet walls served as a backdrop for a room full of rich and colorful art and antiques.

"Have we ventured into the seventeenth century?" she asked in a hushed voice, wide-eyed.

"Opulent and quirky. Reminiscent of Liberace," Evelyn said.

Louise fluttered across the room in a flowing skirt. "Look," she pointed. "That's a late Regency console table." Affectionately, she rubbed her hand across the smooth surface. "Cameron is always adding new pieces. I dinna ken where he finds them, and he *willna* share his source. Why is that?"

"I wouldn't give up my source either." Meredith glanced up at the elaborate staircase. "What are the guest rooms like? Have any of you stayed here?"

"A couple of times last year while Lou was renovating." Elliott nodded toward a man walking in their direction. "Here comes Cameron, the owner. He'll show ye a room, too, if one's available."

"Louise, Evelyn, Merry Christmas." The restaurateur air-kissed their cheeks. "Ye both look ravishing." Then he turned toward Elliott and Meredith, "Not so sure about this old boy, but he has fantastic taste in American women." He kissed Meredith's hand. "California, eh?"

"How—" Meredith smiled. "Louise must have told you."

"I canna lie. And ye're as beautiful as she said." He pointed at Elliott's leg. "Ye've been cut on again."

"For the *last* time," Elliott said.

"Only if ye listen to yer doctors, and judging from the fact that ye're not in a wheelchair, I'd be willing to wager ye'll have another surgery within six months." Cameron turned to Louise and Evelyn. "Willing to wager?"

"Not a chance," Evelyn said.

Cameron laughed then quickly sobered. "I was heartbroken to hear about yer father."

A shadow crossed Elliott's face. "It was a shock."

Cameron squeezed Elliott's shoulder in a tender way that said more than words. "And I heard Kit's been living at the MacKlenna estate for the last three months. Maybe I'll see her soon."

Louise put her hands on her hips. "I doubt it. We havena even seen her, and ye know how much she loves shopping in Edinburgh. We thought for sure—"

"She's living in seclusion," Elliott interrupted, "and we need to respect her privacy."

"Kit's too social to stay secluded," Louise said. "I bet we see her before spring."

Elliott rolled his eyes.

Cameron turned toward Meredith. "What brings ye to Edinburgh?"

"She's digging through the archives for state secrets," Elliott said, snugging his hand into her coat collar and gently massaging her neck.

Cameron's laughter rumbled through the foyer. "If ye find any, please share." He took her arm. "I'll escort ye to the Rhubarb, and ye can tell me where in California ye're from."

"Napa," she said.

"*The Wine Country?*" His eyes grew large with excitement. "Never been there, but it's on my list of places across the pond to visit." When they reached their table he said, "Here comes yer server. I'll leave ye in her capable hands."

A buxom blonde appeared and took their orders. A few minutes later, everyone settled in with drinks.

Louise swatted Elliott's arm. "Ye'll never change."

He rubbed his elbow, looking annoyed. "What the hell was that for?"

"Ye're sitting at the table with three women and ye're drooling over Miss Germany." Louise rolled her eyes. "Ye're *such* a boob man."

Elliott eased back in his chair and sipped his drink. "I'm observant."

"Pish. Ye've never dated less than a D-cup woman in yer life." Evelyn pointed her finger at him. "Ye even hit on Louise all those years ago."

"I didn't know she didn't date men." Elliott recrossed his legs and fiddled with his ghillie brogues' laces. Louise and Evelyn both laughed. Meredith cringed but anchored a smile into place. It remained there during dinner, frozen.

D-cup women. If that's his preference, why is he interested in me?

Waiters approached the table and removed the dishes, and after they had cleared everything away, the waitress brought a bottle of champagne. Elliott took the opened bottle from her. "Thank ye, m'dear. I'll pour."

"Champagne. This *is* special." Louise directed her comment to Meredith. "He never buys champagne."

"I never had to. This was Grandda's purview." Elliott poured about two fingers' worth of the sparkling wine into each of four tall, champagne-fluted glasses and passed them around the table. "'Tis time for a wee toast." He quieted a moment, appearing deep in thought, then said, "Thank ye for joining me tonight and thank ye for making this Christmas Eve special."

They clinked glasses, saying, "Merry Christmas."

Elliott set his glass aside, dug into his silver-mounted, cantle-top sporran, and removed three small boxes. One was wrapped in emerald-colored paper, another sapphire, and the third a deep ruby.

He handed the green box to Evelyn. "This matches yer eyes." The blue one he handed to Lou, saying, "And this one matches yers."

Then he turned toward Meredith. "This doesn't match yer eyes, but it matches yer passion, not just for yer winery but for something much deeper. Merry Christmas, m'lovely."

When Meredith didn't take the box, he opened her hand and clasped her fingers around the small package.

"I can't take this," she said quietly, praying she didn't offend him.

Evelyn held up a pair of emerald earrings. "These are beautiful."

Heat rushed through Meredith's body, and hot sweat broke out under her breasts. *Damn.* She didn't bargain for this.

Louise unwrapped her box, shrieked with excitement, then held up a pair of sapphire earrings. "Elliott, ye shouldna have done this." Then she giggled. "But I'm so glad ye did."

"Open yers, Meredith," Evelyn said.

Meredith pressed her hand against her chest and leaned forward. "I can't accept this gift."

Louise waved her ring-clad fingers. "Of course, ye can. Open the box."

Meredith turned toward Elliott and pleaded with her eyes.

He squeezed her hand. "This comes with no expectation."

"When a man gives a woman a gift, there're always expectations," she said.

He steepled his hands and tapped his forefingers against his lips, thinking. "Wear it tonight and return it in the morning. Consider it on loan."

Against her better judgment, she opened the box. Her next breath caught in her throat. Inside was a ruby art deco stickpin in a white gold setting. "It's exquisite."

"I thought ye'd like it. Put it on."

Her hand wouldn't stop shaking long enough to unclasp the hook. Elliott's warm fingers slipped around hers. "Let me. I've been thinking of doing this since ye walked into the library in this stunning dress." He fished the stickpin through the fabric and

Meredith's nipple hardened as his knuckles brushed her breast. He clasped the hook and slowly withdrew his fingers, taking her breath with him. Elliott rubbed the knuckle that had touched her skin across his bottom lip.

"Beautiful. Just like ye."

Chapter Sixteen

Louise's B&B – Christmas Eve

EDINBURGH HAD QUIETED by the time David drove back down Princes Street after dinner. The clock ticked toward midnight and another Christmas Day. The Edinburgh Wheel had shut down for the night. With the lights off, the structure loomed in the darkness. Meredith envisioned herself sitting at the top, waiting alone for the wheel to start again. The words to John Lennon's song "Watching the Wheels" came to mind. *No longer riding on the merry-go-round. I just had to let it go.* Her overbooked life left little free time to ponder the passage of weeks and months, and the end of the year always came as a surprise. Determined not to find herself in the same situation next year, she vowed to change her ways. Then and there, she made a resolution that regardless of what happened with her breast, she would approach the coming year differently and get off the merry-go-round.

Good luck with that.

ELLIOTT ESCORTED THE women inside the B&B, and as they had done on the previous evening, Evelyn and Louise said good night and retired to their room.

He hung his coat and hat on the hook next to the door, unbuckled his sporran, and left it on the table Louise used for mail and messages for guests. Turning to Meredith, he asked, "Would ye like a cognac?"

"Hmm." She weighed a drink in the library against an early morning departure. "What time do I need to be ready to leave in the morning?" It wasn't being ready that concerned her. Her concern stemmed from fear of being alone with him after champagne, a piece of jewelry, and the tingling sensation inspired by his finger brushing the top of her breast.

"Between seven thirty and eight o'clock. But that shouldn't be too early for someone who runs at five thirty." The crutches' rubber tips squeaked against the marble floor as they walked down the hallway. He paused at the turn to go toward the library and waited for her to answer.

"I'll pass on the cognac. I'm feeling a buzz from the champagne."

He gave her a breathtakingly warm smile. "Okay."

She nodded toward the lift. "I'm going on up." This wasn't what she wanted to do, but it was what she needed to do. Sitting with him in the cozy library was opening the door to more intimacy. After the *boob man* comment made at dinner, she was even more self-conscious about her breasts. She needed to discourage him, not the other way around.

He walked with her. "Will ye need a wake-up call? I'll be glad to roll over and tell ye good morning."

Meredith pushed the up arrow, shaking her head. "I bet that line works for you."

He gave her a mischievous grin. "First time I've used it. How am I doing?"

The door opened, and they stepped inside. "I wouldn't take jewelry from you. I doubt I'll jump in bed with you either."

"Ah, hen." He crossed his hands over his heart. "Ye've dashed a lad's high hopes."

Handsome, sexy, and almost irresistible. When he gazed at her with those dark, penetrating eyes, she melted as fast as ice cream on a summer afternoon. She punched the button and the elevator began its slow rise. Her foot made a tapping sound against the hardwood floor. "You're good at melting a girl's resistance. I've almost fallen for it twice."

He leaned forward, his mouth only inches from hers. "Third time's the charm."

She tucked her bottom lip between her teeth, stepped back out of his reach, and punched the button again, again, and then again. The elevator stopped, and the door opened.

"I think the girls have given ye the wrong impression of me," Elliott said.

She chuckled. "I think Evelyn and Louise are spot on when it comes to you."

He held the door while she exited. "I'm as loving and loyal as a golden retriever."

Meredith cocked her head a bit. "Seriously?"

"Just ask Tate."

She fished her room key from her purse. "Okay. Who's Tate?"

"My golden retriever."

She shook her head. "I don't peg you as owning a golden. You're more of a—" She raised her chin in thought. "Pit bull owner."

"Ah, jeez, Mer. Give a guy a break."

She put the key in the lock, laughing.

"I inherited Tate and a spoiled Maine coon cat named Tabor a few months ago. And Tabor is twice as big as a pit bull."

Before she could mention that he was an unlikely cat owner, too, his mouth was over hers. The air crackled between them with sexual energy that engulfed everything in its wake: the hallway, stairs—hell, the entire house. The delicious salty taste of him flavored every breath. The beat of her heart drummed thickly in her ears. She teetered on the tip of her toes, like a top spinning around and around. If he pulled her to the floor or pressed her against the wall, she would surrender. Only a kilt, a knit dress, her silk thong and bra—flimsy pieces of fabric—separated them. The explosive heat couldn't possibly be hers, but it was, and she burrowed closer, wanting him, needing him in a way she couldn't believe possible.

Slowly, he slid her dress up her bare legs. Strong fingers massaged her, leaving a trail of tingling sensations along the way. She dug her nails into the back of his jacket. Muscles bunched beneath it. Hard muscles. Muscles that said he was all male. If the jacket had been flesh, she would have left scratches, a testament to her burst of hunger. The bottom of her dress gathered at her hips, and a sliver of good sense returned.

"This isn't me, Elliott."

"Feels like ye. Hmm. Tastes like ye. Must be ye." His teeth closed on her ear as his hands pulled her closer to his hips, to an erection dangerously free of restraint trousers would have provided.

"That's not what I meant." She set her hands on his chest. "For a man right out of surgery"—she glanced down—"you surprise me with your…persistence."

He gently stroked her face, then outlined her lips with the tip of his finger. "Relax, hen. It's Christmas."

She could easily fall under the spell he sprinkled like fairy dust, but she couldn't. Not while living with a handful of uncertainties. "That's not easy for me to do." She kissed him lightly. "I'll see you in the morning. Good night."

As she closed the door, she heard him groan. Hopefully, he didn't hear hers.

Chapter Seventeen

Louise's B&B – Christmas Day

A SHORT, crisp knock burst against Meredith's guest room door.

Her eyes popped open. Bright morning sun beamed through the two shuttered guest room windows. She rolled over, checked the time on the alarm clock—eight o'clock. Plenty of time. Her eyes closed, and she sniffed, smelling the soothing fragrance of the rose in the vase on the bedside table. *Elliott.* Vivid dreams of him had invaded her sleep. She snuggled into the silky sheets and pulled the thick down coverlet over her head.

Another staccato knock jostled her memory. *It's Christmas morning.* She threw back the covers, realizing she had overslept. "Coming." Elliott must be wondering what had happened to her.

A scoop-neck cardigan that matched her pajamas lay across the end of the bed. She snatched it up and threw it over her shoulders. Before turning the doorknob, she peeked through the peephole. *Elliott.* She glanced in the mirror to assess the damage. *I look like crap, and he looks like he just left a* GQ *photo shoot.*

She raked her hand through her bed hair, smoothed down her drawstring pajama bottoms, then took a breath and opened the door.

He gave her the rakish grin she'd come to recognize as part of his charm. "Merry Christmas." Then his eyes roamed the length of her body. "Ye look gorgeous fresh out of bed."

Her own special Santa—showered, shaved, and blind as an old dog. Insomnia and jet lag had kicked in, and she'd worked most of the night. Her eyes were probably red and puffy, and not wearing a bra made her self-conscious. She crossed her arms across her chest, thinking it would draw less attention to her breasts.

"Merry Christmas to you, too. I'm sorry. I overslept."

"That wouldn't have happened if ye'd taken me up on my offer."

She laughed. "I'll never fall for a line you've worn out on other women."

"There ye go again, making assumptions."

Lord, help me, please. The morning had just begun and already she was flirting with him. That didn't bode well for the remainder of the day.

"Step aside," he said, pushing a food cart with dome-covered dishes and a carafe of coffee through her doorway using his body, while his hands gripped the handles of his crutches.

"You are multitalented," she said, watching him push the table with his hips.

"I brought ye the works—bacon, sausages, fried eggs, scones, haggis, and fresh squeezed orange juice."

"Did you squeeze it yourself?" she teased.

"Louise kicked me out of her kitchen fifteen years ago after I started a fire in the microwave."

"Hope you're going to share this with me. I couldn't possibly eat it all."

"I've already eaten."

"Then have some coffee." Meredith took over steering the cart and pushed it toward an elegant low table in front of the fireplace. Upholstered Queen Anne chairs were positioned at both ends of the table. "Pour your cup. I'll be right back."

She hurried into the bathroom to brush her hair and teeth and wash her face. Her puffy eyes needed a cold, wet teabag treatment. *Maybe later. He's already seen you. No point standing in the bathroom letting breakfast get cold.*

She squirted lotion on her hands and rubbed some on her face. When she returned, Elliott looked up from the newspaper. His smile looked strained. "Ready for coffee? I'll pour."

"What's happening in the world?" she asked.

He folded the paper and handed it to her, pointing to a section at the bottom. "I made the news; rather, my horse did."

Meredith read the article. "*My God.* Galahad died? He was yours? Oh, Elliott, I'm so sorry. What happened?" She continued reading the press release. "Why didn't you say something? I feel awful for you."

"The veterinary diagnostic lab hasn't issued a preliminary autopsy report yet."

"The article says he just returned from New South Wales."

Elliott tapped the side of his coffee mug. "The airplane was rerouted because of the weather, and he was in the air for twenty-eight hours. The trip might have caused his death. At this point, we don't know."

She put down the paper. "I saw him win at Santa Anita Park. When he turned the final corner and headed for home, he didn't look like he had anything left. Then he raised his ears and took off. He won by—what? Five lengths? Fantastic horse. What a heart."

"Six. That was his last race."

"He certainly went out a winner. How'd he end up at your farm?"

"The MacKlennas lobbied for him, but damn if Kit didn't work a deal with the owner's son. Quite a coup."

"She's your goddaughter who lives in the Highlands, right? Are you going to see her?"

He sipped his coffee. "Not this trip."

"How close is your house to the MacKlenna Estate?"

"Not far."

"If you want—"

He puffed up his chest and poked his tongue to the back of his teeth, jutting out his jaw. "It's not my decision. It's Kit's, and I doubt that will change."

She drew back at both his body language and sharp tone of voice, because she had overstepped her bounds and intruded.

He pressed his fingers into his eye sockets and rubbed, shaking his head. "Forgive me. Ye didn't deserve that."

She blinked. Sharp-toned voices were common in her life. Apologies were not. "You have a lot going on. Surgery and now your horse. I'm a good listener if you want to talk." Now that she knew about the crisis on the farm, she'd definitely keep her own problems to herself. Not that she was likely to tell him about the lump anyway.

He gathered his crutches and stood. "What say we put everything aside for a few hours and celebrate Christmas? David will be here in about forty-five minutes."

"Jeans, boots, fur, right?"

His smile didn't reach his eyes, but she understood why, or thought she did.

After he left the room, Meredith sat quietly for a few minutes, musing over the complicated man that had caused tremors of pleasure to sweep through her. She couldn't analyze it, justify it, or explain it away. It just happened, and for today and maybe tomorrow, she would revel in the warmth of his kisses.

Chapter Eighteen

Christmas Day

MEREDITH STOOD IN the B&B's foyer waiting for Elliott. She quietly tapped her toe while gazing out the window, enjoying the beauty of the snow-covered park across the street. The fact that she hadn't experienced many snowy Christmas mornings added to her nervous excitement.

Louise walked out of the dining room carrying a basket. "I packed food for yer trip."

"Hmm." Meredith sniffed. "Delicious. Fresh bread?"

"Ham, apples, cheese—"

Elliott hobbled up behind her. "Ye didn't need to do that. Alice will have food at the house."

"How's she going to manage that? The kitchen's in shambles and no restaurants will be open."

"Twinkle her nose like she always does." He put his arm around Meredith. "Ye ready?"

Louise looked over Elliott's shoulder. "Where's Kevin? Isna he going with ye?"

"I don't need him. He went back to bed. Ye might see him later."

"Who's Kevin?" Meredith asked.

"Pish," Louise said, talking over Meredith. "The lad will be in the kitchen within the hour. He's feeding a tapeworm." Louise handed Elliott his cap that had been hanging on a hook by the door. "I expect ye to stay warm. Ye just got out of the hospital."

He winked at Meredith. "I'll do my best." He eased down the steps, then they crossed the cobbled drive together, reaching the open door of the car.

"Who's Kev—" Meredith asked.

Louise interrupted again. "And if ye go by the MacKlenna estate and see Kit—"

"She doesn't want to see anyone. *I don't like it*, but I'll respect her decision."

Meredith shivered, although she stood in the flow of warm air pouring out of the heated car. Elliott had used that same tone of voice with her earlier. For the rest of the day, she wouldn't ask him about anyone else unless he volunteered information first.

"It's Christmas," Louise said.

Elliott held up his hand to stop her. "Please, Lou, not today."

Meredith's curiosity leapt dangerously close to the edge of good sense. Why didn't Kit want to see anyone? Obviously, Elliott didn't intend to discuss her, so Meredith buttoned up the urge to ask him why.

Evelyn walked to the door and stood next to her partner. "When will ye be back?"

"Should I leave the door unlocked?" Louise yelled.

"Ye better. I don't have a key. We'll be late. Don't wait up."

Meredith climbed into the backseat of the limo, and Elliott scooted in beside her.

"Do you think Lou wishes she were going with us?"

"I wouldn't be surprised." His voice held a high level of exasperation.

David helped Elliott cushion his leg on the opposite bench seat. Once he was settled, David closed the car door and stashed the crutches in the trunk.

"Since I arrived in town, she's been gnawing a bone about something," Elliott said.

Meredith leaned forward and glanced out the tinted window.

"She's still standing there."

Elliott rolled down the window. "Go back inside or ye'll catch a cold." He rolled up the window. "In twenty years, she's never fixed food for the road."

"Speaking of the road, where're we going?" Meredith asked.

David pulled the car out onto Dundas Street. At eight thirty on Christmas morning, there wasn't another car in sight.

"Fraser House is on Loch Ness close to Inverness. The traffic should be light all the way, but it'll take about three hours. There's not much to see except forests and fields, but pay attention. I'll give ye a test later."

"I'd better take notes."

A sheen of perspiration appeared on his forehead. He wiped his brow without commenting, then shoved the handkerchief into his jacket pocket. "I think ye probably have an excellent memory and rarely write anything down."

"Are you kidding? I'm a compulsive list maker."

He looked at her with eyebrows arched. "Ye forget things easily, then?"

She retrieved a notepad and pen from her bag. "I take notes so I won't."

His lips curled up on the ends in a tight smile as if he were trying to keep the lid on a chuckle.

"Go ahead and laugh. But you never had to deal with my father after you forgot an appointment."

Elliott wrapped his arm around her and pulled her close. "He got after ye, did he? Were ye afraid of him?"

The old familiar bellyache returned with the memories. "Only of disappointing him."

"If ye had to prove yer value to him, he wasn't worth yer effort."

"He wasn't that bad really." She shrugged. "He had expectations. One of them was that if we had an appointment, I was to be there on time."

"Let me guess." Elliott rubbed his chin. "Ye were late to an important meeting."

The ache of disappointment and rejection whirled through her. "Real important, or it seemed so at seventeen. I was a senior in high school. We scheduled an after-school meeting to discuss my spring trip. I lost track of time and arrived at his office forty-five minutes late. I knew what to expect the moment I saw his secretary's face. I found a note on his desk that said"—Meredith made air quotes—"Irresponsibility will not be tolerated."

"He left?" Elliott asked.

She nodded. "He waited a total of fifteen minutes then left town for a two-week tour of northern Italian wineries."

"And ye didn't get to go on yer trip."

Meredith shook her head slowly as if even now she couldn't believe it had happened that way. "The next day I started writing down appointments on three different calendars, a habit I've kept all these years. I even carry a daily to-do list in my pocket."

Elliott ran his hand through her hair at the nape of her neck. "What's on yer list for today?"

She smiled, feeling pleased with herself. "Ignore my phone."

His eyes widened in surprise, and he whistled. "I'll help ye stay on task." Then he pressed his lips against hers, creating an explosive heat deep within her body. She wasn't used to wanting a man like this and the feelings both excited and frightened her.

"I'll try to make it worth the sacrifice," he whispered against her lips.

"You're doing well so far." She kissed him back, letting their tongues dance the tango, a dramatic and seductive dance. Finally, she broke away before the sexual tension building like an engulfing flame proved she was capable of being irresponsible.

David drove the car out of Edinburgh. They crossed the Forth Road Bridge and followed the A90, which became the M90, toward Perth. No cars. No people. Only trees and fields. Nothing to make note of except that Elliott fidgeted. He adjusted then readjusted the straps on the walking boot as if he wanted to rip the damn thing off and throw it out the window.

"Is there something I can help you with?" Meredith asked.

Elliott shook his head. "Damn boot. Six weeks of this will drive me mad."

"I've never had to wear one. Does it itch?"

"No, it's just blasted uncomfortable."

The flush and strain on his face said it was much more than uncomfortable. His discomfort fueled her concern. After the trauma of Jonathan's stroke, she automatically assumed the worst would happen whenever anyone got sick or injured. And Elliott had only been out of the hospital a few days. As stubborn as he appeared to be, he probably left before the ink had dried on his discharge papers.

Now it was her turn to fidget. She needed her phone. But after making such a to-do about turning it off, she couldn't very well turn it back on.

"Am I making ye nervous?" Elliott asked. "Ye seem jittery."

She shook her head. "N-no, not at all," she stammered. "It's the middle of the night at home, but I'm still suffering from communication withdrawal."

He chuckled. "I didn't think ye could go very long. Check for messages, set the phone to vibrate, then put it in your pocket."

"Is that what you've done?"

Although he smiled, it was a tight smile. "I don't have the luxury of disappearing even on Christmas Day." He sounded weary, and not just physically tired.

As hard as it was for her to believe, she knew the winery could function without her for several hours, days even. That she had learned following her father's death when she'd been stuck in a moment of grief—a moment that had gone on for several weeks until Cate bullied her into going back to work, playing the role Meredith's father would have played.

David took the Broxden Roundabout and turned onto the A9 toward Inverness. The four-lane divided road was lined with open fields, rolling hills, trees, a rare house, and a few road signs.

Meredith asked, "How long have you had a house in Inverness?"

"Fraser House has been in the family since 1468."

Her jaw dropped. "*Fourteen?*"

"The family has been around for a while. The house burned during the Jacobite rebellion. The Frasers rebuilt in 1780."

Dozens of questions rushed to the forefront of her brain, but she stemmed the tide of her unrelenting thirst for answers. She could be annoying, as her staff often complained, when she got on one of her question/answer jigs.

He wiped his forehead with his handkerchief. "David, turn the heat down, lad. It's a sweatbox back here."

Meredith looked up and caught David watching Elliott in the rearview mirror. She knew the heat was on a low setting, and if anything, it was cool in the car. Her fingers itched to do the forehead fever-touch test, but the Elliott Fraser she'd come to know would be offended and would probably push her hand away.

"Is there a room with a large fireplace where we can take off our shoes and relax for a while?"

He leaned in so close that his breath stirred tendrils of hair that had fallen loose of her hair clip. They brushed against her cheek and tickled her face. "My wee darlin', ye can have yer pick of fireplaces."

"We're not talking about a *wee* house, are we?" she said, giving lift to her eyebrows.

"The place can be intimidating."

"Because of its size or appearance?"

"There's a wee bit of history in the old walls."

"And a few ghosts, I bet?"

"So they say."

Goose bumps rippled over her skin. She casually rubbed her arms, wishing Louise had packed a thermos of coffee or, better yet, whisky. In the last couple of days, Meredith had become even more hypersensitive, especially to Elliott's intoxicating earthy fragrance with notes of cedar and incense along with the depth and fullness of a honey and spice flavor. Delicious and captivating.

"What's yer family name?" Elliott asked.

"Montgomery."

He gave her a curious glare that asked the same question others had asked through the years.

"I didn't change my name when I married. If that's what you're wondering."

"Did ye come from a large family?"

She curled her goose-bump-clad legs up under her hip and faced him. "My grandmother was a Cameron. She emigrated from Scotland after World War II and met my grandfather, James Montgomery, during one of his business trips to New York City." Meredith took a quick breath and continued. "They married and had three boys. My father was the youngest. The Vietnam War took his two older brothers."

"That happened to a lot of families," Elliott said.

"To your family?" she asked.

"No. If ye know that history, why are ye doing research here?"

"All the genealogy records were lost when the estate house burned at the turn of the century. So no Montgomery family records exist before the birth of my grandparents in the 1920s."

"I think ye said ye didn't have any siblings?"

Meredith dug through the picnic basket, found a bottle of water, and took a long drink. "There was just me to torture my dad."

"What about yer mother?"

"She died shortly after I was born. She was an only child, too, and her parents were already dead."

It wasn't pity she saw in his scrunched face; it was empathy. He knew. He understood her loneliness. Quickly, he rubbed his fist across his lips in a warning signal to his emotions to stay put or die. She knew what he was doing because she often did the same thing.

He cleared his throat. "California Montgomerys?"

"If you've come across any, they aren't related to me."

"No, I doubt they are." A dark tone of disappointment sounded in his voice and probably matched hers. His shoulders hunched ever so slightly, and he seemed to distance himself. After a moment, he turned back toward her. "Did yer dad ever remarry?"

"He didn't date anyone more than a month or two. So no, he never remarried and never had other children. The line ends with me. I'm the last Montgomery."

Elliott chuckled, although the laugh held little humor. "I'm the last Fraser."

"Is Kit the last MacKlenna?" Meredith asked.

He didn't answer.

She wrenched her gaze away from him, biting her tongue, determined to sit on her curiosity until her butt got sore. "I don't know about you, but being the last one doesn't agree with me."

"Didn't ye ever look into adoption?"

"Jonathan wouldn't consider it. I mothered the winery instead of a child."

"Was that satisfying enough for ye?"

"Yes," she answered bluntly, feeling a slight burn in her gut.

"I'm surprised yer father didn't push for an heir—natural or adopted."

"He did, but I wouldn't kowtow to his demands." She picked at the label on the bottle, making the thin plastic bend and pop. "The new wine I'm launching is my legacy. It's not the same as having children, but if the wine is successful, it might have staying power like a…I don't know, maybe an 1870 Lafite."

He smiled. "Have ye tasted the 1870 Lafite?"

"If I drank a ten-thousand-dollar bottle of wine my grandmother would roll over in her grave and my father would stand up in his."

"Ah, wee sweetheart, sometimes ye have to pay extra for special experiences."

His voice lapped against her, soothing yet erotic, like waves spilling onto a soft, sandy beach.

"If yer new wine tastes similar to the wine I liked yesterday, I'll look forward to tasting it."

"*Cailean* is a light, crispy white wine like a pinot grigio or sauvignon blanc. It doesn't have the oaky taste you like."

"*Cailean.*" He seemed to let the name swirl in his mouth, tasting it, paying attention to its texture. Then he pursed his lips and let out a soft whistle. "That's Gaelic for child."

Her cheeks flushed.

Elliott pointed over her shoulder. "We're approaching Blair

Castle." David slowed the car so they could take in the panoramic view.

Meredith turned to see the white stately home that had started life as a medieval castle commanding the wild mountain passes to the Highlands. "It's beautiful. I toured it years ago."

The castle spoke to family and tradition, something she understood.

"I've always felt at home in Scotland." Meredith moaned—a vocal representation of a sweet memory. "Culloden was my grandmother's home. There's no family left there now, of course, but when I was a child, we'd visit and I'd listen to old stories about the Highlands. It always seemed so mysterious." She gave a quick shiver. They rode in silence for several miles, watching the landscape and relaxing, an activity in which Meredith rarely engaged. Elliott probably didn't either.

"We're almost there." His eyes seemed to brighten, his brow less furrowed.

When David drove the car into a clearing, she blinked then blinked again. "Oh my God."

Fraser House was not a house at all but a castle, sitting among a backdrop of rocky cliffs, woods, and hilltops. The hills, filled with hardwoods and Scots pine, rose steeply from the loch and created a formidable frame for the rest of the landscape. Each branch sagged under the heavy weight of snow. Chunks of ice fell to the ground, first from one tree, then another, and another—a snowball fight among the ancient Caledonian pines.

The castle featured a Z-shaped plan with towers and turrets. There were even arrow slots. She gulped. She had envisioned a rather nice house, maybe even a mansion, but not a fourteenth century castle.

"Originally, it had the traditional defensive design of three towers connected by rectangular buildings, but mason workers added the roll-mounted window surrounds, corbeling, and the faerie-taleish circular turrets with pointed candle snuffer roofs."

She laughed. "You sound like a tour guide."

He pulled her into an embrace and kissed her. "I heard my grandda describe the additions so many times, I memorized it." He smiled. "Inside, ye can see original paneling and stonework."

His voice held unfettered energy and she loved the way it rumbled against her skin. It was as if the land had instantly rejuvenated him. "How can you ever leave here? Is there a place more beautiful?" She gazed around drinking it all in. "It's magnificent."

"I'm not sure there is a place more beautiful." He gave her a pensive look. "MacKlenna Farm comes close, but like yer winery, its history is limited to a few hundred years." He swept his hand in a circular motion. "There're miles of trails through the forest and alongside the loch."

"Are we driving the trails?"

"We'll take the sleigh."

"Sleigh? Really? Are you up for it?"

He waved away her concern. "I bought the sleigh during an Alpine skiing trip several years ago but never got around to using it." He glanced at his watch. "I asked for it to be hitched and ready by noon. We're a wee bit early."

A few minutes later, David stopped the car in front of the barn.

"There're facilities inside if ye need to freshen up before we go out."

Meredith envisioned something akin to an outhouse, but found the bathroom more in line with an upscale hotel. A few minutes later, she met Elliott beside a red sleigh straight out of a Norman Rockwell painting. A groom had hitched two bay Clydesdales with white feet, and stacked thick wool blankets on the leather seat. The picnic basket sat on the floor.

With a slight tug, she pulled a striped knit cap down over her ears and jumped aboard. Elliott handed his crutches to the groom. "We'll be out a couple of hours." He then took his place on the bench seat next to her. "Are ye ready?"

"More than ready." She spread the blankets across their laps and tucked the end around Elliott's booted leg. When she glanced up, she noticed David standing in the barn's doorway, grimacing.

"David's not happy."

"He never is." Elliott picked up the reins in both hands and snapped them, clucking at the horses. "Ginger. Fred."

Meredith laughed. "You're kidding. Fred and Ginger?"

"Grandda's responsible for the names. If I had named them, they'd have power names."

"Like what?"

"Highlander Spirit and Winter Jubilee."

"Those sound like racehorses."

Elliott winked. "That's what Grandda said before he tortured these two extraordinary animals by giving them dancers' names."

She wrapped her arm around Elliott's and moved in closer, feeling like a woman who'd been left out in the cold and was finally standing in front of a fire. "Well, then, let's go dancing, Dr. Fraser."

He sighed deeply with obvious regret. "That's one thing I can't do, lass."

Her face heated with embarrassment. "Oh, I'm sorry. I didn't think."

He squeezed her hand that she'd laced with his arm. "At least not vertically."

The flush intensified. "Does everything with you always come back around to sex?"

He belted out a laugh. "Not everything, but almost. I *am* in the breeding business." The roar of his laughter echoed off the hills behind the house. He snapped the reins, and the sleigh's runners glided across snow glistening in the late morning sun. The temperature hovered around the high thirties. Bells, dangling from the harnesses, jingled, bringing to life acres of pristine forest.

"Are ye warm enough?"

She nodded. "I'd freeze to death before I'd give up one moment of this." *This is why he often smells of cedar and Christmas trees.*

Elliott belonged in his Highland hills, rugged and independent. He held the reins as naturally as others held a steering wheel. What hold did MacKlenna Farm have on him that could pull him away from this land? Did a place exist anywhere in the world that could pull her away from Montgomery Winery?

No. Her life's blood seeped into the dry, rocky soil that nurtured her grapes. Separate and apart, she would wither.

The trail took them through the forest where he pointed out red deer and gray spotted woodpeckers. They didn't talk much. Mostly they laughed, hanging in a make-believe world where Derby-winning horses didn't die and young women didn't get breast cancer. They laughed because they could, because Meredith knew—and felt certain Elliott did, too—that they were living on someone else's time. Their lives were too hectic, too full of responsibility to feel this free. She laid her head on his shoulder and gazed at the treetops touching heaven.

Feeling an involuntary sensation warm her body, she asked him to kiss her. He stopped the sleigh, and without any prelude, kissed her full on the mouth—a long, sweet invasion. When she slipped in a breath, his tongue stole its way inside, waltzed across her teeth, and entwined in a continual dance with her tongue. A moan carried past her lips, a husky sound of the need building within her. Time stopped for a heartbeat, and she found herself lost in the feel of the hard planes of his body against hers. The wild smell of outdoors and musk added to her arousal. She deepened the kiss with her tongue as she held tightly to his shoulders, pressing her breasts intimately against his chest. A deep ache urged her to surrender, but not here, not now. She drew back and took a breath. His eyes held the same smoky gaze she'd seen before. Her tongue swiped her bottom lip.

"I don't think the scenery can compete with that," she said, her voice breathy.

He chuckled. "Ah, hen. Hold that thought. We'll continue this as soon as I can get us back to the house."

Elliott drove the sleigh alongside the loch. The turquoise blue water rippled crystal clear. Opposite the wild and remote lake, several hundred yards off the road, the lawn and terraced walled gardens created a formal and grand vista. The wild beat of Meredith's heart matched the rhythm found in the isolation and beauty.

They rode in silence, engulfed by a sense of peace Meredith

didn't think she'd ever experienced. If the day could last a thousand hours, it would still end too quickly.

She'd ridden for miles bundled up in the curve of his arm, but now she noticed him twitching, his teeth gritted. "Are you in pain?"

"No more than usual."

"Let me drive." She reached for the reins.

He shrugged her off. "We're almost home."

She placed her hands over his. "I can drive, Elliott."

Surprisingly, he handed them to her. "They'll recognize the lighter touch and try to pull. Don't let them. They'll get away from ye. Follow the road." He leaned back and closed his eyes. Cold and riding in a bumpy sleigh was not what he needed. She tossed the blankets off her legs and folded them over him. Even from under a pile of wool, he shivered.

"Giddy up." The horses ran at a slow gallop but faster than they had for Elliott. Ahead there was a slight curve with a tree lying across the road. No time to react. The horses swerved. The sudden movement threatened to upend the sleigh. She held tight to the reins and leaned in. She had the wherewithal to throw her arm across Elliott's chest to keep him from falling out, but his head hit the metal on the back of the seat. The sleigh righted with a bad bounce. The shock traveled up her spine. Her teeth caught her lip and held on while tears pooled in her eyes.

Elliott groaned as blood trickled down his neck, his handsome face ashen.

"Oh God." She didn't know whether to stop or go on. The sun disappeared behind the clouds, and the day turned gray and gloomy. A blistery wind blew in her face, making her blink. The knit cap inched up the side of her head, exposing her ears to the cold. The fur coat fell open. The knitted thick wool sweater she wore should have kept her warm. It didn't. Her toes were frozen. Her fingers, almost. She, too, shivered.

Go. Don't stop.

When she spotted the barn's roof, relief welled up inside. She didn't slow the horses but went barreling onto the grounds at a fast trot.

"Whoa." The horses stopped in front of the barn, kicking up snow that found its way into the back of the sleigh. Meredith brushed flakes off Elliott.

The groom stuck his head out the door.

Panting hard, she asked, "Where's David?"

"In here, ma'am."

"Dr. Fraser needs help. *Now.*"

David rushed out, throwing on his coat as he ran. If looks could box someone's ears, then she now had cauliflower stuck on each side of her head. He hopped onto the sleigh's runners and yanked the reins from Meredith's hands. He drove the sleigh down a long drive lined by the ancient trees to the front door of the immaculately restored Fraser House. A misnomer for sure.

David unbundled Elliott, hissing when he saw blood. He grabbed a handkerchief from his jacket pocket and pressed it against the cut on the back of Elliott's head.

Elliott's teeth chattered. "Leave me alone."

"I should leave ye right here." But David didn't. Instead, he wrapped Elliott's arm around his muscled neck. "We'll take this slow." Then, with David supporting most of Elliott's weight, the men entered the house through the front door.

"What can I do?" Meredith asked, struggling to keep panic at bay.

"The library is the second room on the right. Should be warm enough. Wait there. I'll take Dr. Fraser to his room."

"But—"

"Wait," David said again in a no-nonsense voice.

"Can I call the doctor?" Meredith asked.

David didn't answer.

What the hell is going on here? Meredith started to follow. *David said to wait.* She didn't want to wait. She wanted to stay with Elliott, but she wasn't wanted or needed. Well, David didn't need her, but what about Elliott? She pulled off her cap and tossed it in the chair. This didn't feel right. *Why?* The answer eluded her. The fire in the well-appointed library drew her in. Any other time she would have explored, touched the fabrics, examined the art work. Right now, she didn't care if there were first edition books on the shelves or not. She stood close to the flame and warmed her hands. Then memories of her father's heart attack swamped her. The paramedics had shoved her out of the way, just as David had done.

Panic claimed a firm grip on her, and she paced the room. *What if something happens to Elliott and I never talk to him again?* To hell with David's request.

She hurried out into the hallway. A center-sweep of stairs opened to a second-floor balcony. Behind the stairs on the lower level, the room branched off in three directions. *Which way did they go?* She gulped. *Why didn't I pay attention?*

She dropped into the nearest chair and put her head in her hands. *This is my fault. I should have refused to go. I shouldn't have driven the sleigh. I should have…what?* She sat up straight. *I should have stayed home. I have no business here. I'm juggling sticks of dynamite while holding a lighted match between my teeth. Dumb. Dumb. Dumb. I've got to get out of here.*

She dug into her purse for the limo driver's business card. It would be best if she could get a ride back to Edinburgh and let David take care of Elliott.

"Ye must be Meredith," said a woman with a heavy brogue.

Meredith jumped to her feet, looking around for the body that went with the voice. "Yes, I am."

"Heard a wee bit 'bout ye. I'm Alice."

Chapter Nineteen

Fraser House on Christmas Day

A PETITE, HEAVYSET WOMAN holding a stack of linens stood at the first landing of a divided grand staircase with intricately carved detail on the spindles and newel post. A gold and royal blue runner ran down the center of the stairs.

"Did Dr. Fraser go to his room?" she asked.

"Yes," Meredith said, "but I'm lost. I don't know where his room is."

"He shouldna have been out in the cold. He was jostled around for hours in that sleigh. Was it yer idea?"

Meredith bristled. "He had it all arranged. I didn't know…" She stopped. Explaining to the housekeeper was unnecessary. And besides, she already knew she should have discouraged him.

"Canna stop him. He'll do what he sets his mind on even if it's no good for him." The woman reached the bottom step and readjusted the load she carried in her arms. "How about a cup of tea?"

"I thought it would be best if I left."

"Ye plan to walk back to the city, do ye?"

Meredith shook her head. "I was going to call for a ride."

"Nobody will come out here to get ye today. Best thing now is to take yer coat off and have a cup of tea. Dr. Fraser will want to see ye after he's tended to. Call me Alice."

Alice wasn't snarky, just abrupt and opinionated. *She and Louise must get along well.* Thankfully, she had talked Meredith off the running-away ledge.

She followed Alice's tiny footsteps down a long hallway then through a maze of cold but extraordinarily large rooms furnished with sixteenth and seventeenth century furniture and original paintings by eighteenth century artists. Her junior year in college studying art in Paris occasionally came in handy.

The twists and turns disoriented Meredith, making a return trip to the foyer impossible. She was stuck until Elliott decided to ask for her. If he never did, Meredith assumed she'd stay lost in the castle until the end of time. If she had a floor plan, it would be a fantastic place to spend the rest of her life. And it would take a lifetime to explore all the rooms.

"Watch yer step," Alice said when they reached the kitchen, which Meredith was convinced was located in another county. They had walked at least the length of a football field. "Stand over there next to the fireplace. Warm up a wee bit."

Meredith made her way to the fireplace and stood with her back to the fire warming her hands, taking in all there was to see. Workers had dug a two-foot-wide trench through the wide-planked wood floor from the interior wall to the exterior wall on the opposite side of a room. The kitchen appeared large enough to support a five-star restaurant. The appliances were all industrial-sized stainless steel.

Alice filled a teapot with water from a jug, set it on the stove, and turned up the gas flame. "Dr. Fraser wanted ye to visit the wine cellar. It's through that door," she said, pointing to the far corner of the room, "and down the stairs. Tea will be ready in a few minutes."

"I'd rather check on Elliott."

"David's probably on the phone with Kevin. They'll patch Dr. Fraser up. Ye can see him in a wee bit. Now go on to the wine cellar."

"Who's Kevin?"

"Ye havena met the lad?"

"No, but I've heard his name mentioned."

"He's Dr. Fraser's assistant. Been with him now four years, I reckon."

An assistant and a chauffeur are tending to Elliott? Something didn't sound quite right.

"Don't you think he needs a doctor?"

"Those two lads know what they're doing."

Pictures of emergency rooms and intensive care cubicles played in a loop in Meredith's mind. *The lads know what they're doing.* She found that hard to believe. Elliott needed to be in the hospital. Period. If there wasn't any improvement when she saw him, and she doubted there would be, she'd insist he call his doctor or, *damn it*, she would. She shook her head, exasperated with herself for allowing him to take her on a sleigh ride.

Since all she was doing was waiting on water to boil, she decided to check out his collection. A heavy oak door opened on well-oiled hinges, and she descended into a big, cold cellar—a perfect place for long-term ageing. An oak scent permeated the air. *Probably old barrels cut up for racking.*

When she reached the bottom step, she stopped, flash-frozen to the spot. Was her heart even beating? Row upon row of five-foot tall shelves lined each side of a wide middle aisle. She flipped a light switch and another whole section opened up. If her sense of direction was accurate, the back part of the cellar lay beneath the raised courtyard.

Dust danced with her breath. There was no sound except her shallow breathing and her heartbeat, which began to thump loudly in her chest again.

In disbelief, she stepped over to the first row of shelves and began a slow walk down an aisle stocked with dozens, no, hundreds of bottles of wine. The light feeling in her chest was one she hadn't experienced in a very long time. Well, maybe she'd gotten close to the feeling while kissing Elliott in the sleigh. *Close?* She waved her hand, refusing to argue with her internal editor. She pushed thoughts of kissing Elliott aside, amazed once again at the magnitude of a collection that belonged to a man who didn't drink wine.

While lingering for long minutes, intoxicating aromas and tastes jumbled and exploded in her mind. She read labels and calculated market prices. The shelves held wines from Burgundy, Bordeaux, and Alsace in France; Tuscany and Piedmont in Italy; Ribera del Duero, Penedes, and Priorat in Spain; the Duero region and the island of Madeira in Portugal. From the United States, she found cabernet sauvignon and merlots from Washington State, pinot noir from Oregon, and chardonnay and sauvignon blanc from California. Her wines were there, too, although not as dusty as the others.

For a private residence, the collection was astounding. She turned down another row, finding two of the greatest d'Yquem—an 1811 and an 1847. Close by was a 1900 Margaux. Down the next row, she found a 1928 and a 1929 Mouton Rothschild. "Unbelievable." Surprise after surprise. A vintner's dream collection. Suddenly, she gasped and pressed her dusty fingers against her mouth. "I'll be damned."

On a shelf against the wall were two magnums of the 1870 Lafite. Giggling, she reached for a bottle but withdrew her hands. She reached again, but withdrew them once more. Then did it again and again, giggling each time. Finally, she got herself under control, picked up the legendary wine, and blew dust off a mint-condition label.

A towel hung on a hook above the shelf. Her hand shook as she used the rag to wipe the bottle clean. The red wax seal hadn't been broken. "Original cork. Extraordinary condition."

If Elliott decided to sell the wine, what price would Christie's put on a collection that held wines spanning more than two hundred years?

Meredith's dad would have loved visiting this cellar. A stab of sorrow cut a jagged line through her heart. She could see him now. Face beaming, voice growing hoarse from shouting about the robust red wines to anyone who would listen. With a catch in her throat, she said to him, "I'll enjoy this for you, Daddy."

A hot tear dropped on the bottle as she placed it back into its niche. Wiping away another, she turned toward the stairs for a final look.

"I'd love to see the cellar book," she said to no one other than herself.

"It's all on computer now."

Meredith squealed, and her hand flew to her chest at the sound of David's voice raining down from the top of the stairs. Stammering she said, "Y-you scared me."

"Sorry," he said, approaching the bottom step. "Dr. Fraser would like to see ye."

She reached for the railing, taking deep breaths to calm her racing heart. "How is he?"

"Better."

That doesn't tell me much. "Did you call the doctor?"

"No need."

That's highly unlikely. "Which way to his room?"

"Down the hall, last door on the right." She hoped there were signs or breadcrumbs, because she seriously doubted the room was just *down the hall.*

She started up the stairs then stopped. "Do you know how many bottles are in the collection?"

"About twenty-five thousand."

Her hand squeezed the railing, turning her knuckles white. "Twenty-five…"

"Thousand," David said with a chuckle.

"It's got to be worth at least fifteen million dollars or more."

David turned out the lights and set the alarm. "I wouldna know about that."

"No, I guess you wouldn't." She rushed up the steps and bounded into the kitchen. Alice stood at the counter, setting a tray with tea, cups, and sandwiches. "I'm sorry. I lost track of time," Meredith said.

Alice narrowed her eyes. "Been down there awhile. Dinna ken what's so interesting about a bunch of old bottles."

"David said Elliott was asking for me."

"Reckon so. Go on now. David will bring the tea. Go down the hall to the end. Ye'll find him."

Meredith doubted it, but she skedaddled out of the kitchen and jogged down the long hallway. She passed the foyer and laughed. Alice really had taken her on a roundabout.

Meredith found Elliott's bedroom door partially opened. Tiptoeing, she entered the room. A chill took root at the base of her spine as deep, intense color swirled around her. Walnut and mahogany chests of drawers, tables, and ornate oak chairs lined the walls, pervading the air with scents of ancient wood and layers of polish. Her fingers glided across the spines of leather-bound volumes of Sir Walter Scott, Edwin Muir, and Robert Burns gathering dust in elaborately built bookcases.

Waning rays of light drew her to a tall window bracketed with heavy velvet drapes. She pushed aside a swathe of fabric with the back of her hand to take in the view of the terrace and the ice-crystal blue Loch Ness. The hills beyond looked like steps climbing to the sky, their snow-capped peaks pink with the glow of early sunset.

The master suite's collective aura swept her back hundreds of years to when Bonnie Prince Charlie and the Jacobites fought for Scotland and the return of the Stuarts to the throne. She found herself listening for the long-forgotten riotous voices of brave Highland lads who had once gathered there.

An amused chuckle floated across the room. She turned toward the sound, toward Elliott. He was reclining on a hand-carved, four-poster canopy bed draped in swags of burgundy velvet. "This is the only part of the house that didn't catch on fire. Legend says the soldiers ran in here to get away from the flames. Ye feel their souls, don't ye?"

"Yes." She let the curtain fall. "I'm glad to know it's not just me."

He patted the mattress beside him. "Come here."

"I don't want to jostle you."

"This is a Tempur-Pedic. Ye can jump on one side, and I wouldn't feel it."

David walked into the room, carrying the tea service.

"Just leave it on the table," Elliott said.

David nodded and left the room.

"Can I pour you a cup of tea, or do you want a sandwich?" Meredith asked.

"No, but help yerself."

"Maybe later." She removed her boots and crawled across the giant bed. "How's the pain?"

Long, thick lashes rimmed his lowered eyelids. "Better."

"What's in the IV?"

"Antibiotic and fluids. I got a wee bit dehydrated."

"Don't you need a doctor?"

"David was a medic—"

"But—"

"He's trained. Don't worry."

The first time she'd met the driver he had exhibited almost panther-like agility, appearing and disappearing at Elliott's slightest nod. A man of many talents and someone Elliott obviously trusted. Driver, medic, what else?

She stretched out beside Elliott and rose up on her elbow. "I met Alice."

He stroked the side of her face with fingertips that twitched slightly. "David likes ye. That means Alice does, too. He's her wee boy. But the ol' gal's got a rough exterior."

"She's very protective, like everyone else around you. Why is that?"

He shrugged, and for an instant his expression held an imprint of some deep sadness. Then it disappeared, and his grin returned. "Did ye go to the wine cellar?"

She kissed the tip of his nose. "You can't fool me about your wine knowledge. Not after seeing your collection."

Elliott wrapped his arm around her and pulled her close. "The wine belonged to my da. I rarely go below. Was there a lot of dust?"

She pressed her cheek against his soft cashmere sweater. "Enough to make a man or two." Snuggling even closer she said, "Supposedly, women love nestling into a man's side because that's where we came from originally. You know…a rib."

The rumble of laughter in his chest tickled her cheek. "Close yer eyes, my wee Eve, and catch up on a bit of rest. Then we'll eat from the garden."

"Maybe you haven't noticed, but the garden is covered with snow."

"Aye, but what was once there is now pickled and canned and frozen." He cupped the back of her head, entangling his fingers in her hair. "Shh. Sleep."

If he thought she could sleep nestled against him, he had more than saline in his IV.

Chapter Twenty

Christmas Dinner at Fraser House

MEREDITH AWOKE BUNDLED in a down comforter, sensing that she was alone in the room. She blinked, confused, but oh so toasty warm. "Don't make me move," she groaned. Jet lag, late nights, and a couple of hard runs had done her in, and she didn't want to budge.

But where am I?

She popped up out of the covers, listening. A crackling fire in the fireplace issued a lighthouse-golden glow in the darkened suite. Elliott's bedroom. Check. In bed alone. Check. Fully clothed. Check.

Where is he?

As if answering her question, the sound of splashing water came from the bathroom located across the room. *Elliott must be showering.* She needed to find a guest bath to freshen up. But where? If she made her way back to the kitchen, Alice could direct her.

Just as she reached for her boots, David walked out of the bathroom and switched on a lamp. "Dr. Fraser will be out shortly. Can I bring ye a cocktail?"

"If he's in the shower, he must be feeling better," she said.

"He says he does."

Relief sailed out on a breath. "I'd love a glass of the Château Chasse Spleen 1990 I saw in the cellar."

"I'll send for it. Is there anything else?"

"A bathroom."

He pointed to the opposite corner. "Alice put fresh towels in the bath through that door. Ye'll find everything ye need. I'll let Dr. Fraser know ye're awake."

Meredith slipped on her boots, and when she straightened, David was gone. *Dang. That man disappears faster than crostini and brie at a French white wine tasting.*

After a quick shower, she brushed her teeth and reapplied her makeup. Since meeting Elliott, she'd been magically transported to a place she'd never been, a place that existed only in daydreams. Now that she had a taste of the magic elixir, she could easily become addicted. Tomorrow she'd worry about that, but not today. After all, it was Christmas.

Refreshed, she reentered Elliott's room and found him sitting in a wing chair in front of the fire, reading and sipping a cocktail. The setting was timeless, right down to the blue-gray Scottish deerhound asleep at his feet—the lord of the manor and his hunting dog. The animal jumped up and trotted toward her.

"She's beautiful, Elliott." Meredith petted the dog's head, which almost reached her elbow. "What's her name? And please don't tell me it's Gracie."

"Gracie?"

"You know like Fred and Ginger, George and Gracie."

He laughed, his chest shaking in a reassuring way. "Annabella." Hearing Elliott's voice, the dog returned to his side, sniffing the open Amazon book boxes scattered on the floor.

"Where does she stay when you're not here?"

"Alice keeps her. I've thought of taking her to Kentucky, but I don't think she'd get on well with Tate and Tabor."

"I can't picture you with critters that track mud on the floor or shed on clothes. Who or what are Tate and Tabor?" She arched her brow. "Goldfish?"

He grabbed his chest with both hands as if he were having a heart attack. "I'm shocked that ye have such a dreadful opinion of me."

"Oh," she said, slapping her palm to her forehead. "You did tell me about them. Tate's a golden retriever. Right?"

"Not just a golden; a country-music-crooning one."

"And Tabor is some kind of cat."

"A persnickety Maine Coon."

"Tabor is the one who's spoiled, right?"

Elliott nodded. "They were Mary MacKlenna's pets."

"How's Mary related to Kit?"

"Her mother. When she died last year, I inherited the animals."

Meredith lifted a chilled bottle of wine from the ice bucket on the sideboard. "It's my wine." She squeezed Elliott's shoulder and kissed his cheek. "Thank you."

He patted her hand. "David told me yer wine was in the collection. Dad was particular about the wines he collected. That says a lot about yers."

"I'm pleased my labels met his standard." She poured a glass then sat in the chair opposite Elliott, neatly crossing her legs. "Did Mary own your farm in Kentucky?"

He shook his head. "Her husband did. The land has been in the MacKlenna family since 1763. The farm was left to Kit."

"Do you think she'll sell it now that she's living in Scotland?" Meredith's pulse quickened. She was treading a slippery slope, but having questions about Kit ignored and evaded butted heads with her stubborn streak.

"Would ye sell yer winery?" he asked.

"No. I guess that's a *no* for Kit, too." Meredith gave in to the impulse and let her leg swing.

After a moment, he said, "A few years back, the family considered selling off a noncontiguous track, but they were convinced old Thomas MacKlenna's ghost would haunt them if they sold even an inch. Kit is bound by family and tradition."

Meredith gave him a warm smile. "I can appreciate that."

"I think she believed Sean MacKlenna would live forever."

Meredith stared down at her leg and willed it to stop shaking. "I thought my dad would live forever, too."

"Yes, but ye've jumped in and are moving forward. Kit loves racing and breeding but not the business side."

"I'm not sure I enjoy that part either. It's all a gamble. Bad breaks can kill you whether you're growing grapes or racing horses."

"Is yer new wine a gamble?"

"I've done my homework, and we've test-marketed the wine in several locations with good results. But yes, it's a gamble, especially in this economy."

"Ye'd hate to be the one to make the big blunder that could bring down the business."

"I couldn't live with that," Meredith said. "That's why my life is so scheduled right now."

He laughed. Annabella stood and bumped Elliott's arm with her nose. He patted her head affectionately. "Sounds like mine."

"I'd love a few stress-free days, though." She glanced around the room, sensing for the first time how calm she had become in the last few hours. The turmoil in her stomach had eased, and quiet confidence replaced the nagging tension. "I feel less stressed here. You do, too, don't you?"

Annabella lay down at his feet, but he patted the arm of the chair as if her head was still nudging his hand. "This is the only place in the world I can escape the fires, but starting tomorrow, I'll need an oversized extinguisher to put them out."

"Because of Galahad?" she asked.

Elliott nodded. "His death is a forest fire that will grow out of control quickly. I've seen it happen before."

"When are you going home?"

"I'm scheduled to stay here until the first, but now I don't know. How about ye?"

"The same, unless something pulls me home earlier," she said. *Like a doctor's report.*

He sipped his drink. "If I can do damage control over the next few days, we might have time to enjoy part of the Hogmanay."

A quick knock on the door preceded David's entrance. He pushed a food cart into the room. "Where'd ye like the table?"

"Here." Elliott pointed to the space between his chair and Meredith's. David locked the cart and snapped the leaves into place. Once Elliott and Meredith settled themselves at the table, David reached beneath the cart and presented her with a bottle of wine, label forward. It was the 1870 Lafite. An orgasmic feeling welled within her. Her body tingled from big toe to eyelashes. Never in her life had she been so surprised. She gazed at Elliott and saw similar pleasure in his eyes. She should decline the gift, but that would be rude, and she was all but salivating to taste the wine.

"Thank you." The words came out on a long, slow breath.

He reached for her hand, squeezing her fingers. "The expression on yer face is exactly what I was hoping for." Elliott gave a silent nod to David, who then removed the cork and placed it on the table. Meredith cocked her head and studied it, noticing its immaculate condition. She inhaled deeply with anticipation, feeling very optimistic.

He poured two ounces into a spotless wineglass. Her heart thumped wildly. The men could probably hear, but she didn't care. Her hand shook as she tilted the glass at a forty-five degree angle against the white tablecloth and assessed the wine visually. She found no faults with the healthy, dark garnet wine. She rotated her wrist, swirling the wine for a few seconds, then checked the patterns formed by the legs. Next, she placed her nose inside the wineglass and sniffed—celery, mint, cedar, and cassis. Slowly, she sipped and swallowed. The wine had a long, sweet finish.

"*Extraordinary.*" She set down the glass, and David poured more wine. "Are you going to have a glass?" she asked Elliott.

"Not tonight, wee sweetheart." David handed him a fresh cocktail, and Elliott sipped.

She smiled up into his eyes. "You did this just for me?"

"I did it for two selfish reasons. I wanted to see yer expression, and I was hoping to see yer father stand up in his grave."

Her smile widened, imagining the sight. "If we were at the winery, we could probably see him."

David removed the dome lids covering the food.

"So what did Alice conjure up for dinner?" Elliott asked.

"Yer favorite. Prawns in whisky cream, salmon, and potatoes," David said.

"Very Scottish," Meredith said, taking another sip and making mental notes of how the wine flowed over her tongue.

"Alice twitches her nose and food appears," Elliott said.

"That makes more sense than cooking in the midst of a torn-up kitchen."

"She cooked at the cottage tonight." David refreshed Meredith's glass then quietly left the room.

"Alice took me on a roundabout to the kitchen earlier. I think she was trying to get me lost, or else she was showing off the house."

"She's been here fifty years. She's proud of the place and treats it like her own. I'll give ye the ten-cent tour after dinner."

"You don't need to be up and about. Maybe we can come back later this week."

Elliott chewed the prawns slowly, thoughtfully. Then he gave her a teasing smile that made his dark brown eyes twinkle. He dabbed at his mouth with the cloth napkin. "Have ye had a lover since yer husband died?"

She studied him, unsure of how to answer. It was none of his business how many lovers she had turned down due to the timing or the man not being suitable.

He looked her over with roguish scrutiny. "It's not something ye forget how to do."

"Like riding a bike?"

"A horse is probably a better analogy," Elliott said.

She quirked an eyebrow and gave him a lopsided grin. "In that case, I certainly haven't forgotten. I ride my stallion, Quiet Dancer, at least three times a week."

His jaw dropped. "That horse was hard to manage. I thought they put him down after he hurt his leg."

"The injury ended his racing career, but he's a good riding horse. He behaves for me."

Elliott tipped his head back and laughed. "Darlin', with yer long legs wrapped around me, I'd behave, too."

"Ha. You wouldn't behave at all. You're incorrigible."

He picked up the bottle of wine and filled her glass. "There ye go, believing the wee stories about me again."

"You make it easy to believe them." She sipped the wine and smiled. "Are you trying to get me intoxicated so you can take advantage of me?"

He set down the bottle of wine, picked up his cocktail, and gave her an easy salute with the glass. "It didn't work for me last night, but I'm an optimist."

Not sleeping with him had little to do with the length of time she'd known him and everything to do with her previous mastectomy and the one yet to come. She'd always spoken freely about her cancer, but with Elliott, she hesitated. She did owe him an explanation, especially after opening a ten-thousand-dollar bottle of wine. "Elliott, I—"

A knock interrupted her, and David's entrance shelved her confession. "I'll take the wee table if ye're through."

Elliott scooted back in his chair. "Give us an hour, and we'll be ready to return to Edinburgh."

David nodded to Elliott and made an almost indiscernible waving motion with his hand. Annabella stood, wagged her tail, and followed David out of the room.

"What were ye saying?" Elliott asked.

She shrugged. "Oh, nothing."

Feeling the heat of his gaze, she looked everywhere but at him. Her eyes came to rest on the portrait hanging over the fireplace. "Is that your father?"

"It was painted the year he turned fifty," Elliott said.

"Handsome man. You favor him, but then I haven't seen your mother's portrait. Where is hers?"

Elliott drew his brows together and set his mouth in a determined line. After a moment, he said, "Come. I'll show ye my favorite room at Fraser House before we head back to Edinburgh. Bring yer wine."

Slowly, she rose from the table. *He's not going to talk about his mother either. Dang, there's a story there, and I'd love to hear it. I'd love to hear Kit's story, too.* Elliott played life close to his chest, and she doubted he'd ever open up to her.

Meredith picked up her glass and followed him with well-seated knowledge that she was falling for a man who could hurt her more than she'd ever been hurt.

Chapter Twenty-One

Louise's B&B, Edinburgh, Scotland – Late Christmas Night

MEREDITH SLIPPED A royal blue nightgown over her head. The silk shimmied over her fresh-out-of-the-shower body. A quick brush through her hair left her ready for bed. She walked out of the bathroom at the B&B and heard noise from the adjoining room. She pricked her ears. Random sounds—cars, gunshots, screaming, newscasters—that could only come from flipping TV channels.

Elliott had been quiet on the ride home. He didn't talk much about his dad, but Meredith sensed that being home reminded Elliott of how much he missed his father. She understood that feeling well.

They had kissed in the hallway. His hard, aroused body had made his desire perfectly clear. Although what she wanted remained foggy, her body reacted with a single-minded purpose. He didn't want the day to end any more than she did. Although she melted in his arms, she couldn't sleep with him, and her hesitation confused him. Confused her, too.

An hour later, she climbed into bed and pulled the covers over her head. Even in the dim light, she could see Elliott's dark brown eyes fill with calm disappointment when she closed the door.

Did she have excuses or honest concerns? Although she was self-conscious about her reconstructed breast, the surgeon had matched the other side beautifully. Yes, the breast was scarred, but they had faded with time. Then why?

Baffled, she rolled over and punched the feather pillow with her fist. "Urg." Her uncertainty tipped the frustration scale. She buried her face, smelling the freshly laundered pillowcase.

"Urg," she groaned again, kicking her feet. The sheet and blanket came untucked. Now her toes were cold. She'd never been so indecisive in her life. If indecision was the norm for her, her grapes would rot on the vines.

The scent of the Highlands, fresh and woodsy, permeated her skin. Separating the man from the land was impossible now that she had seen him in his element. She kicked her feet again as a vivid sensory image flashed across her mind—the sleigh ride kiss—a kiss unlike any other, a kiss that still sizzled hours later.

A lonely ache resided in the pit of her stomach. A delicacy, something sumptuous like Elliott, would satisfy the yearning. But at what cost? The loneliness would only be worse tomorrow. That's why she'd never considered a one-night fling. So why now? Because a charming, irresistible Scotsman wanted her or because she wanted more of him than a mere taste?

She rolled over and stared at the ceiling. *Go knock on his door.* She wrung her hands, twisting and tugging on her fingers as if they were a sopping wet dishrag. Then she threw back the covers and paced until she stood in front of their adjoining door.

"Elliott," she said, tapping lightly. "Are you still awake?" She waited an interminable minute until the lock turned on the other side of the door.

"Meredith, unlock yer side," he said.

She turned the bolt, and the door swung open.

"I've had my hand on this door a half dozen times." He stood mere inches from her, supported by his crutches and wearing tight gray boxer briefs and his walking boot. She stared at his broad muscular shoulders, and then she set her eyes on his bed. He'd turned down the bedcovers and fluffed the pillows.

"You were turning in. I'm sorry." She pushed on the door as if to close it.

He stuck one of the crutches in the way. "Meredith, what do ye want?"

"Sleep with me," she blurted out. "I mean, go to sleep in my bed."

A grin split his face. "That's a good place to start."

"I miss you."

His gaze swept over her, marking her with a visual caress. He gently tugged on the fabric where the two triangle cups of the empire waist gown overlapped. "Do ye have anything less revealing to sleep in?"

"A 49ers football jersey."

"That would be just as evocative." He teased the swell of her breast.

Her lips parted to say something clever about her team, but he kissed her open mouth, and she moved closer to him, melding into his warm chest.

"I can't stand. We need to get into bed or we'll both end up on the floor."

"Please—"

"Ye're not a teenager whose virtue needs protecting." Emotion thickened his voice.

The decision belonged to her to make in a moment of weakness or in a moment of conviction. She wrestled with the fierceness of her desire. "Take me to bed."

"Or lose ye forever?" he asked, quoting the line from the movie *Top Gun.* He dropped the crutches, sat on the bed, pushed the covers out of the way, and pulled her into his arms.

Heat seeped through his fingers into her skin, stirring her coiled passion and sending fragrant smoke spiraling though her.

"I've wanted ye from the first moment I saw ye." His tongue swept against hers. The taste of whisky, smoky and sweet, filled her mouth. Whatever fears she'd had, her all-consuming need quashed them now. Her body ached and grew more insistent with each kiss and stroke of his fingers, teasing her neck and her face. She wrapped her arms around him and anchored her body to his. The inextinguishable fire burned through her, and she couldn't say no. Not to him, not to his erection poised and throbbing between them.

A groan vibrated in his chest as the kiss deepened. Her pulsating flesh, yielding by degree, screamed a muted cry, and she burst from her self-imposed constraints and demanded all due to her after years of abstinence.

He pressed his forehead against hers, his body trembling. "I don't have protection."

"I don't care." She looked beyond the lacy fringe of her lashes, panting out the words that represented failure and disappointment for most of her adult life but now stood at the gateway to freedom. If he said no, she'd crawl back into her barren womb and never attempt another foray into the sensual realm.

"It would be irresponsible." His whispered words matched the conviction in his eyes.

"*This* is irresponsible." Her impassioned voice echoed her body's desperation. She slipped her fingers beneath the waistband of his briefs and pushed them down over his hips until he kicked them aside.

"I didn't think ye'd change yer mind—"

"Shh." She pressed her finger against his lips.

He lifted her gown, sliding the silk over her knees, her hips, her belly, and gathered the fabric in his hands. She held her arms still, fighting the tightening at the back of her throat. *It's dark in the room. He can't see me.* She raised her arms, and he tossed the gown to the floor.

He kissed her, and the tightening in her throat disappeared, replaced by hard tremors racing through her, growing stronger and more insistent. The entrance to her body stretched taut, and Elliott seated himself within her. A heartbeat or two later, he penetrated deeper still, sparking a storm of golden, erotic sensations.

His gaze traveled up her body, stopping for a moment at her breasts. "God, wee sweetheart, ye're beautiful. Just as I knew ye'd be."

They cleaved to each other with hot, steamy skin, and the taste of his fervor turned spicy and salty and tangy all at the same time. Making love with him might as well have been her first time. Never had a man filled her so completely. She moaned as she rocked against him, enjoying the play of his muscles against her skin. She closed her eyes, panting desperate, greedy breaths, until a tempest rose within her, building to a crescendo. Her nails dug into his back. He applied a modicum of pressure, and then her breathing unraveled and she disappeared within her climax. A perfect rapture.

She opened her eyes slowly, her nerve endings still humming. "That was delicious."

He withdrew and plunged back in. "Sounded like ye enjoyed it."

She sighed, although slightly embarrassed that she'd been so vocal. He pressed hard against her with an answering groan, and his mouth roamed at will. No longer gentle, he devoured the soft curve of her neck and took her lips in an urgent demand. With every torrid thrust, she rose up to meet him, giving back with the same insatiable hunger, and demanding more in return.

"Thank God ye changed yer mind," he said.

The rough timbre of his voice aroused and electrified her. She met his brown eyes, smoldering with heat. And then the words stopped, too late now to say anything more. His movements grew more fervent, his breathing labored, his neck strained and pulsing, until his body shuddered against her, erupting and branding her with his spirit.

Chapter Twenty-Two

Louise's B&B – December 26

MEREDITH POPPED AWAKE with the winter sun on her face. She rolled over onto the other side of the bed, burrowing deep into the blankets. The smell of sex perfumed the sheets. They'd made love twice. Working around his injured leg had been a challenge, and they had laughed through the awkwardness. *Oh, the places his mouth and fingers touched.* Places that still tingled.

She covered her face with her hands and patted her flaming cheeks.

The door to the adjoining room stood closed now. *I wonder what time he left?* She had slept soundly. *Did I snore? Maybe he couldn't sleep and left soon after we…*

A strong breeze blew through the tree outside the window. Bare branches swiped against the side of the house, hurling old insecurities at her. Jonathan had slept with her only a handful of times after the mastectomy, and each time he'd left before the sun came up and always closed the door between them. She rolled over and caressed a pillow that still held Elliott's musky scent, but her nose picked up something else. Something metallic. Another sniff and a sense of urgency rose in the pit of her stomach. She yanked back the comforter and gasped softly.

Blood. *Elliott's blood.*

THIRTY MINUTES LATER, after a quick shower, Meredith ventured downstairs for breakfast, hoping Louise would have news of Elliott. Had he gone to the doctor? If his wound was bleeding, he needed medical care.

Meredith made a beeline to the dining room for a much-needed cup of caffeine. The serving trays on the sideboard were empty, but the coffeepot remained plugged in. By now, the brew was probably overcooked. What should she expect? She was forty-five minutes late. This was a B&B, not a restaurant.

The door into the kitchen swung open, and Louise came barreling out. The two women collided. Meredith rolled her ankle and fell against the sideboard. Louise wobbled yet remained upright.

"Shite," Louise said. "Scared the bejesus out of me." She patted her chest, panting. "Are ye hurt?"

Meredith's heart thumped against the wall of her chest. The fear of injury scared the daylights out of her. She held her leg still, bent at the knee. *Please don't let my foot be hurt.* Seconds turned into a full minute, but she still couldn't put her foot on the floor out of fear. There'd been no break, no crunch, no tear, but still her fear lingered.

"Are *ye* hurt?" Louise asked again.

Meredith bit her lip as she put weight on her foot. A twinge of pain, but nothing significant. "I'm fine."

"Thank God." Louise waved her bracelet-clad arms. "I've had the contractor back twice to fix that blind corner. He canna get it right."

Meredith rubbed her shoulder where she had hit it against the furniture. She'd probably have a bruise. She'd keep an eye on both her shoulder and foot during the day and ice later if there was any swelling.

"I was tidying up the room. I thought ye'd gone out. It's rather *late*," Louise said.

"I overslept. Is Elliott working in the library?"

Louise grabbed dirty dishes and loaded them on a tray. "He's been in there with the door closed since seven o'clock." She seemed tied up tighter than the apron squeezing her waist.

"How was he feeling?" Meredith asked.

Louise picked up the tray, took a step toward the kitchen door, then stopped. "He tries to hide his pain, but this morning he wasna doing a verra good job. If ye ask me, he shouldna have gone out yesterday."

"Have you ever tried to dissuade Elliott from doing something? I don't think it's possible," Meredith said.

"Tell him it will cost a week's wages. He'll back right off."

Meredith thoughtfully gnawed on her lower lip. As far as she could tell, he'd spared no expense entertaining her last night, but she didn't intend to tell Louise that.

Louise jostled the tray, and the dishes clinked against each other. "It's late. I've put all the breakfast food away, but if ye're hungry, a bowl of fruit with yogurt would be easy enough to throw together."

"Don't go to any trouble. I'll just have a cup of coffee." Meredith poured a cup before picking up the newspaper and glancing at the headlines. She quickly scanned the article about the upcoming Hogmanay events. "I'll finish this, then head out."

Louise set down the tray, then fisted her hands at her hips. "What have ye done to Elliott? I've never seen him like this."

The newspaper slipped from Meredith's fingers. "Excuse me. You're asking what I've done?"

Louise stared at Meredith's left hand, which was holding the coffee cup. "He's vulnerable right now, and I dinna want to see him hurt."

Heat hotter than her coffee rose from the pit of Meredith's stomach. "I don't intend—" She stopped, refusing to let Louise bully her into a discussion that was none of her business. "I'm going to work now."

"If ye're planning to interrupt Elliott, I wouldna. He snaps at me when I do, but he might not snap at *ye*." Frost an inch-thick coated Louise's words. She picked up Meredith's cup and placed it on the tray with the other dirty dishes.

Meredith fingered her wedding ring while taking several calming breaths. She had no idea what caused the flighty woman to turn into a snarky, overprotective bitch—a snarky bitch who took her cup of unfinished coffee.

Meredith stopped by the library on her way out. The door was closed, but she heard Elliott yelling about insurance to someone named Harrison. She tiptoed away from the door. Now she could leave for the archives knowing two things: Harrison was in big trouble, and Elliott wasn't bleeding to death.

Chapter Twenty-Three

Louise's B&B – December 26

ELLIOTT STOKED THE fire in the library's fireplace. He knew the fluctuation in temperature didn't come from the room's thermostat but from his own. Cold chills caused the shakes, making holding a pen difficult, yet sizzling memories of Meredith beneath him made him hard and hungry. Intense waves of cold followed by heat broke his concentration at a time when the farm needed his full attention. Now, due to the conversation with Harrison about the insurance company, Elliott was shivering and chewing antacids.

Shots of Demerol dimmed the pain, but nothing pulled down the curtain on his erotic memories. He wanted an encore, even though physically, based on past experience, he doubted his ability to perform. Maybe tonight he and Meredith would order dinner in and have a bed picnic. Sustenance, he didn't need. Meredith, he did, and he would hope for the best.

His phone rang, bringing an unwanted intrusion. "Fraser."

"We've got a problem."

A muscle twitched along his jaw. "Damn, Doc, what now?"

"The gross pathology of Galahad's liver showed a characteristic pattern similar to that of a euthanasia solution."

Elliott straightened in his chair. "Barbiturates?"

Doc cleared his throat. "Someone killed him."

Elliott slammed his fist on top of the desk, then took a breath to cap the boiling rage. Except for the deaths of Sean and Mary MacKlenna, Galahad's death represented the single most devastating event on the farm. Wrong. A murdered horse was catastrophically worse.

Elliott's stomach, filled with breakfast and painkillers, roiled.

"I notified the sheriff," Doc said.

Elliott rubbed his forehead. "What'd he say?"

"There's no law against putting your own horse down."

"The insurance company won't pay the claim if they believe we killed him. The sheriff's attitude won't help." Elliott glanced at his watch. "As soon as I can gather the flight crew, I'll come home."

Doc gave a weary sigh. "I think that's wise. Sandy's good at what she does, but she can't handle the kind of press this will generate."

"I'll send her an email, but tell her and Allie that no one is to talk to a reporter, including Harrison. I'll draft a statement. Sandy should have it within the hour." Elliott hung up, shaking, and not from the chills. He'd get that murdering son of a bitch in his crosshairs, and when he did, there'd be no mercy.

He buzzed Kevin's room and started talking before Kevin said hello. "Pack up. We're going home." Then he called his pilot, David, and Jim Manning. After leaving a message asking Jim to return his call, Elliott shuffled through the house with knifelike pains shooting up and down his leg. "Louise." He found her sitting at the dining room table, head in her hands, reading the newspaper.

She glanced up. "God, ye look horrible. What's wrong?"

He leaned on the crutches. An intense uncontrolled fire burned in his stomach. Once he reported what happened to his horse, the news would knock down the first domino in a long line of carefully placed tiles. There would be no stopping the rest from falling. When the police eventually solved the mystery, and he knew they would, Elliott would be the last domino to tumble.

"Galahad was murdered, and we're in for a fight with the insurance company. I'm going home, and I need Meredith's phone number."

Louise crossed her arms and gave him a pointed stare. "A travel agency made her reservation. I dinna have it. *Ye're* sleeping with her. Why ask me?"

He scowled at her. "What the hell's wrong with ye?"

She gave a little harrumph and a shrug. "I dinna want ye hurt, Elliott."

"I've got a dead twenty-five million-dollar horse, and ye're giving me crap because I slept with a woman." The muscles in his jaw balled up.

The front door opened, and David entered the hallway. "Where's Kevin?"

"He's packing," Elliott said.

David headed toward the steps. "Give us a couple of minutes."

Louise dabbed at her eyes with a napkin. "I'm sorry. I hate change, and it's coming whether I want it or not."

He ran his hand through his hair. Something he rarely did.

Louise walked over to him. "Ye have a strand of hair sticking straight up." She finger-combed his hair. "There now, back in place."

His phone beeped with a text message. He answered it, sent a text to Harrison, and another one to Doc.

Louise reached for his arm. "Come on. I'll walk you to the front door."

David and Kevin came downstairs carrying the bags. "Your laptop wasn't in your room. Is it in the library?" Kevin asked.

Elliott nodded. "So is my jacket."

Louise grabbed his tweed cap off the hook by the door and placed it on his head. "Ye feel like ye're running a fever."

"Nothing's wrong with me." He punched the door open with his crutch. "Tell Meredith to call me."

"Go to the doctor when ye get home," Louise pleaded. "Ye could still lose yer leg."

"They won't cut it off because of a wee fever."

"No, but they'll take it to save yer life," she said with a bite to her words.

Elliott stormed out of the house, letting the door slam behind him.

Chapter Twenty-Four

The National Archives of Scotland – December 26

WHEN MEREDITH ARRIVED at the archives, she discovered the search rooms were closed for the day. If it hadn't been for a sweet woman in records who was working extra to get caught up, Meredith would have been locked out. The woman took pity on her when Meredith plopped down on the icy steps and buried her face in her hands, crying.

Now, a few hours later, she sat in the restroom at the registry house with a cold pack icing her ankle. The ankle didn't swell, but paranoia did. She didn't intend to rush off to the doctor, but if swelling developed, she'd get the name of a specialist from Elliott and have her foot X-rayed. A stress fracture years earlier had gone unnoticed until a secondary injury sidelined her for several weeks. She refused to let that happen again, especially with the qualifying race looming in a couple of months. Looking ahead at the race was a way of denying her probable cancer. Right now, she needed that.

She leaned her head against the wall and closed her eyes. Every time she sighed, a spot on her body tingled—a place where Elliott had touched or licked or nibbled. The ice helped cool her body temperature. Her memories heated her up again.

If she had a conversation with Cate, her intuitive assistant would pick up on a pause or delayed response and accuse Meredith of finding a handsome Scotsman. She knew Meredith well. So she had sent Cate a text explaining that use of cellular devices in the archives was prohibited and that she'd be unavailable for most of the day. And if Meredith remained unavailable, she wouldn't have to talk to her doctor either. It wasn't that she didn't want the results of the biopsy; it was that she didn't want to know today. She wanted time with Elliott before the world came crashing down.

Just one more day. That's all I want.

Chapter Twenty-Five

Louise's B&B – December 26

BY MIDAFTERNOON, Meredith had traced Cullen Montgomery's line back to Major John Montgomery born in 1670. And she'd even had time to make copies of the session record Elliott needed for his research. Several times she'd thought of calling him but didn't have his phone number, and she didn't want to ask Louise. If he hadn't made plans for dinner, she'd suggest a light supper by the fire in the library, or in her room. A warm smile tickled her.

As soon as she walked through the door at the B&B, she sensed in the quiet stillness that the house was in a somber mood. She sniffed, picking up the aromas of meat roasting in the oven and Christmas candles burning in the dining room, but the scent of outdoors that Elliott brought indoors had vanished. Her gloved hands clenched at her side.

"Meredith, is that ye?" Louise called.

Meredith peeked around the corner, slipping off her gloves and scarf. "Yes. Have you seen Elliott?"

Louise stepped out into the hallway, wringing her hands. "He's gone."

Meredith's heart hit the brakes to avoid a messy collision. "To the store?" She knew Louise wasn't implying that he'd taken a quick trip down to the market, but she held out hope nonetheless.

"He went home." Louise's emphatic tone didn't match the hand-wringing.

"To Fraser House, you mean?"

"No. MacKlenna Farm. He went home to Kentucky."

Meredith gasped, thinking of the bloody sheet. She should have knocked on the door and checked on him this morning. *Oh, damn.* "His leg is worse, isn't it?"

Louise shook her head. "It's not his leg. He went home on business."

Meredith stiffened as the sharp edge of betrayal cut through her in rough, zigzag lines. "Did he leave a message?" she asked, but she felt certain he had left without thinking of her.

"He got a call from the farm and off he went." She snapped her fingers. "Just like that."

Tears rushed to Meredith's eyes. She turned away from Louise, not wanting her to see the pain Elliott's departure had caused.

"Would ye like to join Eve and me for supper? I'm cooking a roast."

The crushing weight of Meredith's bad decisions squeezed the air from her chest. "I had a big lunch. I'm not hungry." A lie, yes, but the knots in her stomach would play havoc with food if the two collided anytime soon.

"Excuse me." Meredith edged past Louise and headed toward the elevator. *He left because the farm needed him. How could he do that? We had plans.* She punched the elevator button, and the door opened right away. When she was safely inside with the door closed, she tapped her head against the glass. "How could I be so stupid?" Anger welled within her.

When she reached her floor, she hurried to her room, where she kicked off her boots and slung them across the bed. *Stupid. I gave my body to a man I'd known for three days.* Now on top of her other health concerns, she'd have to be tested for STDs. Tears rolled down her cheeks.

She wasn't sure what she wanted to do, but she knew she couldn't stay at the B&B. Even looking at the bed made her gag.

Elliott's sudden departure had squeezed the joy right out of her, leaving only an empty tube. She'd never been a quitter, but today she didn't have the energy to rebound. Especially now, knowing she'd be leaving Scotland to face worse news at home. Goose bumps peppered her arms, and the stream of tears turned into a gully washer.

Maybe she should go home and spend a few days in San Francisco before returning to the winery. That would give her time to bounce back before the next crisis. She was a bottom line girl, and the bottom line was that she'd had a one-night stand. Time to put on her big girl panties and move on.

Go home, Mer. Put on some new music and dance.

Thirty minutes later, she went downstairs to check out. After dropping her bags by the front door, she went looking for Louise and found her in the library working at the desk. "I'm leaving earlier than planned. My work here's done."

"I'm sorry to hear that." Louise's tone had thawed a degree or two. She walked around to the front of the desk. "Do ye want to keep the room charges on the credit card I have on file?"

Meredith handed Louise a business card. "Yes, and please email a copy of the bill to me." Even though a roaring fire burned in the fireplace and classical music played on the sound system, the vivid red room Meredith had found so warm and cozy was noticeably frigid and unwelcoming.

Louise glanced at the card before putting it in her skirt pocket. "I hate to see ye leave before yer holiday is over."

I'm sure you do.

The doorbell rang.

"Excuse me. I need to get that," Louise said.

"I'm sure it's the car service I ordered."

"I hope ye'll come back," Louise said, following Meredith out into the hallway. "My rooms book early, so give me plenty of notice."

Meredith suspected Louise wouldn't have a vacancy regardless of the dates she requested.

Louise's clogs flapped against the marble floor. "Evelyn is looking forward to a trip to yer winery."

"You have my number. Tell her to call if she can work it out."

Louise's face held a pinched expression as if she were debating with herself. She glanced at Meredith's left hand. Something was on Louise's mind, but Meredith had already had a piece of it earlier and wasn't up for another serving.

The driver carried the bags to the car. The walls seemed to be closing in around Meredith. She had to get out of the house before she suffocated. She opened the door and stepped out into the chill, taking a deep breath of cold air.

"Thanks for the hospitality." Meredith almost choked on the words. She climbed into the limo and said a second good-bye, not to the B&B proprietress, but to a man with chocolate eyes and a whisky-smooth voice that had whispered to her soul on a lonely Christmas night.

Chapter Twenty-Six

On the MacKlenna jet – December 26

KEVIN HAD WAITED on, cajoled, medicated, and fed Elliott, but nothing seemed to ease the stress his boss wore like an old farm shirt, ripped and stained.

They were two hours from landing in Kentucky, and the flight couldn't end fast enough for either of them. Although Kevin had tried to engage Elliott in conversation, he hadn't said more than a few words since leaving Scotland. He wouldn't even talk about the woman he took to the estate on Christmas Day and screwed afterward. It wasn't that Elliott bragged about his women; it was just that he usually shared their preferred wines and foods so Kevin could have them readily available.

The fact that his boss, for the very first time, took a date to the family estate made Kevin even more curious about the mysterious woman. If Elliott wouldn't talk about her, he knew who would. He carried the wine magazine he was reading to the galley, closed the door, and placed a call to Scotland.

"Lou, who's the woman Elliott took to Fraser House yesterday?"

She laughed. "Ye dinna care who he took to the estate. Ye just want to know whose bed he was in this morning. He's not talking about her, is he?"

"He hasn't said much since we left Scotland. He's in a bad mood."

"The woman's married."

Kevin gasped and clutched his chest. "I don't believe that." His voice pitched higher than usual. "Elliott's got a strict code about married women."

Louise made a tsk-tsk sound. "Idol worshiping will disappoint ye every time."

"It's not just me, Lou. Everyone will tell you—Elliott doesn't mess with married women."

"Fine," she said, snapping out the word. "But the woman *was* wearing a wedding ring. I didna mind her joining us for dinner, but when they went to the estate and, well, afterward, I got worried. Scared, really. Funny thing is, I like her, and I think she's a good match for Elliott. But she's *married.*"

"Crap." Kevin sagged against the door. "Give me her name and address. I'll Google her and see what I can find out."

"She gave me her business card, but I tore it up and tossed it into the bubbish. Let me see if I can piece it back together."

Kevin put the phone on speaker and drummed the countertop with his index fingers. Louise was right about his idol worshiping. If Elliott broke one of his cardinal rules, he had a good reason. Wanting sex didn't qualify. There was more to this situation. There had to be.

"Her name is Meredith Montgomery."

Kevin turned off the speaker and put the phone to his ear. "Did you say *Meredith Montgomery?*" He glanced at the cover of the wine magazine he'd been reading. "Is she by any chance from California?" Kevin held his breath waiting for Louise's answer.

"Napa. She owns a winery."

Kevin raised his fist then lowered it with a vigorous, swift motion. "*Yes.*"

"I'm going to put you on speaker so I can put pieces of the card back together," Louise said.

"I only need her mobile number. Can you get that?"

"Here ye go. Write this down," Louise said.

Kevin wrote down the number with a shaking hand.

"There's something else I should tell ye," Louise said. "Elliott wanted her to call him, but I didna give her the message. Now she's gone home."

"She left thinking Elliott slept with her and left town without saying good-bye." Kevin slapped his forehead.

"Something like that."

"Oh, hell, Lou." Elliott didn't always care about the women he slept with, but he did care about his reputation, and he made sure the women he dated were always treated well.

Louise sniffled. "Evelyn's furious with me, but I was only trying to protect Elliott. He's in so much pain and has problems at the farm."

Kevin held the phone between his chin and shoulder and made a fresh pot of coffee while Louise talked and sniffled.

"He doesna need to get mixed up with a married woman," Louise said.

"I don't think she's married," Kevin said.

"She was wearing a wedding ring."

Kevin flipped through the article. "According to this article in *Wine Digest,* she's a widow."

"Shite," Louise said. "How was I supposed to know? Should I call her and confess?"

"You'd probably piss her off," Kevin said. "Let me think of something."

"Call me later and let me know if I need to call and apologize," Louise said.

"You can do that the next time you see her."

Louise sighed. "Dinna think that'll happen."

Kevin smiled, barely able to contain his excitement. "Something tells me it will."

"Kevin," Elliott yelled.

Kevin patted the cover of the magazine. "Got to go, Lou. He's awake." He disconnected the call, poured a cup of coffee, and grabbed the fruit and cheese plate from the refrigerator.

"Bring me coffee and something to eat."

"You don't have to yell. We're the only ones here." Kevin carried a tray and the magazine toward the front of the plane where he sat in the chair opposite Elliott.

Elliott snatched the coffee and a slice of apple from the tray. "Where the hell are we?"

"About an hour from home." Kevin held up the latest issue of *Wine Digest.* "Do you know who this woman is? I know you slept with her. But do you know who she is?"

"Meredith—"

"The owner of Montgomery Winery," Kevin interrupted.

Elliott took the magazine and glanced at the article.

"Her winery," Kevin said, "has created some of the finest handcrafted wines in the world. It's a 160-year-old winery. She's a megastar, and a widow, by the way."

Elliott rolled the magazine and slapped Kevin's knee. "Ye know I don't sleep with married women."

Kevin rubbed his knee. "Lou said she was wearing a wedding ring."

"Gossiping is a good way to get fired." Elliott's voice sounded normal, but his face had an angry red flush.

Kevin slipped a piece of paper from his pocket and dropped it on the table in front of Elliott.

"What's this?"

"Meredith's phone number."

A vertical frown line appeared between his eyebrows. "How'd ye get it?"

"Louise had it."

The frown line deepened. "She told me she didn't."

"Meredith gave it to her when she left the B&B this afternoon, heading home."

"Lou was supposed to tell her to call me."

Kevin's adrenaline spiked. The bearer of bad news always received the brunt of Elliott's Scottish temper, and Kevin seemed to be the only one in Elliott's sphere with the courage to be the bearer. He tasted the words he intended to say, wishing they weren't so bitter. He looked into Elliott's dark angry eyes and said, "She didn't give Meredith the message."

Elliott's face turned a darker shade of red. "*Why?*"

Kevin didn't drop his long-fixed look, although common sense told him to put distance between himself and his boss. He stayed put and said calmly, "She thought Meredith was married."

Elliott scrubbed his face, shaking his head. "I don't have time for this crap. Call Louise back and tell her to fix it."

Kevin leaned forward and put his elbows on his knees. "I'll do that if that's what you want, but I don't think Meredith will take her call."

"I've got a nutcase killing my twenty-five-million-dollar Thoroughbred and a friend screwing me, too." The anger drained from his voice, and he sounded very tired. "Where's Meredith now?"

"Somewhere over the Atlantic."

"She can't take a call now. I'll call her from home."

Kevin picked up the rolled magazine Elliott had tossed aside and flipped through the pages. "Look at this," he said, pointing to a picture. "Her plane's bigger than yours, fully equipped. Call her."

Elliott raised his brow as he glanced at the picture of the Gulfstream G500. Then he handed Kevin his coffee cup. "Get me a real drink."

Kevin strutted back toward the galley. "Maybe she'll stop in Kentucky on the way to California. I'd like to meet her."

"Ye don't hustle my women, and you don't date former girlfriends."

"Whew. Touchy. I just want to talk wine, not the size of your dick." According to the magazine article, Meredith loved Scotland, horses, and a wee half when she was thirsty.

She's the woman for you, Boss, so wake up and get ready.

Chapter Twenty-Seven

Montgomery Winery Jet – December 26

MEREDITH'S PLANE WAS halfway across the Atlantic when her phone rang, flashing a number with an 859-area code. Since she didn't recognize the number and wasn't in the mood to talk to anyone she didn't know, she let the call go to voice mail. Then she clicked over to listen to the message.

"Meredith, this is Elliott."

She tensed at the sound of his voice. The anger burning in her gut over his insensitive departure hadn't cooled one degree.

"All hell is about to break loose at the farm. I had to get in the air. I couldn't wait. I asked Louise to give ye a message to call me. We didn't have yer mobile number. She didn't tell ye, and I'll deal with her later. Call me when ye get this message, or better yet, stop in Lexington for a few days and we'll enjoy what's left of our holiday."

All the heartbreaking anger swamped her emotions. He had hurt her, not intentionally, but he had hurt her nonetheless. It was over now and time to move on.

She tossed the phone aside and went to take a shower. What had started out as an *I'm Gonna Wash That Man Right Outa My Hair* shower turned into the complete opposite when she massaged her breast, feeling the lump. Elliott had fondled her, kissed her, complimented her, but never once had he asked about her scars.

Jonathan had led her to believe she was undesirable, but Elliott proved that wasn't true. In a moment of clarity, she made a decision that might not turn out to be the best one for her, but she made it and would live with the consequences.

Call her gullible. Call her stupid. But don't call her sorry.

Thirty minutes later, she sat back in her chair and made a list for a gut check:

1. There had been a communication glitch.
2. He didn't mean to hurt her.
3. He had promised her dinner.
4. Her life was about to change, and she wanted another moment to hold in her heart.

She snapped her pen against the paper, thinking through each item, focusing on the emotions that were pulling her in four different directions. None of them, however, produced teary eyes or foot-tapping anxiety. Her normally tied-in-knots stomach cheered, "Bring it on."

I'm going in with eyes wide open.

She tapped the call back icon, and the phone rang. A prickly sensation started at her neck and ended at her toes. *Eyes wide open.*

Elliott answered in his whisky-smooth voice, aged by nature. "Fraser."

"It's Meredith."

He let out a breath, sounding relieved. "Where are ye?"

Memories popped like firecrackers. The whisky and sex she licked from his lips hours earlier now teased her tongue—memories, oh, such sweet memories.

"Halfway across the pond," she said breathlessly. "What about you?"

"Almost home."

"What's for dinner?" she asked.

He chuckled, sounding even more relieved. "Whatever ye want."

"A Kentucky Hot Brown?"

"That can be arranged. Anything else?"

She twirled the hair at the nape of her neck like an infatuated schoolgirl. "You're good at making arrangements. I'll leave that to you." She tapped her nails against the window.

"Tell yer pilot to change course, and call me back with an ETA."

She unbuckled her seat belt and stepped into the flight deck. "Can you reroute us to Lexington, Kentucky?"

"The Thoroughbred Capital of the World," the captain said. "Sure. Give us a few minutes, and we'll get you a new estimated time of arrival."

Ten minutes later, she phoned Elliott. "We'll arrive at eight o'clock p.m. Eastern."

"I'll send a car," he said over the sound of crystal clinking in the background. "My assistant will make arrangements with the customs inspector along with hotel reservations for yer crew."

"Sounds like the cocktail hour's begun."

"Nae, wee sweetheart," he said with a lift to his voice. "Not 'til ye arrive."

She chuckled. "Somehow I don't believe that. Enjoy, and I'll see you soon."

Smiling now, forgetting all the angst from before, she clutched the phone to her breast. In her mind, she slipped into the circle of his arms, biceps flexing to hold her closer. Sensual notes infused his woodsy smell and changed his organic scent. A vision of him speaking with his eyes, telling her how much he wanted her, smothered the pain she'd experienced earlier. The imagery held more than the rich texture of his skin or the words he'd spoken into her ear with his soft brogue. It held the roots of the vine he'd wrapped around her heart. Roots that would need nourishing in order to thrive.

Part II

Chapter Twenty-Eight

MacKlenna Farm – Late Afternoon on December 26

"I'M COMING. Don't beat down the damn house," Elliott yelled as he hobbled through the MacKlenna Mansion's wide foyer. He yanked open the oak door darkened with the patina of two centuries to find Jim Manning, the farm's attorney and his friend of twenty years, standing on the portico stomping snow from his boots.

"We should be in Naples, Florida." The lawyer's sour tone reflected the miserable weather conditions.

"I know why the hell I'm not. Why aren't ye?" Elliott asked.

Jim entered the house and removed his snow-dusted overcoat. "My kids threatened not to come home for Christmas if we went south. My wife didn't take to that idea at all. When this storm hit, she changed her mind, but by then we couldn't get a flight out, and you weren't offering your jet."

"It's parked at the airport if ye can get out before the storm of the century arrives."

"The forecast isn't that bad, and I might take you up on the offer if you're staying put."

In spite of Elliott's holiday planning, he'd arrived at the one place he didn't want to be. At least he'd talked Meredith into a visit. She had become his Bethlehem Star on a very bleak night. "Let's talk in the office." He led the way through the elegantly appointed entrance hall. When he reached the light switches installed in an alcove beneath the grand staircase, he turned up the crystal chandeliers.

"You look like hell," Jim said.

"Feel like it, too. I'm barely hanging on this time. Even considering giving the leg up."

Jim came to a sudden stop, squeaking his rubber soles on the hardwood floor. "After *all* you've been through. Why?"

Elliott swung the crutches across the threshold and entered the office. "Give me a prosthetic device and I could run a marathon instead of living with this crap."

"Listen to your damn doctors."

Elliott poked his tongue against the back of his teeth. "Don't start with me."

"I'm not the only one telling you to see a therapist." The attorney threw up his hands and strode over to the bar with the same swagger he'd used on the basketball court when he'd played at the University of Kentucky years earlier. "Why quit now?"

Elliott sat in a leather chair and put his leg on the footstool. "The injury stopped me once before from doing what I needed to do. Came close to doing it again."

"You nearly died in that attack—"

"I did die," he mumbled.

"Your sacrifice saved Kit from a lot worse than she got."

Elliott swallowed hard and gazed off into some invisible distance to look beyond the horror of that night. "Just pour me a whisky."

"Why'd you call? I'm sure it's not to talk about your health. You could get more sympathy from Mrs. Collins."

"We've got a problem."

Jim handed Elliott his drink, loosened his tie, and sat in a wingback chair that framed the fireplace. "Start at the beginning. Don't leave anything out."

"Has anyone ever told ye yer bedside manner sucks?"

"You want sympathy, go—"

Elliott held up his hand to stop his friend from repeating the mantra *Get Help*. He didn't need a therapist. He needed good doctors, good lawyers, and a detailed CFO. "Galahad was murdered, or more accurately, euthanized. If the insurance company's investigation concludes that we put him down, they won't pay the claim."

Jim whistled. "We've got a hell of a problem." He put down his glass, pulled a small notepad and pen from his shirt pocket, and jotted down a few notes. "The insurance company doesn't want another Alydar situation."

"The murder of that horse set in motion the collapse of a financial house of cards. That's not what we've got here," Elliott said. "These horses are worth more to us alive than dead."

"That wasn't the situation with Alydar." Jim put the notepad aside and took another sip of his drink. "No one on the farm would have harmed Galahad. Who did? Any suspects?"

Elliott grimaced from the nasty taste of a cocktail mixed with anger, grief, and frustration. Those questions had kept his mind racing around an endless track for the last several hours. "There's only one person who had that kind of grudge against the farm, and he's dead."

"You're thinking of Gates, aren't you?"

Even the sound of the name evoked visions of demonic spirits. Elliott knocked back his drink and wanted another. He reached for his crutches.

Jim came to his feet. "Here, I'll do it."

"Give me a double."

"How much pain medication have you had today?"

Elliott glared at his friend. "I'm not driving. Pour me a damn drink."

"The police never recovered the fifty thousand dollars he stole from the farm."

"After this long, we'll never get the money back." Elliott took the refilled glass. The barman shorted him on the double, but Elliott sipped his drink without complaint. "I see wheels spinning behind yer eyes. What are ye thinking?"

Jim sat, crossed his ankle over his opposite knee, and fiddled with his pants' cuff. "That he gave the money to someone to do what he couldn't." He met Elliott's gaze with his usual exterior calm.

"I mentioned to Jake there could be a connection to Gates."

"Maybe he hired someone in jail and that person just got out," Jim said.

"Thank God Kit's not here."

"This is all conjecture," Jim said. "If someone's bent on retaliation, he's after you, not Kit." Jim finished his drink. "I'll talk to my investigator tomorrow and ask him to track down Gates's friends and family members. We might get lucky."

"David's available to work the case if ye need him."

The lawyer dropped his foot to the floor and sat straight in his chair. "Let's see what Chuck can find out. I get nervous when a member of SCOTS DG starts nosing around."

"David's retired from the army."

"Those guys never retire."

Elliott had never met a more tight-lipped individual than David, and he'd never asked his friend what he did when he wasn't working security at Fraser House. If Jim's investigator didn't get immediate results, Elliott would make the call.

Breaking into the temporary silence, Jim asked, "Have you filed the insurance claim?"

"Harrison notified the insurance company. It's now in the hands of the claims adjuster—"

"—who'll wait on the final necropsy report," Jim said.

"MacKlenna Farm only owned twenty-five percent of Galahad. We'll have to pay out almost nineteen million dollars."

Manning gave a look that went from startled to sick in one second flat. "Thanks for reminding me."

"We'll take a bath in the global economy if we have to liquidate assets."

"You got anything of value you don't have to liquidate?"

Elliott gave a hollow laugh. "We could rezone the two-hundred-acre tract across the road to a developer."

"You'd have one hell of a battle with the planning and zoning commission. It would quickly get personal and ugly." Jim sipped his drink. "I'm not saying I like the idea, but if you could sell that acreage for development, you'd put a sizable dent in what the farm will owe the shareholders if the claim's denied." He made another note on the pad. "I'll ask my law partner to look into it."

Elliott scowled. "Don't run up the bill on a hypothetical."

"Three months from now it might not be a hypothetical. Pay now, pay later. The difference is that later, you'll want an answer in an hour, and the entire firm will have to stop what they're doing to get you an answer."

Elliott curled his lip. "Bloodsuckers, the whole lot of ye."

Jim stepped over to the bar and refilled his drink. "The biggest problem I see is that the farm sits on the Fayette-Woodford County line where residents of both counties use the words developer and devil interchangeably."

Elliott held out his empty glass. "Won't be the first time someone's called me the devil."

"I think the last one was the redhead from Virginia," Jim said, pouring the other half of the double into the glass.

"How the hell do ye keep track of my dates? Do ye have spies here?"

Jim held up his hand and made a basketball dunking motion. "I live vicariously through you. Haven't you figured that out yet?"

"Not only me, but the entire University of Kentucky men's basketball team. Ye need to get a life," Elliott said.

All Jim said in response to that was an indifferent, "Yeah."

The two men sat in silence, sipping and thinking. The chimes on the tall clock marked the half hour, and still they sat. Finally, Jim said, "You know, Sean will turn flips in his coffin if we sell, but it's a revenue stream the board of directors will need to consider. Galahad's shareholders will have to sue the farm first. That puts us into the next year or the year after before we'd have to pay anything out."

Elliott glanced up at Sean's portrait hanging over the fireplace and shook his head. "Sean's second worst nightmare—a lawsuit."

Jim put his glass in the sink and returned his notebook to his breast pocket. "I'll talk to the insurance company. In the meantime, don't talk to the press or the claims adjuster. Go to the doctor. Watch your back and the stallions'. That asshole could come back for more." Jim checked his watch. "I've got to run. No need to see me out. I'll call you tomorrow."

Elliott gave his friend the thumbs-up.

Jim glanced up at the portrait, too, and let out a heavy sigh. "It's not the same with the big guy gone, is it?"

Elliott shook his head. "Sean was a giant among ordinary men. But I'm glad he's not here to see this." On reflection, Elliott wished he wasn't either. He'd failed his *anamchara.*

Elliott stared out the window into the black of night. "If ye're watching, my soul friend, I'm sorry it's come to this." Cold stillness turned into hot impatience. He picked up the autopsy report Doc had left for him, crushed it in his hands, and threw it across the room.

I'll find out who's responsible. This will not be my legacy.

Chapter Twenty-Nine

Lexington Blue Grass Airport – Early Evening on Decembe 26

THE FARM'S CHIEF of security drove Elliott to the airport to pick up Meredith. He had given himself a shot of Demerol earlier that barely touched the pain. Either his tolerance had taken a dip or his leg was worse this time.

Begrudgingly, he knew he'd have to be at his doctor's office when the door opened in the morning. Dr. Chris Lyles wouldn't be in, thank God, but his PA would see Elliott immediately. After Jim dumped on him, Elliott didn't relish a dose from his surgeon, too. He hadn't wanted to switch doctors and go to New York, but Chris insisted, thinking a new approach to Elliott's care might be more successful.

Jake went inside the terminal to check Meredith's ETA. While Elliott waited in the car at the farm's private hangar, he fiddled with his wristwatch. The strap seemed looser than usual. Was he losing weight? He jiggled his belt buckle. It had extra slack, too. "Damn." *Better not get on the scales in the morning.* Weight loss would give Chris more ammunition to blast in Elliott's direction.

Jake returned to the car and Elliott lowered the window. "The plane should be on the ground in about five minutes. The customs inspector is inside staying warm."

Elliott rolled the window back up. In the dark and silent car,

Galahad's necropsy pictures filled the void. In life, the horse had been a magnificent animal. In death, he looked unrecognizable as the animal Elliott had loved. Long, smooth, well-defined muscles had pulsed with the blood of champions. In the photographs, they were flat and unresponsive.

Elliott pounded his fist on the armrest. *Son of a bitch. Whoever did this, I'll kill him.*

A text message beeped, pulling him from his torment.

"I'm on the ground," Meredith's message said.

His dick swelled in response. He gave the appendage a slight squeeze. "Ye operate on yer own, don't ye, buddy? Don't give a rat's ass about my pain." Elliott wiped perspiration from his forehead.

The plane landed and taxied to the MacKlenna hangar. It took a few minutes, but when the cabin door opened, Meredith appeared at the entrance. She slipped a cap out of her pocket, tugged it on her head and down over her ears, leaving a fringe of dark hair around her neck.

"Damn, ye're cute." His left foot tapped an impatient beat. "Zip up. It's cold." The flight attendant standing next to her must have said the same thing. She zipped her white fur jacket. Then, ducking her head against the cold, she descended the steps toward the customs officer. Jake gathered up her bags and followed the officer and Meredith into the hangar.

If Elliott didn't stop tapping his foot, there'd be a hole in the floorboard. He checked his watch. Waited. Checked the time again. "What are ye carrying in those bags, m'dear?" He reached for the door handle. "Enough of this." Just then, she reappeared at the hangar entrance, laughing, and so was Jake, who held tight to her elbow. "What the crap?" Elliott crossed his arms in front of his chest and sneered at his security chief.

Jake opened the car door and Meredith slid in beside Elliott. When their eyes met, he pulled her into his arms, reading the unspoken message that she wanted him as he wanted her. He paused for only an instant as his gaze was drawn to her lips, parted, full, and glistening. Then he lowered his mouth to hers—warm and welcoming—and he claimed her. He unzipped her jacket, and she leaned into him, pressing her small, soft breasts against his chest.

"Are we going to do it in the backseat with everyone watching?" she whispered against his mouth.

"Only if we can't wait." His need for her seared him, and he moaned. He didn't want to wait, but he would. His fingers inched underneath her cap and pushed it off, freeing her thick, dark hair. He cradled her head while his tongue stroked the interior of her mouth, tasting sweet wine.

"I can wait. And you have a fever," she said, pulling away slightly.

"My whole body's on fire."

"You need a doctor."

"I am one." He kissed her again.

"I'm going home if you don't get treatment."

"I'll go in the morning."

"Okay," she said and kissed him back.

The trunk lid slammed, and he straightened. "We're starting from right here when we get to the house," he said in a husky voice.

Jake climbed in behind the steering wheel. "I put two bags and a computer case in the trunk, and your crew is on the way to their hotel. Is there anything else you need, Ms. Montgomery?"

"I'm fine. Thanks." She nestled next to Elliott. "How far is the farm from here?"

"Fifteen minutes in that direction."

Meredith laced her arm with his. "That should give you plenty of time to give me the short version of what happened to bring you home in such a hurry."

"What did Louise tell ye?"

"That you went home on business."

He settled back into the seat, holding her in the crook of his arm. "Galahad was murdered, and we don't think the insurance company will pay the twenty-five-million-dollar claim. We're in for a battle and a hunt for the killer."

"Oh my," Meredith said. "I'm not surprised you left after getting that kind of news. What's the next step? Do the police have any leads?"

"We're on our own. The police don't care."

She looked at him, scrunching her brow. "Wasn't there a famous horse killed by its owner several years ago?"

"Ye're thinking of Alydar. The most highly leveraged horse in history. Insurance fraud was never proved in that case, but the owner went to prison for other matters relating to his farm's bankruptcy. The equine insurance industry started denying claims in sudden death situations, holding owners responsible."

"How do you prove you didn't kill him?"

"Find the person who did."

"That's dangerous."

"We don't have a choice." He glanced out the window for a moment. "See the white fence up there on the left? That's the eastern edge of the farm. We'll turn off and go in through the side entrance."

"I've heard about the white fences."

"Most are painted black now. It's too expensive to keep them white. MacKlenna Farm will always have white fences, though."

"How many acres?"

"Three thousand. The farm's governed by a revocable trust agreement that established a board of directors. If Kit doesn't revoke the trust within ten years, the farm passes to the University of Kentucky in perpetuity. I'll be long gone by then." *If this mess with Galahad isn't cleared up, I'll be gone sooner.*

Jake turned into a drive, and the gate lifted automatically. Bare-branched trees lined the path to a well-lit, red-bricked mansion. Meredith sat forward in her seat. "The house is beautiful. The Doric columns are exquisite."

"They're affectionately known as the Venerable Old Soldiers, and they have quite a reputation. The farm gets calls every week from brides who want to use the portico as a backdrop for wedding pictures. We try to accommodate as many as we can."

"That's risky for the farm."

"The photographer has to be on the approved list. We've never had a problem."

"What about security? How do you handle employee egress and ingress?"

"Farm vehicles have sensors that open and close the gates. Employees go in and out through the main guarded entrance. That way we don't have to change codes or collect security cards when employees leave."

"What about at night?"

"Security walks through each barn every hour, and when the horses are out, checks the paddocks."

"How did someone know when they could safely get in and out of Galahad's stall?"

"We're looking into that."

"Security's a big concern at the vineyard. That's why I asked. When Jonathan had his stroke"—she stopped and blew out a puff of breath—"a worker found him unconscious in the vineyard. Now security keeps up with everyone. It's annoying, but I'm getting used to the intrusion."

The car approached the circular drive and slowed as they passed the brick skirt of the wide portico. "The MacKlennas built the house in the late seventeen hundreds on the same floor plan as Monticello," Elliott said.

"It even has an oculus." Appreciation flowed through her voice.

"There's a secret passage to the top. I can't navigate it now, but I'll show ye the way."

"A house with lots of secrets, I bet."

Too many. "We'll go in through the garage. Not a dramatic entrance, but safer than icy steps."

Jake parked in the six-bay garage. Elliott led Meredith into the house through the mudroom, and from there, they stepped into the hallway. He pointed toward the front of the house. "The housekeeper prepared the front upstairs room. Jake will take yer bags there. I thought ye'd prefer some privacy, but I hope ye'll sleep with me."

Her cheeks flushed. "After last night, I'd come after you again, but a lot sooner."

He leaned in and kissed her, cursing the damn crutches. "I would have knocked on yer door within the next fifteen minutes if ye hadn't knocked on mine."

"Really?" she asked, her eyes twinkling.

He kissed the tip of her nose. "Really."

Jake entered with her bags and headed toward the steps. "Should I put these in the front room?"

"Yes," Elliott said, "and be sure the heat's on."

"Peter sent me a text asking if he could meet with you in the morning," Jake said. "What should I tell him?"

"I have a doctor's appointment at eight thirty, and I need transportation. Kevin can take me if no one else is available. Tell Peter to arrange a time with Allie later in the morning." Elliott continued down the hall, passing the gold-leaf portraits of the MacKlennas.

"Who are these men?" Meredith asked.

He nodded toward the first portrait as he continued down the hallway toward the office. "That's Thomas I, then Thomas II, Sean I, II, III, IV, V, and VI."

"And the women?"

"That one," Elliott said, passing the first of two smaller portraits, "is Sean I's twin sister. The other woman is her daughter."

Meredith stood in front of the portrait, but Elliott kept walking. "What year was this painted?"

He reached the office door. "Early 1850s."

Meredith cocked her head first one way and then the other. "She's a beautiful woman. Looks familiar."

"She has that look about her. Do ye want wine or whisky?" he asked. For three months, he'd avoided discussing the appearance of the portrait with the staff and didn't intend to discuss it further with Meredith.

"Whisky," she said. "Let me pour. You sit." Relieved, he did, sitting in the same wingback chair in front of the fireplace that he'd occupied earlier during his meeting with Manning. She poured drinks at the bar, handed Elliott a glass, and sat across from him.

"This is not the office I had pictured for you."

"This belonged to Sean. I use it, but I have two others on the farm. I move around."

"You don't look well. Why don't you go to bed?"

At least he wore pressed clothes, because everything else about him must look like crap. "Do ye mind turning in early?"

"Early?" she asked. "My biological clock has no idea what time it is. I'll carry the drinks. You lead the way."

Elliott and Meredith entered the first-floor master suite just as Kevin walked out of the bathroom, wearing gym shorts and a T-shirt and carrying a handful of dirty laundry. Elliott stopped and leaned heavily on the crutches. "Meredith, this is Kevin Allen. Wherever I am, he's usually close by."

"Great article in *Wine Digest,* Ms. Montgomery. I'm looking forward to tasting your new wine."

"I don't have any *Cailean* on the plane, but I do have several other labels. I'll get you a few bottles before I leave."

He rubbed his hands together, smiling. "Thank you." Then he turned to Elliott and said, "I laid everything out. When you're ready to shower, buzz me."

Meredith set Elliott's drink on the table next to the bed. "Why don't I go unpack, and Kevin can help you now. I'll be back in what…" She glanced at Elliott and then at Kevin. "Thirty minutes?"

Elliott nodded.

As soon as Meredith left the room, Kevin dropped the clothes into the nearest chair and rushed to Elliott's side. "You can hardly stand. I don't think you'll be much good to your lady friend tonight." He eased Elliott to the side of the bed.

"Get my medicine bag," Elliott said.

Kevin grabbed the bag off the bathroom counter. "If you have a shot now, you definitely won't be able to—"

"It can't be helped." Elliott blew out a ragged breath. "Damn. Up the dosage. The pain's never been this bad."

Kevin gave him a shot in the hip, disposed of the syringe, put the medicine back into the bag, and zipped it. "When you're ready,

I'll help you get a shower."

"Give me a couple of minutes." He stretched out on the bed, thinking how embarrassed he'd be if he couldn't get his dick up. The way he felt at the moment, he knew he couldn't. He rarely second-guessed his decisions, but he considered that he'd made a mistake inviting Meredith to the farm. She only planned to spend the night, so maybe he'd feel better in a few hours. He could make love once, then he'd put her back on the plane. In a few weeks when the situation wasn't so dire, he'd go out to California and spend time with her. Right now, he wasn't much good to anyone.

"Come on," Kevin said. "You'll feel better after a hot shower."

Elliott groaned. Kevin supported his back as he sat and swung his legs over the side of the bed. "Give me my drink." Elliott tossed back the whisky. The liquid fire burned past his lips and tongue and swirled down his throat. If only it could cut the pain the way it had in the beginning. But that was a hell of a long time ago.

With Kevin's encouragement, he made it into the shower, where he nearly passed out. "Kevin." Elliott grasped the shower bar, holding tight as if to a rope attached to a gondola. If he let go, he'd be in trouble. If he held on, he might be in worse shape. "For God's sake, get me out of here." A few minutes later, he sat on the edge of the bed with a drink in his hand.

"Drink it slow, Boss. It's the last one."

"Oh, go on," Elliott said, waving his free hand. "Get out of here and take the dirty laundry with ye."

Kevin loaded his arms with the clothes he'd earlier left in the chair. "I'll be back at seven to help you get ready for your doctor's appointment."

Crap. Elliott didn't want to go to the doctor. He'd catch hell from the drill sergeant PA who would bust his balls. She'd chastise him more than Lyles would, and he'd hang his head a wee bit in shame. "Don't come barging in here," he said to Kevin in a tone of voice clouded with dread.

"Your secrets are safe with me."

"The hell they are. Ye and Louise gossip like two old hens."

Kevin's face went slack, paling slightly, and his shoulder slumped. "I don't gossip."

"I don't give a crap. It's Meredith's privacy that concerns me."

"Since *when* were you concerned about anybody's privacy?"

"I'll see ye in the morning," Elliott said, ignoring the question. He picked up a throw pillow to toss at Kevin, but Meredith appeared at the door.

"Is this a good time?"

"He's all yours," Kevin said with sarcasm dripping from his voice. He left the room, closing the door behind him.

Elliott forced a smile to his lips. She looked breathtaking in a pair of deep purple lounging pajamas. His dick played dead. *Traitor.* Elliott leaned back on the pillows and patted the bed beside him. "Come here, gorgeous."

She climbed in beside him. "Hmm. It's warm." She rolled over onto her side and leaned her head on her hand, revealing the swell of her breasts below the pajama top neckline. Breasts always got a rise out of him, but not tonight. *Traitor.*

"I turned on the heated blanket. It gets cold in here," he said.

"I like to keep it cold in the bedroom so I can burrow underneath heavy comforters. But tonight, I've got you to keep me warm." She pressed her hand against his forehead. "I think you're warmer than the blanket."

Hell, yeah, he was hot, but not the way he needed to be. "I just took a shower." Never in his life had he been forced to tell a woman he couldn't perform.

"Do you want me to turn out the lights?"

He picked up the remote control from the bedside table. "This does everything—a one-stop shop. There's a button for security, music, lights, and phone."

"What about 911?" she asked, running her fingers through his hair.

Her nails weren't too long or too short. He hated long nails. "Hope ye're not anticipating making a call."

Her eyes widened, and she gave him what looked to be a tentative smile. "After Jonathan's death, I'm paranoid. I need to know where to get help."

"If ye need help while on MacKlenna Farm, push this red button. It automatically calls the security office and Jake's mobile."

She continued teasing his hair. He wanted her fingers wrapped around his dick, not running through his graying temple, but he wasn't getting hard. At least his hair kept her hand busy and his ego less deflated. Her index finger trailed down the side of his face until it reached his mouth, where she traced the outline of his lips, exploring. "Doesn't Jake ever get time off?"

"Some, but he rarely takes it." He found her steady gaze unsettling. God, he hated disappointing her. He focused on the remote out of necessity. "This green button controls the lights."

"Which one fixes breakfast?" A smile teased the corners of her mouth.

"Mrs. Collins does that, and she'll be here by six."

"I'm worried about your fever," Meredith said.

He drew in a deep, ragged breath, and his chin dropped dejectedly to his chest. "I'd make a lousy lover tonight. The pain meds interfere with an erection. The mind's willing, but the body—"

"I can wait until you're well."

"I'll make it up to ye."

She put her arm across his chest and placed her head on his shoulder. "I'll hold you to that."

Chapter Thirty

MacKlenna Mansion – December 27

ELLIOTT'S MOANING WOKE Meredith in a sizzling panic. The digital clock on the bedside table gave off the only light in the room. She touched his forehead—hot and sweaty. Waiting for a morning doctor's visit might be too late. She flipped on the lamp, found the remote on the table, and pushed the red button. The house phone rang immediately.

"Dr. Fraser, this is Jake. What's your emergency?"

"It's Meredith. Elliott needs an ambulance."

"Is it his leg or something else?"

Elliott's pallor sent tentacles of fear that leeched on to her, sucking her breath. She began to shake. "I think it's something else. How long will it take?"

"We have our own ambulance and a paramedic on call. Hold just a minute."

Seconds ticked by annoyingly slow, and with each second, her mouth got drier.

"The paramedic is on his way. He has a key. Tell me when you hear him at the door. His name is Skip."

She jumped out of bed, put on her slippers, and paced. "Come on. Come on."

"Is Dr. Fraser having trouble breathing?" Jake asked.

She leaned over Elliott and listened. "His respiration is shallow, but he doesn't appear to be struggling."

"You should be hearing Skip now. Where's Kevin?"

"Upstairs asleep, I guess." She tried to still her heart, quiet the rapid thump. "Tell the paramedic to hurry. *Please.*"

"Ms. Montgomery, look at the bandage. Is there blood?"

A hot rush of annoyance heated her words. "Yes." Time passed and still no Skip. "*Where is he?*" Her tone demanded an answer.

"Stay calm. He's on his way. Where's Kevin?"

"Upstairs."

"Press the intercom button and wake him. I see red lights at the front of the mansion."

Within moments, the rumble of a man's voice came from the hallway. "Ms. Montgomery."

"He's here," she said into the phone, breathing relief.

"I'm going to hang up now," Jake said. "I'll be there in three minutes."

"We're in here," Meredith called out. Then she pressed the intercom button. "Kevin, we need you. *Hurry.*"

Almost instantly, he replied, "Coming."

A man dressed in black EMT gear entered the room and made his way to Elliott's side of the bed. "Dr. Fraser, can you hear me?" The paramedic checked Elliott's leg and took the pulse in his ankle.

Elliott moaned, and his eyes rolled back into his head.

Kevin ran into the room, wearing gym shorts and no shirt, hair disheveled. "What the hell? How long has he been like this?"

"His moaning woke me." She rubbed her temples. *What time did we fall asleep?* "We drifted off around nine o'clock. I didn't hear anything until just a few minutes ago."

"The pulse in his right ankle is very weak," Skip said. "Has he said anything about his foot being cold?"

Kevin heaved a sigh. "No, and he would have told me. If it's the arterial graft that could account for the severe pain he's been having."

Jake entered the room, clipping his radio to his duty belt. "How is he?"

"My guess," Skip said, "is that he's got a clot in the arterial graft. The pulse in his right foot is very weak. I hope Dr. Lyles is on call tonight."

"I've alerted the hospital," Jake said. "I've got two guys bringing in the stretcher."

"Kevin, get dressed. We'll start an IV when we get him in the ambulance. Get his meds, too," Skip said.

Two security officers rolled the stretcher into the room. They stepped aside as Jake and Skip lifted Elliott and secured him with belts.

"Is there anything else about his condition we need to know?" Skip asked.

"His leg was bleeding yesterday, too," she said.

Skip took a pad and pen from his pocket and jotted down a few notes. "You can ride with us, Ms. Montgomery. It'll take several minutes to get an IV started. That should give you time to dress."

"I'll take her," Jake said.

Meredith fought back a wealth of tears. She had no idea what an arterial graft was or how it could make Elliott's foot cold. Right now the paramedic needed to focus on Elliott's care, not on giving her an anatomy lesson.

"You don't need to do that. With GPS, I'll find my way. I'm used to driving in unfamiliar places. Where are you taking him?"

Skip put his notepad away. "University of Kentucky Medical Center."

"Are you sure you want to drive?" Jake said.

"I might have to come back to the house on short notice, and I'd prefer to have a car available," Meredith said. She picked up Elliott's cell phone from the bedside table. "Is there family we should notify?"

Jake fingered the buckle on his service belt. "The MacKlennas and his father are gone now. They were all the family he had."

Louise and Evelyn were the closest to family members Elliott had. They needed to know about his condition. The similarity struck her. She had no family either. If paramedics rushed Meredith to the hospital, the only person on her notification list was Cate.

After Jake and Skip wheeled Elliott to the ambulance, she hurried upstairs to change. Fifteen minutes later, she drove the Mercedes out of the garage with the GPS set to direct her to the medical center. She cruised through town in the dead of night with Christmas lights shining on the icy streets. When she arrived at the hospital, she saw the ambulance parked at the entrance to the emergency room.

A row of empty parking spaces fronted the ER entrance. She pulled the car into the closest space but couldn't turn off the engine. She couldn't open the door. She couldn't get out. Frozen in her memories of Jonathan airlifted to the hospital and her frantic race to arrive in time to give the doctors his advance directive—no resuscitation. But they had put him on life support by the time she arrived, stripping the decision from her hands. Days later, exhausted, she made the excruciating call to turn off the machine that never should have been turned on. She had failed to follow through with the only promise he'd ever extracted from her.

Could she make a similar decision for Elliott? Of course not, nor would the hospital allow her. She'd only known him a handful of days, albeit very special days, but she knew so little about him. Her fickle heart, though, thought it knew all it needed to know. That's why she'd invited him into her bed, and that's why she was sitting in the parking lot in the middle of the night in front of a hospital she'd never entered in a town she'd never visited.

Deep within her reserves, she found the courage to turn off the car and cut through the snow-covered grass to the sidewalk leading to the ER entrance. A handful of weary-eyed people sat in the waiting room, shoulders slumping under the weight of whatever brought them to the hospital at such a dreary hour. Meredith knocked on the receptionist's window to get the woman's attention and told her she'd like to see Dr. Fraser, who'd just been brought in by ambulance.

"Are you family?" the receptionist asked.

Meredith steeled her back and lied. "Yes." The receptionist

buzzed the door, and she went back to room number ten. The curtain was open. Elliott wore a nondescript print hospital gown, and the ER staff had hooked him up to a bank of beeping machines.

A triage nurse, standing next to the bed, glanced up as Meredith entered the room. "Are you Ms. Montgomery? He's been asking for you."

Meredith walked to the opposite side of the bed and clasped Elliott's cold hand.

"The doctor will be right in," the nurse said and left the room.

Skip poked his head into the cubicle. "I'm going back to the farm, Ms. Montgomery. Is there anything you need?"

She handed him her cell phone. "Would you mind programming Jake's number into my contacts? Right now, I couldn't punch in two digits in the correct sequence."

He took the phone and handed it back a minute later. "Look under *Jake at MacKlenna Farm*."

"Where's Kevin?"

Just as she asked, Kevin stepped into the room carrying two cups of steaming coffee. "I had to get coffee out of the machine downstairs. I don't have privileges like other people." He snarled at Skip, who punched Kevin on the shoulder.

"If you get a real job, you might have a few perks," Skip said.

Kevin glanced at Meredith. "He's jealous. His name is McIntosh. He thinks he should have gone to Scotland for Christmas instead of me."

"I don't want to go where it's cold. I wanted to go to Naples," Skip said. "I'm going back to the farm. You riding back with me or staying here?" he asked Kevin.

"I'll stay. Jake will send a car if I need to go back. But, hey, tell him Tabor sneaked into my room. I closed the door on the way out. No telling what that cat will do if he can't eat breakfast," Kevin said.

The paramedic laughed. "Hate to see the woodwork after that thirty-pound cat scratches it up."

Their jocularity was about to piss Meredith off until she looked into their eyes—dark and focused. Their joking was only a mask to cover their fear.

"Kevin, wait outside." Elliott's gravelly voice barely rose above a whisper. "I want to talk to Meredith."

Kevin, looking not the least bit perturbed, left the cubicle and pulled the curtain closed.

Elliott squeezed her hand. "Don't let them take my leg."

She gulped, but she knew what it was like to lose a part of her body to save her life. "I won't let you die, Elliott."

"I have to know ye'll fight for me."

"Kevin's here."

Elliott shook his head. "He prays for me to get well, no matter the cost."

"I'll do what I can." *But I won't let you die.*

"My phone?" he asked.

She patted her jacket pocket. "I have it. Do you want me to call someone?"

Elliott nodded. "David."

Meredith took a breath before she asked the next question. "Should I call Louise?"

"David will."

"Will he call Kit, too?"

Elliott grimaced. "She doesn't have mobile service."

"But—"

The ER doc pushed the curtain aside and entered the room, cutting Meredith off. "Dr. Fraser, I just talked to your surgeon—"

"Lyles or the surgeon in New York?" Elliott interrupted.

"Lyles. He just finished emergency surgery and is on his way down. How's the pain?"

"Tolerable."

"Is there anything you need?"

Elliott gave the doctor a half grin. "Protection from Lyles."

The ER doctor patted Elliott's arm. "He's very concerned about you."

Elliott gazed at Meredith. Then he closed his eyes and seemed to fall asleep, until he said, "Tell Jake that David's coming."

How can he think of the farm when he's so sick and staring down the threat of another surgery? Her mind filled with the fear she held for him. "What's wrong with his leg?"

"The ultrasound showed a clot in the arterial graft."

The door curtain fluttered, and a man in green scrubs entered. "Elliott, I'm not happy about this."

"Ye think I am?" Elliott said.

"The doctor in New York told me the surgery exceeded expectations. Now here you are. I'm going to take you up to OR and get rid of that clot."

"Ye're *not* taking my leg."

"I don't intend to." The doctor glanced at Meredith. "There's a waiting room on the second floor. As soon as I finish, I'll come out and give you a report. We'll keep him in ICU tonight to keep an eye on him. Otherwise he'll get up and walk around." He squeezed Elliott's shoulder. "I'll see you upstairs."

The doctor left, and Meredith followed him out into the corridor. "Doctor Lyles."

He stopped and turned toward her, his brows furrowed.

Meredith cleared away the lump in her throat. "You wouldn't take his leg without talking to him beforehand, would you?"

"Rest assured, Ms.—"

"Montgomery."

"He lives in fear of that, but I hope that's not something to worry about tonight."

She let out a tight breath of relief and reentered the room. The orderly had unhooked Elliott from the monitors and rehooked him to mobile units. She clasped his hand. "I'll be in to see you as soon as they let me." She kissed him lightly on the mouth.

"If a decision has to be made, make sure I'm awake," Elliott said.

Relieved that she had Dr. Lyles's word, she said, "I will."

The orderly rolled him out of the cubical and down the corridor. She plodded behind them until they reached the patient elevators. "The public elevators are around the corner, or you can take the steps," the orderly said. "We're going to the second floor."

Elliott had a wide-eyed fix on her that she understood. When she went into surgery, though, she knew the surgeon would leave part of her in the operating room. The only thing about Elliott that would change if he lost his leg would be his perception of himself. No one else would perceive him differently. He would be no less a man, certainly not in her eyes.

After Elliott and the orderly disappeared inside the elevator, Meredith wound her way through the hospital until she found the second-floor waiting room. She plopped into a hard-cushioned chair. The time was one thirty, which made it six thirty in the UK.

Where's Kevin?

The resourceful man could be anywhere. If she had to bet, she'd wager he was wherever the nurses were. In his late twenties, about six feet tall with chiseled good looks and a body built to compete in triathlons, he'd have no trouble attracting beautiful women. Elliott had an eclectic group of caring friends, which reminded her that she needed to call David. She dialed his number.

"McBain," he said.

"David, this is Meredith Montgomery. Elliott's in surgery. He needs you."

"Ms. Montgomery, I don't make assumptions, especially where Dr. Fraser is concerned, but I put him on a plane heading to Kentucky. Ye were still in Scotland. Did he turn the damn plane around?"

"No, I arrived in Lexington a few hours ago," she said, shivering from the late-night hour.

"Are they taking his leg?"

Tears slid down her cheeks. Stress, lack of sleep, and fear usurped her physical and emotional coping skills.

"Ms. Montgomery, can ye hear me? Are they taking his leg?"

She couldn't speak. Sentences tumbled from her brain but froze on her tongue, growing thicker with the accumulation of unspoken thoughts.

"*Meredith.*" His tone was deadly sharp now and couldn't be ignored.

"No."

"If it's his life or his leg, he has to let it go."

She stared ahead at the gray cinderblock wall—drab, boring. The complete opposite to what was happening in her life. Weren't her problems enough? Now, to compound the severity of her own situation, she was enmeshed in Elliott's possible life-or-limb predicament. She shook her head, partly because she didn't know what was happening and partly to shake some sense back into her brain.

"Meredith, are ye still there?"

The words thawed and rolled off her swollen tongue. "They think he has a blood clot in the arterial graft. I don't know what that means, but it seems serious."

In her fog and darkness, she sensed more than heard his heightened alarm. "I'll catch the first flight out. Dr. Fraser and I both have satellite phones, and ye can reach us anytime, anywhere in the world."

She grabbed a small package of tissues from her purse and wiped her nose. "Elliott's battery is low. I'm going to call you from my phone so we'll have each other's number, but it's not a sat phone, so occasionally I'm out of reach. Will you call Louise?" Meredith functioned only by rote now, speaking in a monotone.

"She'll want to come with me. Is that a problem for ye?"

Meredith juxtaposed two images of Louise in her mind. The woman she first met in the library and the woman she left in the library. "She doesn't care for me, but she loves Elliott. She needs to be here."

"Ye're a gracious lass. Stand yer ground. I'll send ye a text with my arrival time."

She leaned her head against the wall. If she hadn't been with Elliott, what would have happened to him? He could have suffered for hours like Jonathan, all alone with no one aware he was in danger. Kevin would have checked on him. But would he have been too late? Exhausted, she closed her eyes and nodded off.

David called and woke her a few minutes later. "We leave for London in an hour. From there we've got a flight to Atlanta. We should be in Lexington around suppertime."

"I'll let Jake know."

"Are ye by yerself? Where's Kevin?"

"He's here somewhere."

"I know exactly where he is." David's tone was part father intending to reprimand his child and part employer intent on firing him.

"He doesn't need to sit with me."

David hissed between his teeth. "The lad needs to do exactly what Dr. Fraser would want him to do, and if he doesn't know what that is, I'll tell him."

Meredith straightened in her chair.

"I'll send a message from Atlanta. And, Ms. Montgomery, don't worry about Louise. Whatever bee was stuck in her wee bonnet, it's gone now."

Meredith was sure David had something to do with arranging for a beekeeper, but she wasn't about to question it. "See you soon." Her voice barely rose above a squeak.

Meredith's next call was to Jake to let him know that Elliott was in surgery and that Louise and David would be arriving in the late afternoon. He assured her he would see to transportation, and he would let Mrs. Collins know of their arrival. Before he hung up, he asked Meredith if there was anything he could do for her, and she told him no.

Why is everyone bending over backward for me?

She closed her eyes and rolled her tight shoulders. There wasn't anything anyone could do for her. Four days earlier, she'd left San Francisco with a lump in her breast and a handful of projects to complete. The projects had been bumped way down her to-do list where the writing was too small to read.

Is there anything we can do for you, Ms. Montgomery?

"Yes, heal Elliott so I can have more time with him before I'm cut apart again."

Chapter Thirty-One

University of Kentucky Medical Center – December 27

THE HOSPITAL PAGING system startled Meredith awake. She glanced at the clock on the wall—four o'clock. Adrenaline pumped panic into her veins, and she jumped out of the chair. Why hadn't the doctor come out and given her a report? Did he forget? She rushed out into the white hallway, bright as daylight in the dead of night. No professional staff. No maintenance crew. No one to ask for help. Where were the cheery-faced pink ladies? Did she dare leave to check in with ICU? What choice did she have? She couldn't stay there and do nothing. Convinced she'd been forgotten, she followed the signs to the bank of elevators. When she arrived at the secure door to ICU, she pushed up her sweater sleeves and pressed the intercom button.

"May I help you?"

"Dr. Lyles took Elliott Fraser to surgery at one o'clock, and said he would go to ICU afterward. I'd like to see the patient."

"What's your relationship?"

"I'm his wife." God, that sounded odd, but she wasn't in a mood to deal with HIPAA compliance.

"I'm sorry, but we don't have him on our floor yet, Mrs. Fraser."

Don't have him. That meant he was still in surgery or in the recovery room. She went back down the hall, burst through the exit door, took the stairs two at a time, and returned to the waiting room. The jaunt to ICU and back had taken five minutes. Why hadn't she asked Lyles how long he anticipated surgery would take? What should she do next? Sitting and waiting calmly didn't seem feasible. There was a text message on her phone from Louise letting her know she and David were onboard and set to depart. *Good.* Meredith collapsed in a chair, shivering.

Panic—relief. Panic—relief. Panic—relief. The rollercoaster ride from hell.

For a few moments, she closed her eyes. When she opened them again, she saw Dr. Lyles standing in the doorway, obviously unsure whether to wake her or not. "I'm glad to see you." She stood and held out her hand. "We weren't introduced earlier. I'm Meredith Montgomery—wife, sister, aunt, mother. Whoever I need to be to visit Elliott."

He pointed to the chairs. "Let's sit." He sat back and crossed his ankles. "Elliott and I have known each other for years. If you'd been in his life very long, I'd have known about it." He scratched the side of his face. "On second thought, he'd probably keep you a secret, Ms. Montgomery—"

"Meredith…"

"Meredith… The fact that you're here tells me you're special to him, plus he told me I could discuss his medical condition with you." Dr. Lyles leaned forward in the chair and propped his elbows on his thighs. Then he held his clasped hands down between his knees. "Elliott is a challenging patient. His initial injury was devastating. Most people would have lost their leg at the knee. He insisted we try to save it."

"He's still adamant about that," Meredith said.

Lyles nodded. "I did an arterial graft to keep blood flowing to his foot, but he lost most of his calf muscle in the knife attack."

Meredith shivered. "From a comment Louise made, I thought something like that had happened. But why has it taken so long to heal?"

"He's had several problems over the last five years. The blood flow to the leg remains a challenge. The injury is cosmetically disfiguring, which is an emotional challenge for him, and with most of the calf muscle gone, it's difficult to walk."

Tears rushed to her eyes. "I had no idea."

"His busy lifestyle makes rehab and recovery difficult. His trainer works with him daily, but Elliott never stops, and I'm not sure he sleeps more than a couple of hours."

"He just got out of the hospital," Meredith said. "He probably shouldn't have gone on a sleigh ride."

Lyles sighed. "Typical."

"He's mentioned an implant. What does that do?"

"For a man who wears a kilt, we felt it was important to try to give him a normal looking leg. We put in an implant and grafted over it. Complications set in almost immediately, and we had to go back in and repair the arterial graft, which is what we had to do again."

"Will what's left of the calf muscle increase in size if it's exercised?"

"Yes, and his trainer has done a good job with that, too. That was the reason for the surgery he just had in New York. The surgeon reduced the size of the implant, and a plastic surgeon smoothed out the scars."

"What's made him so sick?"

"He developed a clot in the arterial graft. That's why he was in so much pain."

Meredith sat back in her chair and considered all that Lyles had said. "If Elliott will heal if he slows down, why doesn't he?"

Lyles shrugged. "That's the million-dollar question. Some patients refuse to listen to medical advice. They refuse to make lifestyle changes that will improve their health. Some continue to smoke through cancer and heart disease. Elliott refuses to follow a treatment regimen that will result in healing his leg. It's dangerous for him and frustrating for his medical team. I think he avoids rehab as a way of ignoring what happened and how much it took from him."

This whole concept was foreign to her. Caring for her body was paramount to her emotional well-being. For a man who used to be a runner, how could he treat his leg with such indifference? Meredith wiped the tears from her eyes. "I just feel so sorry for him."

"Don't let him know that," Lyles said. "The last thing Elliott needs is pity, especially from a beautiful woman."

"If his problems are psychological, why doesn't he get counseling?"

"That's the rub of the green, as Elliott's father would say." Dr. Lyles's phone beeped. He checked the message. "Elliott trusts you. Maybe you can get him to go."

"Don't put that on me. I've only known him for four days."

The doctor stood. "If there's anything else—"

"How big is the wound?"

"About golf ball size now. I heard he left New York Presbyterian and flew to Edinburgh. Is that true?"

"That's where I met him."

Lyles shook his head. "I'll keep him for a few days. Then we'll try again. Do you know if David's coming?"

"He and Louise just boarded their flight."

"If Elliott will commit to doing what he's told, David will be the enforcer. He's the only one who can keep Elliott in line."

"I thought that role went to Louise," Meredith said.

"I've never seen anybody as overprotective as Louise. She can be worse than a mother bear. I wouldn't want to get on her bad side."

Meredith rolled her eyes. "I'm afraid I did."

"I can see that happening. You'd be a threat to her," Lyles said.

"How does Evelyn fit into the mix?"

"She plays the role of mediator."

Meredith grinned. "You know them well."

"I spend a week every year at Fraser House. The girls make a point of coming up for a few days." He checked his pager again. "I have patients to check on before I go home. I've enjoyed meeting you."

She pulled a business card from her purse and handed it to him. "Here's my contact information in case you need it."

He glanced at the card and then at her with a raised brow. "You remind me of an older, wiser Kit MacKlenna, and now that I know you're a vintner, it makes sense. She always wanted to own a vineyard. I doubt she'll grow many grapes up there in the Highlands, but you never know when it comes to her. She's a spitfire."

"Elliott doesn't like to talk about her."

Dr. Lyles let out an exasperated sigh. "One of these days he'll stop feeling guilty and stop grieving. That's when he'll heal more than his leg." The doctor glanced at Meredith's card again. "I'll have to try your wine." He stuck the card in his shirt pocket. "Come on. I'll walk you to the elevator. You can probably get into ICU for a few minutes."

"Where's Kevin? Do you know?"

Dr. Lyles laughed. "Have you spent much time with him?"

"No, I just met him."

"Kevin is a paramedic, a hunter, and an equestrian. He and Kit worked together at the Lexington Fire Department—"

"She was a fireman?"

"Paramedic. They were partners. He'd go out to the farm and ride. That's how he met Elliott. They clicked. About a year after Elliott's first surgery, he hired Kevin as his assistant and aide, and even sent him to flight school. Kevin flies them around in Elliott's little Cessna. It adds to his charm, and the nurses love him. So, to answer your question, he's probably in the nurses' lounge. But don't get me wrong, he'd take a bullet for Elliott, probably wearing a smile on his face." They reached the bank of elevators, and Dr. Lyles pushed the up button. "Get some rest, Meredith. Doctor's orders."

After stepping into the elevator, she gave him a tight smile. "I'll try, and thank you."

She made her way back to the ICU. This time the staff didn't ask her relationship to the patient, they just opened the door. Kevin was probably already in there.

The quiet chill, the antiseptic smells, and the beeping monitors were like a warning gate at a railroad stop. They got her attention and brought back a flood of memories. Taking another step would be the same as crashing through the barrier. She turned around, slapped the automatic door opener, and rushed out of the unit where she sat cross-legged on the recently mopped, cold and damp tiles.

Why am I doing this? Although she asked the question, she already knew the answer. Elliott made her feel like a woman, and she could temporarily forget what was ahead for her.

After a few minutes, she unwound her legs, stood, and somehow dug deep enough to push past the awful memories and reenter the ICU.

A nurse directed her to Elliott's room. Beneath the wan face, the tubes, and IVs snaking around his arms and leg, he looked vulnerable. Louise's words came rushing back. "Don't hurt him," she had said. How could Meredith hurt him when he did such a good job of that all by himself?

Beneath the ICU's obnoxious medicinal odors, her discriminating nose scampered through all the smells until she found his unique blend of outdoors and winter sun. *I can't deny the connection that exists between us.* When she touched his hand, shock riddled through her. Cold, clammy fingers lay inert, unresponsive against her palm. "Elliott," she whispered against his lips before she kissed him.

His eyelashes fluttered. "Hi, hen. I can feel my toes."

"He repaired the graft. You should get better soon."

"Get in bed with me."

She tunneled her fingers through his hair. "Not tonight, honey. I have a headache."

His lips curled up on the side.

"Louise and David are on their way."

"Good," he mouthed, then his head lolled to the side, and he drifted back to sleep.

The nurse came into the cubicle and stood at the opposite side of the bed, checking the IV. "You'll have to leave now. We'll take good care of him."

Meredith appreciated the nurse's sympathetic smile. She kissed him again, missing his warm kiss in return. How many hours ago had it been? Twenty-four? Forty-eight? Fear, buried beneath thick antiseptic smells, loomed large in the small cubicle. Dr. Lyles had told her Elliott would recover, but nothing was an absolute. Even those expected to heal died in hospitals. She didn't want to leave, but neither did she want to cause a scene and upset the patients. The only consolation was that Kevin was in the building and David was en route.

Elliott was in danger. Meredith sensed it, and it wasn't just his health. Asking David to come across the pond meant Elliott sensed it, too. Until he could protect himself, the snappy nurse would guard the door and David would guard Elliott.

Meredith checked the time—five o'clock. Her feet dragged down the nondescript tiled floor, mirroring her heart's reluctance to leave him behind. If the situation was reversed, she felt certain he'd fight the nurses, administrators, and doctors to get his way, and more than likely win. He had that way about him.

By reversing directions, she found her way back to MacKlenna Farm and parked the car in the garage. She walked down the hallway and stopped at the portrait of Thomas MacKlenna's granddaughter. The eyes, the chin, the cheekbones seemed familiar. Maybe Meredith would find something in her research.

Curiosity pulled Meredith down the polished oak hallway that spilled into an enormous foyer that smelled old. Not musty or moldy, just old southern tradition. She reached the doorway to the front sitting room, separated from the dining room by two large partially opened pocket doors. Above the fireplace was an elaborate gold-framed painting of a woman, probably in her late forties, with porcelain skin. Her black hair flowed down her back, and vivid green eyes followed Meredith around a room filled with the most exquisite early-American antiques she'd seen outside of a museum. With an appreciative glance at the artwork and collectibles, she decided maybe she was in a museum. The room was centuries old elegance personified.

For a long moment, she stared at the painting. Something niggled at her brain. Something important. Something she needed to know. But what? She hurried back down the hall toward the two women's portraits. An art appraiser she wasn't, but she knew enough about art from the year she studied abroad to notice that the styles were very similar.

She leaned in, put her nose to the canvas and sniffed dust and age. At the bottom of the younger woman's portrait were the initials S.M. She went back to the other painting and looked closely. S.M. "Sean MacKlenna? How interesting."

Determined to return later and study the paintings, she climbed the stairs to her second-floor bedroom. The majestic house seemed alive in the early morning hour, not with noise and activity, but with MacKlenna spirits. She closed her eyes and saw images of people in her mind's eye, and she heard them, too—Scottish brogues, music, servants, children's laughter.

Meredith felt connected to the house in an indescribable way.

Goose bumps peppered her arms and legs. A similar tingly sensation to what she experienced at the starting line of every race filled her with jittery excitement. She touched everything: the plaster wall, the wool carpet, the banister. She sniffed. Sniffed again. *Lemon oil.* What was it about this place that made her feel at home? Her hand slid along the smooth mahogany railing, coated with layers of polishing oil that had turned the wood a deep, golden brown.

Something beyond this world brought her here. Why?

Chapter Thirty-Two

MacKlenna Mansion – December 27

MEREDITH WOKE WITH a headache and upset stomach, symptoms of a hangover without any alcohol in her system. The clock on the bedside table screamed in a silent language, "You've only had four hours of sleep. What do you expect?"

She turned the clock face around. "Talk to the wall." Then she rolled over and curled into a ball in the king-size four-poster cherry bed, but her eyes wouldn't close. The sun bathed the room with warm light peering in between the slats of one unshuttered and two shuttered windows, all decorated with green chintz swags. The fabric coordinated with the earth-tone green walls and white woodwork. Early eighteenth- and nineteenth-century antiques lined the walls. Perfect harmony flowed through the room. Very feng shui.

She tossed aside the covers and walked across the room to get a closer look at three paintings labeled: Chimney Rock, Nebraska; South Pass, Wyoming; and The Blue Mountains, Oregon. The artist must have painted the scenes using earlier renderings as guides, because there were no paved roads, utility poles, or developments. As a child, she'd learned when facing a painting, the question to ask was: "How does it make you feel?"

Lonely.

As she gazed at the paintings a while longer, she was suddenly struck by a sense of joy—not happiness, but joy. She couldn't reconcile those two emotions. All three paintings elicited the same response. She wasn't at all surprised to find Kit's name scribbled in the right-hand corner of the canvases.

I would love to meet you someday, Kit MacKlenna.

Meredith stepped over to the Georgian-style writing desk set in a niche in front of a south-facing window. The shutters stood open, revealing a breathtaking view of the snow-covered, white-plank paddock. A magnificent chestnut stallion, heavily bodied and muscled with three white stockings, stood in the center, head up, surveying his kingdom. She gripped the window frame. The horse was a dead ringer for the stallion in a painting hanging in the winery's office.

Her cell phone rang, and she answered the call before the second ring.

"We're in Atlanta," David said. "Our flight leaves in a couple of hours. We'll arrive around six o'clock yer time, unless there're weather delays. How's Elliott?"

"He was groggy when I left at five. I haven't called to check on him yet. I'll do that and call you back."

Meredith called the hospital and talked with Elliott's nurse, who informed her he had slept well and had eaten breakfast. She then returned David's call and gave him the encouraging news. Louise took his phone and asked Meredith to repeat the update. Louise's voice no longer held the chill of Edinburgh. What had caused it to begin with and what caused the thaw? It didn't matter, really. Meredith was just glad the frosty tone and attitude were gone. She'd learned the hard way that when someone hurt her, she typically avoided the person in the future. Louise would have to earn Meredith's trust, and it would take more than a simple *I'm sorry*.

After a long shower, she followed the sweet strains of Christmas carols and the scent of coffee to a gourmet kitchen painted the color of melted butter, with cherry cabinets, white woodwork, and stainless-steel appliances. The room's natural light from an entire windowed wall allowed the thoroughly modern kitchen to fit seamlessly into the historic home. She never would have picked that shade of yellow, but the warmth drew her into the room and made her want to sit and drink not just a cup of coffee but an entire pot.

A petite, buxom woman with white hair peeked around the open refrigerator door. "You must be Ms. Montgomery."

"Mrs. Collins?" Meredith asked, offering a smile.

"My, my. Jake told me everything," she said, making a tsking sound. "Dr. Fraser would've had himself in one pickle of a mess if you hadn't been there to see to him. Lordy me, that man's got to get a wife, or next time there won't be nobody to pack him off to the hospital. Now." She stopped to take a breath. "What can I get you for breakfast? Pancakes, scrambled eggs, an omelet maybe with cheddar and tomatoes and ham? I can throw on some home fries, too. I hear you're from California. You probably just want tofu. Whatever that is, I don't have it anyway." She glanced back inside the refrigerator. "What was I doing when you came in here? I was looking for something."

Meredith wanted to shrink back into the hallway and disappear as quickly as possible. "Do you have a coffee cup I could take with me to the hospital?"

"Leave without eating? Oh." She glanced at the refrigerator, then back at Meredith. "I guess you do want to get to the hospital." Mrs. Collins pulled a tumbler from the cabinet, filled it with coffee, and screwed on the lid. "Black coffee is what he said you drink. Never known him to be wrong about anything. Here." She jutted out her hand, holding the steaming cup.

Meredith took the coffee. "Maybe tomorrow I'll have time to eat one of your omelets."

Mrs. Collins immediately brightened. "I'll get a dozen of them organic eggs. I hear they eat a lot of them in California. Around here, we just eat whatever they got at Kroger. Don't matter to me if the hens stay in their cages or run loose in the barnyard. An egg's an egg."

Meredith skedaddled, only to be attacked in the hallway by a golden retriever. "And who is this?" she asked. "You must be Tate."

"That's Tate all right," Mrs. Collins yelled from the kitchen, "and he needs to go out. You don't mind taking him for a little walk, do you? He don't need a leash. In fact, if he runs off, just let him go. He'll show up soon enough, just like a bad penny."

If the dog didn't need a leash and could run wild, why did Mrs. Collins want Meredith to take him out? She wasn't about to ask. "Do you want to go outside, Tate? Maybe listen to some country music?"

He barked and ran toward the front door. *Guess you want to escape Mrs. Collins, too.*

Meredith grabbed her coat and walked out, zipping her jacket against the morning's chilly air. She headed straight to the paddock for a better look at the chestnut stallion. Tate ran ahead of her. When she reached the fence, she climbed up on the lowest rail and leaned over the top plank. The horse whinnied and trotted over to her. "You're beautiful." Meredith rubbed his nose and blew into his nostrils. "What's your name?"

"Stormy," a voice behind her said. "He's Kit's horse. Nobody else can ride him."

Meredith turned to see a tall, rail-thin, gray-haired man walking toward her. He was dressed in khakis, wearing a green Barbour jacket—the MacKlenna Farm uniform.

"You must be Meredith Montgomery?" His breath came out in a cloud of white.

"You have me at a disadvantage, Mr.—"

"Harrison Roberts. I'm CFO." Although his eyes were an extraordinary shade of blue, they were bloodshot. "I called the hospital, but they wouldn't tell me anything."

"I talked to Elliott's nurse about an hour ago. He had a good night and ate some breakfast. I'm on my way there now."

Roberts pressed his lips into a tight seam. "Tell him to call me this afternoon. I guess you know someone killed our horse. It's the insurance company's opinion that an employee did it, and they're not going to pay the claim. Elliott's got to straighten this out." Harrison unwrapped a throat lozenge and popped it into his mouth. "Anyway, nice meeting you." He turned and stomped through the snow.

Meredith rubbed her arms, shaking off a general feeling of unease, and glanced around for Tate. The dog had vanished. Meredith gave Stormy a last pat, then hurried back to the house to gather her coffee, purse, and car keys to make a super stealthy getaway from the talkative Mrs. Collins.

On her way off the farm property, she stopped at the security gatehouse and notified the guard that Louise and David would arrive from Atlanta at six o'clock and needed a pickup from the airport. She left her contact information and headed back to the hospital.

The three previous trips down the two-lane Old Frankfort Pike had been in the dark. In the morning sun, every vista the road offered was more beautiful than the last. No wonder it was a historic byway. Miles of snowy pastures dotted with Thoroughbreds, white or black plank fences, and estate homes. It was clear to her now why Elliott felt torn between his Kentucky farm and his Highland hills.

She slowed the car and rolled down the window. Brisk air blew in her face, bringing crisp winter smells and wood smoke. Tears flashed in her eyes, partly from the smoke, partly from worry, partly because she just needed to cry. She pulled over to the side of the road and rested her forehead on the hand-polished wooden steering wheel. On Christmas Day, she and Elliott had created a magical winter wonderland, and she wanted to escape to Fraser House again. Life had intruded into their kingdom, and as much as she wanted the situation to be different, she couldn't change a damn thing. She couldn't heal his leg. She couldn't find the person responsible for killing his horse. She couldn't cure cancer. But she could launch her wine. She wiped her eyes before tears clouded more than her vision, then pulled the car back onto the road.

Chapter Thirty-Three

University of Kentucky Medical Center – December 27

MEREDITH ENTERED THE ICU and found Elliott sleeping. Whiskers shadowed his face. She smiled, liking the rugged, sexy look. With slightly tousled hair, a very different Elliott Fraser emerged. On second thought, he looked that way when he had made love to her. She pressed against the railing as she'd pressed against his body, feeling the hard planes of his muscular frame.

The hospital had stripped away most of his scent. With her discriminating nose, she picked through all the smells, breaking them down until she reached his essence—Scottish Highland pine forest and lavender. Comforted that she'd reclaimed him, she sat in the recliner next to the bed, turned on her iPad, and started through a long list of emails.

Her marketing VP, Gregory, had made several changes and attached the revised documents. She clicked open the PDFs. *Damn.* Balance and shading were all wrong. What was he thinking? It would take her hours to make corrections. Her frustration needed to simmer on low heat before she fired back an email she knew would piss him off.

Something or someone had to go. There weren't enough hours in the day to mark off all the items on her daily list. They carried forward to the next day, ensuring that she started every morning where she should have ended the night before. If she hired a local genealogist, she wouldn't have to finish the time-consuming research. That would help. Before she talked herself out of it, she sent Cate an email outlining the research parameters and asked her to contact the local historical society to find a researcher interested in completing the project. When Meredith hit the send icon, a heap of pressure lifted from her shoulders.

"Hey, gorgeous." Elliott's tired, gravelly voice wafted over her.

She tilted her face, smiling. "How do you feel?"

"Kiss me, and I'll let ye know."

She put her work aside, pulled to her feet, and kissed him lightly on the mouth. He tugged on her heart in a way nothing else did. Not even her wine. "Okay, I'm waiting for an answer."

"Kiss me again."

"You're ornery. You can't even hold your eyes open."

"I don't need eyes to kiss ye." She leaned over him again, and he cupped her nape, pulling her closer. "I probably can't do anything about it, but that doesn't stop me from wanting ye." Their lips touched, warm and inviting, tender without the impatience of unbridled passion.

"Get well. Then we'll see what we can do about the other situation."

He scratched under his chin and around his neck. "Where the hell is Kevin? I need a shave." Elliott's tone matched the abrasive sound of his bristly whiskers.

She put her hands on her hips. "I'll shave you."

His eyes opened, showing a slight trace of fear. "I'll wait for Kevin, but ye can climb in bed with me."

She went warm with pleasure gazing at him. "I don't think that's allowed."

He cocked his head to the side and looked at her from underneath his eyelashes, giving her a teasing dare. "What? Will they kick us out? Then let's do it."

Meredith swiped a quick glance out into the hallway and spoke in a low tone of voice. "Nurse Hathaway will kick *me* out. If she notices your vital signs fluctuating, she'll run in here waving resuscitation paddles."

"I'll unplug so she won't see the blip on her monitor."

"The reason you're in ICU now is because you didn't take care of yourself. You're a lousy patient."

"I bet ye're worse."

"My assistant would agree with you."

He licked his lips. "I need ChapStick."

She dug into her pocket for a stick of lip balm and started to put some on his lips. He shook his head. "Ye first."

"Sneaky." She rolled the balm across her lips, smacked them together, then kissed him, rubbing her lips against his. "I think you're good now."

He smacked his lips. "More."

Just as she kissed him, a man entered the room clearing his throat. Meredith straightened. Her cheeks flamed with the heated guilt of a caught lover.

Dr. Lyles winked.

She winked back. "Your surgeon is here, Elliott. Maybe he'll give you marching orders."

He pushed the up arrow on the remote, and the head portion of the bed rose. "Give me good news, Chris. I'm ready to go home." His voice had lost its undertone of amusement.

The doctor stood at the side of the bed, thumbing through Elliott's chart. "You're not leaving until we're sure the repairs to the graft are providing sufficient blood to your foot."

Elliott's nostrils flared. His eyes widened, ready for battle. "*That* could take days."

The doctor glanced at Meredith, ignoring his patient's outburst. "What time do you expect David?"

"He's scheduled to land at six."

"I'll release Elliott to a private room when David arrives."

"Ye don't have to talk about me like I'm not here," Elliott said.

"David can be the bad cop, and you, Meredith, can go back to doing what you were doing when I came in. It might put our boy here in better spirits."

Her face heated again.

"I saw Kevin down the hall. He said he didn't want to intrude on your time. He'll come in when you leave," Chris said.

"I don't think I can compete with Elliott's need for a shave," Meredith said. "We better get him in here."

Chris lifted the sheet and checked the dressing on Elliott's leg. "I'll leave a message at the nurse's station along with the order that you're not to get out of bed."

"Take the catheter out," Elliott said, scrunching his face. "I don't need it, and ye know I don't. It's just to keep me in bed."

"The notes said you tried to pull it out while you were asleep. You know you could seriously damage your penis," Chris said.

"Asleep or awake, I don't want a tube in my dick or unwanted hands fondling it. I want it out."

Meredith slowly backed away from the bed, unable to look either man in the eye.

"When you get to your room—"

Elliott cut Chris off with a blast of fury. "*Now.* I can use a urinal."

"When David gets here—"

Elliott set his jaw, threw back the covers, and grabbed his penis.

Meredith bumped into the chair, and her shoes squeaked against the floor. Both men shot her a look, and she threw up her hands. "I'm going to step out, and you two can decide what you want to do"—she wagged her finger at Elliott's penis—"about this situation." On the way out, she spotted Kevin at the nurses' station.

"Hi, Ms. Montgomery. If Dr. Fraser's ready, I'll give him a shave."

"He's arguing with Dr. Lyles right now."

"Probably about the catheter."

After a couple of minutes, Chris made his way to the nurses' station. "You can go back in," he said to Meredith. "You'll keep his temper manageable." Before she could ask, he added, "We reached a compromise."

Kevin shook his head. "He got his way."

Was there any doubt?

Chris entered notes on Elliott's chart before dropping the file on the countertop. "I'll be back tonight." Then he left the ICU, walking with a purposeful stride. His obvious displeasure could steam a nice crease in Elliott's khakis.

"I don't think he's happy. Do you?"

"It's not the first time. I'll get the nurse to remove the catheter. Then, when I give him a shave, his mood will improve."

Meredith took a deep breath, and rolled her eyes. "I hope so. I'm going to the coffee shop. I'll be back in forty-five minutes."

Several minutes later, she sat in the coffee shop staring at the menu. *Bacon and eggs or a bagel?* She set the menu aside, chuckling. How could she think about bagels with the memory of Elliott grabbing his penis so fresh in her mind? He had a special affinity for the well- and lovingly-used appendage and showed no discernible reaction to her presence during the discussion. He was a doctor. He had a different view of bodily functions than nonmedical people. But even she knew he wouldn't risk hurting himself by doing something so dangerous.

A cell phone rang with an unrecognizable ringtone. She ignored it until she heard the ring again, coming from her black bag. She dug through the contents and found Elliott's mobile. "Hello."

"This is Jim Manning. Is Elliott there?"

Meredith recognized the attorney's name. "This is Meredith Montgomery. I'm a friend of his. I know you met with him last night. He relayed most of the conversation before the paramedics rushed him to the hospital for emergency surgery."

"Good God, they didn't take his leg, did they?"

"No," Meredith said. "The arterial graft had to be repaired. He's in ICU."

"That's a relief. He mentioned giving up his leg yesterday, but I didn't think he was serious."

He was considering it? Then why'd he make me promise? "His doctor is confident he'll recover. And if orneriness is a sign, then he's well on his way."

"He must be fighting with Lyles over the catheter."

Does everybody know his personal business? "You know him well."

A woman's voice buzzed through on Jim's intercom. "Give me five minutes," he answered. "Elliott's friends know how he feels about certain situations, including what he'll tolerate and what he won't."

A waiter stopped at Meredith's table and poured her a cup of coffee. She pointed to the egg special, and the waiter nodded. "He has a close network of people who care for him."

"Ms. Montgomery, Elliott hasn't mentioned you, but the fact that you've got his phone that's an extension of his body tells me all I need to know. Are you from Lexington? I haven't heard your name before."

"I own a winery in the Napa Valley. Elliott and I met in Edinburgh."

"Montgomery Winery?"

Meredith smiled. "It's always nice when someone's heard of your wines."

"Great article about you in *Wine Digest.* You're launching a new chardonnay. February, isn't it?"

"Would you like an invitation?"

There was a short pause in the conversation while he shuffled papers. Finally, he said, "I have a trial scheduled for the month of February. If our case settles, I'd love to come."

"I'll put you on the guest list, and you can let me know the status of your trial. Now, what can you tell me about your investigator? Have you put him to work?"

"Tell Elliott the clock is running, and I'll get back to him as soon as I have something to report. How long will he be in ICU?"

"He's moving to a private room this afternoon."

"I suppose David is coming now."

She forced a smile. "And Louise."

"David and my investigator worked together on a previous case. Tell David to call me."

"Anything else?" Meredith asked.

"That's it for now. Welcome to the inner circle."

"Out of curiosity, how many members are there?"

A rumbling laugh came from the other end of the phone. "It's getting smaller but currently has seven members. Eight counting you: David, Kevin, Louise, Evelyn, Chris, Ted, you, and me."

"Who's Ted?"

"Elliott's personal trainer."

"What about Jake?"

"He's on the perimeter."

Now it was Meredith's turn to laugh. "I guess that means he doesn't know about Elliott's propensity for threatening to yank out catheters."

Jim laughed again. "I look forward to meeting you. Have a great day, Meredith."

After Jim hung up, she sent Elliott a text message from her phone, letting him know she talked to Manning and would give him a report of the call in person. The message documented that a call took place and was a reminder to Elliott, when he was able to check his messages, to ask in the event she forgot to tell him.

When Meredith finished breakfast, she returned to the ICU and found a smiling, clean-shaven patient sitting up in bed.

"I'll be at the nurses' station, Boss, if you need anything," Kevin said on his way out.

Elliott held out his hand to her. "Come here. I want to kiss ye." He ran his tongue along the seam of her lips.

She pulled away and leaned on the bed rail. "You're an unusual man."

"I'm just a man and we all—"

"Need rescuing. I think I've heard that one before." She stroked his arm with her fingertips.

"Lyles and I've had an ongoing battle about catheters. I got an infection with the first surgery, and I never want another one. I take care of my penis."

She blushed. "So, you've told me."

He studied her face. "I should have worn a condom when we

made love."

"Are you afraid I'll give you an infection?"

"Not at all."

This wasn't a good time to talk about it, so she changed the subject. "I took a call from your lawyer. He said the clock was ticking, and he asked David to call him."

Elliott pressed the reverse arrow button, and the bed began a slow descent. "If I'm asleep, will ye tell him?"

"Yes." She straightened the thin hospital blanket and fluffed an extra pillow for his head.

"Are ye leaving today?" He gazed at her with the same hot, dark chocolate eyes, and she barely kept from tumbling into them again. She kneaded her slightly trembling hands together.

"Tonight."

He clasped his hand over both of hers and squeezed, surprising her with his warm strength. "Ye can work from the farm."

She slipped out one of her hands and slowly stroked up and down his arm, lightly scratching her fingers through the short dark hair. "I wish it were that easy."

"The farm has video-conferencing. It's the same as being on location."

"Maybe that works for your staff, but not mine. I need to go, Elliott. Louise and David will be here. Kevin's here."

The nurse poked her head into the room and told Meredith visiting hours were over.

She slung her bag over her shoulder and her coat over her arm. "They'll move you into a room before the next visiting hours. I'll see you there."

He pulled her down for a kiss. "If ye see Kevin, send him in."

A technician entered the room. "I need to draw blood."

"That's my cue to leave. I'll see you later," she said.

"Meredith, see if ye can arrange to stay longer. Ye haven't had a Hot Brown yet."

She wasn't going to argue with him. When it came time for her to leave, she'd leave. "I'm sure Mrs. Collins could whip something up for me."

Elliott smiled. "Probably, but she doesn't have the magic ingredient that will leave ye begging for more."

Kevin poked his head into the room. "Need anything, Boss?"

"He's all yours, Kevin. I think he's well on his way to recovery," Meredith said. "I'll be back later." She tossed Elliott a kiss and left, wondering what ingredient he could possibly put in a turkey, bacon, tomato, and cheese sandwich that would make it magical. Knowing Elliott, it was probably a spice that would set her on fire. She chuckled. He didn't need a spice to do that.

Chapter Thirty-Four

University of Kentucky Medical Center – December 27 (Late Afternoon)

MEREDITH'S BOOT HEELS made a clicking sound against the tile floor of the private suite on the third floor of the hospital while she paced, listening to Cate. Her assistant had ducked out of a meeting to take Meredith's call and was expounding on a litany of issues: a heated discussion with the wine master, a threat to sue the printer, and a crying fit with the culinary gardener over his child's outbreak of chicken pox. Meredith's normally organized and efficient executive assistant was teetering on the edge. She could either talk Cate down or hope the fall would snap some sense into her. Meredith's earlier conversation with Gregory was almost as chaotic. What the hell was going on at the winery? If she didn't return soon…

Her ears perked up at the sound of clacking gurney wheels out in the hallway. *Elliott?*

"Go back to the marketing meeting. I'll call you later," Meredith said, hanging up on her assistant.

A burly young man dressed in hospital greens wheeled Elliott into the room. His chocolate eyes came alive the moment he saw her. A wink from those sensuous, dark depths held power that could *almost* make her forget the troubles at home. Fear got a quick chokehold around her neck to remind her that she didn't want anyone to have that much power.

"I didn't know if ye'd be here or not," Elliott said.

"I told you I'd be here." She stood beside the bed as the orderly hooked Elliott to the monitors. "How's the pain?"

"Better."

The orderly funneled the cord to the call button remote through the bed rails and placed the remote next to Elliott's hand. "Is there anything else you need, Dr. Fraser?"

"The secret to getting out of here," Elliott said.

The orderly laughed. "You'd be surprised how many times a day I'm asked that. Your nurse should be right in." The man left the room.

"Give me some good news and tell me ye've made arrangements to stay for a few days."

"I can't. I just got off the phone with the office. It sounds like everyone is having a crisis."

"Can't ye handle them from here?"

Meredith puffed up. "You left Scotland because you had an emergency."

"Damn, Meredith. I had a twenty-five-million-dollar dead horse. Ye've got an event almost two months out. What's so important that it can't be handled remotely?"

Meredith bit her tongue to smother the retort so the smoldering fire didn't erupt into bright orange flames.

"Here's his room," they heard Louise say from the hallway.

Meredith cringed.

Elliott barked a humorless laugh. "Great. Perfect timing."

Meredith retreated from the intensity of his eyes by lowering hers.

"Elliott?" Louise asked, peeking around the wall dividing a small entry hall from the rest of the suite. "Are ye here?"

"Ye're in the right place, Lou."

She flitted in, in all her butterfly glory. "We came straight from the airport. How do ye feel? Dreadful, I'm sure." She hugged him and then glanced at Meredith. "Thank ye for letting us know. He never would have told us."

Meredith, be gracious. "I'm glad you're here. I need to go home."

"Oh," Louise said, surprised. "Can't ye stay longer?"

Elliott glanced at Meredith. An expression of disappointment twisted his mouth. "She's got work that won't let her enjoy the holidays."

Meredith bit her tongue hard enough this time to almost make it bleed.

David followed Lou into the room. "How's the leg?"

"Been better."

"Any news?" David asked.

"Call Manning. He already has his investigator working on the case," Elliott said.

"Chuck?"

"I'm sure that's his name. Ye've worked with him before," Elliott said.

David flipped on the room's perimeter lights, pulled his cell phone from his pocket, and scrolled through his contacts. "Does Manning want me to call him or Chuck?"

"Manning," Meredith said.

David punched numbers on his sat phone. After a few seconds, he said, "David McBain calling for Jim Manning. Yes, I'll hold. No, I'll take his voice mail." He paused a moment, then said, "This is David McBain. I'm with Dr. Fraser now. Ye can reach me on my mobile." He left the number and disconnected the call.

In less than thirty seconds, his phone rang. "McBain. Yes, sir. I can do that. I'll be there in an hour." When he concluded the call, he said, "Chuck and I are meeting at Starbucks in Chevy Chase."

All the previous times Meredith had seen David, he'd worn a black suit and cap. Now dressed in the MacKlenna Farm uniform of khakis, polo shirt, and a green Barbour jacket, he seemed more relaxed and less threatening. With the musculature of a bodybuilder, the agility of a dancer, and the facial bone structure of a romance cover model, he created an imposing impression regardless of what he wore.

Louise yawned. "In half an hour, I'll probably be asleep."

"Do ye have a car, Ms. Montgomery?" David asked.

"Elliott's Mercedes."

"I'll take Louise to the farm before I go meet Chuck. Where's Kevin?"

Meredith shrugged.

Elliott punched the nurses' call button.

"Can I help you, Dr. Fraser?"

"I'm looking for Kevin."

"He's on his way in."

Kevin entered before she finished her sentence. "Hi, David. Hi, Lou."

"I've got an appointment and should be back in a couple of hours," David said to Kevin without acknowledging his welcome. "Ms. Montgomery is leaving town this evening. I want ye to stay until they give Dr. Fraser his nighttime meds. Then ye can take off."

Kevin lifted his chin, giving a nod to Elliott. "I'll be waiting in the wings if you need me. I've got a clear view of the door."

"Thanks, Kev."

"I'll call and give ye a status report after the meeting," David said. "Come on, Louise. I'll take ye to the farm."

Louise kissed Elliott's cheek. "I willna be back tonight. I'll see ye in the morning."

When they left, Elliott patted the side of the bed. "Before we were so rudely interrupted, I think I was trying to talk ye into getting into bed with me."

While David and Louise had visited, Meredith had remained stilted, arms folded. Now that they were gone, she pushed up her sweater sleeves and said, "No. You. Weren't. You were insisting my job wasn't important enough to hurry home and put out fires. You might not think wine's important, but there're millions of people who do. And I"—she pointed to herself—"am *one* of them."

"That's not what I said. Of course yer job is important, but catering or dress decisions could be made remotely, leaving ye free time to enjoy yer holiday."

Free to be your playmate.

She grabbed the railing to keep her hands occupied, so she wouldn't smack him. "Are you so full of drugs you can't hear what you're saying? I'm president of a multimillion-dollar winery with several hundred employees." The pitch of her voice grew higher and louder. "I have responsibilities. I can't toss them aside because it's the holidays."

"Calm down. Ye know I didn't mean it that way."

His patronizing tone irritated the hell out of her. The slow burn that had started in her stomach inched up her throat. "I don't see how else you could mean it. You're in the hospital. I have work to do. I'm going home."

He threw up his hands. "*Fine.*"

A nurse's aide came in with a pitcher of water and patient hygiene products. While she stored them in their appropriate places, Meredith peeked through the blinds and hurled her thoughts into the darkness where they had unlimited space to spin and form a funnel cloud. The cloud was about to touch ground and cut the fragile bond between her and Elliott.

The aide left, and the silence in the room was rock-band loud.

"Let's talk when you get out of the hospital," Meredith said. "You need to focus on getting well, and I need to—"

"*Work.* Ye've made that perfectly clear."

His attitude scraped her patience with ragged fingernails.

There was a knock at the door.

Tears pressed against the back of her eyelids. She had to get out of the hospital. The constant reminders of what had happened to Jonathan and worry over Elliott had given her a massive headache that got worse by the hour, and the ticking clock tracking her probable hospital admission in a few weeks had tapped out her reserves.

"Go away," Elliott yelled at the intruder.

Lyles strode into the room, penetrating the fog of dissension Meredith knew was palpable in the air. "Your temper hasn't improved, has it?" he said.

A deep emptiness opened inside her, and her composure crumbled. She ran a nervous hand through her hair. "I'll leave you to your patient. I've got a plane waiting for me." Her own harsh breathing sounded above the silence as she stared at Elliott staring at her. She reclaimed her coat and bag off the sofa. "I'll call you." Then she left. It wasn't a grand exit, but she didn't embarrass herself either.

"I'm not even going to ask what the hell happened here," Meredith heard Lyles say as she hurried from the room.

A part of her wanted to go back and talk to Elliott about what was going on, but she had to get away from the medicinal smells and the annoying paging system.

Yes, she could handle the problems at the winery without going home, but ever since meeting him, her orderly life seemed to be unraveling at a time she desperately needed to hold all the ends together. She needed distance to sort out her feelings and put their tenuous relationship into perspective.

She hurried down three flights of stairs, avoiding eye contact with hospital personnel. At the bottom of the steps, she hit the exit door with both palms against the push-pull door latch and stumbled out into the frigid December night. *Why did I come here?* As she walked toward Elliott's car, she saw the answer scrolling in an old-fashioned ticker-tape manner across the inky sky. She came to find out if Christmas Day was a fluke.

She thought she had her answer, but until her health was factored in, it didn't matter what her heart believed.

Chapter Thirty-Five

MacKlenna Mansion – December 27 (Early Evening)

THE MOUTH-WATERING SMELL of roasting meat hit Meredith as soon as she entered MacKlenna Mansion on what had to be the longest day of her life.

During the drive from the hospital, she'd compared herself to a wilted flower, brown around the edges and too far gone to be revived, but a melt-in-your-mouth, home-cooked meal proved her wrong. She all but leapt into the kitchen.

Mrs. Collins had left a note on the counter with instructions on warming up sweet potatoes and apples to accompany the pork tenderloin, along with a bottle of a Montgomery chardonnay chilling in an ice bucket. Meredith touched the sides, testing the temperature. Cold to the touch but not freezing—castle temperature. "Perfect. What a precious lady."

"If"—a disembodied voice came from the far end of the kitchen—"ye can ever get her to shut up." Meredith jerked her head toward Louise's voice. She sat at the kitchen table, thumbing through a magazine.

"I thought the MacKlenna spirits were answering me," Meredith said.

"That would be a boisterous conversation. There're several haunting the farm, ye know." Louise closed the magazine and walked over to the counter. "Kit got a ghost of her own when she turned ten. A handsome nineteenth-century lawyer type. There's a closet full of pictures of him upstairs." Louise glanced at Meredith, giving her a pointed look. "Black hair, blue eyes just like yers."

Meredith uncorked the bottle. Instead of filling their glasses, she stopped, caught in a memory of a handsome, dark-haired man dressed in nineteenth-century clothes—her great-great-grandfather. As a child, she stood in front of his portrait trying to mimic his enigmatic smile. She shook off the memory. "How did Kit feel about her ghost? Was she scared?"

"Maybe at first," Louise said. "Later, his presence became normal to her. I dinna think she thought much of it."

"Did you ever see him?"

Louise sat on a barstool and wiggled her butt to get it settled on the cushion. "He never showed up for anyone else. The day Kit fell off her horse and broke her back was the first time she ever saw him. The ghost plopped down beside her and held her hand, or tried to. Canna verra well hold the hand of a ghost. She fell in love with him that day. Ten years old and in love with a ghost."

Meredith rested her hip against the edge of the counter, crossed one leg over the other, and removed the cork from the opener. "What did Elliott think of that?"

"Oh, he teased her. Finally, she quit talking about her"—Louise made air quotes with her fingers—"see-through person."

"If I see a ghost, I won't tell him." Meredith rolled the cork between her fingers, noting it was one of the winery's new corks, sporting the Twitter name. The neckband also carried a new design for the varietal color bar—amber yellow for chardonnay. The changes made her wines more distinctive, and they had been Gregory's marketing initiatives.

Louise turned the opened bottle around to look at the label. "Montgomery Winery. This is one of yers."

Meredith smiled. "Very thoughtful of Elliott. Do you want a glass?"

"I thought ye'd never ask."

Meredith bit her tongue to keep from making a catty retort,

poured, then handed Louise a glass. "Chardonnay is like a rainbow. It brightens up the drabbest day."

"Just like a cocker spaniel." Louise saluted Meredith with her glass. "Shall we go to the den and put our feet up? Ye can tell me about yer new amber elixir." Louise led the way to the room behind the kitchen. "My taste buds are rather finicky. Do ye think I'll like it?"

"If you're interested in the nuance of a chardonnay, but less oaky and with a brighter fruit flavor, then yes, I think you will."

Louise sat in an overstuffed armchair, upholstered in a green and yellow vintage chintz fabric. "Elliott willna come in here unless he has to. He gets all jumpy and loses his temper. Finally bolts after a few minutes."

Meredith glanced around. The large open fireplace held enormous logs that crackled, spitting red and gold tongues of fire, giving the room more than a whisper of masculinity. "What's not to like? There's a sixty-inch flat screen TV with surround sound, paintings of stallions, and an extra-long, deep-seated cushioned sofa to stretch out on for naps. There's no wet bar, but surely he can carry his whisky from one room to another."

Louise shrugged one shoulder. "He says the room makes him uncomfortable."

The large picture window overlooking the pasture and floor-to-ceiling French doors leading to a screened porch gave the room an open yet intimate atmosphere. Elliott's reaction baffled Meredith. She sniffed the air. "There's an older woman's presence here."

Louise's face appeared stony. "What makes ye say that?"

"I smell it. Feel it. Are you going to tell me there's an old woman's ghost, too?"

Louise chuckled. "Not that I've heard, but there is an old sea captain."

Meredith raised an eyebrow. "A confederate soldier I could believe, but a sea captain?"

"Sean's the only one to report the captain sighting, and I think Sean only saw him once, a few months before he died."

"Well, I don't think the room holds the scent of the open sea. It smells more like roses."

"Kit called this her granny's room, and Granny Mac loved her rose garden. The two of them would sit for hours and chitchat while Kit sketched and Granny Mac knitted sweaters and socks and scarves that she gave away at Christmas."

"Elliott had on a knitted black sweater the other night. Looked gorgeous on him."

"Granny Mac. She hated him in black, but that's what he wanted. She was the most gracious southern woman I've ever met. Born and raised in Rock Hill, South Carolina. She had an accent as sugary as sweet iced tea. Elliott thought of her as a surrogate mother. She adored him. When she was dying from lung cancer, he never left her side. Cleaned up after her, sang to her. He did the same for me when I had breast cancer—"

Meredith's breath hitched.

"—Ye couldna ask for a better caregiver," Louise continued.

Meredith clasped her hands as if that would control her heart racing to string a thread of hope that Elliott would accept her disfigurement. "When did you have cancer?"

Louise patted her chest tenderly as if it had residual pain, and Meredith mirrored the reflective touch.

"Three years. Evelyn willna talk about the mastectomy, but honestly, I live in fear the disease will come back." Louise sipped her wine and fell into what appeared to be a meditative trance. After a moment she said, "I should have had the other breast removed, too, but my doctors didna recommend it, and Elliott asked why I'd want to be mutilated even more." She shrugged. "He's such a boob man." Her voice sounded indifferent, but there was a level of hurt there. A level of hurt in Meredith, too. The reference stung the first time she heard it. This time she felt attacked by a sea full of jellyfish.

"He wouldna hug me for months afterward," Louise continued. "I never knew if it bothered him because I lost a breast or if the surgery reminded him of how close he came to losing his leg. It doesna matter. It's all behind us now." Louise unfolded an afghan and spread it across her legs. "I worried that I wouldna be attractive to Evelyn, but she isna bothered by my scars."

Meredith tried to swallow the thickness in her throat and catch hold of her unraveling thread of hope. She took a deep breath and changed the subject. "You've met Harrison Roberts, haven't you?"

"Odd fellow. I dinna have much use for him. Why?"

"I met him this morning—"

A Maine Coon cat about the size of a small dog scampered into the room and leapt up on Louise's chair. "Hello, Tabor." She ran her fingers through the tabby cat's long fur. "Elliott inherited Tabor and Tate after the MacKlennas died."

"Elliott mentioned their deaths. What happened to them?"

"A drunk driver ran into them a hundred yards from the entrance to the farm. Sean and Mary died instantly. Kit's friend died in her arms."

"She was a paramedic. That had to have been so hard on her."

"She felt guilty for surviving and guilty because she couldna save them."

The soft ticking of a clock on the mantel created a not-so-gentle reminder that life continued in spite of tragedy, in spite of cancer. "Do you know why Kit's living in seclusion?"

Louise whirled a curl on the side of her head as if stirring a cauldron of secrets. "She's been gone three months. I didna ken her plans beforehand, and of course, Elliott willna talk about her other than to say we have to respect her decision." Louise sipped her wine. Her face seemed locked in concentration, gazing inward. A few moments later, she continued, "Kit softened Elliott's rough edges. We all need someone to do that for us, else we'll wander around lost in a maze, disillusioned by inadequacies we refuse to claim. Without Kit…well, ye've seen his temper."

Meredith gave a quick laugh, and not because the comment held any humor. "He's in contact with her, isn't he?"

"If anybody is, he is."

"Wouldn't she want to know he's in the hospital?"

"Lordy, if ye only knew. This isna Elliott's first surgery. It's his sixth and each time he's gone right back into the hospital."

"He doesn't want to get better," Meredith said under her breath, but loud enough for Louise to hear.

"He hangs on to the guilt of what happened that night when he got hurt."

"Lyles said he lost most of his calf muscle in a knife attack, but that's all he said."

"Elliott was attacked by a man Kit fired and Elliott wouldna rehire. It was brutal. He beat Elliott up, stabbed him in the chest, sliced his leg for meanness, and then he attacked Kit." Louise's voice trailed off and tears pooled at the bottom of her eyes, waiting for the tipping point when the glistening drops would spill and splash down her cheeks.

Meredith crossed her arms, clutching them in front of her. She sensed where the story was going and wasn't sure she wanted to hear what Louise had to say.

"The man's name was Wayne Gates. He cut the side of her neck, threw her to the ground, and attempted to rape her. Her friend Scott arrived a second before Gates…"

Meredith fell back against the sofa. "Dear God. They both went through hell."

"Gates died in jail before he went to trial. Spared Kit the agony of reliving the ordeal in public."

"And Elliott."

Louise emptied her glass. "He blocked it all out. If ye ask him what happened, he'll recite the article in the newspaper without emotion. He flatlined on the operating table—"

Meredith moaned, shuddering at the memory and shock of a monitor going flat and silent.

"It's a miracle he's alive."

She gulped the last of her wine then glared at the empty glass, feeling betrayed that her wine abandoned her when she desperately needed to be grounded in the familiar. "I need a refill." She staggered into the kitchen while vivid memories of the man who had carried her into the unfamiliar erotic world swirled in her mind, stirring up a rumble of timpani rolls against a backdrop of a silent monitor with a straight-line crawling across the bottom.

"I'll join ye," Louise said, following on Meredith's heels.

"Why hasn't Kit reassured him?"

"Dearie, that precious child tried for years. She sat by his bed twenty-four hours a day while he was recovering. Seeing the pain in her eyes probably made him feel even guiltier. He's one complicated man."

After hearing Louise's stories, Meredith understood why. She refilled their glasses. "Are you hungry? Shall we eat?" She didn't know what else to do.

Chapter Thirty-Six

University of Kentucky Medical Center – December 27 (Early Evening)

NOT LONG AFTER Meredith left the hospital, Harrison stopped by, sneezing as he entered the room. Kevin followed him in, glaring at his back. Elliott gave his aide a nod and tapped his watch. He wasn't in the mood to listen to Harrison's Chicken-Little-Doomsday rant.

"Take yer cold and go home, Harrison," Elliott said. "There're enough germs in this place."

The CFO folded his arms, held his hands under his armpits, and said in a short, clipped voice, "You have to deal with the insurance adjuster."

Elliott raised his eyebrows, framing an answer. "As far as I know, the insurance company hasn't responded. And Manning's working on an answer if the claim's denied."

"What's he going to say?"

"As soon as he has a report, I'll pass it along."

Harrison sat in the chair next to the bed, shivering. Sweat coated his forehead. Either he had a fever or more trouble had invaded his structured life.

"Where's the money from Hazy Mountain Stud for their interest in Galahad?" Elliott asked.

Momentary panic flashed in Harrison's eyes. "Their managing

director called this afternoon demanding we return the funds."

"Let Manning deal with that."

"I gave them his phone number."

"His name's Doughty, right? What'd he say?" Elliott asked.

"'Fuck you.' I couldn't believe he'd talk to me like that. I had a mind to hang up on him, but he calmed down."

Elliott shifted slightly in the bed to get a better look at Harrison. He'd never seen his CFO in such a disheveled state. "Go home, Harrison. Ye don't feel well. There's nothing ye can do right now."

Harrison straightened, and his eyes darkened. "What do you mean? I have to do something."

Kevin stepped over to the bed. "You've had a long day, Boss. You need to rest." He turned to Harrison. "Mr. Roberts, come back tomorrow? Dr. Fraser might have news from Manning to pass along."

Harrison stomped toward the door. "If you don't hear from him in the morning, I'll call him myself."

"You do that, and be sure to let us know what he says," Kevin said.

Harrison's heavy step made his boots squeak against the tile floor, leaving black marks in his wake. He yanked open the door, and the handle hit the back wall. "Sorry." He closed the door behind him.

"What the hell is wrong with him?" Kevin asked.

"He has a personality shortage," Elliott said.

"Shortage would imply he had some."

"I don't need him to entertain us. I need him to balance the books. He does that well enough."

Kevin pinched his lips together, staring at the door, and then finally said, "Or used to."

David entered on the heels of Harrison's departure. "I passed yer money man in the hall. His eyes were bouncing like a ball on a racquetball court."

"Put him on yer list," Elliott said. "I've never seen him like this. His son was arrested last month on a DUI charge. Maybe the kid got in trouble again, or maybe it's something else."

Kevin sat in the chair Harrison had vacated. "He wrecked his car, too."

"The kid or Harrison?" David asked.

Kevin rolled his eyes. "Harrison, Jr. Happened the week before the DUI. He was driving his mother's Lexus."

Elliott scrolled through the emails on his cell phone. Nothing from Meredith. Not a text. Not a smiley face. Not even a *kiss my ass.* He reread the one she'd sent early that morning, so he knew she had his email address. She'd probably sent a dozen messages to her staff since leaving the hospital. Obviously, she didn't have anything to say to him. God, he hoped he hadn't screwed things up with her. If he didn't hear from her tonight, he'd call her in the morning.

Elliott returned his attention to the discussion of Harrison and his son. "A conviction will cost him a summer job on the farm."

"Harrison will fight you on that," Kevin said.

"Can't help it." Elliott set the phone on the tray table floating above his bed. "The zero tolerance policy applies to everyone, employees and new hires. It's Harrison's job to support board initiatives."

David pulled a notebook from his jacket pocket, made notes, and then flipped back through a few pages.

"What'd ye learn from Chuck?" Elliott asked.

David closed the door. "Chuck tracked down two of Gates's brothers. One's in prison in Texas convicted on drug and assault charges. A rape conviction got the other one locked up. There's a younger brother, too. He's stayed under the police radar. His last known address was in Louisville but that's been six months. We'll find him."

"That's it?" Elliott asked.

"We'll get yer man. But ye've got to give us more than a day."

"Ask Allie to give you Sean's personnel files. See if he made any notes about employees that might be useful."

"How far back ye want me to go?"

"All the way, or ask Allie to do it."

"I'll do it myself," David said. "Anything else?" He glanced around the room. "Did Ms. Montgomery leave?"

Kevin glared at Elliott.

"She left an hour ago," Elliott said.

"And, ah, crying," Kevin added.

"*Kevin*." David gave the aide a cold, hard stare for a few awkward seconds.

Guilt sifted through Elliott's conscience like a pitchfork mucking a stall, making him squirm in pain and disgust.

"Go home. Be back here at oh-seven-hundred," David said.

Kevin double-thumbed on his cell phone. "Do you think Dr. Lyles will let you go home tomorrow?"

"I don't know. Bring me pants and a shirt on hangers. Not in a suitcase. I'll be dressed and out of here as soon as he springs the jail doors."

Kevin turned to leave, but Elliott grabbed his arm. "Wait. How do ye know she was crying?"

"I passed her in the stairwell. She didn't see me. She was wiping her eyes."

Elliott punched the button on the remote and dimmed the lights. He could hide from his circle of friends in the dark, but not from himself. He was nothing more than a feedbag full of stupid.

Chapter Thirty-Seven

MacKlenna Mansion – December 27 (Late Evening)

AFTER DINNER, Meredith left Louise in the den watching a British sitcom and went to her room to pack. Cate had sent her an email after the marketing meeting, and reading between the lines implied the tense two-hour meeting ended in disaster. Meredith called Cate after reading a limited transcript of the conference. "How did Gregory lose control? He assured me—"

"He had a difference of opinion with the web designer who was following your instructions." Cate's normally exuberant voice lowered to a mumble. "He quit."

"Who quit?"

"Gregory."

"*What?* And no one called me." Meredith paced the room. A slow burn of impatience crept up her spine.

"It just happened an hour ago."

She picked a boot up off the floor and threw it into her suitcase. "I'm on my way home. I'll deal with the situation when I get there."

"Don't cut your trip short."

"We're six weeks from the launch, which appears to be going to hell in a handbasket." Meredith threw the other boot in on top of her clothes and it bounced back out of the bag. "I'll be home by nine o'clock."

"Where are you?"

"Close enough to get there in time."

"But—"

"Leave everything you have on my desk, and I'll see you in the morning." Meredith hung up before Cate asked more questions Meredith didn't intend to answer.

Her next call was to her pilot to confirm their departure. Then another to Jake, who immediately arranged to have someone pick her up and take her to the airport. She lugged her bags to the front door and went in search of Louise, finding her asleep in the chintz chair just where Meredith had left her. She gingerly shook the woman's shoulder. "Louise."

She jerked awake. "*What's the matter?* Is Elliott all right?"

"I'm sure he's fine. I just wanted to say good-bye," Meredith said.

Louise rubbed her eyes and gave her head a little doggie shake. "If ye leave, his mood will go from sour to downright rancid."

"I think it already has."

She stood and folded the blanket that had covered her legs. "Before ye run off, I need to tell ye something. I was thinking about this when I fell asleep."

"I'm not sure—"

"Just hear me out." Louise held up her hand and tugged on her thumb. "One, Elliott has never chased after a woman. Two"—she tweaked her index finger—"if ye're out of his sight, ye're typically out of his mind. Three"—she moved on to the next finger—"he's never given a woman a second chance. Four, he's demanding and has little tolerance for anyone who doesna meet his expectations. Five"—she squeezed her pinkie—"I've never seen him so crazy over a woman before. Stallions, yes, but never a woman."

Meredith heard the grin in Louise's voice, although her face remained stony.

Louise continued. "I think ye should go home."

Meredith swayed on her feet. "I'm—"

"Dinna get me wrong," Louise interrupted. "I dinna want ye to leave, and Elliott needs ye, but his attitude needs an adjustment.

Kevin phoned earlier and told me ye were upset. Kevin doesna gossip, but sometimes he gets so worried he has to talk. So, he calls me. Kevin wanted me to encourage ye not to give up. We both think Elliott might decide it's worth healing if he has to go after ye."

Louise's honesty both surprised and bewildered Meredith.

A wan smile softened Louise's face. "I'm sorry about the way I treated ye in Edinburgh. When Elliott invited ye to Fraser House, I knew he was interested in more than sex, and I thought ye were married."

Meredith glanced down at her wedding ring and twisted it around her finger. Maybe it was time to rethink her decision to wear the band. While she didn't trust Louise to keep whatever she was told confidential, she did appreciate her openness.

"I've never known a man with such a giving heart," Louise said. "He's tender and loving and affectionate, but he doesna believe he's worthy of the kind of love he craves. I think he might accept it from ye. But that Scottish temper of his might send ye away before he figures that out. Have patience and let him get through this recovery. Ye'll see the man ye had a glimpse of in Edinburgh. That's who he really is. If he wasna, his inner circle would have disintegrated a long time ago." Louise squeezed Meredith's arm, and she felt the warmth of Louise's reassurance. "This may sound like a selfish offer because our number one concern is Elliott, but if ye'll give him a chance, the rest of us will stand in the gap for ye."

"And do what I can't do?" Meredith asked.

"We'll give him some tough love, which we havena done before," Louise said.

No one had ever made that kind of offer to Meredith. Not her father. Not even her husband. Her heart tightened a bit in her chest.

A security guard had his arms loaded with Meredith's bags by the time the two women reached the front door. Meredith handed Louise a business card like the one she had given her in Edinburgh. "Here's my contact information. If anything happens, please let me know."

"Of course, dearie. Now, run along. Do what ye have to do and hurry back."

If Louise had asked Meredith when she would return, she couldn't have answered. If Elliott couldn't hug Louise after her surgery, what made Meredith think he'd want to hug her once he knew about her mastectomy? She couldn't deal with that right now, so she shoved the thought into the deepest recesses of her mind. Her solo dance with denial.

The wind blew across the portico, and the oak door slammed shut behind her. She jumped, startled. After a moment, she shook off the shivers, dodged patches of ice, and climbed into the backseat of the Mercedes.

Her mind seemed muddled, covered with a black cloud threatening to storm. Confused? Yes. Fearful? Yes. Angry? At her staff, yes. And very, very tired.

She glanced back at the house. Louise's profile remained visible through the door's sidelights. It would take a while to digest all that she had said about Elliott.

The waxing moon bathed the snow-covered yard in silver-colored light. Each individual snowflake glistened like a Swarovski crystal, giving the mansion an otherworldly beauty. She sniffed, fighting back tears and got a whiff of Elliott hidden beneath the leather interior of the luxury sedan. The scent was a full-bodied cabernet sauvignon with black currant and dark chocolate notes with a long sweet finish. Their lovemaking had been exactly that. She held her arms tightly against her belly as if a squeeze would hold onto him, onto the memory.

The driver stopped at Stormy's paddock, giving the right of way to the groom leading the horse through the well-lit gate on his way to the barn. The stallion's big brown eyes, gleaming in the beam of the car's headlights, were full of pathos and determination.

You miss her, don't you?

He shook his head as if he'd heard the question, and then something moved in Meredith's peripheral vision. She glanced back, gasped, and jerked around in her seat for a better view.

"*Good God,*" Meredith said.

"Is there a problem?" the driver asked.

"Do you see that?" she asked, pointing.

"What?"

"It's…it's behind the gate."

The driver glanced back. "Don't see anything."

"Shapes in the shadows," she said, giving a forced laugh to her voice. But she wasn't staring at a random shape, a trick of the light. She was staring at a ghost—a handsome man with black hair tied in a queue and large, expressive eyes. Then he faded into the night.

Meredith had a photographic memory when it came to names and faces. She had seen the ghost's face before, albeit an older version. But it was the same face.

The face of her ancestor, Cullen Montgomery.

Chapter Thirty-Eight

Montgomery Winery – December 27 (Late that Evening)

MEREDITH LANDED IN Napa at nine o'clock, bone weary. Normally, she adjusted to the difference in time zones while traveling, but this trip tossed her headfirst into a tailspin. Maybe it was her health. Maybe it was Elliott. No matter how many times she pushed away thoughts of his lips, his hands, they came back uninvited, along with his condescending attitude.

The moonlight flooded the interior of her car while she drove to the winery. At a stop light, she scrolled through emails. Nothing from Elliott. But she was the one who had said she would call, and she hadn't. Maybe tomorrow. Maybe the next day. One day soon, she would go back to the farm. Invited or not. After all, her ancestor was haunting the place, and she had to discover why.

If she thought she left trouble behind in Kentucky, that was nothing compared to what faced her at home. She'd have to make concessions to Gregory to get him to come back. Concessions she wouldn't make unless under duress. Well, guess what? He wasn't holding a gun to her head, but she needed him at least through the launch, and he knew it. She suspected, although Cate hadn't said anything, that Gregory wanted autonomy. That meant she had to let go of the marketing department. A department she had grown and nurtured over twenty years. It wasn't easy to step aside.

Meredith pulled into the driveway. Cate's car was parked in the drive. Meredith wasn't surprised. Her assistant was the equivalent of a bomb-sniffing dog when it came to uncovering information. Cate would want to know where Meredith had been and what she intended to do about Gregory. She was probably sitting on the heated terrace, waiting. For Meredith, that meant a chilled bottle of wine and company.

A security guard drove up behind her. "Welcome home, Ms. Montgomery. Would you like me to carry your bags?"

"Thanks. Just let yourself in. I'm going to meet Cate in the back." Meredith punched the trunk release button, grabbed the laptop, and then tossed the car keys to the guard. "Will you put it in the garage for me?"

"Sure."

As she climbed the steps to the terrace, she heard Cate say, "I'll talk to her as soon as she gets here. I know what you want, Gregory. I'll talk to her. I promise. Love you, too. Good-bye."

Love you? What the hell is that all about? Meredith backed down the steps, waited a moment or two, and then called out to her assistant. "Cate, where are you?"

"On the terrace, and the wine's chilled."

The landscape lighting design gave the property the dramatic appearance of the moon shining through a canopy of trees, casting soft light onto the walking paths, gardens, and stone terrace with a pergola and fireplace. No matter the season, the temperature on the stone oasis remained comfortable year round.

Meredith sat in a wrought-iron chair across from her assistant, thinking through several scenarios. What was the best approach? She surprised herself wondering what Elliott would do in a similar situation, and she heard him say clearly, "The conversation is between you and Gregory. Not you and Cate."

Meredith poured a glass of wine without looking at the label and sipped. The blended taste of fresh pineapple, bright green apples, and juicy pear burst like a sparkler in her mouth. She picked up the bottle and held it tenderly, befitting a new parent. "*Cailean.*"

Cate smiled. "I had to sneak it out."

A chill tripped down Meredith's spine. "The wine is supposed to be under lock and key."

"But I have the key."

Meredith's mouth twisted into an uneven frown. "If a bottle gets out, the leak could put a damper on the launch, and this could be the most successful one in the winery's history."

"You need your VP of marketing to make that happen."

"I'll talk to Gregory tomorrow."

Cate stared at her fingers tapping against her wineglass. After a moment's pause, she glanced up and asked, "You know what's on his mind?"

Meredith wasn't an ostrich when it came to the winery. Gregory's dissatisfaction stemmed from a lack of authority to make marketing decisions. The same frustration she'd voiced while working in that position. Her father never relinquished control to her. Could she give it to Gregory? "We'll talk about it."

"Can you let go of the department?"

"This is between Gregory and me." Meredith's voice sounded calm with no noticeable wobble, but if her stomach was any indication of the state of her nerves, then she was as jittery as an old woman with palsy on a good day. Her overactive nerves weren't just because Gregory balked under the constraints of her leadership, but was a sign of the deeper concern she had over health issues. A familiar tug took place in her heart—the need to reach out to a compassionate friend warred with her need for privacy. And right now, privacy won out. "What have I missed that didn't make it into an email?"

Cate harrumphed. "If you won't talk about Gregory, will you tell me where you've been?"

"I stopped in Kentucky to see a friend."

"You don't have any friends in Kentucky."

If there was a downside to working with someone for years, Cate just pounced on it, forcing Meredith to confess or lie, neither of which she wanted to do. So she mentally flipped a coin and then said under her breath loud enough for Cate to hear, "I do now."

"Well?" Cate's eyes grew wide. She waited expectantly for an explanation.

"He's just a friend."

"*He?*" Cate grabbed her cell phone off the table. "It will only take one call to find out who *he* is. Why don't you tell me and save me the trouble?"

Meredith's assistant was extremely resourceful and often found information that eluded Meredith. She was curious to see what Cate could discover. "Go for it."

Cate punched in a number. "Hey, this is Cate. I'm updating Meredith's travel log. Where'd you stop last night? Really? How many cars did you rent? They did? Who'd they work for? No. No. That's all I need. Thanks." Cate punched more buttons on her cell. Waited a minute, punched some more. Then she read from her mobile device. "Dr. Elliott Fraser, fifty, single, veterinarian, and CEO of MacKlenna Farm. Originally from Inverness, Scotland, Dr. Fraser has called MacKlenna Farm home for over thirty years." She stopped reading and glanced at Meredith. "There's more, including several pictures. Should I continue?"

Meredith shook her head. "I've already read it."

Cate laughed. "My God, I was kidding when I said to find a smooth-talking Scotsman. Well, I wasn't really kidding, but I didn't think you would. Tell me something not in his bio." She drank her wine, but her eyes never stopped tracking Meredith's face.

"He's demanding and has a horrible temper."

"So what else do you have in common?"

Meredith whistled. "That's below the belt."

"Maybe. But it's true. You never yelled at your staff before you became president."

"Under the circumstances—"

"There are no *under* the circumstances," Cate said. "You're sailing *through* your circumstances."

A sudden chill wrapped around Meredith thicker than her fur coat. "It's a hell of a stormy course."

"Rough seas will eventually calm down, or you'll get a bigger boat. You know that," Cate said.

The wind sighed through the bare trellising surrounding the

house, reminding Meredith of her responsibilities. "I didn't have this pressure when Daddy was alive." She had a different kind of pressure. It wasn't the pressure to succeed, but the pressure to prove she could.

"You don't have to carry it all."

"I'm the first woman to run this business. I can't fail." Maybe her ancestor was haunting her and not MacKlenna Farm. Maybe he was afraid she would bring the whole kit and caboodle tumbling down, and he popped in to be sure she didn't. She glanced around the terrace wondering if he'd make an appearance at the winery, too.

"If you don't let up on the reins, you won't have anyone working for you."

Meredith flinched at the iciness in Cate's tone. "Does that include you?"

"I can tell you to your face what others are saying behind your back."

"What? That I'm a bitch?" Meredith said it matter-of-factly, but the insinuation cut out a sliver of her heart. She dearly loved the men and women who worked at the winery. Many of them had been around since her childhood. They were family.

Cate didn't say anything, and silence lengthened between them. *Damn the tension-filled silence.* Meredith had been a participant in too many silent conversations lately. She pinched the bridge of her nose as she considered an answer. "It'll be better after the launch."

"If you don't make some changes soon, you'll be launching this wine by yourself."

"I'll call a staff meeting tomorrow."

"And tell everybody what?"

Meredith pushed her chair away from the table, but she didn't stand and run, even though that was exactly what she wanted to do. "Damn it, Cate. Give me a break."

Cate reached for Meredith's hand, which was gripping the edge of the table. "Don't call a meeting until you meet with Gregory."

Meredith let out a slow breath, squeezed Cate's hand in return, then let it go. "You've always been honest with me, and I wouldn't want it any other way." Meredith sipped her wine. "I guess the staff will be disappointed to have me back in the office."

"Why *did* you come back?"

"You called me with bad news."

"But I told you not to cut your trip short."

Meredith cocked an eyebrow. "Now I see why."

Cate emptied her glass and set it on the serving tray. "Are you going back?"

"To Kentucky?" Meredith shrugged. "I don't know. I need to stay in town right now."

"If you'd give Gregory—"

"*Tomorrow, Cate.*" Her assistant was not only her employee, but also her friend. If Cate didn't stop pressing, she'd push through the limits set by both relationships and suffer consequences Meredith didn't want to impose. She let out a breath she wasn't aware she was holding. "I'll talk to him in the morning. Go home and call him. Ask him to meet me at Gillwoods Café at ten o'clock."

"Your calendar is clear for the rest of the week, if you want to go—"

Meredith held up her hands, wishing they were a protective brick wall. "Go. Home."

Cate maintained eye contact for a second or two, then broke away, collected her purse and phone, and left. A couple of minutes later, Cate's late-model BMW roared to life.

"Damn it." Meredith snatched her glass from the table and walked to the edge of the stone terrace. She was weighed down by a heavy heart and even heavier load on her mind.

In the valley below, her vineyards stretched for miles, lit by a quarter slice of moon. She reached out and grabbed a fist full of air—a moment of time. She opened her fist, but there was nothing there. The moment was gone. That was her life—moment to moment. Some appeared as roses. Some appeared as brush. She couldn't change yesterday. Nor could she guarantee tomorrow. All she had was now.

She stepped back over to the table and emptied the bottle into her glass. She then lifted the goblet in a salute. "To this moment—scrub brush or silky rose. It'll never come again."

Chapter Thirty-Nine

Montgomery Winery, Napa Valley, California – December 28

MEREDITH ARRIVED AT the winery's office around seven the next morning. The stone one-story building housed only the executive staff. The kitchen, tasting room, and wine store were in another similarly constructed building connected to the office by a covered pass-through. She grabbed a cup of coffee from the kitchen. After checking the menu for the afternoon tasting, she continued to her office.

When she entered the president's suite, she stopped and glared at the mail overflowing from her out-box. Her heart palpitated, and her chest grew tight. It would take an hour she didn't have this morning to clean out the box. Although Cate had drafted responses and paper clipped them to the original letter, nothing went out without Meredith's final review.

Not only the in/out-box overflowed, but the desk chair held a two-inch stack of memos and other documents from staff that required her immediate attention. Everyone knew if they wanted Meredith to read their notes and memos immediately, they should put the documents on her chair. She couldn't sit without picking them up. If you landed on top of the stack, chances were good you'd get a quick response. She'd even heard stories of employees coming in late at night to move their memo to the top of the stack. Meredith shook her head. Something had to change. She couldn't continue the way she was going. Obviously, stress was making her sick.

Today, the top document was the Springsteen revised contract. "Whew. Thank God." Anxiety dropped a notch. Now, if she could commit to a menu, she could check the two biggest items off her list.

The desk phone had a blinking message light. She entered her code and played her messages. Gregory confirmed a ten o'clock meeting at Gillwoods. *Great.* She'd need a few minutes between now and then to organize her thoughts and decide on her bottom line. Although that would remain fluid until they shook on a deal.

She placed her laptop and purse on top of the mahogany desk that had belonged to her father, grandfather, his father, and his father before him. Where the antique originally came from, she didn't know, but the previous occupants had left their mark. Her father had set the desk against the wall and covered the top with glass. Spilled coffee had seeped underneath and stained the wood, creating ugly white patches around the edges of the glass.

Her great-grandfather had moved the desk from the villa at the turn of the twentieth century and set it in the center of the room so he could see the vineyards from the picture window. Sun exposure had weathered the desk unevenly.

Her great-great-grandfather had a front panel removed so air could circulate underneath. Her great-great-great-grandfather kept the desk in the corner of the library and rarely used it. Her great-great-great-great-grandfather, Cullen Montgomery, had preferred a roll top with dozens of cubbyholes. That desk now stood in the waiting area with a phone for visitors to use.

The mahogany desk had miraculously survived the fire of 1890 and became sort of a Montgomery talisman. Meredith treasured it, felt inspired working there, and although the desk needed to be refinished, she couldn't bear to let it out of her possession.

She glanced up at her father's portrait hanging over the fireplace. "Morning, Dad. Wish you were here." He was an imposing man, but then all the Montgomery men had cut a dashing figure—dark hair, blue eyes, chiseled features, and brilliant. She could use a healthy dose of their brilliance to see her through the day. *What would you do about Gregory, Dad?*

She could hear his answer. "Would losing him make your life easier or more difficult?"

That was simple to answer. More difficult.

Most mornings, the deep hunter green walls embraced her, but not this morning. She felt itchy, almost claustrophobic. Maybe she should have the walls painted a neutral color. Make the office softer, more feminine, put her own mark on the room instead of continuing her father's.

She checked her watch—nine thirty. As soon as she met with Gregory, she'd drive to San Francisco. Her doctor's office had left a message at home. The fine needle aspiration report had not found cancer cells, which thrilled her but concerned her doctor. He explained that the needle could have missed the tumor and taken a sample from normal cells. Because of her history, he scheduled an appointment at the San Francisco Breast Care Center for further evaluation.

Since she was going into the city, she scheduled a dress fitting with her designer. She might not be in the mood after leaving the center, but at least she'd be able to check another item off her list. *Keep moving forward.*

Meredith had the caterer on the phone when Cate entered the office and handed her a note. Her "Kentucky friend" was on the line. Meredith covered the receiver. "Tell him I'll call him back in a few minutes." The caterer wouldn't let Meredith go until she settled on a menu. "Done. I'm checking this off my list," she said at the conclusion of the call. Then she sat back in the chair and rolled her shoulders as if they were stiff. Her insides were like a pinball machine going bing, bang, bing. If Louise's five-point analysis held any validity, Elliott needed to call her, and he had. Time to call him back.

He answered on the second ring. "Fraser."

A hospital page blared in the background. "It's Meredith. It sounds like you're still in the hospital. How are you?" There was silence until she heard a door close.

"Sorry about that. I had to clear the room." He let out a relaxing sigh. "Much better now."

She stood and walked over to the picture window. "Any word on how long you'll be in there?"

"I'm going home tomorrow with or without Lyles's permission."

A twinge of anger coursed through her at his cavalier attitude about his health. "Hmm. Not sure what to say about that."

"I told him ye wouldn't come back to Kentucky as long as I was in the hospital."

"You got that right. I don't like hospitals."

"Bad memories, huh?"

She braced her hip against the wide window ledge that held a collection of antique wine openers. She picked up one with a sterling and staghorn handle and tested the weight in her hand. "Let's just say I've never had a good experience in one."

Silence again.

She put down the opener and went back to her desk. This wasn't going well. They were avoiding the elephant in the room.

"I didn't mean to imply yesterday that what ye did wasn't important," he said.

Bingo.

"If I thought that, I'd be saying my da's passion for wine wasn't important either."

If she heard right, he just apologized in a roundabout way. "You *are* feeling better."

"I don't apologize often, Mer, but I was wrong. If ye can make time in yer schedule, I'd like to see ye again. Come back and let me show ye a real Kentucky welcome."

She plopped down in her chair. Her heart pounded. Decision time. What would it be? Yes or no. "Did Kevin write you a script to follow?"

Elliott laughed. "Sort of. He threatened to quit if I didn't call and apologize."

She shook her head. How could she not see Elliott again? Yes, he did have a way of pissing her off, but he also made her feel alive. And there was the little matter of her ancestor's ghost. *Admit it. You're itching to go back.* She pressed a hand against her stomach to calm the turmoil of indecision.

"I'd come to California, but David and Kevin won't facilitate an escape," Elliott said.

She clicked open her Outlook calendar. There were no appointments scheduled for the next four days other than the big ones: a doctor's appointment and an appointment with Gregory.

"Let's pretend we're back in Edinburgh," Elliott said.

"You don't even know when you're getting out of the hospital, and I've got appointments today that will impact the rest of the week. If they go well—"

"Ye'll come back?"

"Let me see how things go," she said.

"I'll call ye in a few hours."

How long would she be at the clinic after her conversation with Gregory, and depending on the test results, how long would it take to calm down afterward? "I have commitments through dinner. I'll call you."

"Ye don't have a good track record when it comes to calling. I'll call ye tonight at eight o'clock yer time to confirm yer travel plans."

"But..."

He laughed, and the call went dead. *Dang.* Was she that transparent or was he so used to women coming at a flick of his finger?

She gazed out the window at the vineyards blanketed with a morning fog that mimicked her mind, which normally clipped at a steady rate of speed on a well-known path. Now it sputtered along on a bumpy, unchartered course.

Get through today, then go with the flow and see where it takes you.

Chapter Forty

Gillwoods Café, Napa, California – December 28

AT TEN O'CLOCK, Meredith entered Gillwoods Café in the Napa Town Center. The family-style restaurant, which featured all-day breakfast, had opened in Napa in 1997. It was one of her favorite places to meet for coffee. And the bakery, with its to-die-for, mouth-watering cinnamon rolls, always had one piping hot just for her.

She glanced around, searching the booths and tables until she spotted Gregory sitting at a two-top in the corner, drinking coffee from the café's logo mug and reading from his iPad. She punched up her nerves with a shot of determination and sat down across from him.

"What will it take to get you back?" she asked.

He compressed his lips, saying nothing, and then looked at her. "Hello, Meredith. Good to see you, too."

She kept her face placid, intending not to react to his hostile tone.

He set the iPad aside. "For starters, fire the web designer."

She was expecting that to be one of his conditions. "They're not that bad, Greg. And they've worked for us for years. There're loyalties to consider."

"The website has been down for five days."

A waitress approached the table, and Meredith ordered coffee.

"Who would you use?" she asked. "We can't hire one of the competitors in the valley. That'd be bad for business."

"We'll handle it in house."

Meredith glanced at the waitress and smiled as she poured coffee into a mug and then refilled Gregory's. When the woman walked away, Meredith said, "You don't have time to take on more work."

"I'd like to bring someone on board."

"As what?"

"Director of social media. He'll handle Twitter, Facebook, a blog, and the website."

Meredith leaned back and crossed her arms. A director of social media wasn't the issue. She'd have hired one if he'd only asked. "I know social media is important. I'm willing to tweet."

"If you'd like to, great. But we need someone to do it regularly. Once we start, our customers will expect regular updates on what's happening at the winery. Can you do that? Do you want to do that? I don't."

"I'm willing to write blog posts, too."

"You don't have time to keep up a blog."

She fiddled with her spoon. "What else do you want?"

"I'm only interested in one thing. If you can't deliver, I'm not coming back."

Meredith's phone rang and flashed her doctor's name and number. She turned off the device and dropped it into her purse. This was a scrub brush moment, and she had to see it through.

"You need to run the company, not the marketing department," he said. "Step aside, and I'll go back to work."

She opened her mouth to say no, but the word wouldn't form on her tongue.

"The winery is a private company with over two hundred employees and no succession plan. Who's going to lead if something happens to you? What if you get sick again and have to be out for several months? What would happen if you fell in love and wanted to spend more time with the lucky man instead of your grapes?"

"So that's what you're after? The executive office."

"If you think that's what this is about, you're not watching the market as closely as I thought you were. If *Cailean*'s a success, we could do a hundred million this year. That's too big for one person. You've got to let up on the reins. If you do, you'll have time to chase your dream. Other than rescuing that broken down racehorse, you've done nothing to fill up the stables you built."

He's right about that.

"God, Meredith. I'm not asking you to cut off a body part."

He could have used a different analogy.

"I've been marketing wine for twenty years," he continued. "I'm good at what I do. That's why you cherry-picked me from Kendall Jackson. Let me do my job."

I thought I was.

The early lunch crowd filled the booths around them. The smell of sauerkraut for the turkey Reuben sandwiches filtered her way and irritated her already queasy stomach. "Do you really think we could make a hundred million dollars?"

Greg smiled for the first time since she'd sat down across from him. "Let me do what you hired me to do."

"I have high standards. From what I've seen coming out of your office lately, the work falls below my expectations. Why is that?"

His eyes grew large, and he pushed back from the table. "The work on the brochure has been top of the line. You've done nothing but pick it apart since this project began. Why is *that*?"

"I'm not getting into a—" She glanced around to see if restaurant patrons were listening to their conversation. As far as she could tell, they weren't, but she did lower her voice. "—pissing contest with you over whose work is better."

"Really? Well, take a good look at the corrections you've made. You've trashed all my initiatives and revised the slicks to retain *your look*. A look that's been around for a decade. It's time to freshen up the website and our printed material. It's all dated and turns off buyers."

"That *look* has done well for us. There's no reason to change it. It's our brand."

"Our brand needs a facelift. If you don't believe me, I'll show you the market research."

"Where'd you get the research?" she asked.

"I had it done."

Her face flushed with the heat of anger. "Behind my back." Now it was her turn to push away from the table.

"I should have told you, but I had money left in my budget. I went for it. The results were well worth the time and expense."

That was it. She threw up her hands. "I'm done here."

"What if you get sick again?" he asked.

"That's the second time you've asked that. Do you know something I don't?" None of her doctors would have talked to Cate about her health issues. Gregory was hitting her in a vulnerable spot.

"I'm prepared to walk away. Are you prepared to let me?"

Was he intentionally trying to provoke her? "If you think you're indispensable, you're wrong."

They were now at a standstill. He was prepared to walk, and she was prepared to let him. Damn egos. Any other time, she would have let him go, but right now, that would make a huge mess of her life.

She put her elbows on the table, tented her hands, and tapped her fingertips together. "Here's the deal. I'll step back, and you can hire a director of social media. The ball's in your court. But I swear, if you drop it, you won't find another job in the valley or the bay area."

"Deal," he said, shaking her hand with a dry, strong grip.

"Deal," she said, returning his shake with a slightly sweaty palm.

She walked away knowing neither of them left anything on the table. Gregory got what he wanted—her out of the way. She got what she needed—a very capable marketing VP and less responsibility.

There'd be no negotiating during her upcoming appointment with her doctor, though. Either she had cancer or she didn't. If she didn't, she'd go back to Kentucky, have a great weekend with Elliott, and try to find out why Cullen Montgomery was hanging out at MacKlenna Farm. If she did have cancer, well, all bets were off.

Chapter Forty-One

San Francisco Breast Care Center – December 28

MEREDITH PULLED INTO the small, crowded parking lot at the San Francisco Breast Care Center. Sweaty palms made for an uneasy grip of the steering wheel. She found a space in the back, farthest from the door, and squeezed in between a new Lexus and an older model VW Jetta that had a woman in the driver's seat. Meredith turned off the ignition and sat perfectly still. Tears welled in her eyes. Within three hours, she'd all but surrendered to Elliott's request and did surrender to Gregory's demand. Both men were happy. *But what about me?* She should feel lighter, giddy with anticipation, but she didn't. How could she?

The door to the building opened and closed as women—old and young, some dressed in designer suits, some in jeans and jackets—walked in and out. None of them smiling. Although she had survived a previous battle, she could still lose the war. Others had. Beautiful, courageous women who suffered with long-term pain once their breast cancer metastasized. She grieved for them, the ones she had known, like her dear friend Sally, and the ones she hadn't.

"Don't let fear get a foothold," her dad's assistant of many years used to say. "Once it does, it'll bully all of your other emotions." Right now, fear was a noisy troublemaker. She tried to quiet it, but…

Her cell phone rang. She dug into her bag. Her fingers ripped into the contents, tossing aside a wallet, passport, tissues, ChapStick, power cord, hand sanitizer, nail polish. The phone rang again. "Damn." She upturned the bag. On the third ring, she grabbed the phone off the floor and punched the send key. "Meredith Montgomery."

"Ye're crying. What's wrong?" Elliott asked.

Tell him anything, but don't tell him the truth. "I just had a conversation with Gregory about the direction of the marketing department."

"Let me guess. He wants ye out of his way."

She wiped her eyes with a tissue. "You're perceptive."

"I'm not a marketing expert, but the slicks I saw were well done. Ye didn't like them, which meant something else was going on. Ye probably ran the department before yer father died and ye don't want to let go."

"Like I said, you're perceptive."

"Yer situation sounds familiar. A couple of years ago, I was the farm's chief vet. I got tired of horses kicking and slamming me against the wall, so I stepped down to concentrate on developing a compound for joint inflammation that Sean and I were working on."

"Are you going to tell me you got in your replacement's way?"

"And acted like an ass—"

Meredith laughed, and so did he.

"Yeah, well, some things never change. I rewrote several of his orders. He went to Sean threatening to quit if I didn't stop. Sean told me to either back off or take the job back. I didn't want it, but I didn't want to completely let go either. Somehow, Sean smoothed Doc's feathers. He didn't tell me how.

"Then, only a few weeks before Sean died, an offer for the drug came in from a pharmaceutical company. We signed the agreement the next day. Based on the last quarter's earnings, we're set to make some real money."

"Gregory told me *Cailean* could make us a hundred million dollar company. If we get that big, I can't do his job and mine, too."

"Giving up control isn't the worst thing in the world. Ye might find something else that makes ye happier."

She didn't say anything. She just let his words seep in and fill in the corners and crevices. "Why'd you call me just now? I thought you said you'd call at eight."

"I woke up from a nap, thinking about ye. I wanted to hear yer voice."

I wish you could give me a hug.

"If I was there, I'd give ye a hug." He laughed again. "Probably wouldn't stop at a hug, though. As soon as yer body rolled into mine, I'd be ripping off yer clothes."

"Okay, I'm going to hang up before this becomes one of *those* calls."

"I don't want ye over the phone. I want ye here where I can make—"

She laughed again. "I'm hanging up. I've got a meeting to go to."

The woman in the Jetta opened the driver's door and stepped out of the car. She wore a butterfly-print head scarf. She gave Meredith a wan smile then shuffled toward the clinic's entrance. Would that be her in a couple of months, making her way to another chemo appointment? With her first cancer, treatment hadn't included chemo or radiation. She touched her head and ran her fingers through her hair. *I'd look awful without hair. No one would buy a sick woman's wine.*

"Meredith, are ye there, or am I hanging on to a dropped call?"

She sniffed. "I'm still here. I think I'm getting a cold."

"Ye're too fit to get sick. Ye're upset, and there's more going on than the conversation with Gregory, isn't there? Do ye want to talk?"

"Not really. I'm just tired. I've got a lot on my mind."

"Ye need a break."

She leaned her head against the window. "I wish we were still in Edinburgh."

"I need to bring Edinburgh to the farm. Would that get ye back here sooner?"

"Haggis and a Ferris wheel at MacKlenna Farm. Wow. Lexington's first Hogmanay. You might start a new tradition."

"The farm needs one." Elliott's voice reflected a sad tone.

No matter what happened once she walked through those looming clinic doors, she could have one last weekend in his arms. "A couple of quiet days would be fine with me."

"It'll be New Year's weekend. We need to celebrate. *Kevin*," Elliott yelled.

"You don't have to yell. I'm right here," Kevin said.

Meredith shook her head at the mumbled conversation taking place in a hospital room on the other side of the country. "Elliott, I've got to go. I'll call tonight."

She disconnected, unsure he even heard her say good-bye. She had no doubt he would spend the next few days creating a mini version of Edinburgh's four-day winter festival. Whatever he planned would be spectacular.

Chapter Forty-Two

San Francisco Breast Care Center – December 28

MEREDITH SAT IN a plastic chair with sturdy metal legs, an institutional mainstay, and cleaned the fingerprints from her phone. She'd turned it off in case Elliott called back to ask her to come tonight instead. Even if he promised the Edinburgh Wheel, she couldn't leave any sooner than she'd planned.

If she slept with him again—who was she kidding?—*when* she slept with him again, she'd have to tell him about her mastectomy. The slight nuances in her reconstructed breast would be visible to his discerning eye. She sighed with the full weight of her worry. Then why put herself through it? For a non-risk-taker, risks were stacking up at her feet.

The radiologist entered the room, carrying his iPad. He sat at the desk next to Meredith. "The fine needle aspiration was negative. You could still have a tumor that the needle just missed. Because of your past history, your doctor is concerned, legitimately so. My recommendation is that we do an ultrasound."

"Can I get conclusive results today?" she asked.

"Let's see what we find, if anything," he said.

"If it's malignant, I can't do anything about it before February 16."

He sat back, crossed one leg over the other, and scratched his chin, playing with an invisible goatee. "Let's not talk about what you can't do until we know what, if anything, we're facing."

"One of the biggest events in my life is coming up. I can't—"

"Worrying about tomorrow or two months into the future won't do you any good. When we have all the facts, we'll deal with what happens next. Let's start with an ultrasound and go from there."

She wanted to make light of what was happening, to find a joke, a reason to laugh instead of shake. This shouldn't be happening to her again. Hadn't she already sung to this audience? Yep, and she didn't need a comeback tour.

"This situation is complex, Meredith, but you've been through worse."

His platitude stung. If it was meant to comfort her, it didn't. Instead, it buried its stinger in her gut, spreading venom, and she exploded. "What do you think was worse? My first cancer, or praying for a brain-dead husband? How about my father dying in my arms, hoping he'd regain consciousness long enough to tell me for the *first time* that he loved me? Which one of those was worse, do you think?" She slid over the edge of a cliff, dangling above a cavern. "Maybe we should start with my mother dying in labor because she was too sick to give birth to me. *Which one was worse?*"

The doctor cleared his throat.

She had asked rhetorical questions and didn't expect answers from him. Her cheeks heated, partially with embarrassment, partly from anger. "I'm sorry. I've had too much happen to me lately."

"All those things are awful, but you survived." He stood and patted her shoulder. "I'll go and get Lisa to take you across the hall to change. She's a patient advocate and will stay with you during the testing to answer your questions."

A young woman with pert breasts and brown hair pulled into a ponytail entered the room. "Hello, Ms. Montgomery. My name is Lisa. If you're ready, we'll go across the hall for the ultrasound."

They walked through an interior waiting room, passing a fire burning in the fireplace and multicolored fish swimming in an aquarium. Calming fixtures. Meredith counted a dozen women wearing short flowery gowns over their street clothes, sitting on upholstered sofas. Some read books; some dipped tea bags into mugs of steamy water. There was camaraderie in the room. A laugh, a chuckle, a sigh. Everyone was there for the same reason. To find out if their breasts had betrayed them.

Lisa led her down the hall to an exam room, where she left Meredith to change.

A few minutes later, Lisa and the radiologist entered. "You had an ultrasound last time, didn't you?" he asked.

Meredith nodded. "You'll tell me what you see, right?" She lay down on the table and glanced up at the screen.

"I will. I want to do a breast exam first. Then we'll do the ultrasound." He palpated deep into the tissue. Meredith saw a twitch around his mouth and knew the moment he felt the lump.

"You feel it, don't you?" Meredith asked.

"Let's see what it looks like." The radiologist moved the ultrasound transducer around the whole breast, up to the nipple and back around again. "There's a low density, irregular, spiculated mass at the posterior depth in the left breast. We need to do a core biopsy."

"Right now?" Meredith asked.

"Yes. We'll take three to six samples."

"Will that tell you for sure?" She tried to keep the quiver out of her voice—impossible. She was shaking-in-her-Jimmy-Choos scared.

"Yes, but it'll be tomorrow before we get the results."

While the doctor prepared to do the procedure, Meredith closed her eyes and thought of Elliott and the sleigh ride and Christmas night. And then she thought about him some more as a needle pierced her skin.

Chapter Forty-Three

San Francisco Breast Care Center – December 29

TWENTY-FOUR HOURS LATER, Meredith sat at a conference table across from the radiologist who had performed the biopsy. She clasped her hands in her lap to keep from twiddling her hair or picking at her nails or tapping on the tabletop.

The doctor pointed to the image on his laptop screen. "You have an invasive lobular carcinoma."

Her heart beat fast and furiously. Her mouth went dry, and her hands shook. *Invasive carcinoma. I'm going to die.* The room began to spin. She grabbed the edge of the table and held on fast as her life spun out of control.

The doctor poured a glass of water. "Drink this."

She reached for the glass, then had second thoughts and dropped her shaking, clammy hand. Tears fell down her cheeks. "Are you sure?"

He nodded.

"What's…what's the survival rate?"

"Prognosis varies with the grade and stage."

"What's mine?"

"Grade two. The tumor is about three centimeters. What I recommend is that we do a lumpectomy and determine if it's spread to the lymph nodes."

"I already explained that I can't have a mastectomy now."

"This isn't a mastectomy. It's only the removal of the lump. If the margins are clear, we won't have to do the mastectomy. We'll also do a sentinel lymph node biopsy, which will require a pregnancy test. You're not pregnant, are you?"

"No, I'm not." Her hand stopped shaking long enough to hold the glass and take one long sip. "Will you do that today?"

"The surgery center had a cancellation, and they can work you in this afternoon."

"It can't wait until February?" she asked, even though she knew what his answer would be.

He eyed her from under a thicket of graying eyebrows. "I wouldn't advise it."

She squeezed her clasped hands so tightly the blue veins pumped more noticeably beneath the thin layer of skin. "Since I'm already here, let's do it."

"Do you have a friend you can call to be with you? You don't need to be alone."

She endured his stare, holding her composure, precarious as it was. "I'm alone every day. Today's no different."

Chapter Forty-Four

University of Kentucky Medical Center – December 29

ELLIOTT SAT IN the hospital bed, balancing two cell phones, a laptop, and a legal pad. "I'm sending the plane to Edinburgh to pick ye up," he said into one of the phones.

"I'll fly commercial," Evelyn said. "Dinna spend that kind of money on me."

He glanced at the yellow legal pad on the tray table and counted. "I've got eight people on the same flight."

"*Good God, Elliott*," she said, forcing him to yank the phone away from his ear. "Are ye doing all of this to get laid?"

He shook his head, chuckling. "I think I'll get lucky without a party, but it'll be New Year's. If I have to be here and reminded of what happened last year, then I'm having a hell of a party to see me through the night."

She mumbled an obscenity. "A bottle of whisky and a hot woman will get ye through any night."

"I dare say the same is true for ye."

"As long as the hot woman is Lou. By the way, where is she?"

"Shopping with Mrs. Collins."

Evelyn cackled. "Oh my God, the woman drives Lou nuts. What are they shopping for?"

"Food." Elliott attached a document to an email and clicked send. "An email should be popping into yer in-box."

"The city's wearing a blanket of frigging snow, and ye want me to run all over town filling yer order."

"Can ye handle it?" he asked.

"Of course, I can handle anything. This party will cost a fortune."

"Dear God," he belted out in dramatic fashion. "We do not ask ye to give us wealth. But would ye mind showing us where it is?"

Evelyn laughed. "Ye *are* feeling better."

"I am. Now, if ye run into any trouble, call me. We don't have much time."

"I'll send ye a status report. Ciao."

Elliott smiled for the first time since he'd crawled into bed with Meredith four days earlier. If he could keep all the plates spinning, this would be one hell of a party; the kind of party that could keep him quoting Burns until the wee hours of the morning, except that he had different plans for those particular hours.

Kevin rushed into the room. "I got the Ferris wheel, but it's going to cost you. And you know David won't let you ride it anyway."

"We'll talk about that later. When will it get here?"

"Tomorrow."

"Allie." Elliott's executive assistant sat at a table across the room, a laptop open in front of her. "Call our insurance agent, and let him know about the Ferris wheel."

"Did that."

"Did ye invite Dr. Lyles and his wife?"

"Yep," she said. "And I also have RSVPs from all of the members of the board of directors."

"What's yer count?"

"We have one hundred twenty-five confirmed," she said. "Wait. Here's an email from Jake. Oh, good. He's got the men lined up to install the tent tomorrow."

"What about the heaters?"

Allie gave him the *check* signal with her index finger. "Heaters and portable dance floor. Done."

Elliott groaned. "I won't be dancing."

Kevin's face brightened. "If Ms. Montgomery needs a partner—"

"Don't you have a date, Kevin?" Allie asked.

"Yes, but I can—"

"I've seen ye dance, Kevin. Ye lead with yer damn dick," Elliott said, feeling usurped by his aide.

Allie laughed. "Better stay away from his woman, Kev."

"I heard Mrs. Collins was bitching this morning because she was supposed to have the weekend off. Now she's cooking for a mob. Did somebody calm her down?"

"I talked to her," Elliott said.

"And it will cost you," Allie said.

Elliott jammed the cap onto his pen. "The next person who reminds me of the cost of this *soiree* won't get an invitation. *Got it?*" Allie's cheeks reddened, and Kevin found something interesting on the floor to examine. "Allie, as soon as ye've updated the spreadsheet, send it to me, then go home. Kevin, get me something decent to eat."

"They're delivering dinner right now. Don't you want to wait and see what's on the tray?"

"No. Get me the grilled salmon and vegetables from Malones. Go to the Tates Creek restaurant. It's closer than Harrodsburg Road."

David entered the hospital room, stopped at the foot of Elliott's bed, and glared at Allie. "What're ye doing here?"

"Working?" She shot Elliott a look, rolling her eyes, and whispered, "I told you he wouldn't be happy."

David turned a pointed gaze at Elliott. "What are ye planning?"

"A get-together for New Year's," Elliott said.

David shook his head. "A tent-sized party, I'll wager."

Allie patted David's arm. "It's okay, really. He didn't get out of bed. He took a nap, and he ate well."

David removed his coat and tossed it on the sofa. "He followed orders. Is that what ye're telling me?"

"Cheerfully," Allie said.

"That must mean Ms. Montgomery's coming back, and he's trying to get out of here."

"Dr. Lyles said he could go tomorrow, and Ms. Montgomery's arriving tomorrow night."

It usually irritated Elliott when his staff talked about him as if he wasn't in the room, but knowing that tomorrow he'd have Meredith naked in his arms made everything, with the exception of hospital food, tolerable. He was also monitoring his pain medication. He didn't want drugs interfering with his performance.

"If he goes home, I'll set a schedule. Someone will need to be with him constantly."

"What about Ms. Montgomery?" Allie asked.

"I don't think she's going to help him to the bathroom to pee," Kevin said.

"Yuck! Well, I'm not going to either. Now, I am leaving. I'll see y'all back at the farm," Allie said.

"Don't forget to send the spreadsheet as soon as ye've updated the list."

She waved good-bye and closed the door.

David sat at the table and booted up the laptop he'd left there earlier. "Kevin, if ye're going out to pick up dinner, will ye get me whatever ye're getting?"

"Will you tell the food-service worker to take the dinner tray back? I hate wasting food." Kevin slipped on his jacket and gloves and left.

Elliott lowered his bed to a reclining position, groaning a bit as he rolled and stretched his tight shoulders. "What'd ye learn at the police station?"

David formed a zero with his thumb and index finger. "They don't have anything on the Gates lad. I talked to the investigator who worked the case five years ago. He said Gates's brothers were pieces of shit. He didn't know how the younger one stayed clean with scum for role models."

"Maybe he isn't. Maybe he just hasn't been caught."

"That's where I'd put my money." David started typing. After a couple of minutes, he said, "Sorry. I had to add a note to my daily report." He closed the laptop and faced Elliott. "Chuck did hit on a bit of good news, though. He was canvassing young Gates's neighborhood in Louisville and discovered the lad worked in construction. Tonight he's making a list of Kentucky companies with projects in the Louisville-Jefferson County area. We'll divide it up tomorrow and go one by one until we get a break."

Elliott uncapped his pen and drew an outline of the state of Kentucky while David talked. He then divided the state into thirds by area codes. "Are ye searching the Lexington area?"

"The whole state, if necessary," David said.

Elliott drew an odd-shaped circle encompassing Louisville and Southern Indiana, Lexington, and the Northern Kentucky and Cincinnati area. "Let's hope it doesn't come to that." He tapped his pen against the pad. "Where'd they all grow up?"

"Somewhere in Indiana."

Elliott circled Indianapolis on his map. "Ye may have to hire help. Ye're looking at a large area to canvass."

"Chuck has operatives he can pull in if we need them."

"Bring them on board now. We don't have time to screw with this."

David removed a small spiral notebook from his shirt pocket and thumbed through a few pages. "This will cost ye."

Elliott tossed his pad onto the tray table. "That's all I've heard all day. It costs what it costs. Get it done, but I don't want anyone at the farm to know what we're doing, and that includes Louise and Evelyn."

"What about Kevin?"

"Keep him in the loop, but don't tell Allie yet."

"I'll need an advance from Harrison to hire more investigators."

"I'll front the money and get reimbursed later." Elliott had already joked with Kevin that he'd have to sell some Apple stock to pay for a portion of the party. The Ferris wheel, musical entertainment, and food flown in from Scotland were extravagances that he wouldn't charge to the farm.

David made a phone call. "Dr. Fraser said to bring in extra help now. Okay. I'll get it to ye in the morning." He disconnected and said to Elliott, "Chuck needs access to twenty-five thousand dollars."

"What does that mean? Cash in an envelope?"

"His people are legit. I'll set up a special account we can draw from."

"Kevin can get a cashier's check to ye in the morning." Elliott reached for his pad and tore off the top sheet. "Here's a sketch of the state to give ye an idea of the size of the search parameters."

David took the paper and studied it. "Any news from Manning?"

"He talked to the adjuster. They're still waiting on the final necropsy report, but from what they know so far, they don't intend to pay the claim."

David folded the paper in half and inserted it into his notebook. "What'd Harrison say?"

"He cried."

"Ye'd think it was his money," David said.

"I didn't tell ye about his accounting errors that cost us twenty-five thousand dollars. Makes him more than cautious right now, especially since another slip up means he's out of a job. He's sixty-two. If he gets fired in this economy, he won't land on his feet."

David let out a long, slow whistle. "When do the auditors review the books?"

"Last two weeks in January."

A young woman brought Elliott's dinner into the room, but before she could set it on his tray, he said, "Take it back. I won't eat it."

"Are you sure?"

He nodded. "Harrison still has the support of the board, but I'm not so sure he has mine."

"Has he ever?"

"I was impressed with his resume when he was hired, but that was ten years ago. A few mistakes and, well, I'm not that impressed any longer."

"I'll look through his personnel file. Maybe there're some notes about him."

"I doubt they're relevant to this investigation, but they might be helpful to the board if the members decide to let him go. Allie said she left the box of files in the office at the mansion. Ye should have everything ye need."

"Harrison won't take dismissal lightly."

"Nothing will happen until after the audit, and if he's done anything improper, he'll know the auditors will uncover creative accounting, and he'll expect to be fired, if not arrested. But I don't think it'll come to that." Elliott's phone rang and Meredith's number flashed across the screen. He smiled like a stupid teenager. *Damn. I get hard thinking about her.* "It's Meredith. Will ye give me some privacy?"

David left the room.

"Fraser."

Chapter Forty-Five

Montgomery Condominium, San Francisco – December 29

"HOW'S THE PARTY PLANNING?" Meredith was sitting on the sofa in her San Francisco condominium following a lonely clam chowder dinner that she'd ordered in. Now she wanted nothing more than to curl into a ball and sleep for as long as she could, which probably wouldn't be long enough. Her breast was tender from the procedures, but it hadn't taken the doctor long to remove the lump, do the SLN biopsy, then send her home in a taxi.

"It'll be a star-studded evening," Elliott said.

"Are you wearing a tux or kilt?"

"A kilt. I've got several friends coming in from Scotland who'll be in Highland dress."

"Not only a star-studded affair but an international one. How about I provide the wine?"

"Will this be a pre-launch party to taste yer new chard?"

"That's tempting, but I can't risk letting a review get out before the February event. I'll bring other labels. How many are on the guest list, and what's the menu?"

"So far one hundred twenty-five, but I don't have the menu. Cameron is catering."

"The Prestonfield House Cameron?" Her voice couldn't hide the excitement of biting into one of his delectable entrees again.

"Ye wouldn't believe what I had to promise him."

"Let me guess. A trip to San Francisco." She laughed, and for just a moment, cancer slipped from the number one position in her mind. "After the special accommodations he made for us, I'd be thrilled to give him a tour of the valley."

"We'll talk about it later. Tell me about ye. How'd yer afternoon go?" The soft lull of his voice sprinkled her with warmth and compassion.

Do not tell him. Do not.

Tears slipped from her eyes, creating fresh, salty tracks down her face. Needing and wanting more than the sound of his voice, she hugged herself, but her arms couldn't give her the depth of comfort she craved from him. In her heart, she knew the pain of his withdrawal if he knew she had cancer would be a hundred times worse than the loneliness now stripping her insides down to a hollow core. She didn't trust him, but that wasn't limited to Elliott. Right now, she didn't trust anyone.

"Tense," she said, swiping at her tears, "but I got through it. I have two meetings in the morning then I'm all yours for four days."

"All ye'll need to pack is something to wear to the party because the rest of the time—"

"Whoa. You'll have a house full of guests. We'll have to be sociable."

"The hell we will."

She laughed. "I'll be glad to see you."

"I promise to be on my best behavior."

Somehow, she doubted that.

Chapter Forty-Six

Surgeon's Office, San Francisco – December 30

THE NEXT MORNING, as Meredith was going through her emails, she received a call from her surgeon's office. The lumpectomy and sentinel lymph node biopsy reports were on his desk, and he wanted to see her as soon as possible. She didn't want to go. So she went for a run to give the endorphins a chance to do their magic. Normally, she ran through pain, but after a mile her breast hurt too much. She walked home, trying to wrap her brain around all that was happening.

Three hours later, she sat in her surgeon's office. "I don't want to be here." She uncrossed her legs and placed both feet firmly on the floor.

"I know you don't, and I wish we were chatting over a bottle of wine instead, but…"

"We have to take care of business first. So tell me. Do you have good news or bad news?"

He focused on her sharply. "I have both."

She ran damp palms up and down the tops of her thighs, leaving handprints on her double weave trousers. "Tell me the bad first."

He leaned forward, placed his forearms on his desk, and tapped his fingers together. "The margins were not clear on the lump I removed. We didn't get all the cancer, and you need a mastectomy."

Tears fell down her cheeks. Since finding the lump, she had

sensed that she would lose her other breast, too, but actually hearing the word *mastectomy* was like slamming into a rock wall. If she hadn't been sitting, her trembling legs would have collapsed beneath her.

She wiped away tears with the back of her hand. "You said there was good news. What could possibly be good in this situation?"

"The cancer hasn't spread to the lymph nodes. With surgery and probably radiation, you should have a good outcome." He sat back and reviewed his notes. "It will take a couple of weeks to coordinate schedules with your plastic surgeon and oncologist."

"I can't have surgery until after February sixteenth."

He glanced at the calendar on his desk. "That's a long time to wait."

"I'm launching a new wine, and there's too much to do right now."

"Your health is more—"

She held up a hand to stop him. "I've heard that lecture already. Waiting another three weeks isn't going to impact my heath. Is it?"

"Probably not," he said.

"Good." She dropped her hand. "Now, let's schedule the surgery for the eighteenth or nineteenth. Anticipating this outcome, I have an appointment with my plastic surgeon next. Her office can coordinate with yours." Meredith stood, holding the back of the chair until her legs grew steady. "Your invitation to the launch has been mailed. I hope you'll come."

"Wouldn't miss it," he said, walking her to the door. "If you change your mind and decide to have surgery earlier, I'll work you into the schedule."

She shivered slightly. "I *won't* change my mind."

The walk to the plastic surgeon's office in the adjoining building was short and bittersweet. Unlike five years ago, she knew what to expect. The cold and dreary day matched her somber mood perfectly. Not even the winery's sweet Harvest Riesling could bring about a smile. Then her lip turned up slightly. Maybe a taste of wine couldn't, but a soft lingering kiss from Elliott… She sighed, cupping the side of her face. Yes, his lips could do what even sweet wine could not. Although some tension eased from her body, it held steady at a higher than normal level.

She pushed open the door and walked inside the doctor's calm yellow-tinted office with paintings and fixtures in various shades of blue and green—friendly and welcoming. But, for Meredith, not at all relaxing. She knew months of procedures awaited her. Why hadn't she had both breasts done at the same time? Of course, she knew the answer. The procedure wasn't recommended, and she wouldn't have agreed if it had been.

An hour later, after an exam and photographs, she sat across the table from a gentle and kind professional, everything she wanted in a doctor who would mold her left side into a sphere of mammary perfection.

"You can only have one TRAM flap, so that option isn't available this time, but we can do a latissimus dorsi flap. That will move fat, muscle, and blood vessels from—"

"No," Meredith said. "That will weaken my shoulder and back. I can't do that."

"Then we'll have to go with the tissue expander and silicone implant."

She knew her options going in and had already decided what she wanted. "What dates do you have open after February sixteenth?"

"I can work you in sooner."

"I have commitments through the sixteenth. Can your staff work with my surgeon's people to find a suitable date after that?"

The doctor removed her glasses, held the end pieces between her index fingers and thumbs, and rocked the glasses back and forth. "It's not in your best interest to put this off. You know that."

Five years ago, she'd been naïve and uninformed and had let her doctors make decisions based on what they thought was best for her. This time, however, her treatment would be different, because she was different. She'd be her own advocate and make decisions in concert with her doctors or, as in this case, bulldoze the opposition until they came into alignment with her conditions.

She stood and extended her hand, much as she'd done with the surgeon. The gnawing in her stomach would send her to a gastroenterologist next. Getting through the doctor appointments would go a long way in reducing the stress, but she still had a confession to make to Elliott.

"You're the best plastic surgeon in California, and I'm relieved you can fit me in. I'll wait to hear from you."

She exited the yellow office, and for the next four days, she'd shut the door on her cancer.

Chapter Forty-Seven

MacKlenna Mansion, Lexington – December 30

LATER THAT DAY, Meredith's plane touched down at Lexington's Blue Grass Airport. Elliott had told her that unless her arrival coincided with his release from the hospital, he wouldn't be there to greet her. When she exited the plane, she found David waiting at the bottom of the steps. She tightened a coat of disappointment around her.

"Is he still in the hospital?"

David's breath condensed in the cold air. "We just got him settled in at the farm. He's waiting for ye."

Meredith climbed down the stairs. "How's he feeling?"

"When I left the house, he was singing."

Christmas Eve was the only time she'd heard his Rod Stewart-esque, raspy singing voice. "He's multitalented."

David took her bag. "Let me carry this. It's a wee bit icy out here."

She laced her arm through his and summoned up a smile. "I'm glad I live in Napa. It's rare to have snow."

"A few days of this has rejiggled my memory. Made me wish for the desert again."

She squeezed his arm. "Cold weather is much better than a battlefield."

"Aye. A wee house here is safer." He glanced at her with his keen eyes. "D'ye feel weel? Ye look a wee bit tired."

She was tired and worried and her breast hurt, but she'd keep that to herself. "I worked during the flight. I should have taken a nap." She pointed over her shoulder toward the plane. "I brought several cases of wine, but I don't think they'll fit in the car."

"Jake has two men on their way to offload the wine, but I'll get yer luggage."

"I have everything I need in the bag you're carrying. They can bring my luggage with the wine."

He guided her in the direction of Elliott's vehicle. "If ye're ready, then, we'll be off." He opened the back door, and she climbed into the Mercedes.

"How long is Elliott's list of restrictions?" she asked.

David glanced in the rearview mirror. "There's just one. He can't walk with or without crutches."

"So he's spearheading the party from a wheelchair."

"He's being secretive about his weekend plans. But as long as he doesn't walk, I'll leave him alone."

Meredith opened her compact and checked the lipstick she applied before landing. "So that's my job. To keep him off his feet."

David turned right onto Versailles Road at the Keeneland intersection. "If anyone can do that, ye can."

She shook her head, laughing. "I don't deserve that confidence. I'm a new inner circle recruit."

"Well, speaking for the rest of the members, ye're a welcome addition."

A temporary addition.

They drove past Calumet Farm's pastures encased in white plank fencing. Red-trimmed white barns sat atop rolling hills. "You couldn't ask for a more beautiful entrance into Lexington."

"Dr. Fraser could arrange a tour, if ye're interested."

She took one last look as they merged onto New Circle Road. "I haven't seen all of MacKlenna Farm yet, and it's what, a hundred years older than Calumet?"

"Kentucky history isn't my forte," David said.

Your forte probably involves guns and remote locations that need satellite phones. "Elliott said he has friends coming from Scotland for the weekend. Is Evelyn coming?"

"She'll arrive in the morning," David said.

"I'm sure Louise will be happy to see her."

"Yes, ma'am."

Meredith sent Elliott a text. *On New Circle Road. Should I ask David to speed?* A one-word answer came back. *Yes.* Tingles of anticipation battled anxiety for domination. What reaction would he have to her revelation? Louise's comments gave her little hope for a positive outcome. What if she didn't tell him? In the dark, he hadn't noticed her scars. If they kept the lights down, maybe…

David entered the farm through a different entrance than she'd used during her previous visit. "I haven't been this way."

"Dr. Fraser moved into the cottage for the weekend. It's a short walk from the mansion."

Elliott hadn't said anything about moving, but a couple of days in a quaint cottage sounded intriguing. David stopped in front of a two-story, white-bricked, Neo-Classical residence. "If this is a cottage, Kentucky has a unique dictionary." She'd never seen one with columns, a slate roof, copper gutters, and balustrade-topped side porches.

"The original frame house was demolished in the 1930s. When they rebuilt the house, they kept the name. Dr. Fraser lived here for thirty years until he begrudgingly moved into the mansion a couple of months ago."

David opened her door, and she climbed out. "Elliott requested privacy, so I'll let ye go in by yerself. His bedroom is on the main floor. Follow the hall, turn left. Ye'll probably hear him singing."

She lightly squeezed David's arm. "If he misbehaves, I'll call you. Where will you be?"

"At the mansion. I can be here in sixty seconds."

"Where's Kevin?"

"Inside." David removed his aviators and leveled his intense dark brown eyes at her. "The lad's discreet. Ye willna know he's there unless ye need him. If ye'll leave yer phone on the table by the door, he'll notify ye if ye receive an urgent call."

"*Leave* my phone?"

"Just until dinner. Dr. Fraser gave up his phone, too, and put a hold on all calls into the residence. He didn't want yer reunion interrupted."

Reunion? A portion of her anxiety vanished with a deep exhale.

"We're all glad ye're back, Ms. Montgomery."

The spicy fragrance of the outdoors that she had come to identify with Elliott wafted over her as soon as she crossed the threshold and entered a rich-red-wine and beige colored entry hall. She inhaled deeply, letting the scent tease her lungs. Then, from somewhere in the house came his breathy singing.

"*By yon bonnie banks and by yon bonnie braes, where the sun shines bright on Loch Lomond.*" If possible, the words and tune brought out more of the original flavor of his brogue. The sound danced across her heart, alive and vibrant.

"*Where me and my true love were ever wont to gae, on the bonnie, bonnie banks of Loch Lomond.*"

She left her phone on the table and followed the Pied Piper through the foyer, past a grand staircase hugging the wall, and down a wide, well-lit hallway lined with paintings of old Scottish castles. If she stopped to study one, she'd want to study them all. Right now, all she wanted was Elliott's enticing mouth-watering promise of epicurean pleasure.

"*Oh! Ye'll take the high road, and I'll take the low road, and I'll be in Scotland afore ye…*"

The walls of the master suite matched the color of the waters of Loch Lomond, and she wanted to jump naked into the clear, cool lake. A massive, century-old, four-poster bed stood as the focal point of the room. Until she spotted Elliott, reclining with his hands stacked behind his head, wearing a black sweater and a pair of khakis, a walking boot, and socks but no shoes. Her breath—and her heart—stopped, caught in another magical moment.

"*But me and my true love will never meet again…*"

Breathless, she patted her chest to jump-start her heart, and she joined him on the chorus. "*On the bonnie, bonnie banks of Loch Lomond.*"

Smiling, he raised himself up on his elbows. "Don't make me wait another second to hold ye."

She pitched her bag and hurried to his side. "Are you sure you just got out of the hospital?"

He pressed his lips against hers, encircled her with arms that belied his weakened condition, and pulled her close. The scent of balsam and cedar, clean and delicious, tickled her nose, and she tasted cinnamon tea on his tongue, different for him yet highly erotic. The flavors and scents created a boutique cocktail that teased her senses. He slid his hand beneath her sweater and cupped her breast, sending confusing signals to her brain. She wanted him to touch her but feared his possible reaction.

"Ye're shivering. Do ye want me to turn up the heat?" he asked.

"I think you are."

He nipped at her chin and throat, turning her skin into kindling for the wildfire he set with only a kiss, an accelerant more powerful than anything on the market. "What restrictions do we have?"

"I can't use my right leg at all." He dragged his gaze from her mouth to her eyes. "I can't even put weight on my knee."

"Sounds like we need to be creative."

The late afternoon sun filtered through the blinds. There wasn't a lot of light but enough that he would notice her faded scars and nipple. It was no longer a question of whether or not to tell him but how to start the conversation.

She took a deep breath and slipped her sweater over her head. Her breasts spilled from the underwire cups of a leopard-print, lace-trimmed cami. Panic eased up to her throat.

"God, ye're gorgeous." His fingertips glided across her cleavage. He slipped the straps off her shoulders. His right carotid artery pulsed noticeably. He wanted her, of that she had no doubt. But would he still once he knew the truth?

Panic now cut off her breath.

He pulled down the cami, freeing her breasts.

She swallowed hard, waiting for words that wouldn't come.

He cocked his head, studying her. "What's with the bandages?"

She placed her fingers over the two Band-Aids covering the biopsy and lumpectomy incisions. "I had two moles snipped off yesterday. My breast is a little sore." She avoided his eyes. "It's nothing." She prayed for courage to tell him about her first mastectomy.

"What's wrong, Mer? Ye look like ye're about to cry."

Just say it. "I had cancer five years ago. They took my breast." *I have it again, but I don't want to talk about that.*

The color left his cheeks. He looked at her breasts first one way and then the other. "They left ye a wee nice one in its place." He ran his finger around her nipple. "Yer surgeon's an expert. I would have figured it out, but yer breasts are perfect." He cupped her left breast. "Do ye have an implant in this one?" He massaged her. "I don't feel one."

"That side is all me."

"That's why a wee mole would concern ye."

Mole?

He massaged her right breast. "This one is as soft and natural as the other." He sucked the nipple into his mouth. When he released her, he wore a crooked smile that worked in concert with his mischievous eyes.

"It doesn't disgust you?" she asked.

"*Disgust me?* I'm the one with scars from here to there. Never. Yer scars are noble. Ye fought a horrible disease and beat it." He kissed her breast again and then ran the tip of his finger around the areola and across the faded scars. "I made love to ye and didn't know."

"I should have told you, but I—"

He pressed his hand over her lips. "Ye didn't have to tell me. I would have figured it out, but it doesn't matter." He cupped both breasts, gently skimming his fingers around them. "I'll be careful. I'm sure this side is a wee bit sore."

Her nipple grew taut from his attention, and sensations rippled through her, jumbling her thought processes.

"It's all behind ye. Five years. Ye beat the odds." His voice, warm with affection, caressed her. She shivered, and he pulled her close. "Talking about it probably brings up bad memories."

"I had a difficult time."

Elliott stilled. "That's why ye haven't had sex. Isn't it?" He held her gaze.

An incredible weight lifted from her, and she grew tempted to tell him she had cancer again, but she couldn't. It would interject uncertainty into their fragile relationship. His lips touched hers in a firm, possessive kiss, and he told her with his mouth that she wasn't damaged goods to him.

"Now, would ye please take off the rest of yer clothes?"

She stripped in a slow tease. Her slacks whispered as they settled onto the floor. For the first time in five years, she stood in front of a man unashamed. She leaned over and kissed him. "Help me take your clothes off."

He yanked off his sweater, unbuckled his pants, and pushed one-legged trousers down over his hips. The boxer briefs followed. His erection lay flat against his abdomen. He jerked open the drawer to the bedside table, grabbed a condom, tore open the wrapper, and rolled it down his penis.

"Come here."

Drunk on relief, she eagerly lowered onto him until he filled her.

Elliott let out a deep, ragged groan.

A groan slipped through her lips, too. She tiptoed her fingers through the smattering of chest hair. Corded muscles that defined his chest rippled beneath her touch.

"Ye're in control. Take it fast, slow, whatever feels good for ye. Watching ye is a fantasy come true."

A vixen took possession of her body, and she ground against him. "When'd you first have this fantasy?"

His eyes brightened with laughter. "When ye walked into the library. Didn't ye notice my hand shake when I poured yer drink?"

His erection twitched inside her, stroked her inner walls, and waves of pleasure tickled her spine. She pushed up on her knees and then slid back down him slowly, causing him to pull air through his teeth. "Jeez, Mer. Keep that up, and I won't last long."

"You gave me a slow once-over and pretty much telegraphed what you wanted. What do you want now?" She squeezed and ground her pelvis against him. The air around them crackled.

"I'm just along for the ride," he said, his voice deep and husky. He grabbed her hips and tugged her even closer.

She leaned forward and dangled her breasts above him. "I don't want to feed your ego, Fraser, but I've never felt like this."

He nipped her nipple with his teeth.

"Ouch."

His lip twitched as he fought back a smile. "I just wanted to be sure I had the right one."

After all the anxiety she'd experienced, that one statement washed it away. "Kiss me."

He cupped the sides of her head, pulled her to him, and kissed her. Then, in a flash, he rolled over, pinning her beneath him. He jerked, his eyes rolled back in his head, and he yelled, "*Damn.*"

She came up quickly on her elbows. "What happened?"

He rolled off, broke out in a cold sweat, and let out a pain-filled growl. "I forgot," he said, hissing.

"*Kevin,*" Meredith yelled. She grabbed the blanket folded over the end of the bed and covered up before he ran into the room.

"What's wrong?"

"He put weight on his leg," she said.

Kevin grabbed another throw and covered Elliott's groin. "What do you need, Boss?"

"Hurts like hell."

"Do you want a shot?"

Elliott hissed out dozens of rapid breaths.

"I'll get the medicine."

Kevin came back with a syringe, rolled Elliott slightly, and shot the drug into his hip. "I need to check the dressing." He removed the walking boot. "You got lucky. No bleeding."

"Get me a drink," Elliott said as Kevin laced his leg back up.

"Can't do that, Boss, but I can get Ms. Montgomery one."

Elliott waved him off. "Go on. Get out of here."

Meredith lay on her side and teased her fingers through his hair. "What'd he give you?"

"Demerol. It'll take an hour before I can try again, but my fingers still work." His chest rose and fell rapidly.

She kissed his cheek. "I'll wait for you."

Kevin came back into the room with a glass of wine and a bottle of Evian.

"Damn, Kevin. Bring me whisky."

"Can't do it. David can hurt me more than you can right now." He gathered up the medical kit and left.

Meredith ran her fingers through his hair. "Close your eyes. Sing me a song. I'll be right beside you."

After a few minutes, he started singing again, although not as boisterous as he had earlier. "*'Twas then that we parted, in your shady glen, on the steep, steep side of Ben Lomond…*"

He nodded off before he sang another verse. Meredith finished her wine and closed her eyes only to be awakened later with a kiss. "If the lass has a mind to wake, I've a mind to take her for a ride."

"To Loch Lomond?" she asked in a sleep-coated voice.

He swept his tongue along the seam of her mouth. His lips were both warm and inviting, and she melted into him. Still ensnared by sleep, she rolled on top and slid down his length, rocking against him while he stimulated her in slow, sexy circles. Pleasure pulsed through her belly and down between her legs. She moaned deep in her throat, urging him to give her the final push that would send her spiraling into the unknown.

And then it happened. She arched her back, breathing faster, and her entire body quaked. He held her hips and moved her in a rhythm that quickly had him convulsing beneath her. She fell limply on his chest and kissed him. "I'll get a warm washcloth and be your body girl." She went to the bathroom and returned with two hot washcloths. She handed him one, and he started to wash himself. She pushed his hand away. "That's for me."

"Oh," he said, grinning.

She washed him then reclined on her elbows so he could do the same to her. After washing her sensitive skin, he tossed the wash-cloth aside and pressed a kiss on her pubic mound, bringing more heat to the fire burning within her.

"Don't think about what I'm doing, wee sweetheart. Relax."

His fingers moved deeply and slowly within her. She relaxed her shoulders. Her head lolled to the side, and she watched him from beneath lowered lids.

"God, that feels wonderful," she said.

"Yer body's humming." He locked his face in concentration as if she were a puzzle to solve, a masterpiece to create, a delectable treat to devour.

Awash with sensations, she let her mind go blank, soaring into a deep, cloudless blue sky. Her orgasms kept building, overlapping until she climbed the last peak, and her body screamed *replete.*

"I feel like I ran a marathon."

"Come here. Let me hold ye," he said.

She slowly turned and nestled against him. "I'm not sure I can walk."

"Ye don't have to yet." He stroked her lightly with his fingertips from her neck to the base of her spine, up and down, teasing her. "Ye fell into a trance and held me spellbound with an erotic dance."

"Nothing like that has ever happened to me." She stretched like a lazy cat in the mild winter sun. "I need to refresh my drink."

"Kevin will do that."

"No," she said, coming up off the bed. "He will not. If we hadn't had an emergency, I would never have allowed him in here."

Elliott chuckled. "Oh, wee sweetheart. He knew what we were doing."

"I don't care. Well, I do care. He's so young."

"Twenty-eight. He's delivered over a dozen babies in the backseats of cars. He's a big boy, and he's even had sex himself."

Elliott's eyes twinkled. "From the sounds I've heard coming from his room, I think he enjoys it."

"You two have a strange relationship."

"He puts up with a lot of abuse when I have surgery, but he never gets angry."

"He gets scared."

Elliott arched his brow. "Why do you say that?"

"I'm talking out of school." She scooted off the bed and slipped on a robe she found slung over a chair. "What do you want to drink? And should we make dinner plans?"

"Whisky. Neat. Louise planned a small dinner party, and we're supposed to be at the mansion at eight o'clock."

Meredith glanced at the clock. "It's six thirty. I need a shower. And I won't bring you any alcohol."

"Ye, too? Won't anybody get me a drink?"

"Nope, but I'll bring you some water."

"There should be a tray with setups in the kitchen. Down the hall on the left."

The stainless steel and granite kitchen had two microwaves, two dishwashers, plus double the counter space normally found in a house of this size. Meredith had a surprising rush of jealousy thinking of Elliott's dates who had attended soirees at the cottage. She'd never been jealous of anyone. Why now? She shook off the question, afraid of the answer.

A large serving tray on the counter held an ice bucket cooling a Montgomery pinot grigio, a bottle of Balvenie, glasses, bottled water, and a plate of grapes and assorted cheeses. *Kevin, you're a doll.* She poured a glass of wine and carried the plate and water back to the bedroom. "Is Kevin joining us for dinner?"

"He's bringing a date." Elliott leaned against the headboard and put his hands behind his head. The muscles in his arms and shoulders bulged.

The sight of him took her breath, and her feet stopped moving. "I hope I can face him without blushing."

"Ye were blushing for me earlier." He gave her one of those

smiles that tickled every nerve ending.

She set the tray on a table beside the bed. "When?"

He sipped from the bottle of water. "Ye had a pink flush on yer breasts when my tongue—"

She clasped her hand over his mouth. "Shh. You don't have to tell me."

"Does that embarrass ye?"

His voice rumbled through his chest, jumped the track, and rumbled through hers. Jonathan had only made love to her that way once. When he never used his tongue on her again, she assumed something was wrong with her. But Elliott's eager moaning said he couldn't get enough of her.

She popped a piece of cheese into her mouth, grinning. "I think I could have another orgasm."

Smiling, he set his water aside. "Well, then come here."

She straddled his face and held on to the headboard. Her smooth-talking Scotsman certainly had a way with his mouth and tongue. When she finally dropped on the bed, exhausted, she doubted she'd ever be able to get up again.

He watched her, wearing a Cheshire smile. "Ye amaze me."

She gave him a sultry look. "Well, I Kegel." She rolled over on her side. "I'm surprised at the way my body reacted. You know how to pull the best from me."

"Well, I hope to do a lot more pulling." He tweaked her nipple. "Ye have a very responsive body."

"It's responding to you." How could she be forty-two and never have known what her body was capable of feeling? Now that she knew, she'd never accept anything less from a lover. She rolled into the crook of his arm. "What's next for your leg?"

"Chris will put the implant back in, but only if I commit to re-habbing."

"What'd you tell him?"

He stroked his fingers through her hair. "That I wanted to dance with ye the night of yer launch."

"That means you'll have to go back next week for surgery."

"Thursday, depending on blood work."

"I've got to go home Monday. With appointments on Tuesday, I can't stay." God, she hated this. Why couldn't they live in a bubble for a few weeks until this out-of-control passion burned out? Then she could get on with what she had to do.

"Let's talk about what happens Monday once we make it to Sunday. Deal?"

She gave a long exhale, knowing there was nothing to talk about, but she forced a smile and said, "Deal."

Chapter Forty-Eight

MacKlenna Mansion, Lexington – December 30

SHORTLY BEFORE EIGHT O'CLOCK, Meredith entered through the front entrance of the mansion and held the door for David as he wheeled Elliott across the threshold.

"Are those bullet holes?" she asked, rubbing the indentations in the door.

"Civil War," Elliott said.

"I'd love to hear that story," she said.

"There's a large journal in the office that goes back to 1795. The story of the battle is in there. Nothing noteworthy. Captain McCabe, a Union officer, was visiting the MacKlennas and led the charge against a small Rebel force."

"Nothing small about it from what I heard," Louise said, giving Meredith a hug. "Welcome back, dearie."

"Elliott said Evelyn's coming tomorrow," Meredith said.

Louise waved jewelry-free hands. "I'll be glad to see her, too." She rubbed her fingers. "I left in such a hurry, I forgot my jewelry."

"Good thing, too," Elliott said, rolling his eyes. "That clanking annoys me."

A man standing close to Elliott's wheelchair laughed. "You only have yourself to blame. You gave her most of those rings she wears."

"But not to wear all at one time," Elliott grumbled.

The man stuck out his hand toward Meredith. "I'm Doc. Heard a bit about you, Ms. Montgomery."

Meredith blinked. *Doc? The vet?* "I'm so sorry about Galahad."

Doc cleared his throat. "Yeah, well, thanks. It's a huge loss for the farm."

An attractive woman on the high side of sixty laced her arm with the vet's. "I'm Doc's better half, Betty."

"And I'm Allie," a petite blond bombshell said, wrapping her arm around Elliott's shoulder, "his assistant."

Meredith smiled. "Elliott's mentioned you." *Although he didn't tell me you look like a Playboy bunny.*

A man came up beside her. "And I'm her fiancé, Bill."

"Best horse trainer in the business," Elliott said.

The front door blew open and a gorgeous, leggy brunette rushed in, rubbing her arms. "It's cold."

Elliott smiled at the newest arrival. "Are ye flying solo tonight, Sandy?"

"Hi, sweetie." The woman kissed his cheek. "Roger's parking the car." She glanced at Meredith. Sandy's eyes opened wide in surprise. "You came back. No one told me." She shook Meredith's hand with a firm handshake. "I saw the announcement about your new chardonnay in *Wine Digest.* I'm watching the campaign closely. I've been very impressed with your VP of marketing. He's positioned the new label to take a large market share."

"Sandy is a former Miss Kentucky and one of the best Thoroughbred marketing managers in the business," Elliott said. "We're lucky to have her."

Meredith detected familiarity between the two, but how familiar had they been? And did it matter? One day, she, too, would be a number in a long line of Elliott's ex-girlfriends. Wondering who else was on the list was pointless and added knots to her already tense shoulders.

The door blew open again. Meredith fixed her eyes on the man who entered the foyer. If the state had a Mr. Kentucky contest, the winner just walked into the house—a younger version of George

Clooney. Although gorgeous, he didn't have Elliott's bad-boy killer smile.

"Glad ye could make it, Roger," Elliott said. "Meet Meredith Montgomery."

"The vintner?" Roger asked.

"Yes," Meredith said.

"I'm Roger Longley, Sandy's date."

Sandy wiggled her ring finger. A large emerald-cut diamond graced her hand. "He forgets sometimes," she said, winking.

"Roger is also one of the top brain surgeons in the country," Louise said. "He's agreed to operate on Elliott." She handed the doctor a cocktail. "Ye're not on call, are ye?"

The George Clooney doppelganger shook his head. "But I've had a cancellation for Monday. I can work you in at eleven o'clock, Elliott."

"The medical community is begging to study my brain to figure out why I'm so irresistible to women," Elliott said.

Without missing a beat, Meredith arched her brow and asked, "So they can develop an antidote?"

Peals of laughter rolled down the hallway like an unfolding red carpet. Doc slapped Elliott on the shoulder. "Good God, you've finally met your match." He paused a minute and studied her. "She reminds me of Kit, and she's not going to take a bit of your crap either."

Elliott grinned sheepishly.

"What's so funny?" Kevin asked, entering the parlor from the dining room with a beautiful redhead on his arm. It was beginning to look like the preliminaries of a beauty contest in which Meredith was too old to compete. She saw her forty-two years stacking up on top of gray hair, dry skin, and cancer.

"Susan, this is Meredith Montgomery," Kevin said.

"Kevin can't stop talking about you," Susan said. "He even brought over a bottle of your wine last night, which was delicious, by the way."

Meredith smiled, thinking what an extraordinary couple they

made. Both were good looking, athletic, and exuded self-confidence. "I'm glad you enjoyed it."

"I had to drag Susan out of the hospital with a promise of good food and more wine," he said.

"I hope you weren't a patient," Meredith said.

"No, but I have no doubt Kevin's helped patients escape before." Susan glanced out the corner of her eye toward Elliott.

Kevin put his hands on his hips. "I'd never do anything to jeopardize a patient's health."

Meredith wondered about the prescription pain medication she'd seen him give Elliott. Were narcotics in his best interest?

"Susan's a third-year resident," Kevin said.

Another eyebrow-raising moment for Meredith. Susan, like the other women, was both beautiful and intelligent. While beautiful women had never intimidated her, somehow having young, gorgeous women surrounding Elliott made her second-guess her clothes, her hair, and her makeup. She snatched her composure before it drifted out of reach and asked, "What's your specialty?"

"Oncology," Susan said.

"I think that field would be difficult. I commend you." Meredith felt the heat of Elliott's gaze, but she didn't dare turn toward him yet. Not until her heart moved out of the way and she could swallow her emotions.

"My mom has stage-four breast cancer. I inherited a gene defect that puts me at risk. I have decisions to make about my own health."

Cut them off while you're still healthy. While she would encourage women to do that now, before struck with cancer, she wouldn't have agreed to surgery because a test put her at high risk.

Kevin wrapped his arm around his date. "The family just called hospice to come in."

Meredith's mouth went dry, and the room turned very warm. "Your mom is lucky to have you."

Susan's eyes seemed to dim, casting a shadow over her face. Kevin hugged her and kissed her cheek. Meredith watched them, ashamed at her insensitivity toward her doctors who felt and bled and hurt for her. And she had snapped at them, thinking they cared only about her disease.

"Ms. Montgomery."

Meredith turned toward the voice to find Jake stepping to her side.

"I thought you'd want to know that your wine is now stored in the wine cellar."

"I appreciate you taking care of that." She glanced at the woman at his side, who had long, black hair and high cheekbones with Native American features. Another gorgeous woman.

"This is my wife, Linda," Jake said.

"She's a damn good vet," Doc said. "One of these days she might leave Three Chimneys and work for me."

Linda gave him a don't-bet-your-ass laugh. "I'll come to MacKlenna Farm, Doc, but only after you retire."

Doc pressed the heel of his palm to his forehead. "Oh man, that hurts." Linda mussed his gray, thinning hair, giving him an absent-minded professor look. "I'll tell you what," he said. "If Elliott doesn't stop micromanaging my practice, I might retire sooner than you think."

Elliott looked annoyed, then his lip twitched. "Maybe I'll just fire his ass and hire ye, Linda."

Doc pressed his palm to his forehead again. "Oh man, you're both hurting me now."

Mrs. Collins appeared under the arch between the dining room and the parlor. "Dinner's ready."

David crossed the room toward Elliott as the crowd headed toward the dining room.

"I'll push him," Meredith said.

David nodded and followed the others.

"I've been watching yer face," Elliott said, kissing the tips of her fingers. "Susan upset ye talking about her mother. Yer cancer is behind ye. Ye don't have to fear it now."

It's come back, Elliott. And I don't trust you enough to tell you.

She grabbed the wheelchair's handles, and her knuckles turned white around them. "It's never a sure thing. It can always come back."

"It's not going to, Meredith. Ye beat it. Now let's go eat dinner."

Meredith bristled at his dismissive tone of voice. She pushed the wheelchair into the dining room.

Elliott pointed to the last chair next to the end at a long mahogany table that could easily fit twenty. "Sit here." He then rolled the wheelchair to the head of the table.

The waitstaff poured wine and served hot bread. As everyone munched on the buttermilk biscuits, Allie's fiancé, Bill, asked, "What happens financially, Elliott, if the farm has to pay the shareholders? Nineteen million is no small payout."

Elliott put down his butter knife and wiped his mouth with the cloth napkin. "If the shareholders sue the farm, we'll have a year or two while the case is litigated. That will give us time to liquidate assets or sell off a portion of the farm to cover the loss, if it comes to that."

"Can the farm absorb the hit?" Jake asked.

"The farm's been around almost two centuries. It's not going anywhere," Elliott said. "Ye don't have to worry about yer jobs, if that's what's on yer mind."

Whispers of relief spread quickly around the table. Without staring, she watched above the rim of her wineglass, sipping, noting tension slip from eyes and jaws. Her eyes met Elliott's. He smiled, not a bedroom smile with twinkling eyes, but a polite one. *Thank goodness.* If he smiled at her the way he did in bed, she'd melt into a messy puddle on the floor. From a distance, his eyes and lips could titillate as well as his fingers and other body parts that she couldn't think about without wearing a heated blush.

"If you're interested in riding," Doc said to Meredith, pulling her back to the here and now, "Stormy could use a workout."

"Do you think he'll let me? I thought he was a one-rider horse."

"Ye can handle him," Elliott said with a quirky grin.

She ducked her head and politely wiped her mouth. She doubted anyone at the table missed Elliott's double meaning. "I'd love to explore the farm. Is there any place I shouldn't ride?"

Jake choked and grabbed his throat, but he gave the okay signal with his other hand. "I'd stay away from the cemetery," he finally said. "Stormy threw Kit how many times, Elliott?"

Elliott's jaw tightened, and he said in a gruff voice, "Several."

"It's those damn ghosts. We can't see them, but the horses can," Doc said. "Stormy's especially sensitive when it comes to the see-through people."

Elliott moved food around the plate's flowery pattern as if trying to make designs with the vegetables.

Doc elbowed Meredith. "Elliott's even more sensitive than Stormy, but he claims he's never seen one."

Elliott dropped his fork, clanging the silver against the china. "Doc, ye know—"

"Then tell us what you think of the farm's ghosts," the vet said.

Elliott put his elbows on the table and tapped his fingertips together. "Kit saw her ghost the day she turned ten. The apparition made several appearances every year. I never saw him and I'm glad for it." He picked up his fork and jabbed a piece of turkey. "And that's enough talk of ghosts."

"We won't mention them again if you'll tell us who's entertaining at our Hogmanay," Kevin said.

"Don't ye want to be surprised?" Elliott asked.

"Allie and I are spearheading the event, Boss, and we don't know the most important part of the night."

"Wynonna," Elliott said under his breath.

Allie tapped her nails against her wineglass. "We think you should tell—"

"Wynonna?" Shock riddled across Kevin's face.

"Wynonna?" Allie's face mirrored Kevin's.

"You got Wynonna for the party?" Kevin stood and bowed. "Kemosabe, you're my hero." Before he sat down, he strummed an air guitar and sang, "*I know that look. Don't you throw that mojo on me.*"

David joined Kevin singing the song and even played drums with his fingers tapping against the table. Then Allie and Jake joined in. Meredith thought she had fallen into the dinner scene in the movie *My Best Friend's Wedding*.

On the last note, everyone except Elliott applauded and threw out titles of favorite Wynonna tunes to sing next.

Doc elbowed Meredith again. "The MacKlennas loved music. Depending on Elliott's mood, he either sings or cries."

"Wynonna came for the Derby last year, and we all fell in love with her," Allie said. "But Kevin fell the hardest."

Kevin slapped his chest, giving a crestfallen impression. "But she only had eyes for Regal Now."

"No way can you compete with that stallion," Bill said, laughing, holding his hands a good twelve inches apart.

Kevin reached behind Susan, winking, and punched the trainer in the arm. "You don't know what I got. Shut up."

"You're comparing him to the wrong horse, Bill. Check out Regal Tomorrow," Doc said.

Bill doubled over, laughing. "Have you seen Regal Tomorrow lately? Even that colt's got Kevin beat."

The laughter continued until there wasn't a dry eye at the table. Meredith thought of her own staff, and while the very diverse group was close, there had never been the kind of camaraderie she found at this table, where love abounded. Was it possible to instill that now at the winery and start a new tradition? *Change begins at the top.* She hadn't even told Cate about her tumor. How could this kind of compassion develop among coworkers when she withheld information that would draw people together? In her heart, she wanted it, but that damn glasshouse mentality kept her frozen inside its walls.

From the corner of her eye, she spotted Elliott lift his index finger an inch from the tabletop and lowered the digit to tap twice. Her watchful gaze then drifted to his face. He smiled and patted her hand.

David, sitting at the opposite end of the table, pushed back his chair. "I don't want to stop the party, but I have orders from Dr. Lyles. I have to take the host back to the cottage."

Elliott laced his warm fingers with hers. "Stay, if ye want."

She placed her other hand on top of his. "I'm with you, babe."

A few minutes later, bundled up, they made their way back to the cottage with David pushing the wheelchair.

"I caught you tonight," she said.

"At what?" Elliott asked. "And please don't say I was staring at one of the other women at the table."

Meredith heard a snicker and wasn't sure if it came from David or the wind. "Well, I should hope you weren't lusting after—"

"I have eyes for only one woman. If ye need convincing, I will, in just a few minutes."

"Either you have a guilty conscience or you've been accused of ogling women other than your date." She heard the same snicker again and turned toward David, whose stony face was visible in the landscaping lights planted along the path to the cottage.

"So what did ye catch me doing?" Elliott asked.

"Signaling David."

Elliott chuckled. "I bet ye didn't."

"Ha, I did, too. You raised your index finger and tapped the table twice."

David laughed this time. "She almost caught ye."

"What do you mean, almost?"

"Ye saw the signal to expect a signal."

Meredith stopped, but David kept pushing the wheelchair. "Wait a minute. You gave him another signal?"

"While ye were watching my finger, ye weren't looking at my other hand, were ye?" Elliott said.

"The first signal is only the warning. The second one is the message," David said.

Meredith caught up with the wheelchair. "What would happen if David missed the first signal?"

"Ye were watching me," Elliott said. "Ye weren't watching him. So ye missed his signal."

Meredith stopped again. "What was the signal?"

"A double blink," Elliott said.

"This is just a game. Isn't it?"

"It was until we tried it out at a meeting," David said.

"So you, Kevin, and David know the same signals."

"Yes," Elliott said.

She followed David and the wheelchair up the ramp to the cottage's back door. "Why didn't Kevin end the party? Didn't he see it?"

"It wasn't meant for Kevin. He has the night off," Elliott said.

Meredith held the door, and they entered the kitchen. "Are you going back to the mansion?" she asked David.

"I'll stay here tonight."

Elliott tossed his cap on the kitchen table. "He's afraid I'll forget about my leg again and try to run sprints in the middle of the night."

Meredith cringed. Would Kevin have reported to David what happened to Elliott earlier? If she found Kevin running into the bedroom embarrassing, she'd find David at the bedside discreetly covering Elliott's condom-clad penis humiliating. As hot as her face felt, it had to be the color of a Montgomery pinot noir. "I'm going upstairs to change and check email."

David pushed the wheelchair through the kitchen and out into the hallway.

"Give us thirty minutes," Elliott said.

She bounded up the stairs. *The inner circle holds no expectation of privacy.* From this point on, she'd hold her secrets as close to her chest as cards in a poker game. There would be no *tells* from her. Not a heavy breath, not a twitch or a shake, not even a sigh. Maybe the MacKlenna type of camaraderie wasn't such a good thing after all.

In her room, she booted up her laptop. There were three emails from Gregory. The first one advised her that he'd interviewed the candidate for the social media position, that it went well, and that he wanted her to meet with the man on Tuesday. His second email included PDFs of the marketing brochure, complete except for her article on the history of the winery. If she spent Tuesday afternoon and all day Wednesday working, she could have her part written. What about Elliott's surgery? Her stomach tightened at the thought of leaving him, but what could she do? She had responsibilities, and he had his clan.

She opened Greg's next email.

> *Meredith, I hate to do this electronically, but since I won't see you, I wanted you to know that I'm proposing to Cate on New Year's Eve.*

"I'll be damned." She quickly wrote back that she couldn't be happier. Now with Cate planning a wedding, Meredith knew she wouldn't burden her friend with news of her cancer. She closed the computer and chewed on her bottom lip. *I'm by myself on this one.* She walked into the bathroom and stared into the mirror. *Don't fall into the black hole tonight, Mer. There's a handsome Scotsman downstairs waiting for you.*

Chapter Forty-Nine

MacKlenna Mansion – December 31

FOLLOWING A NIGHT of making love, Meredith woke alone—again. The covers were twisted and partially tossed on the floor, and the smell of sex wafted around her, teasing her with delicious memories. They had fallen asleep in each other's arms. Elliott had awakened early, kissed her good morning, murmured what he wanted to do to her later, and left to take a shower before an early conference. She had immediately gone back to sleep. Had she ever felt so unmotivated to work? Never. The Zac Brown Band's song "Knee Deep" came to mind. *The only worry in my world is the tide gonna reach my chair.* Knowing the feeling would last temporarily gave her more freedom to enjoy it.

Stretching languidly, she wondered why no woman had ever captured Elliott—a loving, passionate man. As she considered the question, his hospital behavior came to mind. *Maybe he acts like an ass more often than those in his inner circle are willing to admit.* Then she thought back to last night's dinner. The people at the table were not all inner circle members, and they loved him, too. If his acceptance of her reconstructed breast demonstrated his compassion, then she certainly understood their devotion to him. Where did that leave her? Right where she'd been since she met him. Facing breast cancer.

She searched the bed and found her gown tangled up in the

wrinkled, knotted covers. Elliott had pulled it off her before she'd even put her head on the pillow. Magic hands, magic tongue, and magic…well…everything about him had a magical touch.

If she was going horseback riding, she needed to get up and get moving, but coffee came first. She turned the corner into the kitchen and barreled right into David, who grabbed her arms to keep her steady on her feet. "Did ye sleep well?" he asked, releasing his grip.

She didn't answer right away. Her eyes and her brain locked on the Glock in his shoulder holster. Although guns didn't scare her, David wearing one reminded her of the dangerous cloud hovering over MacKlenna Farm until the person responsible for murdering Galahad was arrested.

"I did." She glanced around the kitchen. "Where'd you put Elliott?"

"He's working in his office."

"At the mansion?"

"Here at the cottage." David pointed toward the hallway. "It's across from the living room."

"I think I'll pop in and see him before I go riding." She headed out of the kitchen.

"His attorney and board of directors are with him," David said.

She made a quick U-turn. "Thanks for letting me know."

"Don't get me wrong. Elliott's eyes would light up, but I think ye'd be embarrassed." He poured a cup of coffee and handed it to her.

"You've got me figured out." She took the cup and sipped.

"I think ye expect privacy, and his lifestyle doesn't put a high priority on that." David leaned his hip against the counter and drank his coffee. A comfortable silence settled between them. After a couple of sips, he said, "Kevin should have been more sensitive when he barged in on ye yesterday."

The heat of embarrassment went from her scalp to her chest. She looked down at the polished oak floor. "You wouldn't have come running if you heard Elliott screaming?"

"I would have come running."

She looked into his eyes. "Then what are you saying?"

"Knowing he was with ye, I wouldn't have been there as quickly." David quirked his shoulders. "We have different roles in Dr. Fraser's life. Kevin's his aide. That means he's always within hearing distance, regardless of the situation." David refilled his cup. "How's yer coffee?"

"It's good. Did you make it?"

"Hard to mess up in one of these *do-all* machines."

She noticed the time on a wall clock. "Oh, goodness. I need to get dressed." She chewed her lip. "They'll see me if I go up the front steps, won't they?"

"Take the rear stairs."

She looked around, puzzled. "Where are they?"

He put down his coffee cup and waved for her to follow. Across from Elliott's bedroom, David opened a door that she'd assumed was a closet. A solid wood spiral staircase hugged the back wall. "This will take ye to the guest suite."

"What was this?"

"A bathroom. Elliott had a half-bath built at the other end of the hall."

"Handy. Where does it come out? I've opened all the doors in the bedroom."

"The wardrobe."

Meredith laughed, shaking her head. "The Lion, the Witch and the Wardrobe. Instead of Narnia, you fall into Elliott's bed. What a sense of humor."

David's mouth twitched. "If ye're going riding now, I'll call the stallion barn."

"Tell them I'll be there in thirty minutes." She trucked up the steps. At the top, she pushed the wardrobe's doors, and they flung open. She had tried to open it before but the knobs wouldn't turn and she assumed it was locked. The design and creativity both awed and tickled her. "God, the man's got an ego." *With a tongue like he has, he deserves to have a big ego.*

She took a quick shower before dressing in winter riding breeches, jacket, and tall boots. With a bounce to her step, she headed out to go riding. Her eyes widened when she entered the main stallion barn. Definitely five-star horse accommodations. The rubber-matted floors of the six seventeen-by-seventeen-foot stalls were covered with straw. The walls were paneled in dark oak. A brass nameplate hung on each stall door. Several of the stallions' names were familiar to her. They had all won a Grade One stakes race. *Impressive stable.*

The stalls surrounded an open, brick-floored area with a pointed ceiling rising to a cupola. Gorgeous. A natural horse smell permeated the air. Off to the side was a padded-walled room where the stallions covered the mares. The floor consisted of cut-up tires. Only the best for multimillion-dollar Thoroughbreds.

A groom had already put Stormy under tack and wrapped the reins around the back of the saddle for safety. She approached the horse's front shoulder and patted him, cooing softly.

Bill walked out of the breeding shed. "Good morning, Meredith."

"Is there anything I should know before I mount up?"

The trainer put his hands on his hips, elbows jutting out, and rocked back and forth on his boot heels. "Stormy's not difficult, but he is a stallion. I don't know how much experience you have."

"Elliott said I should be able to handle him. Would you mind giving me a leg up?" She pulled the reins from around the saddle, grabbed them in a half cross, put her right hand on the pommel, and caught a lock of mane.

Bill stood next to her. "You ready?"

She bent her knee. "Ready." With his assistance, she sprang up and came down nice and soft on Stormy's back.

"I'm impressed. Even legging you up, you did most of the work. Came down light in your saddle."

"I ride a retired racehorse." She slipped her feet into the stirrups and then tied a double loop knot in the reins. "He bolted the first time I tried to mount him. I learned to come down on his back as gently as possible."

"What's his name?"

"Quiet Dancer."

Bill whistled. "No wonder Elliott said you could handle Stormy. He's a pussycat compared to your horse."

"Let's hope so." She eased Stormy out of the barn and into the razor-sharp sunshine bursting from a trough of blue sky. "Okay, boy. How about we do a fly-by in front of the cottage?" She doubted Elliott would be watching, but on the off chance he was, she wanted to wave. A rush of disappointment swamped her when she didn't see him. "Oh well, where to now, Stormy?"

They followed the path that circled the stallion barn complex, then headed out into the pasture where she gave the horse some slack in the reins and squeezed her thighs. He galloped at a fast pace with hooves thundering on the snow-packed grass. They raced alongside the fence that stitched a meandering seam through acres of rolling hills. When they reached the corner of the pasture, she turned and headed north, arriving at the one place everyone had told her to avoid—the cemetery.

After a cautious look around the knoll, she dismounted and tied the reins to a wrought-iron fence encircling the small cemetery nestled under a large oak tree. The massive branches testified to its age, old and endearing, and probably planted at the same time the MacKlennas dug the first grave.

Thomas MacKlenna's monolith commanded the plot of ground filled with a couple of dozen graves. The gate squeaked when she pushed it ajar. Careful not to walk on a grave, she sidestepped her way to the farm founder's monument and read the inscription on the native limestone marker:

THOMAS SEAN MACKLENNA II
HE SAW WHAT OTHERS DID NOT.
HE LIVED WHAT OTHERS COULD NOT.
HE DREAMED WHAT OTHERS DARED NOT.
JANUARY 25, 1770—JANUARY 25, 1853

The wind slithered by her, rustling a pile of dead leaves in the fencerow, sounding like whisperings of indiscernible secrets. A double layer of goose bumps covered her arms. Circling the cemetery, she found Sean and Mary's markers. A year earlier, Kit had stood over her parents' graves. Grief was not foreign to Meredith. How was Kit coping with the anniversary? Probably similar to the way Meredith coped—with tears.

She brushed snow from a concrete bench and sat. There had been so much heartache and more to come, at least for her.

"It's all behind you," Elliott had said. "You beat the odds." But she hadn't beaten anything, except her heart into an unrecognizable shape, and since it wasn't a pliable organ, it couldn't be returned to its original condition.

A swirl of light and white vapor appeared in front of her. She jumped up, retreating toward the wrought iron fence behind her, but she tripped over a footstone and landed flat on her back in the snow. The body of a person began to form. First the legs, then the torso, arms, and head. She could see through him, but his form and features were very distinctive. He wore a double-breasted frock coat with a wide velvet collar, a fancy silk vest, and an ascot. His eyebrows furrowed, then released.

"*It's you*," Meredith said.

He held out his hand to help her up, but her hand passed through his. She scrunched her face, relieved that she was wearing gloves. *Okay, that was weird.*

He made an elegant bow, lifting his hat and fixing her with an enchanting smile.

"You're Cullen Montgomery. Why are you here?"

Stormy neighed softly, and the ghost patted the horse's head. His big brown eyes stared at the ghost, unafraid. The ghost looked at Stormy, then at Meredith, then back at Stormy. The horse nodded his head as if the ghost were communicating with him.

"I can't tell what you're trying to say to me," Meredith said.

The ghost took flight and floated above the cemetery, swirling around headstones until he perched atop a granite stone in the back corner. Meredith read the inscription beneath him.

KITHERINA KOONCE MACKLENNA
LIVED HER LIFE AS A GRACIOUS
SOUTHERN WOMAN
OCTOBER 14, 1930—DECEMBER 1, 2008

"This is Granny Mac's grave, isn't it?" Meredith asked.

The ghost rested his elbows on his knees, nodding slowly.

"I don't know what you're trying to tell me." She let out a weak laugh. "What do you want me to know?"

His eyes darkened, reminding her of her father. He ran his hand along the edge of the monument, floating above the headstone again before evaporating in the cold December air.

She turned in frantic, dizzying circles searching for him, peering into shadows and behind monuments. "Come back," she pleaded, but he didn't reappear.

Kit's grandmother and I have nothing in common.

Nothing? What about Granny Mac's cancer? Panic gushed into Meredith's throat. When Granny Mac lay dying, Elliott never left her side. He cleaned up after her and sang to her. Is that what her ancestor wanted her to know? That Elliott would take care of her. The thought of Elliott cleaning up after her or wiping sweat from her hairless head made her sick. She rushed the fence and threw up on the other side of the wrought iron.

That won't happen. I'll never tell him.

Gripping the fence's spindles, she slid to the ground and wept. Snow seeped into her riding pants, chilling her, and she began to shiver from cold and fear.

Get up. You can't stay here like this.

She stood, legs shaky. What in God's name had happened? Her resolve and fearlessness were melting faster than snow during an early March warm spell. Unless she stopped the thaw, she'd be nothing but a puddle of muddy water, useless for anything more than growing weeds. Everyone told her to stay away from the cemetery. Why hadn't she ridden in the opposite direction?

Meredith grabbed Stormy's reins, jumped up on the crumbling rock wall adjoining the cemetery, mounted, then galloped into the brisk December wind with tears forming icicles on her lashes.

Chapter Fifty

The Cottage at MacKlenna Farm – December 31

ELLIOTT SAT AT the head of the conference table, striving to present an image of authority instead of an invalid. He and David had gone two rounds over Elliott's insistence that he sit in a conference chair. David wouldn't budge, insisting Elliott needed the support of the wheelchair's leg extension. Now that the meeting steered into a second hour, he had to admit losing the bruising match had enabled him to keep his mind focused on business, not on pain.

Jim Manning, with Harrison's assistance, had spent the first hour explaining to the five members of the board of directors the ramifications in the event the insurance company refused to pay the claim. At the end of Manning's presentation, the board moved into executive session, excluding Doc, Harrison, Jake, and Allie. As the board's attorney, Manning stayed.

The chairman of the board asked Elliott, "Now that we know we might have to liquidate assets or sell a portion of the farm, what's your plan to prevent that from happening?"

"Find the person responsible," Elliott said.

"And if you can't?" the chairman fired back.

"Prepare for a lawsuit." Elliott put a leash on his frustration while the board members grumbled among themselves.

Manning stacked his papers, slipped them into his briefcase, and clicked the latch. The sound drew attention to him. "We have a handful of detectives working on this. We'll find who did it."

"Harrison usually notifies me when he has unusual expenditures. Who's paying the bill?" the only female board member, a retired financial controller, asked.

Elliott tented his fingers. "I don't want anyone outside of this room to know what we're doing. To protect the integrity of the investigation, I paid the advance."

"That says to me you suspect someone on staff," she said.

Elliott shook his head. "It's only to prevent unintentional leaks."

"What have your detectives discovered?" The chairman's Groucho Marx bushy brows formed a straight line above his nose.

"When we have something, we'll give ye a report. For now, it's best for the farm if information concerning the direction of the investigation is limited to those who need to know."

Another board member pushed his chair away from the conference table, scraping the floor. "*You* suspect one of us?"

"Hell, calm down." Elliott's tone matched the ripple of tension in the room. "Ye wouldn't have learned about the investigation if I doubted the integrity of the board."

The chairman folded his notebook with a snap. "I think we're done here." He stood. "Keep us in the loop with whatever you can share."

Elliott sucked in a breath of relief as the board members gathered their coats and left the room.

Jim took a sip of bottled water. "David and Chuck might not find the person responsible for killing Galahad."

Elliott wheeled the chair away from the table and turned toward the window's scenic view of the paddocks and stallion barns. "I've lived on MacKlenna Farm and loved it for almost thirty years. If it loses its reputation and assets over this incident, I personally will be held accountable. Two hundred years of honor and tradition will come to an end, and so will my tenure."

"No one will ask for your resignation." Jim tossed the empty water bottle into the trash can as if it were a basketball.

"They won't have to."

Manning shrugged. "Well, it won't be accepted."

Elliott inhaled deeply, hearing the whisper of breath at the back of his throat. Then he exhaled, letting go of a bit of stress. "Ye're coming to the party, aren't ye?"

"Wouldn't miss it. Now, tell me about Meredith Montgomery. She's not your usual playmate."

"She's *not* a playmate. And as soon as this mess with Galahad is resolved and I can walk again, we're leaving the country for a long vacation."

"Doesn't she have a launch coming up?"

"I'm sure her underlings can handle most of it."

Jim leaned against the table, folding his arms across his chest. "If you think that, you don't know her very well. Have you read the article in *Wine Digest?* If not, read it. You might learn something about this woman you profess to be so interested in."

"I don't drink wine. Why would I read a magazine devoted to it?"

Jim shook his head. "Sometimes you can be the biggest ass. Are you looking for a way to sabotage the relationship? If so, you'll manage to do that before the weekend is over."

Elliott pshawed. "Ye don't know what ye're talking about."

"No. I'm just a dumb ex-jock you pay five hundred thousand dollars in legal fees to every year."

"She had breast cancer." The words shot out, loud and distracting like his deer-hunting rifle.

"How long ago?"

"Five years."

"What's your problem? You think your dick will catch it like an STD?"

"What if it comes back?"

Jim pushed away from the conference table and joined Elliott at the window. "This isn't about Meredith having cancer. This is about you taking a risk and loving someone who might leave you."

Everyone does. Why not her? "Go to work."

"I am at work," Jim said.

"Counseling isn't yer expertise."

Jim loosened his tie. "The hell it isn't. That's half of what I do for you."

"I need a drink."

"You need therapy, and I'm tired of telling you."

"How come our conversations always end in the same place?"

"You tell me. You're brilliant at what you do. You have one of the most recognizable and regarded names in the Thoroughbred industry, and I'm talking worldwide. You have the perfect blend of business acumen, horse sense, and marketing ability. But when it comes to your health and your personal life, you're fucked up."

"She loves Scotland, horses, and whisky."

"Well, there you go. She's definitely your kind of woman."

"And she can sit a horse. Look." Elliott pointed out the window. Meredith cantered Stormy toward the stallion barn. God, she looked gorgeous. Perfectly aligned in the saddle; as perfectly aligned as she had been riding Elliott hours earlier. His dick hardened, and he shifted slightly in the wheelchair.

"You really should read that article. Besides being an equestrian, beautiful, and wealthy, her handicap would put most golfers to shame." Jim slipped on his overcoat and picked up his briefcase. "Think about what I said. I still have that list of psychiatrists for you to consider. Maybe I'll email you the names because you'll never ask. At least if you have the list, you might get a hair up your ass one day and make the call."

David knocked before entering the room. "Yer trainer is here."

Jim walked toward the door. "I heard Wynonna is performing at the shindig. My bride and I are looking forward to it."

"That's why I didn't want the board to know any more than necessary. There're no secrets on this farm."

David pushed Elliott out into the hall.

"Call me if you need anything," Manning said on his way out.

When they were alone, Elliott asked David, "Did ye talk to Meredith this morning?"

He wheeled Elliott into the exercise room located off the kitchen. "She looked rested and excited to go riding."

"Tell her I'd like to have lunch with her."

"If I don't see her before I leave, I'll tell Kevin to give her the message."

Elliott stripped off his sweater and put on a University of Kentucky T-shirt. "Ye still on track to finish canvassing Jefferson County construction companies today?"

David helped Elliott ease to the exercise bench, where he slipped off his one shoe and dropped his trousers. "And Jeffersonville, Indiana. Then we'll head east."

Elliott pulled up a pair of gym shorts. "We've got to get a break."

"We've got too many people working this case not to find Gates. I'll call if I have any news. I won't get back until late tonight."

Ted walked in carrying two bottles of water. "You ready to start? This isn't going to be easy."

"Don't kill him," David said to Elliott's trainer. "He's got a bonny lass waiting for him."

Ted laughed. "We've been working together… What? Ten years now? I don't think there's ever been a time when a beautiful woman wasn't waiting."

"This one's different," Elliott said.

"Wow." Ted widened his eyes for emphasis. "I think I heard that back in the summer and before that, hmm, February maybe, and before that—"

Elliott did an iPhone swipe with his finger. Instead of changing screens, he changed the conversation. "Let's get to work. And don't hurt my fucking leg."

Chapter Fifty-One

MacKlenna Farm – December 31

MEREDITH STOOD UNDER jets of pulsing hot water, letting the cemetery trauma wash down the drain. Was the inference she drew the one her ancestor intended? She had no way of knowing, so she had to let it go. If Elliott knew something had upset her, he'd drag out the reason. *Which one do you want to hear? That Kit's ghost is my great-great-great-great-grandfather or that I have cancer. You can't deal with either one.* And neither could she. Not today.

She turned off the water and grabbed a towel. Today she needed to review Springsteen's tour rider and the downtime rider to be sure she met all accommodations. Bruce and the band's requirements for some semblance of home on the road were quirky, but not as outrageous as other celebs she'd dealt with. A guitar security guard, cinnamon raisin bagels, fresh fruit, and whey powder she could handle, but the request for beluga caviar didn't belong with the band's working-class image. Quirky. You bet.

She rubbed a three-butter lotion bar on her arms, breasts, belly, and freshly shaved legs while still warm and damp, hydrating her skin and giving it a naturally sweet chocolate and fresh scent. She'd discovered yesterday that Elliott found the aroma of unrefined cocoa butter intoxicating, and he couldn't stop lapping her up with an erotic dance of his tongue. She shivered, deliciously wanting more.

Her cell phone rang with a call from an 859 number she didn't recognize. "Meredith Montgomery," she said.

"This is Kevin. I'm coordinating calendars. Are you free for lunch at one o'clock?"

The clock on the bedside table read eleven fifteen. "Are we eating at the mansion or here?"

"The mansion."

"I've got some work to do that will keep me busy until the last minute. I'll meet him there. Does he have anything on his calendar for this afternoon?"

"I know he was checking the movie listings, in case you're interested."

"Thanks, Kevin. We'll talk about it at lunch."

Quickly, she dried her hair, put on makeup, and dressed in jeans and a sweater. Before pulling up the contract, she set the alarm on her computer.

At twelve fifteen, she hurried over to the mansion.

Parked in the driveway were service trucks with logos indicating that a florist, a catering business, and an electrician were on site. As soon as Meredith entered the house, she considered turning around and leaving. Chaos abounded. The cleaning crew busily dusted and vacuumed, four women with baskets of flowers filled vases and containers with gorgeous color, and two men with J&H Electrical on their jackets tracked snow into the clean foyer to the disapproval of the cleaning staff.

Then she heard Elliott's voice booming above the commotion. "We're having a hell of a party. Don't fuss at me."

Louise hustled down the hallway toward Meredith. "Thank God ye're here. Take him. We dinna care where. Just get him out of the house. He's driving us nuts."

Meredith laughed. "So, what's new?"

"Nothing a'tall, dearie. Just please put him somewhere he canna cause trouble."

Kevin burst from the parlor. "Take one of the limos." He handed her a printout of movie listings. "Wynonna's entourage is due here for rehearsal, and we're not ready. Cameron Thomson just arrived from Scotland with the food, and Mrs. Collins is shooing everyone from *her* kitchen."

"And I havena had a chance to say more than hello to Evelyn," Louise said.

"I'll kill him if he doesn't get out of here," Allie said, following on Kevin's heels. "He expects a minute-by-minute accounting. We've got everything under control but *him*."

Meredith pressed her hand against her mouth to hide a smile. Her staff would have similar complaints. "Where is he?"

"In the dining room," Evelyn said, coming down the stairs. "Get him out of here. He canna do what he usually does, and he doesna need to be doing whatever that is anyway."

Louise slipped her arm around her lover. "Meredith is taking him away now, aren't ye?" she asked, giving Meredith a pleading look.

"How could I say no?" She entered the dining room to find Elliott at the head of the table, typing on his laptop. She leaned over and kissed him. "Do you want to go to bed or to a movie?"

He pushed away from the table. "I don't want to see a fooked movie."

She straightened, narrowing her eyes. "Change your attitude."

"Consider it changed, wee sweetheart." Then he yelled, "Mrs. Collins."

The woman ran into the dining room. "I've too much to do to jump when you yell."

"Will ye pack us a lunch? We're leaving."

She threw up praying hands. "Thank you, Lord."

Elliott wheeled his chair into the foyer. "If anyone needs anything, tell me now. I'll be out of contact until dinner."

"Nothing," Allie said.

"Dinna need anything," Louise said.

"Enjoy yerself," Evelyn said.

Kevin grabbed Elliott's jacket and cap from the coat stand. "Do you want me to push the wheelchair?"

"No. Meredith and I will be at the cottage. Mrs. Collins is sending over lunch. Don't bother us." He put on his coat. "Make sure Jake checks the tent carefully. Support, leaks, heat, sound. Everything."

"We're on it, Boss," Kevin said, opening the front door.

"And ask him for a report on security detail for the farm and the party."

Allie wheeled the chair toward the door. "It's all on the hundred-point bullet list you gave us."

"Be sure to notify the fire department," Elliott said. "And put my laptop back on my desk."

Meredith noticed Kevin and Allie rolling their eyes at each other. As soon as the front door of the mansion closed behind them, Meredith could have sworn she heard a collective sigh of relief. "What were you doing in there? They all wanted to shoot you."

"I asked Allie to review her spreadsheet with me. I wanted to be sure she and Kevin were on target. Ye would have thought I'd asked for her first born."

Meredith set the wheelchair's brake while she slipped on her gloves. "What'd you do to Louise?"

"I asked for the menu."

"You gave them jobs to do, but you didn't trust that they would do them. Is that it?" She released the brake and pushed the chair down the ramp from the portico to the brick walk.

"I know they'll do what they're supposed to do. I just wanted confirmation."

His staff gave Meredith a glimpse of what would happen at the winery the day before the launch. What could she do to ensure *Cailean* would launch without snafus and keep her from pulling out her hair? She cringed at the thought of her hair coming out in clumps. Why did everything always circle back to her cancer?

"How was yer ride?" Elliott asked.

She stiffened and said quickly, "Perfect." Then after a moment she added, "Do you think Kit would sell Stormy? I'd like to buy him."

"He's not for sale."

Chapter Fifty-Two

The Cottage on MacKlenna Farm – December 31

SEVERAL HOURS LATER, Elliott and Meredith leaned against the headboard naked, checking email on their laptops with empty dinner trays on the floor next to the clothes they'd ripped off.

"Thank God," Elliott said.

Meredith looked at him curiously, her head to one side. "For what?"

"David talked to a foreman who supervised Gates on a job last year. Said he got a call a few months back asking for a recommendation. He didn't write down the name of the company, but he was certain it was a Kentucky construction company."

"That's good news. Now you know you're on the right track."

"It will be when we find him, prove he killed Galahad, and that he never worked at MacKlenna Farm."

She put her laptop aside, scooted down under the sheet, and rose up on her elbow, watching him. "Proving he was never an employee should be the easy part."

He gave her nipple a tweak. "Not necessarily."

"Ouch," she teased. "Please don't tell me the farm hires illegals."

He quit teasing her nipple, stroked her entire breast, and then her neck. "We're a legit operation. But until the farm stopped growing tobacco in the early 1990s, paying day workers in cash was the norm. It'd be hard to prove he did or didn't work here." His voice grew husky.

"Why would he want to claim he did?"

Elliott nuzzled her neck. "If his goal is to ruin the farm, and he's caught, what's he got to lose?"

"Would he even know to claim he was an employee?"

"He's an asshole. There's no telling. David will find Gates, and when he does, he'll get the information he's looking for."

"That sounds ominous." Her voice grew breathy from the heat Elliott created with his lips and fingers.

He tugged her toward him. "Come here and let's pick up where we stopped before lunch interrupted us."

Chapter Fifty-Three

MacKlenna Farm – New Year's Day

NEW YEAR'S DAY MORNING arrived in a blur and, while Elliott met with David and Chuck, Meredith intended to go riding. Elliott had told her he'd be tied up most of the day and would meet her at six o'clock for cocktails before the party started at seven. Allie had made her an afternoon appointment for a facial, waxing, and manicure. Other than a morning ride and an afternoon at the spa, she had nothing on her calendar until she ran into a gorgeous thirty-something-year-old man in the kitchen.

"Hi. I'm Meredith Montgomery."

A warm, solid grip met hers. "Ted Jenkins, Elliott's trainer."

She smiled at the black-haired, black-eyed man dressed in gym shorts and a T-shirt that accentuated his muscled chest, arms, and abs. Her perusal stopped there. "You're the one member of the inner circle I haven't met or talked to in the last ten days."

"I've been on vacation. Missed the jaunts to Scotland and the hospital."

"Either you have a healthy tan all year, or you've been someplace warm."

"Hawaii."

Now she laughed and held out her hands pretending they were balancing scales. "Hawaii"—she lifted one hand—"or Christmas at Fraser House." She lifted the other. "That's a toughie."

His brows knitted together. "Fraser House, huh?" He leaned against the counter, crossed his ankles, and studied her. "Stressed, meticulous, wealthy." He cocked his head and squinted. "A year either side of forty. No cosmetic surgeries on your face. Nice rack. Good skin tone. Vegetarian. Daily exercise. Probably power yoga, weight training, running, plus two or three riding sessions a week. Am I right?"

Meredith picked her jaw up off the floor.

He seemed not to take his remarks too seriously, giving her a light shrug. "I've got time for a yoga class, if you're interested?"

"I'm going riding."

"Then you need to stretch."

She found Ted arrogant and obnoxious, but he had her placed in the top hole of the pegboard puzzle found in every Cracker Barrel restaurant from Texas to New York. A hard task for anyone after only saying hello. That earned enough respect from her to take a second look at the young man. If he was Elliott's trainer, he must be good. She'd had several yoga instructors she disliked but enjoyed their classes. What the heck? Yoga, then riding. Why not? "Let me change clothes. Where should I meet you?"

"In the training room."

"Where's that?"

He pointed over his shoulder to the far side of the kitchen. "Through that door."

She scrunched her face as she mentally tried to place a gym into what she knew of the floor plan. The door must open into a hallway that led to the back of the other wing. "I'll go change. Is there a password to get into the gym?"

Ted gave a deep rumbling laugh that tickled her. "No, but the Grinch might ask for your first born."

"Well," she said, throwing up her hands, "he'll never get one from me. See you in a few."

Two hours later, sweating, Meredith entered the kitchen to grab two bottles of water out of the refrigerator. "You'd be a hit in the Valley. If you're ever interested in moving west, I'll give you the name of a studio that would be a great fit for you. Lots of stressed-out, professional vegetarians."

"Tempting, but I couldn't leave Elliott."

"How long have you worked together?"

Ted took a long drink of water. "Ten years now."

"Then you knew him before he got hurt."

"He was a long-distance runner. I helped him train for his triathlons. After he got hurt, we developed a new fitness regime. He works out twice a day, depending on his schedule, which changes daily. Usually an hour in the morning and an hour late at night."

Or who he has in his bed. "What does he do when he goes out of town?"

"I usually travel with him, but I've been on vacation. Just got back yesterday."

"You do an incredible job. His body fat must be close to zero."

"We try to stay at ten percent."

Meredith wiped sweat from her face using the exercise towel wrapped around her neck. "Thanks for the workout. I needed it."

"I'll be here tomorrow morning if you want to switch to weights or do yoga again."

"Same time?" she asked.

"Either before or after Elliott's workout."

Meredith threw her empty water bottle into the recycling bin under the sink. "See you tomorrow." She walked away, but he called her back.

"Elliott said you were special. Honestly, I razzed him because I've heard it too many times, but he got it right for once. Hang in there. He's not doing so well right now."

"Physically, I know," she said.

"It's not just his leg. It's the anniversary of Sean and Mary's deaths, and this business with Galahad is eating him up. I'm afraid he's abusing pain medication and drinking too much again. God, I know he's in pain, but David and Kevin don't monitor his dosage like they should. Somebody needs to watch him now that Kit's not here, and I'm not around all the time."

"Neither am I, Ted. And that's a conversation you need to have with Kevin and David."

Ted broke eye contact. "I have."

"I've learned there're topics, like Kit, that you don't broach with Elliott."

"I'm so mad at her." Ted's face flashed with anger. "That's the main reason I didn't go to Scotland. If I got anywhere near her, I'd go bust the estate's door down and haul her ass back here. She's got more guts than any woman I've ever met, and for her to cower out is not the Kit MacKlenna I know." He brushed his sweaty arm across his forehead. "I don't mean to be gossiping." He finished his water and threw away the bottle. "I'll see you at the party."

"Are you bringing a date?"

Ted relaxed his shoulders and smiled. "My partner's name is Laurence. He's a PT at Central Baptist Hospital."

"Oh. *Oh*," Meredith said again.

He must have read surprise on her face. "Most straight men have a problem with gay trainers, but it's never been an issue with Elliott. He's tolerant, except if you mention seeing a ghost. Then he'll snap faster than a woman with PMS."

Meredith didn't want to laugh, but the remark coming from Ted was too funny. "You're right. Well, thanks again." She hurried off to change back into her riding clothes. A few minutes later, she headed over to the barn, thinking through all Ted had told her and what she'd discovered on her own. People loved and adored Elliott. He had a world-renowned reputation for honor and integrity, and he was a passionate and considerate lover. But she didn't trust him. Not with her secrets, and not with her heart.

Meredith bumped into Harrison rushing out of the barn. "Excuse me," he said, not even taking notice of who he'd run into. Then he glanced up and met Meredith's eyes. "Oh, it's you. I thought you went home."

"I did, but I came back for the party." She worked at being polite, difficult to do with ants crawling up her legs.

"Don't you live in California? That's a long way to go to turn around and come back. Expensive, too."

"Napa." If she didn't get away from him, she'd soon be stomping her feet to shake off the ants.

"The Valley, huh? Do you grow grapes?"

Be gracious. You're a Montgomery. "I own a family winery."

He gave his chin a slight lift. "I'm a wine aficionado myself. What's the name? I'll have to sample your wine if I can find any at my local liquor store."

"Montgomery Winery."

Harrison's Adam's apple bobbed. "That's no small winery. Hey, didn't I read you're about to launch a new signature wine?"

"February sixteenth."

"If you come for another visit, bring some," he said, jumping down from his arrogant stepladder and rubbing his hands together with childlike glee. "We'll have our own little tasting."

Surely, she and Louise weren't the only ones to see his creepy side. "Elliott's serving my wine at the party tonight. Let me know what you think. Now, if you'll excuse me, there's a twelve-hundred-pound stallion in the barn waiting to go for a run." She walked past him, shaking off the tingling sensation.

Stormy stood in his stall, already under tack. Ears up.

"You going to ride now, Ms. Montgomery?" a groom asked.

She glanced at his name tag. "Yes, Peter. Thanks for getting him ready."

"No problem, ma'am. Stormy's one of my favorites." He opened the stall door and led the horse out to the center of the dark-paneled barn. She bent her knee, and Peter gave her a leg up. "He's acting a bit frisky. Don't let him get away from you."

Stormy felt different today. She couldn't put her finger on it—anxious, maybe. Or maybe the anxiety belonged to her. No, she didn't think so, not after Ted's yoga class. She decided not to stay out as long as she did yesterday. "I'll be out about an hour."

"I'll be here when you get back," Peter said.

After a half hour spin around the barns and paddocks, Meredith lightly nudged the Thoroughbred's quivering flanks with her knees, and he took off across the pasture in a gallop. The sweaty silklike skin covering his rippling muscles glistened in the morning sun.

An icy branch broke off a tree with a loud snap and landed in the fencerow only a few yards away. Stormy planted his feet, reared, and spun on his haunches, almost pitching her over his shoulder. Then he took off, galloping toward a three-foot-high rock fence.

He's going to jump.

She didn't know the type of ground beneath the snow. Was it icy? Could he keep his footing? Would he refuse at the last second and toss her over the fence? She tightened her legs. Stormy sailed over the rocks but caught his rear leg. He landed off, snorted loudly, and limped. She pulled him up and swung down. His left rear leg was bleeding. He drew it up close to his body.

"It's okay, boy. It's okay. Let me have a look." He gave her a fearful whinny and turned his head into her, leaning it against her chest. She hugged him. "I'll take care of you."

When she saw the extent of his injury, bile rushed to the back of her throat. The left rear leg was a bloody mess. He had cut the skin on his long bone down to his ankle. She gagged, almost throwing up. *I've got to wrap it. I've got to do something.* There was a trail of blood from the wall to where Stormy stood several feet away.

She yanked off her scarf. "I'm going to put this around your leg. I won't hurt you." She kept her voice low and calm, although she didn't feel calm at all. Her neck and shoulders bunched into tight knots.

He grunted but stood still while she wrapped his leg. Her hands shook. She gave up trying to tie a knot and tucked the loose ends inside the wrap instead. "There. That will hold until Doc can fix you up."

She wrapped her arm around his neck. "I'm going to call Doc. You can't walk home." Her cell phone was in her jacket pocket. She called the farm and asked for the vet. "It's Meredith. An icy branch broke off and scared Stormy. He took a rock fence and scraped the skin off his rear leg. It looks bad."

"Where are you?" Doc asked in a gruff voice.

"In the fencerow, parallel to Old Frankfort. There's a large white house directly across the street."

"Keep him still. We'll bring a van."

She unsaddled the horse and continued to talk calmly to him. "Doc's on his way." If he had a permanent injury, she'd never forgive herself. She considered calling Elliott but decided to wait until she knew what was wrong. The thought of giving him bad news today made her want to cower in the corner. "I hear the van. Just a few more minutes."

Doc and Peter hurried toward her. "How is he?" Doc asked.

"Staying still."

He untied the blood-soaked scarf. "Damn." He ran his hands up and down the horse's leg. Doc's face reddened, his jaw tightened. "We need to take him to Rood & Riddle Equine Hospital. He needs X-rays, and my machine is being serviced."

"Can I go with you?" she asked.

"What?"

"Can I go with you? I want to be sure he'll be okay."

"No. Go back to the house."

"What will I tell Elliott?" she asked.

Doc rubbed his forehead. "Get in the truck."

Peter backed up as close as possible, leaving room to extend the ramp. Then he jumped out to get Stormy onboard.

"Take him on slow. Don't let him move around," Doc said.

"I ain't gonna let something bad happen to another horse," Peter said.

Meredith climbed into the front seat, shivering, more out of fear than because of the temperature. "Shouldn't we tell Elliott?" she said to Doc.

"Not until I know what's wrong with him. What happened?"

She tapped her foot against the floorboard, going over what happened again and again. "When the branch snapped, it sounded like a tree crashing to the ground. Stormy pulled up, reared, then took off. He caught his back leg on the rock wall. I hope he's all right. I'm not sure Elliott could handle more bad news."

Something close to bitterness twisted Doc's mouth. "Let's see what the X-rays show."

She fidgeted in her seat, staring at her tightly laced fingers. She untangled them, placed her hands on her thighs, and sat stiff and ramrod straight.

They could have flown to California quicker than Doc drove to the northwest side of Lexington. He called the hospital en route, and they were expecting Stormy when the van pulled up in front of the admission office located in the center of the compound. Doc and a staff vet took the horse while Meredith stayed in the waiting room. An hour later, Doc and an older man came out to meet her.

"How is he? Can I see him?" she asked, not waiting for introductions.

"Stormy skinned the lower part of his leg and broke off the top part of the outside sesamoid," the hospital vet said. "The leg is swollen now. As soon as the swelling goes down, we'll take more pictures to see if there's additional damage. I don't think there is, but we won't know for sure until we get a better look. We'll keep him in a stall with his leg bandaged for several days."

"Does he have permanent damage?" Meredith asked.

The hospital vet hesitated a moment. "If he were racing, I'd recommend retiring him to stud."

She glanced at her cell phone. "Elliott should know about this, but I can't tell him."

"We'll leave it to Doc."

"Great," Doc said. "This time I get to tell him his horse is alive but has a bum leg."

The vet slapped Doc on the shoulder. "When he's healed, he'll need to do only light work for a while, but I doubt he's ridden much since Kit moved to Scotland."

"How am I going to explain to Elliott that I hurt Kit's horse?" Meredith asked.

"From what Doc said, Stormy got away from you."

"To Elliott, that won't be an acceptable reason," Meredith said.

"Stormy had a rough spring and summer," the vet said. "I don't know where Kit took him, but they were gone a couple of months. He lost weight, and it took several weeks to get him back in condition. He could have injured the leg while he was gone. We don't know."

"Where is he now? Can I see him?"

"We keep our orthopedic patients in Barn Four. You can see him anytime, but check in at admissions, and someone will escort you to his stall."

A horse whinnied, and Meredith stretched her neck to look down the corridor.

"That's not Stormy. He's already been moved to the barn," the vet said.

"I guess I should call Elliott," she said.

"Wait just a bit longer. He'll want the results from the additional X-rays. Matter of fact," the vet said, "I'll just bring the results with me tonight and talk to Elliott about Stormy's condition."

She scrubbed her face with her hands. *Stormy will be okay, and Elliott will be furious.*

Peter hustled into the waiting room. "Doc, you just got a call. They need you at the broodmare barn."

The vet turned to go. "See you tonight at the party unless there's an emergency here and I can't get away."

As Meredith slid into the truck, she checked the time. "Do you pass Midway on the way to the farm?"

"We can go back that way," Doc said.

"I have a three thirty appointment at a salon on Winter Street." It seemed heartless to leave Stormy and go to the spa, but what else could she do? Stormy was in good hands.

Peter put the truck in gear. "I'll get you there in time, Ms. Montgomery."

Doc stared out the window, appearing deep in thought. Finally, he roused himself as though coming out of trance and said, "I'll tell Elliott when I get the blood work later tonight. No point in ruining his evening. I'll take the heat if he blows up."

"I thought the hospital vet intended to tell him," Meredith said.

"It's my job, not his," Doc said.

Her stomach churned with an icky feeling, but Doc was right, and she nodded in acquiescence. He wasn't the only one who would take heat over this. She could bank a bet that Elliott would blame her…if not for causing the injury, for keeping silent.

When Doc dropped her off at the spa, he seemed hard-edged, but she chalked it up to the situation.

"Will you ask Jake to send a car for me at four thirty?" Meredith asked.

"I'll tell him," Peter said.

As the truck sped down Winter Street, she stood there watching, trying to pigeonhole Doc's behavior into a slot marked *Concerned Vet,* but something didn't fit. She tried to shake it off. People showed worry and concern in different ways. Look at her. She was all but ignoring the fact that she had breast cancer. She'd let it go for now, and see how the evening played out.

But what if…

Forget the what ifs. If Elliott got angry at her, there wasn't anything she could do except go home. In the meantime, she'd try to picture her guilt as a thick vapor dissipating into the atmosphere, cleansing her lungs. And as an extra precaution, she'd indulge in a triple-scented layer of the three-butter lotion bar.

Chapter Fifty-Four

MacKlenna Farm – January 1

ELLIOTT WAS DRESSING for the gala in his suite at the cottage when his phone beeped with a text message. Kevin picked up the device from the bedside table. "It's Meredith. She's running late. Will be ready by six thirty."

"What the hell has she been doing all day?"

"Yoga with Ted. Horseback riding. Trip to the spa." Kevin slipped the phone into Elliott's jacket pocket.

"And she couldn't find time to get ready?" He didn't tolerate tardiness in employees, barely tolerated it in his associates, and quit dating a woman if she ever showed up late.

"It's New Year's. Cut her some slack." Kevin stepped into the walk-in closet and found a clothes brush. "She'll be beautiful and worth the wait."

"Text her back. Tell her I'm going on to the mansion and will send a car to pick her up at six thirty. I don't want her walking over there in a long gown."

Kevin brushed Elliott's jacket. "You sure you want to do that?"

Elliott slipped on his jacket before settling into the wheelchair. "If I wait for her, I'll be late." He straightened his kilt and sporran. "Where's Susan?"

"Her night off got bumped," Kevin said. "She has to work until ten o'clock. She'll get here when she can."

David entered the bedroom. "It's snowing."

Déjà vu. A similar conversation had taken place a year earlier. But the weather wasn't the cause of Sean and Mary's death. "I insist ye send a car to pick her up," Elliott said. "I don't want her driving out to the farm."

"She's got that big-ass-four-wheel-drive—"

Elliott pointed his finger at Kevin. "Send a car." Elliott wheeled out of the bedroom and threw a quick glance at the door to the spiral staircase. "Damn women. Why are they always late?"

"As much time as ye've spent entertaining her in the last couple of days, ye should be in a better mood," David said.

Kevin laughed. "He's in a foul mood because he hasn't…well…seen her since daybreak."

"I'm glad ye two keep up with my sex life."

"How can we not, Boss?" Kevin laughed again. "Ah…ah…ah…ah. The sounds are repetitive." He opened the door to the garage. Then he and David picked up the wheelchair and lowered it down the two steps.

"Don't let her hear ye talk like that. She'd be embarrassed," Elliott said.

"I'm not talking about her. I'm talking about your groaning. You've got all but a rebel yell there at the end."

Elliott shook his head. "Don't ye have anything better to do?"

Kevin slapped his chest. "How am I supposed to come to your aid if I can't hear you?"

Elliott patted his pocket to be sure he had his New Year's cigar. "I don't want ye that close anymore."

Kevin glanced from Elliott to David and back to Elliott. "Damn. This is serious. You're really into her, aren't you?"

Elliott remained silent. He didn't want to admit his feelings to himself, much less to his closest confidants.

David opened the car door. "Ye don't have to say anything. It's written all over yer face." He helped Elliott into the backseat while Kevin stowed the wheelchair in the trunk.

They drove around to the front of the mansion. Battery-operated Luminaria lit the drive, adding a soft glow to the landscape. A light dusting of snow covered footprints and tracks and gave the grounds a fresh, unspoiled appearance.

A dozen college students stayed warm in a valet tent. David pulled into the garage, and several minutes later, he wheeled Elliott into the mansion's foyer. Holly, poinsettias, and scented candles filled the house with the smells of Christmas. A string quartet entertained in the parlor. Serving staff stood by to check coats and fill drink orders.

"Bring me a whisky, neat," Elliott said to the nearest waiter.

Louise flitted into the entryway, bedazzling in a long, flowing purple gown. "There ye are. Where's Meredith?" she asked, kissing him on the cheek.

He pushed up his jacket sleeve to check the time. "She's now fifteen minutes late." He missed her, damn it. He should have gone upstairs and checked on her before he left the cottage. They would have had time for a quick go at it. His dick hardened. It did that whenever he thought of the scent of her skin, the silky texture of her hair, the pulse beating rapidly in her long neck. Discreetly, he pressed his hand against his sporran, which weighed down his aching discomfort.

Louise squeezed his shoulder. "Allie could only get her a late appointment at the spa. That's why she's late."

Elliott sipped his drink and inspected the decorations and greenery. A directional sign pointed down the twenty-foot-wide entrance hall to venues set up in each of the six rooms that spidered off the hallway. "Did ye get the mistletoe?"

"A kissing ball is hanging from each doorway, but dinna tell me Elliott Fraser needs help stealing kisses," she chided him.

"Meredith is not into public displays of affection. I want to be sure at midnight she can't avoid kissing me."

"If ye're afraid ye willna be kissed at midnight"—Louise shook her head and rolled her eyes—"this *is* serious."

Elliott sipped his drink to contain the grin welling up inside.

Servers came through carrying hors d'oeuvre trays. He sampled the smoked salmon and caviar canapés. "Good. Was this yer recommendation?" he asked Louise, and patted his mouth with a cocktail napkin.

"I told Cameron ye wanted caviar. I left it up to him how he served it."

Elliott ate another one.

A server handed Louise a glass of wine. "Ye said years ago that if ye ever found a woman who loved horses, Scotland, and whisky as much as ye, ye'd free up a corner of yer life. But I dinna think Meredith is the type of woman who'd settle for a corner."

He wiped his fingers on the napkin before picking up the drink he'd set on the side cabinet. "I can't offer her anything more right now."

Louise raised a dark, wing-shaped eyebrow. "Why not?"

"If we don't find out who murdered Galahad, we'll have to pay out the stakeholders, and the board of directors will want someone's hide. Most likely mine."

"It's not yer fault."

He rolled his chair closer to the wall to get out from underfoot. "It's not a matter of fault. It's a matter of responsibility." He currently had the board's support, but he knew from experience the wind shifted quickly where money was concerned. If the shareholders won a multimillion dollar judgment against the farm, support for Elliott would falter faster than a lame horse in a race.

"Ye can walk away. Come back to Scotland. This isna yer home. It's a job."

"I owe Sean, and I'll take care of this place as long as they let me." The doorbell rang, and the chairman of the board and his wife entered. Elliott nodded.

Louise stepped in front of him, blocking his view of the door. "Ye owed Sean for rescuing ye thirty years ago. That debt's been long paid."

"Damn it. I'm not having this discussion. And that debt extends beyond the grave."

"No, it doesna." She lowered her voice to a whisper. "Ye canna spend yer life wallowing in guilt over a mistake ye made when ye were twenty."

"Ye don't know anything about it."

"The hell I don't. I've just let ye believe I didna. That woman was looking for trouble, and ye obliged her."

"I ruined her life."

Louise leaned over and grabbed the chair's handles, putting her face only inches from his. "Ye did not. After yer affair, she and her husband reconciled. The last I heard they had ten grandchildren."

Elliott held out his empty glass to a passing waiter. "I don't believe it."

"Ten, Elliott. While ye've been hiding out at MacKlenna Farm, other people have been living full lives."

He glanced over her shoulder to see another board member entering the house. "Why don't ye go back to whatever ye were doing and let me talk to my guests?"

"Ye always shut me out when ye dinna like what I'm saying." She set her wineglass on a server's tray. "Why aren't ye with Meredith? Ye planned this evening for her. Now ye willna even be with her when she drives up to the house and sees how you've transformed MacKlenna Farm into Edinburgh."

Through the front door's sidelights, he spotted the tip of the Ferris wheel. Louise was right, and because of his stubbornness, he'd miss seeing Meredith's eyes light up. "*David*."

David stepped from the parlor, sipping a drink.

"Take me back to the cottage."

"Did ye forget something? I'll go get it."

"He sure did, and he needs to get his arse back over there right now," Louise said.

David rolled the wheelchair toward the garage. Several minutes later, Elliott sat at the foot of the cottage's staircase, rotating the wheelchair's wheels up and back, up and back.

The guest room door creaked open, and Meredith's heels clicked across the upstairs hardwood floor. Elliott's breath hitched when she appeared at the top of the stairs, wearing a long strapless gown made from the Montgomery purple tartan.

If I ever met a woman who loves Scotland…

Chapter Fifty-Five

MacKlenna Farm – January 1

STANDING AT THE top of a long, curved staircase, Meredith smiled. "I thought you'd left me."

Elliott cleared his throat. "I came back."

She tossed her fur over her arm, grabbed the dark wood railing, and glided down the steps. His intense gaze deepened as she moved closer to him. *God, he takes my breath.* The wheelchair didn't diminish his sex appeal. If anything, his vulnerability increased it. A single dose of Elliott Fraser was hazardous to a woman's health. A double dose was deadly.

His gaze stayed fixed on her. "I want ye right now." His need added flavor to his raspy voice.

Her wobbly legs carried her to the bottom step without tripping. "Do we have time?"

"No."

A wild sensory image flashed across her mind. "Maybe we can duck into a coat closet later," she said, laughing, drinking in his fresh, spicy, woodsy scent.

"A beautiful woman deserves much more than a large closet," Elliott said.

His voice resonated sensuality, and she wanted nothing more than to forget the party and climb into bed with him. "I don't need much."

He held out his hand. "I want to dance with ye tonight."

"Hard to do in a wheelchair."

"I'm not strapped in."

"Maybe you should be."

Their easy banter couldn't hide the sexual undertone. It sizzled around them. Sparks glistened like crystals, floating in the air—a truly magical moment.

David entered the foyer from the office, stopped short, and smiled. "Ye look fetching, Meredith."

"And you look fetching in your kilt."

He bowed slightly. "Here, let me help ye with that." He held her fur while she slipped it on.

Elliott glanced at his watch. "It's six forty."

She flicked her hair over her collar. "I'm sorry I'm late."

"Allie should have pressed for an earlier appointment."

"She did. Even invited the owner to the concert, but they couldn't work me in."

"I could have done it if she'd asked," Elliott said.

Meredith patted his shoulder. "You really don't like to be late, do you?"

David smiled as he wheeled the chair through the foyer.

A few minutes later, they settled into the backseat of the Mercedes. "Close yer eyes. I have a surprise," Elliott said, entwining his arm with hers. "And keep them closed until I tell ye to open them."

She placed her hand over her eyes but separated two fingers.

He frowned. "Hand me the blindfold, David."

She squeezed her eyes shut. "Okay. I promise not to look." She'd have to grit her teeth to hold steadfast to that promise.

David pulled the car out of the garage. "I'll go around and pull up the main drive."

A few minutes later, Elliott tugged on her hand. "Now ye can look."

She gave a long gasp of surprise. "*Oh my God.*" She rolled down the window, and while the car proceeded along the tree-lined drive, she breathed in the sights and sounds and smells. Couples ice-skated on the pond. Others rode in horse-drawn carriages.

As the car approached a lighted arch with a suspended sign that read *MacKlenna Hogmanay,* the true magic he had created came into view. A smaller version of the Edinburgh wheel lifted guests high into the air. Squeals of delight flowed down.

"Where'd you find a Ferris wheel on such short notice?"

"When Kevin sets his mind on something, he won't accept defeat."

She pointed out the window. "A food stand?"

"Haggis and hot cones of chips."

"Just like Edinburgh," she said.

"I wanted everything to be authentic," Elliott said.

"Channel Twenty-Seven is here," David said.

Elliott glanced out the window. "Damn."

"They'll want an interview," David said.

Elliott had never developed Sean's PR skills, and after dealing with the press over Galahad's death, Elliott had had enough contact with news hounds to last a while. "Run interference and send them Sandy's way. They just want admission to the concert."

"Should I tell her to let them in?"

"Tell her to use her judgment."

"Do ye want to enter through the front door or pull into the garage?" David asked.

"Front door."

David pulled the car to a stop next to the valet tent where a young man assisted him with getting Elliott seated in the wheelchair. Once settled, David wheeled the chair up the ramp and through the front door.

Meredith slapped her hands against her cheeks. "Look at what you've done." The outside was worthy of a Broadway production, but inside, the crew had created another kind of magic. The waitstaff wore kilts, and street theater actors roamed the house, some juggling, some reciting Burns. Traditional Scottish Ceilidh dancers performed in the library.

"Do ye know the dance?" David asked.

Meredith nodded. "Do you?"

"Elliott, would ye mind if I danced with yer lady?"

He waved them on.

The three dancing couples stopped and welcomed Meredith and David, and then the music started up again. A crowd gathered, clapping and stomping their feet.

"You're an excellent dancer, David."

"Not as good as he is," he said, pointing his head in Elliott's direction.

She glanced at Elliott. Although he smiled, sadness watered his eyes. She touched David's arm and nodded toward Elliott. They bowed out of the dance.

"Why'd ye stop?" he asked.

She leaned over and whispered, "Because I wasn't dancing with you."

A man and woman approached. "This has to be Meredith." The man extended his hand. "I'm Jim Manning. My wife, Judy."

Jim looked exactly like what Meredith expected of Elliott's long-time friend and attorney—tall, dark eyes and hair, handsome, well-dressed, polished, and personable. She liked him immediately.

"Great party, Elliott. If this is what they do in Scotland, Jim and I are going next year," Judy said.

David stepped behind the wheelchair and grasped the handles. "Everyone is being asked to take their seats." He nodded toward the Mannings. "Ye're to be seated at Dr. Fraser's table."

French doors leading to the north portico stood open. A covered, heated walk connected the columned porch to a walled dining tent. David pushed the wheelchair to the table for eight where they joined Dr. Lyles and the chairman of the board, along with their spouses. David left but returned shortly with crutches and a lapel mike, which he pinned to Elliott's jacket.

"Looks like I get a reprieve," Elliott said to Meredith. He stood, gained his balance, then hobbled to the podium. "May I have yer attention?" The buzz of voices quieted.

Meredith watched the man she had come to—what? Adore,

admire, love? She thought back to the night she walked into the library at Louise's B&B. From the moment she set eyes on him, she thought him deliciously composed, and while he occasionally acted like an ass, her first impression hadn't changed. He was a remarkable man and an incredible lover, and she would miss him when the time came to say good-bye.

"Welcome, lads and lassies, to MacKlenna Farm's Hogmanay." Elliott spoke over the party horns and cheers. "My inspiration for this event came from a very beautiful woman—"

"That's no surprise," a man yelled from the audience.

Elliott chuckled. "For those of ye who haven't met my guest, please give a warm Kentucky welcome to Meredith Montgomery, owner of Montgomery Winery in Napa."

The lighting technician widened the spotlight to include her. Under the glare of the light, Meredith's heart went to her throat. If Elliott hadn't mentioned the winery, she'd have scooted her chair out of the spotlight, but she never missed an opportunity to promote her wines. She picked up a chardonnay, held the bottle aloft, and smiled.

"Woohoo," Kevin and Allie, sitting at the table behind her, shouted above the applause.

When the spotlight released her, Jim leaned over and said, "In the twenty-five years I've known Elliott, he's never publicly introduced his date. Are you paying him to promote your wine?"

Meredith set the bottle back on the table, laughing. "If I was, he'd have mentioned the label I'm launching in February."

"I told my bride if I could work it out, I'd take her."

Judy peeked around her husband's back and tapped Meredith's arm. "And I'm holding him to it."

"Well, if he can't get away, come by yourself. You can stay with me."

Judy winked at Jim, smiling. "That'll put pressure on you for sure."

When the room quieted again, Elliott continued. "A year ago a drunk driver killed"—he stopped and cleared his throat—"killed

Sean and Mary MacKlenna." With the announcement, the air whisked from the room, taking all sound and movement—still as death. Elliott's voice wobbled. He took a breath. "Their absence has been felt beyond this farm. Tonight, I would like to make a toast."

The shuffle of feet and chairs echoed through the tent as everyone stood, glass in hand.

"May their memory be ever in our minds," Elliott said. "May their love be ever in our hearts. May their passion for life be ever our standard. To Sean and Mary MacKlenna."

There weren't any dry eyes at Meredith's table, and tears leaked from Elliott's.

"To Sean and Mary." A cloud of palpable grief smothered the crowd's voices. Then the melodic sound of a piper playing "Amazing Grace" on the Great Highland bagpipe burst through the cloud. After a few stanzas, the entire pipe and drum band joined in, marching in formation to the center of the dance floor.

Tears rolled down Meredith's cheeks. Elliott hobbled over to her, dropped the crutches, and took her into his arms. "Thank ye for being here." His chest heaved against her.

Kevin walked up beside him and picked up the crutches. "You need to sit, Boss."

Elliott took his seat, and when the band started its next song, servers entered the room carrying the first course. By the time everyone had salads, the New Year's excitement had swept away the melancholy. Every time Elliott laughed, Meredith's heart shed a tear. Every time he smiled, her heart cracked. Every time he looked at her with eyes that made her melt, another sliver of her heart splintered off. At the rate she was going, there'd be nothing left by the time her plane took off in the morning.

At nine o'clock, Wynonna came out on stage, and so did Tate. The dog never left her side. When she took a break, the backup band came out and encouraged people to get up and hit the dance floor. Meredith felt certain that if Elliott had been able, they'd have been the first couple out there.

Kevin leaned over her shoulder. "Do you want to dance?"

Meredith shook her head.

Elliott kissed her on the mouth. "Go. Enjoy yerself."

"You don't mind?"

"Ye can dance all ye want with Kevin," Elliott said, glaring at his aide. "He's usually a gentleman."

"You're my role model, Boss." Kevin pulled away her chair and led her out onto the dance floor. The music rocked, and she thoroughly enjoyed dancing with a young, energetic man with some nice moves.

Wynonna returned with Tate tagging along. The audience enjoyed another hour's concert, plus four or five encores. Finally, she said good night. The band returned to the stage, and Meredith and Kevin returned to the dance floor.

At eleven thirty, David wheeled Elliott from the tent. Meredith pointed toward the exit, and Kevin turned to see them disappear through the doorway. "He's probably going to the bathroom." A couple of minutes later, David returned for Jake and Jim Manning. Meredith again pointed to get Kevin's attention. "David will signal if he needs us."

When David reentered the tent and walked toward her, the trickle of fear slid down her spine and turned into an open spigot. She braced for bad news.

David put one arm around Kevin's shoulder, the other around Meredith's. "We've got a situation." As calmly as they could, Meredith and Kevin followed him out.

"What's going on?" Kevin asked.

"The asshole killed another horse."

Meredith's overheated blood froze in her veins. *Elliott can't take any more.* They made their way through the kitchen toward Granny Mac's sitting room.

"I don't give a fuck what it takes. Ye get that son of a bitch." Elliott stood at the French doors with his hands on his hips. He'd tossed his jacket on a chair and pulled his tie undone. She gulped at the unbridled anger twisting his face. "That fucker took Galahad and now Stormy."

"Stormy?" Meredith said on a gasp.

"Is dead in his stall," David said.

"That's impossible. We left him at Rood & Riddle this afternoon." She glanced around the room. "Where's Doc?"

"What the hell are ye talking about?" Elliott asked.

"Stormy got away from me. Jumped a rock fence and hurt his leg. Doc and I took him to the hospital. He'll be okay."

"Why the fuck didn't ye tell me?"

"Doc wanted—"

Dashing into the room, Doc said, "I wanted the full report and prognosis before I told you."

Elliott glared at the vet and then at Meredith. "Why the hell were ye riding a horse you couldn't control?"

"Calm down, Elliott," Doc said. "An icy branch broke off a tree and scared him. You know how he is. He did it to Kit enough times."

"But she never got him hurt."

A sizzling sensation started at the back of Meredith's neck and ended at her ankles. Then her heart kicked her in the chest, sending her stumbling into the wall.

Elliott's eyes grew madman wide. The corded muscles in his neck strained and pulsed. He pointed at Doc. "Ye took my horse to the hospital without telling me. And ye—" He pointed at Meredith. "Ye lied to me." His hot temper rose as if he'd swallowed fire. If flames shot from his mouth, she'd be incinerated.

She choked from his accusation, which was worse than anything her father or husband had ever said to her. In that moment, he destroyed her feelings for him.

"If Stormy isn't in his stall, then who is?" Kevin asked.

Doc collapsed into a chair and covered his face with his hands, shaking and groaning.

"Who's in Stormy's stall, Doc?" Elliott demanded.

Doc dropped his hands, revealing the look of death on his face. "I moved Sugar Butter in there this afternoon to keep an eye on him."

"A ten-million-dollar stallion with a full book is *dead*, and Stormy's recovering at Rood & Riddle. Is that what ye're telling me?"

"That's about it," Doc said.

"This is the biggest fuck up I've ever seen, and it all happened because *she*," Elliott said, glaring at Meredith, "thought she could ride a goddamn stallion."

Was this really her fault? No. She didn't kill his horse and certainly hadn't set out to harm Stormy. She backed out of the room, wincing with remorse that she hadn't told him earlier. She fought the panic that rose in her throat.

Kevin went after her. "He didn't mean that. He didn't mean to hurt you."

She opened her mouth to speak, but words wouldn't tumble out. She felt like a knitted scarf unraveling one stitch at a time in rapid succession. Soon, nothing would be left but a long piece of crinkled yarn. "But he did," she said.

Kevin's face paled. "He cares about you."

"Is that how he shows that he cares for someone? By embarrassing and humiliating them?"

Kevin winced as if he'd been slapped.

"Sometimes we say things we don't mean, but it doesn't make the pain we cause less severe." She filled a glass of water at the sink and gulped it down. If she'd had a glass of wine, she would have gulped that instead. "I'm through. I've got too much going on in my life right now to deal with him." Pain sliced through her stomach, and she all but threw up. "I saw some of this when he was in the hospital, but I cut him some slack." She shook her head. "Not anymore."

"What are you going to do now? Leave?" There was a quake in Kevin's voice.

A waiter brushed by carrying two bottles of wine. Her wine. Her name. Her life. Reality set in, smacking her with the force of a two-by-four.

She leaned against the counter, thinking through what she needed to do. "I can't leave." Her voice was soft, yet controlled.

"You don't have to," Kevin said. "You can stay here at the mansion, or I'll take you to a hotel."

"No. I can't leave the party. My wine is on every table in that tent. I won't run away like a teenager with a broken heart. I have a responsibility to the winery, to the Montgomery name. I won't leave until the party is over." She was a marathoner and knew what it was like to hit the wall, to feel like she couldn't take another step, but she had always finished because that was what she was trained to do. "I've lived my entire life putting Montgomery Winery first. I'll continue to do that." She stood tall, squared her shoulders, and dried her eyes. "I'm going back to the party, and I sure could use a dance partner."

He cut a glance back toward the sitting room; his lips pressed together forming a straight seam. His stony expression didn't change. If anything, it deepened; more raw, more wounded. Meredith had the sense that he was struggling with disillusionment. The man he idol-worshiped had fallen off his pedestal.

"Let's go dancing," he said.

She hugged him, and even though she tried not to compare him to Elliott, she couldn't help but notice that he was not only a bit taller but a bit stronger, too. His scent packed a punch, not subtle like Elliott's. The bottom notes were musk, vanilla bean, and sandalwood. Any other woman would be turned on by the evocative scent. But not her. She didn't react to what she smelled. She reacted to what she didn't.

They reentered the tent, smiles plastered in place. If disappointment and hurt reigned in their hearts, they were determined that no one would know it. They danced until three o'clock, when the backup band finally played the last song. The foursome—Meredith, Kevin, Ted, and Laurence—sat and opened a bottle of champagne.

"To your new wine," Kevin said. Meredith leaned into him, and he wrapped his arm around her. "When are you leaving?"

"My plane will be here at seven o'clock. What time is it now?"

"After four," Kevin said.

"Will you take me to the airport?"

"Laurence and I will take you," Ted said. "Hell, if you've got room, we might go with you."

"Love to have you," she said.

They finished the bottle and opened another one, and at four thirty, they all walked over to the cottage with a promise from Laurence that he'd cook breakfast. Meredith's body ached in a way it never had from any of her races. She was emotionally and physically spent. When Elliott entered the kitchen, she froze, feeling his tension from across the room. His grief-stricken face garnered no sympathy from her.

"I'd like to talk to ye," he said.

She walked past him, out into the hallway. "I'm going upstairs to change and pack."

"Ye're leaving? Can't we talk?" Elliott asked.

"As far as you're concerned, I'm already gone." She hurried upstairs, where she slipped out of her gown and knotted it up, not caring if she ever wore it again. "And the same goes for these damn shoes." She took them off and threw them in the trash.

The door to the wardrobe opened. "I can't let ye leave like this." Elliott hobbled into the room without crutches. "What I did to ye was unconscionable. When I heard Stormy was dead, all I could think of was how much I had failed Sean. Ye became the embodiment of my failure for reasons that are hard to explain, and ye probably wouldn't believe it if I did."

Meredith looked ahead, imagining the finish line. Once she crossed it, she could stop running. She could tune out all the distractions and focus on the one thing that mattered, *Cailean*.

"You know, Elliott, I really don't care. Your sorrys don't mean anything to me. You're as close to Jekyll and Hyde as any man I've met. When I think of you, a tear will come to my eye long before a smile comes to my face."

She walked into the bathroom, locked the door, stripped, and then eased into the hot, steamy shower. Over the years she had learned that you had to take life as it came at you, or else hit it with a baseball bat. And that was exactly what she intended to do.

Swing.

Chapter Fifty-Six

MacKlenna Mansion House – January 2

THE SUN WAS rising from behind the clouds as Kevin backed his BMW out of the garage. Meredith sat bundled in the passenger's seat, wiping tears from her face. Elliott watched from the bedroom window, stretching his neck until the rear of the car disappeared behind the tree line that followed the curve of the driveway.

A blade sliced through his heart as surely as one had sliced through his leg. Deep, racking sobs shook his body. His knees buckled, and he dropped to the floor. He had a tearing, burning sensation in his chest. Maybe a heart attack would kill him and end his suffering. No, not possible. He would continue to kill himself daily in small chunks, masking his pain with whisky and painkillers.

Tears dropped on his pressed shirt and khaki pants. For once, he didn't care that he wasn't immaculately groomed. He combed his hair with his fingers, mussing it intentionally.

The best thing in his life had just walked out, crying. He'd never bring a smile to her face again. He had lost her. He had lost everything important to him.

They always want to come back.

He stopped crying for a moment, believing that was true, believing that he was some kind of superstud who could have any woman he wanted. He knew how to gaze at them with soulful eyes. How to manipulate them into believing what he wanted was their idea. How to make them fall into his arms and into his bed. He knew all that, but what he didn't know was how to get a woman he wanted to come back.

He had failed with his mother.

He had only been a lad of ten when he had discovered her in Roger Graham's arms. They didn't know that Elliott was in the barn that morning. Roger had come for her. They were going to run away together. Elliott tried to stop her and had grabbed her leg. She told him he was a young man and didn't need his mother. "Ye'll be fine," she had said. She rubbed at a spot on his shirt. "Be sure ye clean and press yer clothes. When I see ye next, ye'll look handsome."

He had watched them drive away, and he had cried.

"Stop crying, lad," his father had said. "If a woman doesn't want ye, let her go."

Elliott had run from the barn and found his way into the wine cellar, believing there had to be a way to get her back. His father came after him. "If ye're going to drink away yer pain, drink whisky. Wine's no good for that."

"Then wine's no good for anything," Elliott had said.

Now, he covered his face and sobbed just as he had done in the wine cellar that morning.

A car roared in the driveway.

Meredith's coming back. He peeked over the windowsill, but it was Mrs. Collins's late model Chevy. He dropped back to the floor. *Meredith's not coming back. Not to a drunk.*

When his father had received news that Elliott's mother and Roger Graham had been killed, Elliott had said to him, "If I had stopped her from leaving, if I'd worn a clean shirt, she'd be alive."

"No, Elliott. People are responsible for their own actions."

Later that night, Elliott found his father asleep, an almost empty whisky bottle in one hand and a crumpled picture of his mother in the other.

No woman would come back to a drunk.

Elliott had taken the bottle and drank the rest of the whisky, threw the picture of his mother in the trash, then stumbled off to bed. But before he could sleep, he burned the shirt with the spot his mother had tried to remove. When the shirt had finally turned to ash, he cried until he had no more tears to shed. And those were his last tears until Sean and Mary had died.

And now, curled on the floor at the cottage, he cried with the same heartbreak as that ten-year-old lad. But this time, he wouldn't reach for a bottle of whisky.

Chapter Fifty-Seven

January 5

THREE DAYS LATER, the staff had put away all evidence of the party, Louise and Evelyn had returned to Scotland, and Elliott had moved back to the mansion. He called Meredith several times, but she refused to take his call. He had sent a dozen text messages, too, but she didn't respond. Kevin wasn't speaking to him either, and David spent most of his time traveling around the state investigating the Gates family. Elliott was ignored by even the continuously talking Mrs. Collins.

He resided in a lonely world.

The mudroom door slammed. "Elliott," David yelled.

"I'm in the office," Elliott said.

"Get yer coat."

Elliott spun the wheelchair away from the desk. "Where are we going?"

"Just got a call from Chuck. He located Gates living here in Lexington."

"Hot damn." The only way he could straighten out his relationship with Meredith was to get this horse business behind him, so he could get away from the farm and focus on her. Finding Gates was the biggest hurdle on the track.

Elliott settled into the passenger's seat of a MacKlenna Farm truck. "This doesn't have GPS."

"I plugged the address into my phone. The directions are coming in now. It's in north Lexington," David said.

"Is Chuck meeting us?"

David nodded. "We're not taking any chances with Gates or any possible evidence he might have. We're playing this by the book."

"Why not call the police?" Elliott asked.

"And tell them what? That we think a man without a record possibly killed two multimillion dollar horses?"

"That's a start. He's got motive," Elliott said.

"Maybe. Let's talk to him first. See what he has to say."

Thirty minutes later, they turned onto Gates's street. From a block away, Elliott spotted a police cruiser's flashing lights. A sinking feeling hit his stomach. "God, I hope that police car's not at Gates's house."

"As of early afternoon, he wasn't on their radar. The police must be interested in someone else." David slowed the truck and they both checked mailboxes for street numbers.

"What number did ye say?" Elliott asked.

"Two-five-two," David said.

Elliott pointed to his right. "This one's two-forty-eight."

"Police are at two-five-two," David said with frustration spilling over in his voice.

Two cruisers with lights flashing were parked in front of a one-story, ranch-style house. "Shite," Elliott said. "What the hell has our boy gotten himself into?"

David picked up his phone off the dash and composed a text message. "Maybe Chuck has heard something."

"Look at that ambulance. Notice anything strange?" Elliott said.

"Nothing's happening. Paramedics are just standing around."

Elliott's head throbbed. He'd had several headaches lately and knew they were stress related. "Let's hope he has a roommate with a problem, and that this has nothing to do with Gates."

The headlights of an approaching vehicle flashed inside their truck. David glanced in the rearview mirror. "Company's coming."

Elliott turned around to look. "It's a damn news crew. Got

WLEX plastered on the side of the van. They must have heard a report on the police scanner. Go ask."

"I could do that," David said, "but they'd want to know why the CEO of MacKlenna Farm was here. Ye want to talk to them?"

"Hell, no. I put reporters in the same category as IRS agents. I don't talk to either unless I have an attorney present."

David's phone beeped. He read the message. "Chuck's inside. I'm going in. Ye stay put."

Elliott opened his door. "The hell with that. I'm going, too."

David switched off the ignition. "As soon as ye get out of the car, the reporters will have a camera in yer face."

Elliott didn't want to be on the ten o'clock news, but he didn't want to be left out either. The sidewalk looked icy. A slip would set him back. He closed the door. "Hurry up. I want to know what the hell's going on."

David stepped out of the truck, tucked his hands in his jacket pockets, and walked toward a police officer standing in the driveway. Elliott couldn't hear what was being said, but he had a good view of the front door. David flashed his credentials, and the officer pointed over his shoulder.

As David headed up the drive, two police officers came out of the front door and strung police crime scene tape from the driveway to the door. Elliott leaned forward in his seat, tapped his fingers on the dash, and watched. *This doesn't look good.*

Headlights flashed inside the truck again. Elliott glanced over his shoulder, expecting to see another news truck, but it was the coroner's car. Elliott's shoulders sagged, along with his hopes. He had pinned them all on catching Gates with a syringe and a bottle of pentobarbital. *What a dumb-ass I am.* He had wanted to believe Gates was responsible, because it was convenient.

Was that the only reason?

Hell, no. Elliott wanted revenge. He wanted to beat the crap out of Gates for what he did to Elliott's leg. The brother wasn't the perpetrator. Elliott knew that, but he didn't care. A Gates was a Gates. Any of them would do.

He checked his watch. David had been gone for five minutes. Where the hell was he? Five minutes turned into ten, and the car windows steamed. He called David. The call went to voice mail. The windows weren't the only thing steaming. Elliott left a terse message. "Report back, now."

Another five minutes passed. Elliott considered his options. He had none. He grabbed his crutches and opened the door. To hell with the news crew. He'd take his chances. When he reached the driveway, David saw him, scowled, and jogged toward him.

"Why didn't ye answer me?" Elliott said.

"I was talking to the police."

"Hey, that's Dr. Fraser from MacKlenna Farm. What's he doing here?"

Elliott looked around for the disembodied voice. He spotted the familiar face of a reporter from Channel 18. "Let's get out of here," he said to David.

But it was too late. The reporter and a cameraman bulldozed their way through the crowd of neighbors that had gathered.

"Dr. Fraser. Why are you here? What does this shooting have to do with MacKlenna Farm?"

Elliott hustled back into the truck.

"Was this man a farm employee?" the reporter asked.

"No comment." David closed the door and jumped into the driver's seat.

"They got us on tape, and the farm doesn't need the publicity." Elliott snatched his phone from his pocket and scrolled through his contacts. The station's general manager was a personal friend. He could call in a favor. As he punched in the numbers, he reconsidered. The reporter would do some research before they showed the video clip. It would only be a matter of hours before they made the Gates connection. Elliott leaned back against the headrest and sighed heavily.

"Was there any sign of Gates in the house?" he asked, hoping the coroner wasn't there to pick up Gates's body.

David turned on the blinker and merged onto New Circle Road.

Snow had started falling again, and the trucks had only plowed one lane. The going was slow. "The lad was dead. Shot in the head. Cops are saying it was a drug deal gone bad."

"I placed all my bets on Gates. Now I have nothing but worthless betting tickets." Elliott smacked his fist into his open palm. "Did the police say anything else?"

"No signs of forced entry. One bullet to the head. None of the neighbors saw or heard anything."

"How did the police know about the shooting?"

"Chuck called them when he got here. The front door was open, and he spotted the body on the floor."

David's phone rang. "Chuck? Good, yes. I'll put ye on speaker so Dr. Fraser can hear."

"The police found a box of cash and drugs," Chuck said. "Looks like he was dealing."

Elliott pulled a notepad and pen from his pocket. He clicked the pen's cap up and down, up and down, up and down. "What kind of drugs?"

"Prescription…" Chuck's voice faded in and out. Bad connection. Elliott leaned forward, closer to the phone. "Pills, cocaine, pot. A bit of everything."

"Anything that would kill a horse?" Elliott asked.

"Nothing like that."

Elliott sat back and threw up his hands. Somehow, he'd lost the horses, lost the girl, and lost the implant. No one had to spell it out for him. Three strikes. He was out—again.

Chapter Fifty-Eight

MacKlenna Farm – January 7

AT DUSK TWO DAYS LATER, David walked into Elliott's bedroom at the mansion, yelling for him.

"Over here," Elliott said from the far corner of the dimly lit room.

"Hi, Anne. I thought he was alone, or I wouldn't have barged in."

"Just finishing." She wiped oil off Elliott's back and legs. "I can work you in if you want a massage, too, or a tennis match later."

David sat in the chair next to the massage table. "Thanks, but I don't have time right now for tennis or yer healing hands."

She laughed. "I don't think Elliott appreciated my *healing hands* today."

Elliott sat and draped a towel around his waist. "She beat the crap out of me."

"Someone needed to." David's stoic expression didn't change. Seconds later, it still hadn't. The heat of his blue-eyed glare caused the muscles in Elliott's shoulders that Anne had loosened to tighten once again.

"I heard what happened on New Year's," Anne said. "If that woman had been me, I would have slapped the hell out of you."

Elliott's cheek stung as though Anne had slapped him. "Gee, thanks."

"You need to quit those drugs. They affect your personality. Slow up on the whisky, too." She grabbed her jacket and slipped it on.

"Ye going to tell me to see a shrink?"

"Why?" She removed her iPhone from the docking station. Tension smothered the air in the room as soon as the calming massage music ended. "I've been trying to get you to see my therapist for the last five years. I've given up." She dropped the bottle of oil and her iPhone into her backpack. "I hope your mood improves before I come back on Saturday. Work on that, will you?"

"Not likely to happen," David said.

Anne pointed her finger at Elliott. "Call your girlfriend or get on your damn plane and go see her."

"This isn't about Meredith. It's—"

"What?" Anne scrunched her face. "If you don't think so, you're dumber than I thought."

David laughed. Elliott glowered.

She slung her bag over her shoulder. "You don't have to see me out. I'll get some money off the dresser." Anne took a few bills from a large bundle. "I'll leave Allie a note to put the next appointment on your calendar. Ciao." She left, closing the door behind her.

"Ye shouldn't leave that much money lying around," David said.

Elliott shifted to the wheelchair. "No one is around here except Mrs. Collins, and she refuses to enter the room. Calls it Satan's den."

David pushed the wheelchair into the bathroom. "Mrs. Collins isn't the only person with access to the house." He turned on the water and stepped aside.

Elliott sat on the shower bench and washed off the rest of the oil. "So what did ye learn at the police station?"

"Gates's prints were on the box and the cash."

"That shouldn't be a surprise. The guy was a scumbag." Elliott opened the shower door and stepped out, holding tightly to the railing. "The apple doesn't fall far from the tree. No good. Just like his brothers."

Clean clothes were neatly folded on the counter. After Elliott dressed, David wheeled him into the office.

"I sense there's something on yer mind. Even ye are more talkative than this," Elliott said.

"It doesn't add up," David said. "Gates held a steady job, got his work done, paid his bills on time, and had a small amount of money in the bank. He didn't cause trouble and had never been arrested." David poured two cups of coffee at the wet bar and handed a cup to Elliott. "He might be a dealer, but I don't think he's our man."

Elliott tapped his fingers against his coffee cup, took a sip, and tapped some more. "Of course he is. We just need to find the link."

"Do ye know anyone who doesn't carry a mobile?" David asked, flipping pages in his notebook.

Elliott shook his head, sipped the hot brew. "Everyone has a phone."

"Gates didn't. At least they didn't find one."

"Then they haven't looked in the right place."

"And where's that?" David asked.

"Damned if I know, but I bet it's with the gun the killer used."

David flicked his pen against the page he was reading. "Probably at the bottom of a lake."

"Not likely," Elliott said. "All the water around here is frozen."

Chapter Fifty-Nine

Montgomery Winery – January 27

MEREDITH HAD WORKED nonstop for the last four weeks. Whenever thoughts of Elliott entered her mind, she found something else to do. And she had plenty, but she always took time to talk with Kevin when he called. He had promised to come to the launch, and she looked forward to dancing with him again.

He had called her the week before to let her know that Elliott had had surgery, and if he did what he was supposed to do, he'd heal and be done with the overly long process of putting him back together. She would hope for the best, but it really didn't concern her. *Right.* Cate didn't believe her, and neither did Kevin. That's why he kept calling. He saw the chink in her armor and kept needling her.

Sitting at her desk in her office at the winery with her feet up, she glanced once more at her to-do list. The genealogy was done; the article was written and forwarded to the printer. Gregory had taken over the project and given it to the new director of social media. She hadn't even seen the genealogist's research. *Hands off* was her new policy. Weeks earlier, the project had been a top priority. Now, like many other things, it had slipped down the list.

Her stomach roiled for the third or fourth time that day. She ran into her private bathroom and threw up. There wasn't much in her stomach. For the last two days, keeping anything down had been an effort. At the sink, she patted her pale face with a damp washcloth. For some reason, cancer was making her sick this time.

Cate entered the office, calling, "Meredith."

"In here."

Cate stood at the bathroom door. "Good God, you look horrible."

Meredith tightened her ponytail and smoothed down her shirt. "I feel horrible, too. I can't keep anything down, and all I want to do is sleep or throw up. I haven't been out to run in almost a week, and my muscles are screaming."

"You need to go to the doctor. I'll make an appointment. Go home. You've probably got the flu."

Meredith held the cold washcloth against her forehead. "I've got too much work to do."

"Go home," Cate said. "If you have the flu, you'll just make the rest of us sick, too."

Begrudgingly, Meredith agreed, but before she could get out of the bathroom, she threw up again.

Chapter Sixty

Napa Valley – January 27

AT TWO O'CLOCK, Meredith sat in the examining room at her internist's office, waiting. He had examined her and done blood work. An hour wait for the results had turned into two. She didn't mind. She had her iPad and was able to work. It didn't matter whether she threw up at home or at the doctor's office.

Kevin sent her a text: *Can you talk?*

She texted back: *Sure.* A minute later, her phone rang.

"Hey. Ted and I are making flight arrangements. Should we fly into San Francisco and rent a car or fly to Napa?"

"I'll send a car to San Francisco to pick you up. When do you arrive?"

"The day before, but don't worry about us. We'll rent a car."

"Check with the Mannings. Maybe you can share a ride."

"I'll do that."

Meredith scrolled through the pictures on her iPad until she found one of her and Elliott on Christmas Eve. The memories brought tears to her eyes. She cleared her throat. "Send me your itinerary so I'll know when to expect you."

Neither one said anything for a second or two. The silence provided a painful reminder that they had agreed not to talk about Elliott. Her heart bounced up and down, begging for information, but she put on the skids and didn't ask.

"Nothing new on the investigation," Kevin said, breaking the silence. "And Elliott's temper—"

"Kevin, we agreed…"

"It was a stupid agreement. He's all but crying for information. He's in the worst shape I've ever seen."

Meredith hissed at the news.

"Don't get me wrong. Lyles is pleased with his progress, but Elliott's in a foul mood and even a parade of women stopping by to visit hasn't improved his temper. He's not sleeping—"

"Kevin, I don't care."

"He's not sleeping with any of them, Meredith, because you're in his head."

"How's the investigation going?" His women didn't interest her. Well, she was glad to hear he wasn't sleeping with anyone, but she didn't care. His bed would never see her again, although she rarely thought of anything else.

"He's not drinking."

"How's Stormy? You said he was back at the farm."

"He's not taking pain medication either," Kevin said.

"Stormy?"

"No, Elliott."

"Have you talked to Evelyn? She said she was coming to the launch, but I haven't heard from her," Meredith said.

"His leg is finally healing."

"*Kevin.*"

"Crap. I've got to go," he said. "Elliott's yelling for me."

The doctor opened the door and entered. She put her phone away. He gave her a fatherly pat on the back. His eyes narrowed, and his brows pulled down in concentration.

Meredith's heart leaped into her throat. "What's the matter?"

He sat, leaned forward, and crossed his arms in his lap. "When was the last time you had sex?"

A heated blush colored her face and neck. *Oh my God, I've got an STD. That bastard. I'll shoot him.* "Why?" she asked with a dry mouth.

"Within the last month?"

Oh God. I probably caught herpes. "About three weeks ago."

He patted her knee. "You've been a patient for over twenty years, Meredith. I didn't think we'd ever have this conversation."

Her heart was beating at racing speed, and her hands turned clammy. *I probably have gonorrhea. What the hell is that anyway? Shooting's too good for him. I'll cut his balls off.*

"I've been on a conference call with your oncologist, surgeon, and ob-gyn, who scheduled an appointment to see you immediately."

"Can't you put me on penicillin?"

He chuckled. "Penicillin won't help you."

Good God, she probably had every STD out there. Why didn't she insist he use a condom?

"Then what will?"

"Nine months."

"What?"

"You're pregnant."

Every nerve ending fired. Her head swam, and she fainted.

When Meredith regained consciousness, she was lying on the exam table. She batted her eyes to focus. When the doctor's face came into view, so did the instant replay. *Pregnant.* "Impossible. I can't get pregnant."

"Not only can you, but you are."

Her entire body shook. She curled into a protective ball. Tears formed tracks on her cheeks. "I have breast cancer."

He pulled a chair up next to the table. "There are chemo drugs that don't pass through the placenta. Your oncologist suggested you could have chemo now and postpone surgery."

If she thought her head was spinning before, it was nothing like what it was doing now. She covered her mouth, gagging. The doctor grabbed the trash can, but Meredith had nothing left in her stomach.

"There's no way," she said, wiping her mouth with a Kleenex, "that I'll put poison in my body and trust that my baby won't be exposed to the drug. I'll deal with the cancer after he's born." The spinning finally stopped. She sat slowly, inch by inch, testing her stomach and her head.

"The other option is doing the mastectomy without reconstruction," the doctor said.

She crossed her arms and hugged them to her chest. "I had Versed and fentanyl for the lumpectomy, but I'd have to have a general anesthetic for a mastectomy. I was told I had a reaction to the anesthetic during my last one. No. Surgery isn't an option either."

"Your blood pressure dropped, but that doesn't mean it will happen again."

"But if it did, the baby would suffer." She shook her head. "No."

He stood, took her hand, and helped her off the table. "Nothing has to be decided right now. Get some rest. My secretary will schedule appointments for you. Talk to the baby's father—"

"*No*," she said more adamantly than she intended. Her cheeks heated. "He won't be involved in the pregnancy or in the decision-making."

The doctor scratched his chin, thinking. "You have breast cancer. Chances are good that you'll beat it. But what if it's worse than we anticipate? Do you want to leave your child without a mother or a father?"

She punched the big, burly doctor in the arm. "You don't fight fair."

"Not in this situation, little lady."

"You haven't called me that since I was a teenager."

"Meredith." He looked at her over the top of his glasses. "You may not like this guy, but he is the father of the baby you're carrying, and he needs to know."

"You're wrong. Finding out he's going to be a father is the worst thing that could happen right now. I won't involve him."

"Think about your baby."

"I am," she said.

"Then think some more."

Chapter Sixty-One

MacKlenna Farm – January 31

ELLIOTT WAS SITTING at the table, chewing on a drumstick when David entered MacKlenna Mansion's kitchen.

"Do I smell Mrs. Collins's fried chicken?"

"Yep. Fix a plate. There won't be anything left after Kevin eats. There's mashed potatoes, gravy, and biscuits, too."

"I didn't think this kind of food was on yer new health food diet."

Elliott wiped his greasy fingers on a napkin. "She insisted I needed comfort food."

"If anybody needs comfort, ye do."

Elliott pushed back from the table. "What'd ye find at the library?"

David loaded a plate before pouring a glass of tea. "A librarian identified Gates. Said he came in two to three times a week. He'd pull books from the stacks but never checked any out. He did use the computer, though, and always had a jump drive with him."

"I guess the police didn't find a jump drive in the house."

"Nope," David said, sitting down at the table.

"So what happened to it?"

David took a long sip of tea. "Guess it's with the phone." He bit into a piece of chicken and sighed. "The best there is."

Elliott refilled his coffee from a carafe. "What about the books?"

"That's the interesting part. Thoroughbreds and veterinary medicine."

Elliott slapped his fist on the table. "*I knew it.*"

"Here's something else," David said. "Chuck's been snooping around the town in Indiana where the Gates brothers grew up. Seems the younger Gates was a vet's assistant when he was in high school. The vet said he had a special affinity with horses. Always gentle with them and that he considered going to vet school."

"How the hell does someone go from loving horses to hating them enough to kill them?"

"What makes ye think he hated them?" David asked.

Elliott leaned back in his chair, sipping coffee. "Have to. Can't right out kill one unless ye do."

"If there's a story there, Chuck will find it."

"What else ye got?"

David grew pensive. "Did ye know Harrison had a gambling problem?"

Elliott's chair legs hit the floor, and coffee sloshed onto his pants. "Damn." He wiped the spill with the greasy cloth napkin, making it worse. He tossed the napkin onto the table. "Had? Like years ago? Two years? Yesterday? What?"

David did a quick visual check of the room. "Is there anyone else in the house?"

"Kevin"—Elliott glanced up, paying special attention to the corners, crevices, and air vents—"and whoever else is keeping watch over the flock."

"I don't care about the 'see-through' people."

Elliott dry-washed his hands. "Well, ye should."

David gave him a thoughtful glance for a moment, then rolled his shoulders as if checking the weight of the holster. "I found a note buried in Sean's journal. Almost missed it." He flipped through his notebook. "Here it is: 'Talked to Harrison about his gambling. Loaned him twenty thousand dollars to cover losses. He agreed to get counseling.'"

Elliott's eyes widened and his jaw dropped. He made a circle in the air with his finger, indicating he wanted a replay.

"Harrison had a gambling problem."

"*Had?*" Elliott asked.

"There's no indication that it's still a problem or was at the time of Sean's death," David said.

"The way Harrison's been acting, I'd bet he's gambling again. What was he doing? Cards? Sports?"

"The track."

Elliott covered his face with his hands. "Ah, Jesus. Why didn't I know? Ye can't keep something like that quiet."

"Obviously, he did. He had someone place all of his bets."

Shaking his head, Elliott said, "Sean never said a word. How long ago are we talking about?"

David put his hand on Elliott's shoulder and pressed hard.

Elliott's face went slack, waiting.

"A month before the incident in the barn," David said.

Elliott pushed against David's restraining hand, but he applied more pressure to the shoulder. "Ye're not going anywhere. So calm down."

"If he's connected in any way, I swear I'll kill him," Elliott said.

David released Elliott's shoulder. "Ye're not going to kill anybody. Ye won't even step on a bug."

"Fifty thousand dollars is still missing. That would go a long way in repaying gambling debts."

"Harrison wouldn't need fifty thousand if Sean loaned him money to pay off his debts."

Elliott needed a drink to swallow this development. "Pour me a whisky."

David looked at him squint-eyed. "Ye falling off the wagon?"

"I wasn't on the wagon."

"Ye need to be."

"Stop lecturing and get me a drink."

David took his empty plate to the sink. "Ye know where the whisky is. Ye want it, ye get it."

Since New Year's, everybody had developed an attitude. He

didn't like it and felt eerily alone, but if either David or Kevin quit, he'd probably start biting his nails or, worse, biting heads.

"By the way," David said, "I've hired a bodyguard. He's a retired Fayette County policeman and comes highly recommended. He's moving into the house tonight."

"I don't need—"

The doorbell rang. David looked at the clock over the sink. "He's early. And ye do need a bodyguard when I'm not here. Until ye're mobile and until the killer is caught, ye're in possible danger."

David went to answer the door, leaving Elliott staring at the greasy spot on his trousers. Kit would laugh. Hell, Meredith would roll on the floor. He scrolled through the pictures on his phone until he found the one Louise took of him and Meredith under the mistletoe at the restaurant on Christmas Eve. *God, she's beautiful.* It had been a month since he'd seen her, and not an hour went by that he didn't ache for her.

"Elliott."

His head snapped in the direction of her voice. "Meredith." He tried to stand.

"Don't get up."

Relief, unlike anything he'd ever experienced, washed over him. He had a second chance, and he wouldn't blow it. He refused to let another strong woman walk out of his life. This wasn't about flowers or romance. This was about giving part of himself. Whatever she wanted, he would give. More time. More attention. More love. He would put *her* first. Not in a corner, but in the center.

"I need to talk to you," she said.

He ached to touch her, but he didn't reach out. "I didn't think ye'd ever come back."

"I didn't intend to, but…" She sat and crossed her hands under her breasts. "I have something to tell you, then I'm leaving, and I won't see you again."

He sat straight in his chair and placed his shaking hands on the table. "Then don't tell me." He wanted to kiss her, feel her skin against his face. But he remained still, afraid he'd do something that she didn't like and she'd fly off in her airplane. He couldn't let her do that. Not yet. Not until she understood how he felt about her.

"I lied to you," she said.

He closed his eyes and swallowed hard. *She's married.* He opened them and gazed at her. Her face appeared white and drawn, her eyes red, and even now they held tears. He sighed heavily. "Ye're married."

She laughed. "I wish it was that easy."

God, he needed a drink. "If ye're not married, I can take anything. What is it?"

"I…I—"

"Say it," he said.

"Have cancer."

Fireworks exploded from every nerve ending. His skin sizzled, both inside and out. Granny Mac died. Lou survived. He was batting five hundred. The way his life was going at the moment…well, he couldn't think of that now. Surely, the fates wouldn't send him a perfect woman only to take her away.

"It's an invasive lobular carcinoma," she continued. "They removed the lump, but the margins weren't clear. The good news is that it hasn't spread to the lymph nodes."

"The Band-Aid ye had on yer breast. It wasn't a mole, was it? That was from the lumpectomy? Why didn't ye tell me?" His heart was racing now. He grabbed the napkin off the table and wiped his eyes.

"You didn't need to know."

"Why the hell not?"

She stood and paced the room, back and forth.

"Meredith, s*top*."

She did instantly, like a motorized toy with a dead battery.

"There's more, isn't there? What aren't ye telling me?" Desperation sounded in his voice. Her hands gripped the back of the chair.

Small bluish-purple veins popped out. She studied him with her huge baby blues, a touch of tears shimmering in them. He clutched his gut, convinced there was a knife cutting him to shreds again. "For God's sake, *tell me.*"

"I'm pregnant."

Chapter Sixty-Two

ELLIOTT'S NEXT BREATH caught in his throat and hung there. He went completely numb. Time stopped. Leg pain stopped. Everything stopped. Since his first sexual encounter when he had been a lad of sixteen, he'd lived in fear of those words. His eyes drifted from her face to her belly. "Pregnant?" The words came out in a coarse whisper.

"I don't expect you to be involved unless…"

"*Unless?* My God, there is no *unless*. Ye're carrying my child, and I couldn't be happier." He felt a sudden chill as she recoiled. Her shoulders slumped, and her chest heaved with each breath.

"A baby doesn't fit with your lifestyle—"

"Who do ye think I am? Whoever it is, ye've got it all wrong."

"I don't think so. You've spent your life hop-skipping from one woman to another."

A burst of wind blew through the bare branches of the dogwood tree in the center of the garden visible from the large kitchen window. Shadows danced against the wall. The parade of women in his life had been nothing more than shadows. He knew that. They had been sexual partners without emotional commitment. That's what he had wanted. That's what they had wanted, too. Wasn't it? A knot formed in his throat, capturing his breath, holding it there. That's how it had started with Meredith, too, but…

"There have been women in my life who've meant a great deal to me," he said.

"Family and friends," Meredith said. "They don't count."

After a significant silence, Elliott said, "I want our baby. What do I have to do to convince ye of that?"

"You're a confirmed bachelor. What would you do with a baby?" she asked.

"The same thing I did with Kit for twenty-five years. She's part of the reason I never married or had children of my own. I couldn't bear the thought of leaving her." He put his elbows on the table and ran his hands through his hair. "I found her on the front porch when she was an infant—"

"*Found?* As in lost?"

"More like misplaced, but that's a story for another time. I fell in love with her from the get-go. Beautiful round face, green eyes. I was with her when she took her first step. Picked her up off the ground when she fell off her pony. Wiped her tears. Her butt, too."

"So you're saying…what? That you want a child?"

"Yes, but I never met a woman I wanted to have a child with. The first time I saw ye, I fell in love again, and I've been afraid ever since."

"Why?"

He pushed back in his chair. The legs scraped against the hardwood floor. "I thought ye wouldn't be interested because of my scars, my past."

"Elliott, that's not true—"

"I pushed ye away, not because I didn't want ye, but because I was afraid."

Meredith didn't say anything, and silence grew between them.

After what seemed an eternity, he said, "It would help if ye said something."

"I have cancer."

He lowered his head and squeezed his eyes and the bridge of his nose, thinking. Maybe for the first time in years, he was feeling something other than pain. Something that made his frozen heart crack open. He gazed at her. "I'm not an expert, but I believe pregnant women have survived breast cancer. I can afford the best treatment in the world. That's what ye'll get."

"I won't put my baby—"

"Our—"

"At risk."

"I think I read that there are some chemo drugs that don't cross the placenta."

"I don't trust that."

"There's anesthesia that won't hurt the baby."

"I had a reaction to the anesthetic five years ago. I won't take that risk either."

That old familiar rise in blood pressure heated his body. "Ye've ruled out chemo and surgery. What's left? Wait nine months while the cancer spreads?"

She held on to her arms, shaking. Her ankles wrapped around the chair legs.

"Are ye cold?" he asked.

"Yes. No. I've just got the shakes."

Even if he'd never studied body language, he could easily read her. Her movements screamed *don't touch me.*

"Tomorrow," he said, "we'll go over to the medical center and talk to Granny Mac's oncologist. We can conference in your doctors and develop a treatment plan."

"The launch is in two weeks. After that, I'll get a second and, if necessary, third opinion. But until then, my priority is my wine."

The emphasis Meredith placed on the word *wine* tagged a lost memory in Elliott's subconscious and pulled it up front and center. He heard his mother yelling at his father. *"Ye spend more time with yer damn wine than ye do with me."*

He gritted his teeth, torn between the urge to yell at Meredith and the urge to shake her until good sense prevailed. "Yer priority is yer survival, not yer wine."

"That's why I didn't intend to tell you." She stopped and took one deep breath and then another one. "I knew you wouldn't accept my decision."

Tears leaked from his eyes. "Why did ye?"

She got up and walked over to the kitchen sink and filled a glass with water. "Two weeks isn't going to make a difference."

"Two weeks won't, but how long have ye known? A month?"

She took a long drink then carried the glass over to the table. "I've known about the cancer, but I only found out about the baby a few days ago."

"Ye still haven't answered my question. Why did ye decide to tell me?"

She sat and placed the glass on the table. "I'm going home to finish what I started months ago, and then—"

He took her hand in his. "What ye started? What about what we started?"

"We crashed and burned, or have you forgotten?"

He was nothing more than a horse that had cornered the rail, fading fast with only an eighth of a mile to the finish line and nothing left in reserve. He and Meredith needed to be in each other's arms, comforting each other.

"Boss. Boss."

Elliott thrust out a breath and allowed some semblance of a smile. The cavalry had arrived.

Chapter Sixty-Three

"WHERE ARE YOU?" Kevin yelled. "You're not going to believe this."

Elliott knew Meredith was crazy about the lad, and his presence could possibly defuse the wee bit of tension between them. "In the kitchen."

"I just got a text from Meredith's assistant, Cate. Meredith's on her way—"

Kevin entered the kitchen and came to a dead stop with his face turning beet red. "Busted." He glanced first at Meredith then at Elliott. "Cate and I decided we're both going to quit if the two of you can't work this out." He turned and left the room. A few seconds later, the front door slammed.

Elliott stared at Meredith. She stared at him. He stood and pulled her to her feet. "Let me hold ye."

She hugged her elbows. "I don't know what to do."

"Stop thinking with yer head, and start feeling with yer heart."

The front door slammed again. A moment later, Kevin reentered the kitchen carrying Meredith's bags. "I paid for the taxi. What do you want me to do with these?"

Elliott raised his eyebrow. "Ye kept the meter running?"

"I wasn't going to stay," Meredith said.

"Ye could have gotten back on your plane. Why the luggage?"

"Gregory had to go to Washington. I was going to stay in a hotel tonight."

"Put her bags in—"

"The room upstairs," Meredith said.

"My room." Elliott sounded forceful, but he didn't care. She wasn't going to leave. He didn't feel cocky. Just self-assured. He knew where her sexual buttons were, and he intended to push all of them—several times. If he didn't win her over tonight, he might not get another chance.

Kevin turned one way then the other before marching off in the direction of the master suite, announcing over his shoulder, "I'm putting these in Elliott's room."

"Kevin, come back," Meredith said.

He leaned around the doorframe. "Sorry, Meredith, but he signs my checks."

Meredith watched him walk away with her bags. She turned to Elliott saying, "You created a monster."

"Remind me to tell ye how I met him."

"Lyles said he'd been a friend of Kit's."

"What else did he tell ye?"

"Not much." She nodded toward Elliott's leg. "How's it going?"

He placed his hand over his mouth, stretching out the lower lip before letting it spring back. "I'm motivated this time."

"I'm glad to hear that."

Okay, they were stalling. Time to make a move. "I need to sit and stretch my leg. Can we go into the other room?"

"Your room?"

"Well, yeah."

She scratched her forehead. "I'm not sure this—"

"Meredith, just go with it. Let's talk. That's all, but I can't do it in here." He could, but he wasn't going to. He aimed to press his advantage, so for effect, he slumped for a wee bit. A slight twinge of guilt swept across his heart, but he dust-panned it away. Yep, he was manipulating her, and he'd continue to fight dirty if he had to.

She followed him into the bedroom. "What happened to the wheelchair?"

"I'm allowed to use the sticks as long as I don't go any farther than the kitchen and back to my bedroom." He eased onto the bed and stretched out, watching her eyes, tense and worried, bluer than usual. Slowly, they softened. He blew out a quiet breath of relief. She kicked off her shoes, curled up on her side, and pushed up on her elbow like she had done so many times before.

"I've missed you, but you hurt me."

"I know I did, and I'm sorry." He gently cupped her cheek. She pulled away slightly, but he didn't drop his hand.

"You'll hurt me again. Won't you?" Her body still shivered.

Elliott had heard those words before. From his mother. Not directed toward him, but at his father. He was beginning to see with adult eyes the problems in his parents' troubled relationship.

Another tear slipped down his cheek. Then another. "God, I hope not. I couldn't live with myself if I did."

She wiped his tears with her thumb. "You're angry about something that goes much deeper than what's going on now. At least that's what my therapist told me several years ago."

"Did you find out what it was?"

For an instant, her eyes were naked with vulnerability. "Mom died when I was born. I told you that earlier. As a child, I felt responsible—"

"Ye were a baby."

"I know, but I grew up believing that if I hadn't been born she would be alive and my dad would be happy."

Elliott kissed her, and this time Meredith didn't withdraw at his touch.

"Ye're not angry now, though?"

"I read the medical reports. During childbirth, the placenta separated. The doctors saved me, but Mom had a reaction to the anesthetic. They lost her. After her death, they discovered that she had a bifurcated uterus. The placenta had attached to the weak interior wall. It was a miracle I survived."

"Is that why ye don't want surgery again? Ye're afraid."

Blood drained from her face, and her upper body sagged—a crumbling façade. Tears fell in thick streams down her face. Her emotional floodgate creaked open. Elliott made no attempt to bolt the door. He could easily have distracted her with a touch here, a kiss there, but he knew deep in his heart that she needed to unleash the mountain of gnawing fear and disappointment. He reached for a box of Kleenex and wiped her face. Her tears cut into him, creating deep grooves. How could he have been such an ass? For years, he'd inflicted pain, disregarding the feelings of others. His insensitivity would end *now*. It might require him to bite off his tongue, but he'd do what he could and pray for strength to do what he couldn't.

"If the anesthesiologist has a record of yer history," he said, "the doctor will be prepared. Ye'll be in good hands."

Meredith's salty tear-coated fingers covered his mouth. "I don't want to talk about it. Please."

He kissed her palm. "Okay."

She leaned into him, sobbing louder.

Granny Mac and Lou had cried on his shoulder. So had Kit, only months earlier. But with Meredith, her pain seeped into dry places within him that had been sealed up most of his life, and that's why he cried, too. He tried to keep his sobs quiet, but they poured out in wavy patterns and played in concert with hers.

In the midst of her guttural cries, interspersed with gasps of breath, came the words, "*It's not fair*." She pounded on his chest. He grasped her hands, uncurled her fingers. Her nails had cut into her palms, leaving white oval-shaped indentations. He took the brunt of it. The anger, the frustration, the fear. Warm tears soaked his shirt. At one of the most vulnerable times in her life, he had hurt her, hurt her deeply. And he'd carry the guilt forever, hearing her pain-filled sobs. They would bounce around in his memories like echoes reflecting off red and yellow canyon walls.

Kevin stepped into the room, turned the lights down, and closed the door. And all the while, they cried, until finally all the tears were shed. She rolled back onto the pillow, heaving, as did he—exhausted. Yet in a way, his body was now buoyant, purged of the deadly emotions that had weighed him down.

"Ye've carried all that around for years, haven't ye?" He pushed her sweat-soaked hair off her face. "Ye've tried to run it off, but even twenty-milers couldn't get rid of it."

"I wasn't aware of how much I was holding on to."

"We never do. But our stomachs and our hearts know. The stress puts wear and tear on our bodies. But we ignore it, pop antacids, yell, and micromanage everyone around us. As long as we can keep control, we won't succumb to the one thing we fear the most."

"What do you fear the most?" she asked.

"If ye had asked me a month ago—hell, twenty-four hours ago—I couldn't have told ye."

"And now?"

He had no rapid-pulsed fear of telling her anything, but his jumbled mind struggled with verbalizing his revelations. "I—" He stopped and waited for the words forming on his tongue to catch up. "—have always been afraid of not measuring up and being left behind."

She hiccupped. "You don't seem like you're afraid of anything. I noticed that about you when we first met. You're like the rocky soil that nurtures my vines—fearless, indestructible."

"It takes practice." No one cheered his success right now, least of all himself. He had succeeded in doing what he had set out to do as a lad of ten. He had sworn then that no one would ever see his pain again or hurt him as his mother had done.

"You can be human like the rest of us and let your foibles hang out."

He chuckled. "What's the expression about the pot calling the kettle black?"

She wiped tears with the back of her hand. "Since we're confessing…"

"Let me guess. Ye're afraid of failing."

"I'm that obvious?"

"No, ye're too confident. No one would ever believe it. But what I want to know is what will happen if ye do? Will the world end?"

She sat and leaned against the headboard, tucking her feet beneath her. "People will talk about me."

"What could they say that's so important?"

Her well-formed, sexy shoulders lifted in an easy shrug. "That I didn't deserve whatever it was I was trying to do, to get. That's why I work so hard."

He thought back to the compulsive work habits he'd seen in Scotland and later when she'd visited the farm. "Who cares what *they* think?"

She combed her fingers through his longer than usual hair. He'd skipped the last two or three weekly barber appointments, and although he wasn't sure he liked wearing it longer, everyone else seemed to.

"Because it reflects…because I'm a Montgomery."

"Ye're much more than a name."

"My name is everything. It's who I am. What I do. How I live my life."

"So ye're obsessive about yer new wine because ye're afraid it'll fail."

"There's too much at stake. I can't think about anything else."

"Ye're letting yer wine become more important than yer health."

She raised her eyebrows theatrically. "Well, there's that black pot again. Something's been rattling your cage for years or your leg would have healed a long time ago."

"Maybe."

Being open—even partially open—and honest with a woman he was having sex with was new for him. He tugged her back down on the bed, and she sprawled beside him. "Tell ye what. I'll give ye two weeks. I'll even carry yer to-do list and pencil and check off the items as ye get them done, but after *Cailean* is launched, we're focusing on two things: yer health and us."

She reached for a bottle of water off the nightstand and took a long swig.

"Can I get ye a glass of wine?" he asked.

"I'm not drinking now."

"They say one glass of red won't hurt the baby."

She snorted a laugh. "Chemo won't hurt the baby. Surgery won't hurt the baby. Wine won't hurt the baby. Somehow I don't believe it."

"Sex doesn't hurt a baby," Elliott said.

This time she let loose a real laugh. "Neither does running."

He pulled her over on top of him. "Yer laughter makes beautiful music."

"I've missed your singing." She kissed him. He put his hand behind her head and held her to him, kissing her back.

As strong as his need for her was, he took it slow. Her breath brushed against his cheek. He smiled when he breathed in the faint scent of wine. For him, he smelled hope. He pulled her sweater over her head and unclasped her bra. *Snap.* When her breasts fell free, she flinched slightly.

"I don't care if ye have two natural breasts or two man-made ones. Ye're beautiful and desirable and always will be."

"You say that now—"

"And I'll say it later." He touched her.

She pressed the pads of three of his fingers against the side of her breast. "The lump was right there."

"Did ye find it yerself?"

"I've had a lot of practice searching for them," she said.

"We'll conquer this, Meredith. I'll be with ye every step of the way." Her brows drew closer, and her face tightened. He read her face. She didn't believe him.

"Lou said you wouldn't even hug her after her surgery."

"She told ye, huh? At first, I was afraid I'd hurt her. Then I was afraid she'd be self-conscious." He used his hands and pantomimed weighty breasts. "She's large, and the absence of one was very noticeable. I was insensitive, but I didn't know how to approach her."

"You should tell her."

He slipped his hands down Meredith's back, beneath the waistband of her jeans. "I didn't know it still bothered her." He held tight to Meredith and pushed her against his crotch. His dick throbbed.

He wanted to rip off the rest of her clothes, but this was not that kind of night.

The air around them took on a pulsating life of its own.

She pushed his shirt up, and her fingers threaded through his hair-roughened chest. He lifted his arms and pulled the shirt over his head. "Is there anything else ye'd like me to take off?" he asked.

She scratched the whiskers on his jaw.

"Want me to shave, huh?"

She said no with a small shake of her head. "I like the rugged look. The longer hair and stubble are so…un-Elliott-like." Something about the way she said it, the way she was looking at him with those alluring baby blues, made his heart pound with a thunderous knock against his ribs.

"I haven't been so meticulous lately."

"You've had a lot going on with your leg and the farm."

His mouth went dry. He sipped from the same water container. Since he'd capped the whisky bottle almost four weeks earlier, he drank more coffee, more water, and had to pee all the time.

"Everything changed after ye left. When ye didn't give me a chance to make things right, my priorities shifted. I had to get my health back. We might not find out who killed the horses, but the farm will survive. Whether I'm CEO or not doesn't really matter. Lou was right. This place isn't mine. I don't owe it any more than I've already given it."

"Are you going to quit?"

"Not yet. Got to get through this mess first. Get on solid footing again." His throat became painfully tight. He'd never acknowledged this, even to himself.

"And do what? Go back to Scotland?"

His neck pulsed, singularly describing his old fear in relation to a new one. "I won't be separated from my child. I couldn't live like that."

Her weary gaze connected with his. "Something might happen to the baby. My body—"

He kissed her, cutting out whatever she was going to say. The effects of the tender touch of their mouths tingled on his lips. "This *will* work. Let's take it one day at a time." He spread his hand against her chest. The thumb touched one nipple, the pinkie the other. Goose bumps popped out from her neck down. He grabbed a fleece throw blanket and wrapped it around her. "I won't leave ye. Ye won't go through this alone. All I ask is that ye listen to the doctors, trust that I'll help ye, and believe we can conquer this disease."

Her mouth quivered. "Just don't pressure me until after the sixteenth."

"I said I'd give ye that time, and I will." He'd use those days to have conversations with doctors all around the world. When she was ready to act, he'd have appointments scheduled at the best breast cancer centers, along with cutting-edge doctors on standby ready to treat her.

"Would ye feel pressured if I asked ye to take off the rest of yer clothes?"

Her smile had lost the sparkle he'd seen so many times in Edinburgh, but she laughed softly. Her beautiful, expressive eyes were still awash in tears. "I didn't plan…"

He lifted her chin with his index finger. "What?"

"I didn't come here to make love with you. Actually, that was the farthest thing from my mind, but I can't think of anything I want more."

Whatever he expected to hear, it wasn't that, but with those words, he became lost in the softness of her body, the scent of her hair, and the silky feel of her skin next to his. They fumbled with their clothes, tossing them here and there. Finally, he had her naked beside him. Although deep in his heart he had held out hope that this would happen, the logical part of his brain had said, "No way." He put his hands to her cheeks, eased her head forward for the kiss he planned to give her, but he froze, and the throb of his pulse beat against his temples. "Ye have specks of gold in yer eyes."

She kissed his nose, his cheeks, his chin. "It's a family trait. You usually don't see them in blue eyes."

He brushed his lips across the smooth white skin beneath her jaw. "Only seen them in green."

"I bet the baby will have your chocolate eyes," she said.

"Hope not. Yers should be passed on." He lifted her and positioned her right where he wanted her. The muscles in his arms and shoulders coiled and bunched as he held her above him. Then, slowly, like a cat stretching in the sun, she eased down on him until he was buried inside her. He was home, and there was no other place he'd rather be.

Chapter Sixty-Four

En Route to Lexington Airport – February 1

THE OVERCAST MORNING spilled its gloom into the backseat of Elliott's Mercedes. He was heartsick that Meredith wanted to go home after only one night at the farm, but he wasn't going to encourage her to stay. He'd rather walk barefoot through the barn than put pressure on her. Their relationship, although back on course, chugged dangerously along a track still under construction.

Thinking back over the last twelve hours, he had to smile despite the gloom. They had made love, then slept curled tightly in each other's arms. Meredith had gotten up twice during the night, sick to her stomach, but she hadn't complained. Now, as he sat there with his fingers interlaced with her warm hand, his heart beat wildly with admiration for her true grit. How that would play out over the next few months, he didn't know, but he set his hopes high above the rainbow because that's where dreams come true. Call him a hopeless romantic, but he knew he loved her, and he intended to spend many, many years with her in his arms.

"If I can get away this weekend, I'll be in Napa late Friday night," he said.

"Let's play it by ear. It might be easier for me to travel. I know you don't want to leave the farm right now."

He squeezed her hand. "Ye're sick. I don't want ye suffering from jet lag, too."

She let out a little hiss of exasperation. "I'm pregnant. Not an invalid. I should be able to come down at least for Saturday night. Don't tell Gregory I said this, but my life has been so much easier since I gave up trying to do both of our jobs. He's got everything under control. The only things I have left to do for the party is go to my last dress fitting."

"Then stay for a few days."

"The launch isn't the only project going on at the winery. In a few months, we'll unveil the nation's largest rooftop solar cogeneration system. It's just one of our sustainable energy initiatives."

"A green company."

"Very green."

He lifted her hand to his mouth and kissed it. "I'm proud of ye."

She gave him a sparkling smile that told him she not only felt better physically but emotionally, too. "You can be proud of me for something else I did."

"Really? What?"

"I didn't make a to-do list when I woke up."

"Jesus." Elliott glanced out the window searching the sky that sunlight struggled to penetrate. "Yep. I think the world might come to an end today."

She laughed. "Oh, stop it. It's not that big a deal."

He gave her nape a squeeze with one hand before pulling her close. Her warm breath blew soft caresses over his face. His tongue slid inside her mouth, giving and tasting. "I can't wait five days. I'll fly up Wednesday."

She nibbled at the corner of his lips. "Sure you can."

"Easier for ye. Yer projects aren't stalled like mine," he said.

She kissed his chin, his neck. "What's the board of directors saying?"

"Not much, but they're anxious. We've got to have a break in the case, or they'll have my neck in a noose." He slipped his hand beneath her sweater and started to cup her breasts. He stopped. It wasn't that he didn't want to touch her; he did. But he thought he needed to downplay their importance to him. He ran his fingers up and down her spine slowly, teasing and tickling. She wiggled. He lifted her chin, and his lips found hers. Hunger exploded when his tongue slipped into her mouth, and a husky sound of her need past her lips.

"What about the shareholders?"

He flicked his tongue over hers. "They're busting my balls."

She grasped his shoulders and held on tight. "That sounds painful."

"It's manageable." He stroked the inside of her mouth, savoring the lush interior. Maybe he wouldn't let her leave after all.

"I have something else I need to tell you before I go," she said.

He kissed her neck, smelling her three-butter lotion. "I want ye for lunch and dinner."

"Stop a minute. I need to tell you this. I want everything out on the table."

He nibbled on her ear. "The table's rather crowded. Can't it wait?"

She pulled away. "I want to be completely transparent."

He did a quick gut check. No racing heart. No heated anger. Somewhat amazed, he gazed at her with a slow arch of his brow. "If I'd heard those words yesterday, my stress would have gone from zero to a hundred in a snap. So tell me."

"You probably don't want to hear this."

He entwined his fingers in her hair and tugged her back toward him. "No drama. Just spit it out."

She licked her bottom lip. "When I was here before, I saw a ghost."

Surprisingly, he laughed. Not even a ghost sighting could upset him right now. "Ye, too, huh?"

She gave him a pouty look, extending her lower lip. "I'm serious," she said. "I saw him twice."

Elliott was about to suck her lower lip into his mouth when David knocked on the window. He pointed toward the runway. "Plane's landing."

Elliott gave him the okay signal and turned his attention back to Meredith's lip. "A ghost is only a trick of the light. The human brain is hard-wired to see faces. We see them in clouds, too. Ghosts don't exist."

"It wasn't a trick of the light, and he didn't look like Casper with only a face either."

"Which one did ye see? The old sea captain or the dark-haired, handsome dude?"

"The dark-haired dude."

He studied her pensive expression. Obviously, she didn't doubt what her eyes told her. "Sometimes ye can see the ghost, and sometimes ye can't? I wonder why that is?"

"You're making fun of me."

He wasn't, but he was teasing her and thoroughly enjoying it. He didn't care about the damn ghost. If she thought she saw one, so be it. As far as he knew, the black-haired dude had never hurt anyone. Elliott wasn't sure he could say the same about the sea captain and the cutlass he carried strapped to his hip.

"Ye saw a ghost. I believe ye. Next time ye see him, have a nice chat and tell him I said hello."

She put her hand on her hips. "You don't believe me, but I know what I saw. I even looked through Kit's sketch pads. We saw the same ghost. I'd love to talk to her about her sightings because…because"—Meredith took a deep breath—"the dark-haired dude is my great-great-great-great-grandfather, Cullen Montgomery. He's a few years older in the picture I have at home, but it's definitely the same person. What I want to know is why is he here?"

The smile didn't just slip off Elliott's face. It slid off faster than snow down a slope during an avalanche. "Why didn't ye tell me this before?"

"Because you made such a big deal about not believing in the see-through people."

Elliott shook his head like a dog. "It's impossible. Ye're mistaken."

A flicker of disappointment appeared in her eyes. "You're

closed-minded when it comes to ghost sightings. I accept that, so I won't include you in my research. But what I need to know from you is if there are any MacKlenna Farm journals from the nineteenth century that might mention a connection between the MacKlennas and Montgomerys."

"There's Old Thomas's daily journal in the office and some old journals up on a shelf in the library. I'll ask Mrs. Collins to get the cleaning staff to dust them off."

"Are they as dusty as your wine cellar?"

"Nothing's that dusty."

She kissed him. "Thank you. It's important to me."

The Montgomery Winery jet taxied toward the MacKlenna hangar. "Yer ride's here. Are ye sure ye won't change yer mind and stay a few more days?"

Meredith skewed him with a look that told him not to press.

The door to the cabin opened, and the Montgomery Winery flight attendant stood in the doorway.

"I've got to go," Meredith said. "I'll call you later."

He pulled her into his arms for one last kiss. Their open mouths fused hungrily. The tip of his tongue dueled with hers. Neither of them played gently. "Hurry back, my wee sweetheart."

"Late Friday."

"Come sooner if ye can." He teased her ear with his teeth, blowing warm breath on her cheek.

"Keep this up, and I'll come right now," she said.

"Don't let me stop ye."

She straightened and patted her chest, trying to catch her breath. "Whew. You sure can get me going." She reached for the door handle. "If you see any see-through people this week, tell the dark-haired dude we've got a date Friday night."

"They don't show up when I'm around."

She leaned over and kissed him. "Maybe they'll make an exception."

If Cullen Montgomery showed up and explained himself, that would either solve Elliott's problem or cause a bigger one.

She reached into her computer bag and withdrew a thick folder. "I wasn't sure whether I would give these to you or not. But it makes sense for you to have them."

"What's in the file?"

"My medical records, films, reports, doctors' names and contact information. I signed release forms so you can talk to them if you have questions. But don't forget our deal. Two weeks."

Elliott took the folder. "I won't forget."

He watched her hustle up the stairs to the cabin door. She turned and waved. He waved back, but she couldn't see him through the tinted glass.

In less than twenty-four hours, his life had flip-flopped. He still had to find a solution to the farm's situation, but it would no longer consume him. Researching the latest breast cancer treatment protocols would become his twenty-four/seven job. If he had to resign as CEO, he was prepared to submit his resignation.

The only woman he had ever loved was back in his life, and he would fight for her and his unborn child.

Chapter Sixty-Five

MacKlenna Mansion – February 1

DAVID STOOD AT the wet bar in Elliott's office at the farm, quietly tapping his fingers on the counter. The Keurig brewing system spat out an eight-ounce cup of the medium roast. "Ye want sugar or cream?"

"Ye know I drink it black."

"Yer old habits are dying so fast I didn't know if that one had, too."

"Ha-ha," Elliott said.

David set a cup of the brew on the desk with a napkin and a Spalding's donut. "Ye going to tell me what happened before Meredith left or not?"

Elliott stared out the window overlooking the paddock. The brown grass and gloomy day fit perfectly with his mood. "What makes ye think something happened?"

"For starters, ye're staring out the window at nothing."

Elliott turned the wheelchair away from the window and wheeled himself to the desk where he picked up his coffee. "It's complicated."

"Sounds like crap to me. Now a horse killer"—David gestured with his hand—"that's complicated. Sleeping with a beautiful woman, that's black and white."

"Ye got that ass backward. Women are always more complicated."

"If that's the case, drink up fast. Coffee helps ye find yer way through the cobwebs." David returned to the coffeemaker to fix another cup.

"A man named Cullen Montgomery is the ghost of MacKlenna Farm."

David turned toward him. His face held little expression. "He has a name now?"

Elliott drank a few sips, waiting for clarity that didn't come. "Meredith said the ghost is her ancestor, her great-great"—he counted on his fingers—"great-great-grandfather."

David's mouth dropped open. "What?"

"She saw him. The ghost of MacKlenna Farm. Kit's ghost. Meredith identified him as her ancestor, Cullen Montgomery."

David carried his cup across the room and sat in one of the leather chairs positioned in front of the desk. "There must be a connection between the MacKlennas and the Montgomerys. Why else would the ghost haunt MacKlenna Farm?" He propped one booted foot on his opposite knee and crossed his arms over his barrel chest.

Elliott picked up a framed picture of Kit from the desk, an old picture, but one that came with a dozen memories. He could still hear the excitement in her voice after winning her first dressage show.

"If there's a connection, Meredith is determined to find it." Elliott ate his donut and thought about his goddaughter and Meredith. They would have loved each other.

David wiped crumbs off the desk, tossed them into the trash can, then walked over to the coffeepot. "Want another cup?"

"No," Elliott said. "Bottled water."

David made another cup for himself and snatched a bottle of water from the built-in refrigerator. "What could be keeping the ghost here? Maybe he knew Meredith would show up one day."

"Then we owe it to her to see that her ancestor gets settled in the afterlife."

David barked out a laugh. "Do ye want to have a séance?"

Elliott shrugged. "If it would tell us why he's still here, yes."

David bent over laughing until tears came into his eyes. He grabbed a napkin and wiped his face. Then he started laughing again.

"I'm glad ye're having a good laugh at my expense."

"If someone had told me that ye'd stop drinking and start believing in ghosts, I'd have asked what they were smoking." He held up his hands in surrender. "Don't get me wrong, I think the change is long overdue, but it's a wee bit of a shocker."

It was a shocker to Elliott, too. He still missed the whisky, but he missed Meredith more. His outburst on New Year's was alcohol related. If he had to quit permanently to ensure that never happened again, he would. For her, he'd do anything.

"When's Meredith coming back?" David's voice still held a hint of laughter.

"Friday night." Elliott rolled the chair's wheels back and forth in small jerky motions. He itched to park the damn chair in the closet and slam the door. Lyles wanted to see him Friday morning. Maybe Elliott would get his marching orders and trade the chair in for a walking boot. He jerked the wheels a wee bit faster, anticipating standing in front of Meredith when he saw her next.

"Meredith doesn't have any family, does she?" David asked.

Elliott shook his head.

"That means she's pregnant with the last Montgomery—"

"*Fraser*," Elliott said.

"What if there's a connection to the MacKlennas? The baby could be the last MacKlenna, too."

A flash of pride grew inside Elliott. "My son will never be the last of anything. He's the beginning of the rest of my life."

Chapter Sixty-Six

MacKlenna Mansion – February 3

TWO DAYS LATER, Elliott sat in his wheelchair in the middle of the kitchen, drinking Gatorade from a bottle. Sweat poured down his face. An old, wet triathlon T-shirt clung to his heaving chest. Muscles in his arms and shoulders throbbed. His trainer had worked him hard. Too hard. Elliott chalked it up to the fact that Ted was still angry over the way Meredith had been treated. Even knowing that she and Elliott had patched up their differences didn't improve Ted's attitude. Elliott cut him some slack and didn't complain when Ted piled on a few pounds of weight more than Elliott was accustomed to lifting. He'd seen this personality quirk from his trainer before. Ted was slow when it came to handing out forgiveness.

"Elliott," David called.

"In the kitchen."

David entered the room, stopped, and glared at Elliott. "There's a cabinet full of glasses." He opened the one closest to the sink and grabbed one. "Ye're not the only one who drinks out of the gallon Gatorade bottle."

"Give me a pen." Elliott took a black Bic pen from David and scribbled his name on the neck of the bottle. "There. Ye're on notice. This is mine."

David tossed his coat on the counter, along with his hat and gloves, but held on to a rolled up newspaper. "Mrs. Collins needs to shuck those old coats in the hall. Nobody wears them, and there's no room on the tree."

Elliott frowned. "What the hell's wrong with ye?"

David paced, slapping the paper against his palm. Unease didn't slide off him. It rolled in a fevered pitch. Elliott had seen David this agitated only once, shortly after his return from Afghanistan. It lasted a few weeks while he adjusted to being home. The Highlands, the land, and the people made the transition easier.

"What'd the police want?" Elliott asked, hoping to get his friend to focus a wee bit.

David stopped pacing as if he'd come to the end of a ledge. "They found the gun that was used to shoot Gates."

"*Where?*" Elliott asked.

David tossed the paper onto the countertop. Then he cocked his hip against the cabinet, crossed his legs at the ankles, and shoved his hands under his armpits. Frustration tightened his face. "A strung-out freak robbed a convenience store last night. He didn't make it out of the parking lot. He fired. The police fired back. Killed him."

"What does that have to do with the gun that killed Gates?"

"A ballistics match."

Elliott picked the newspaper up off the counter, thumbed through to the local section, found the article describing the shoot-out, and read it quickly. "Jesus. So that's it? Gates was killed by a strung-out dopehead. End of story."

David rubbed the back of his neck. "They've closed the case. Chuck called off his team."

Elliott tossed the newspaper back on the counter. "There's still a horse killer out there. Call him back."

"I did. He said he's been working the case for almost two months, and there're no leads. He's behind with other jobs. Said to call him if anything develops."

"Give my babysitter something to do. He's a retired cop. Maybe he can find something we've missed."

"I'll talk to him," David said. "He's not needed here now."

"As far as I was concerned, he never was," Elliott said.

"Ye've put thousands of dollars into this investigation. It's time to cut yer losses," David said.

All Elliott had believed about the case had been proven wrong. He squirmed in his seat. How could he have been so misguided? "What about Harrison? He's too spineless to have orchestrated the killings, or done it himself, but if he's gambling, that could cause problems for the farm."

"We've checked with bookies from here to Vegas. Nothing. Chuck combed through his trash and his bank accounts. Nothing. He looks clean."

"The farm's lost thirty million dollars. Even selling off part of the land won't cover the loss. One horse, maybe. Two, never. Some asshole set out to ruin us and succeeded." Elliott had gone over the numbers a dozen times. He'd reread the insurance policies and the syndication agreements. No matter which way he sliced it, MacKlenna Farm was saddled with the liability and headed for the auction block.

"What's next?" David asked.

Elliott took several swallows of Gatorade. As he replaced the cap, he said, "Bankruptcy. The only hope is that another Henryk de Kwiatkowski will come forward and save it from liquidation like Kwiatkowski saved Calumet."

"Any superheroes on the horizon who could do that?"

Elliott shook his head. "No one was expecting Kwiatkowski to rescue Calumet Farm before the gavel dropped." He blew out a long breath as he wiped his forehead with the sleeve of his wet T-shirt. "Ye've done yer job. Time for ye to go home." Although he knew David needed to go, he hated losing him. Not only was David a friend and confidant, but Elliott needed someone around to kick his ass when he got out of line, He could count on David to do that.

"Ye've got the money, why don't ye bail it out?"

"If I was a MacKlenna, I'd do it, but the Highland's estate is my home place now that Da is gone." Elliott glanced out the large window overlooking the south paddock. Stormy trotted around the boundaries like a king surveying his domain. Maybe the land didn't belong to Elliott, but Stormy did. Kit had surprised him, leaving a bill of sale for the horse with her journal. Stormy wouldn't be shackled with a new owner.

"When ye heading back to Scotland?"

"Probably not until summer," Elliott said.

"I'll stick around and go to Napa for the launch. Book a flight home from there." David opened the fridge and gathered up eggs and bacon. "There's something I've been meaning to ask. What was the deal with the joint compound ye created?"

"What brought that up?"

David cracked a couple of eggs into a bowl and added salt and pepper. "I found a loose sheet of paper in the box with the journals. Looked like Sean jotted down a few notes but never included them in the daily book."

"What'd it say?"

David placed several strips of bacon in the microwave. "Nothing specific." He placed a skillet on the stove and turned on the burner. "The note mentioned that Doc wanted to discuss the compound. Sean agreed to set up a meeting after the first of the year, but he died. The meeting never happened."

"Did you ask Doc?"

"He brushed it off. Said he didn't know what I was talking about."

"I don't know what he could have wanted from Sean. Doc wasn't involved. He'd made a couple of suggestions during the experimental stage that didn't pan out."

"So, he didn't get a share."

"No reason he should," Elliott said.

David poured the eggs into the skillet. "It's made ye a multimillionaire."

"My Apple stock did that."

"So Doc wasn't pissed that he was cut out?"

"How could he be cut out of a gig he wasn't part of?"

With one hand, David moved the eggs around the skillet with a spatula. With the other he removed the bacon from the microwave and placed the slices on a paper towel. "Ye two have never gotten along."

"Has nothing to do with the compound. Why the interrogation?"

"I wanted a gut reaction."

"Well," said Elliott.

"Sounds like he had a problem. He went to Sean who agreed to a meeting, but Sean died. Ye and Doc have worked together without incident this past year. I don't think there's anything there."

Kevin entered the room, dripping in sweat. "Anything where?"

David scraped the eggs onto a plate. "With Doc."

"You talking about him being pissed because he got cut out of the joint compound? I'd be pissed, too," Kevin said.

"He didn't get cut out," Elliott said.

"That's not what I heard."

"What'd ye hear?" Elliott asked.

Kevin pinched a slice of bacon. David slapped his hand with the spatula. "Ouch." Kevin glared at David. David glared back.

"What'd ye hear?" Elliott asked again, annoyance in his voice.

"I heard him and Kit arguing about the drug. She told him to talk to her dad. Did he?"

David popped two pieces of bread into the toaster and moved the bacon out of Kevin's reach. "According to a note I found, yes, but a meeting never occurred."

"Ask him," Kevin said. "Doc hates vetting. He's planning to retire. A small share of the compound could make it nice for him."

Elliott put what was left of the Gatorade back into the refrigerator. "Wonder why he never said anything to me?"

"Because you'd blow him off." Kevin attempted to snatch another piece of bacon but settled for a bite of eggs. David threatened him again with the spatula.

"It's too late now," Elliott said. "Sean's interest in the compound might be tied up in the bankruptcy."

David dug into his eggs to Kevin's chagrin. "The farm's not

bankrupt yet," David said between bites.

"There're laws about transferring assets prior to bankruptcy. It'd never be approved."

"I'm sure he's forgotten all about it by now," Kevin said.

Kevin's phone beeped with a text message. "Susan got us an appointment at the oncology department at Markey Cancer Center at ten thirty. We've got to get ready."

"Who're we meeting with?" Elliott asked as Kevin wheeled him out into the hallway.

"She didn't say."

Kevin's evasive tone of voice told Elliott he knew more than he was saying. "What is it, lad? What're ye not telling me?"

"Nothing."

"*Kevin.*"

"Be prepared, Boss. That's all I can say."

Elliott grabbed the wheels, stopped the chair, and swiveled around to confront Kevin. "For what?"

Kevin blew out a breath that hissed between his teeth. "They're going to recommend Meredith terminate the pregnancy."

Chapter Sixty-Seven

Markey Cancer Center – February 3

TWO HOURS LATER, Kevin and Elliott sat in a conference room on the second floor of the Whitney-Hendrickson Building at Markey Cancer Center with a nationally recognized team of physicians. Sean had made a significant contribution to the center following Granny Mac's death, and Elliott assured the administration that another donation would be forthcoming. If the doctors could cure Meredith, he'd give the center whatever they wanted.

"Dr. Fraser, our goal is to cure Ms. Montgomery's cancer. Protecting the unborn child makes this more complex. Both chemotherapy and radiation may be harmful to the fetus," the chief of radiology said.

"I thought there were some forms of chemo that didn't cross the placenta," Elliott said.

"Recent studies have found that chemotherapy treatment after the first trimester can be safe for the baby," the breast care center director said.

"Would ye recommend a mastectomy followed by chemo?" Elliott asked.

The chief of surgery and surgical oncology section head said, "I'd recommend terminating the pregnancy, followed by mastectomy and radiation. The risk of birth defects is already high since Ms. Montgomery had the sentinel lymph node biopsy with radioactive dye."

"She had a pregnancy test before the sentinel lymph node biopsy. Why didn't the test show positive?"

"It was too early in the pregnancy."

Elliott scrubbed his face with his hands. "What happens if she does nothing until after the birth?"

"The cancer will spread, and the odds of a positive outcome diminish," the director said.

"Can ye do the mastectomy now and hold off on the chemo until after the baby is born?"

"Yes, although I'd recommend starting chemo during the second trimester."

The doctors might as well have told Elliott he had terminal brain cancer. Their recommendations had sucked the life from him. Why hadn't he used a condom? If she decided against treatment in order to protect the baby, then his carelessness could cost Meredith her life.

"It's also my recommendation to terminate the pregnancy. Then we can fight the disease aggressively," the director said.

Those words formed into sharp needles that punctured Elliott's skin. He rubbed his arms, but the sensation didn't go away. He played the one and only card he had. "Do ye have any research that proves ending a pregnancy to have cancer treatments improves a woman's prognosis?"

The director shuffled papers, stalling. Finally, she said, "No. There isn't any."

Elliott threw up his hands. "Then I know Meredith won't agree."

"I have in my notes that Ms. Montgomery initially put off treatment because she has an event next week," the director said. "Why don't we give her time to get through that, then meet again the following week? She may be more open to treatment options."

The medical team consulted their calendars and agreed to set another appointment in two weeks. Elliott left the meeting with a painful lump in his throat. His limbs felt too heavy to move, and for once, he was thankful to be in a wheelchair. The drive home, although only a few miles, was a slow, quiet trip.

Kevin pulled into the driveway and passed through security. Elliott waved at the guard. "If I'd only used a condom…"

Kevin pushed the garage door opener and watched the door rise. "I think there were two consenting adults in that bed."

Elliott opened his door and got out. He stood on one foot, waiting for the chair. "It's ultimately my responsibility."

Kevin lifted the wheelchair from the trunk and pushed it toward Elliott. "You'd like to think that, wouldn't you? But it's her body, and her decision to make."

"Then I'll have to make sure she makes the right ones going forward." Elliott scrolled through his contacts and called his jeweler.

"This is Elliott Fraser. Is Shelia there?"

"She's with a customer, Dr. Fraser. Can I have her call you?" Shelia's assistant asked.

Elliott tugged on his chin. "Tell her I called and wanted an update on the ring I ordered."

"She told me this morning it would be ready on Friday. I'll call and tell you when to pick it up."

Elliott disconnected the call just as Kevin opened the door to the mudroom and yelled for David. "I win the bet."

"What was the bet?" Elliott asked.

Kevin laughed. "That you'd propose this weekend."

Elliott stood and stepped across the threshold. Kevin lifted the chair, then Elliott sat back down. "I don't have a plan in mind."

"Nah, Boss. You'll give it to her. You won't be able to wait." Kevin began humming "Here Comes the Bride."

Fear crawled through Elliott's stomach, punching and kicking along the way. "The bet shouldn't be when I'll propose, but if she'll accept."

Chapter Sixty-Eight

Montgomery Winery – February 13

MEREDITH SAT ALONE at a round table for ten under the giant rectangular tent erected two hundred yards from the winery's welcome center. Miles of vineyards surrounded the tent. After hosting dozens of fundraisers for nonprofits over the years, her father had had a concrete pad built and installed underground utilities. Not only did the winery hold special events there, but several nonprofits held annual fundraisers. The money spent on constructing the facility provided a tax write-off for the winery, and offering the grounds to nonprofits guaranteed sold-out events for the charities. Good for the community. Good for business.

She sat back in a white folding chair with a white padded seat. On event day, the one hundred tables, providing seating for a thousand, would be covered with white tablecloths. Lush, dreamy floral arrangements in a variety of colors would decorate each table. The napkins, in a coordinating bright green, would also provide splashes of color. If she closed her eyes, she could see the space as it would look on the sixteenth—eye-poppingly gorgeous.

The week had been exhausting, and nausea had plagued her nonstop. Knowing that she was sick because she was pregnant made the queasy stomach and occasional vomiting tolerable. Cate's constant nagging to make an appointment with a specialist, however, created a problem. After the launch, Meredith would have to bring her assistant into the loop.

Experience from hosting dozens of events had stenciled a last-minute checklist on her brain.

- Portable kitchen installed and functioning
- Port-a-pots
- EMT, police, and fire scheduled
- Lights and sound check scheduled
- Trailer for celebrities
- Valet parking
- Photographers
- TV stations notified
- Dress/shoes/hair appointment

Cate had a list, too, but this time Meredith trusted her to get it done without looking over her assistant's capable shoulder. Memories of Elliott's staff wigging out before the MacKlenna Hogmanay played over and over in her mind. Meredith didn't want people making faces behind her back.

The director of social media had turned out to be a godsend, and Gregory had more than earned a promotion. There was little left for Meredith to do for the party than show up. And show up she would, with a handsome Scotsman on her arm. God, she missed Elliott.

The text message she'd just received said he'd be in an emergency board of directors' meeting when she arrived later that night. He didn't like the idea, but several owners of the horses who were killed were saber rattling, and the board needed to calm the owners' nerves before they ran off to the courthouse to file lawsuits.

She hated to see the farm go bankrupt, but it wasn't his farm, and he wasn't liable for the debt. Her ancestor's ghost concerned her, though. Would he stick around the farm? Maybe she could talk him into coming to California where he belonged. She laughed. Cullen Montgomery, ghost of MacKlenna Farm. Boy oh boy, she'd love to know how that came about. Since ghosts couldn't talk, she was unlikely to find out.

Meredith strolled around the tent. The workers had just completed the construction of the dance floor on the north end facing the stage and were now working on the bar. For past events, the bar had been located at the opposite end from the dance floor. This year, Meredith had a circular bar designed for the center of the tent. The focal point was a twenty-foot tall bottle of *Cailean* rising from a platform built into the interior of the bar. Very impressive. The concealed wiring made it look suspended in thin air. She rubbed the chill bumps on her arms.

"What do you think, Ms. Montgomery?" the construction foreman asked as the final support went into place.

She took a deep breath. "It won't fall down, will it?"

"No, ma'am. It's in there pretty tight," he said.

She kept on walking without fretting over a possible disaster in the making. The event's hundred-pound weight of worry was now on Gregory's shoulders instead of hers. She had a different hundred-pound weight that couldn't be turned over to anyone else. Several extra pounds had been added to the weight a few minutes earlier when her ob-gyn called. One of the doctors treating her called once a day. She suspected they had set up a tag team.

Her ob-gyn had broken the news that the breast center had used radioactive dye during the sentinel lymph node biopsy after her pregnancy test came back negative, explaining that it was too soon after conception to give a positive reading.

"So what does that mean?" she had asked him.

"It may affect the fetus," he had said. "We'll be able to tell more in a few weeks."

The news had left her stunned and shaking. Tears rolled down her cheeks now as she recalled the words: *May affect the fetus.*

Her legs moved faster. Fear crawled up her spine, scratching and gouging. At the entrance, she burst through the canvas door and followed the well-tended brick path lined with daffodils. The path snaked around the outside of the tent toward the blacktop road. The road led through miles of vineyards now alive with growing cover crops. She ran past the pruning crews, methodically cutting away. Some nodded. Some waved. They were used to seeing her run.

As her feet pounded the pavement, a thought repeatedly pounded her brain. *May affect the fetus.* One mile turned into four, then into six. And still she ran. *May affect the fetus.* Ten miles became twelve. In the warmer temperature, sweat poured off her body. When the Italian-style villa came into view, she slowed down and ran the final half mile at a comfortable pace. The vibrant wild mustard flowers bloomed, growing in rows between bare grapevines. Soon her vines would bloom, and another growing season would be upon them. This year, along with her grapes, her baby would grow, too.

When she hit the driveway, she slowed to a walk. The grounds crew was busy grooming her yard. In a few days, a thousand visitors would stream onto the property. A thousand people would taste her wine. A thousand people whose opinion mattered. Had she done all she could do? Probably not. But today she could live with that.

She entered the kitchen through the back door, grabbed a banana and a bottle of chocolate milk—carbs and protein—then plopped down on the floor in her home office to stretch. She loved the joke: How do you tell you're a runner? Answer: Because you know you should stretch, but don't. As part of her new regime to reduce her stress, she stretched.

Sitting on the floor sipping milk, she rubbed her hand over her belly, something she found herself doing often. There was no baby bump, of course. Not yet. But she knew the little guy was there, depending on her to keep him healthy. She had to do all she could for him. She wouldn't be bullied into treatment because it was good for her. Whatever she did had to be good for both of them.

I don't care what they say. You'll be born healthy. You'll survive.

Chapter Sixty-Nine

Montgomery Winery – February 13

THE EXUBERANCE MEREDITH experienced following her run went to hell in a Gucci bag when the caterer had an attack during a telephone conference with her and had to be rushed to the hospital with nausea, vomiting, and pain radiating to the back.

Meredith paced in her office waiting for the caterer's wife to call with a report, which she did three hours later.

"It's pancreatitis caused by gallstones. He'll be in the hospital for a week."

Meredith broke down and cried. Not only was he the best caterer in the area, he was also an old friend.

Cate rushed into Meredith's office after getting the news secondhand. "He'll be all right, and you have a plan B caterer. You insisted I line one up. Cost a fortune, but you wouldn't have it any other way."

Meredith nodded between sobs. "Get him on the phone."

Cate handed Meredith a tissue. "I can't right now. He's on a flight from Mexico."

"How do you know?"

"I called him yesterday to check on his schedule in case we needed him."

Meredith wiped her eyes, but a fresh supply of tears took their place. "The contract said he had to stay in town."

Cate turned to the catering tab in Meredith's event notebook. She thumbed through the contract then pointed to a paragraph on page two. "Only two days before the event."

Meredith read the paragraph. "Did he negotiate that? I would have required a week."

"You did, and he negotiated."

Meredith finger-combed her hair, pulled it into a ponytail, twisted the tail into a bun, and secured it with a clip. "Get him here as soon as he lands."

"I'll send a car for him. And speaking of airports, it's time for you to get out of here. Elliott's waiting for you."

Meredith scanned the contract to make sure there weren't any surprises. "I need to talk to the caterer as soon as he arrives. Have him call me."

Cate tugged on Meredith's arm to get her up out of the chair, but Meredith wasn't ready to leave. Cate tugged harder.

"Okay. I'm out of here," Meredith said, "but only if you promise—"

Cate threw up her hands, shooing Meredith. "*Go.* I've got this under control."

Meredith gave her assistant a long hug. They held on to each other. Cate wasn't a runner. In fact, she hated all forms of exercise. In the past two years, the pounds had accumulated. Now as Meredith hugged her friend, Cate's soft, full body wrapped Meredith in a warm embrace. She started crying again.

"I don't know what I'd do without you," Meredith said. She had an ache in her chest from carrying such a huge secret. One of the hardest things she'd ever done, other than talk to Elliott about the cancer and pregnancy, was to not tell Cate. Although Meredith second-guessed her decision, she knew it was the right thing to do. Putting up with Elliott's pressure would probably become a full-time job. Adding Cate's to the mix, well, that would be more than Meredith could handle.

On her way out the door, Cate handed her a file.

"Is this something I have to do, or can it wait?" Meredith asked.

"It's the Montgomery family history that Gregory wrote from your notes and the report from the genealogist. It's very interesting." Cate smiled. "I think you'll enjoy it."

Meredith put the file in her briefcase and noticed there was already a folder in the pocket. "What's this?"

"Notes and copies you made in Edinburgh," Cate said. "Knowing you, you'll want to double-check your notes while you're reading."

Meredith rolled her eyes. "I can't believe I'm so predictable."

The intercom buzzed, and the receptionist said, "The car service just arrived."

"Tell the driver I'm on my way out."

"I could have driven you," Cate said.

"Someone needs to stay here and get the work done." Meredith hugged her assistant again. "If you need anything, call."

Cate all but shoved Meredith out the front door. "Go. Enjoy your weekend. Get some rest."

"Call me—"

"*Go.*" Cate closed the door, leaving Meredith on the porch alone.

"Oh, well," she said, walking toward the limo. *Two days of relaxing in Elliott's arms. No talk of hospitals or serious discussions or life-altering decisions.*

The driver held the door open, and she scooted into the backseat.

For two days, no stress, no worries.

Chapter Seventy

Montgomery Corporate Jet – February 13

WITHIN MOMENTS OF wheels up, Meredith opened her briefcase and pulled out the file Cate had given her.

OUR HISTORY & LEGACY

Montgomery Winery has a rich heritage. It was the first premium winery and has become the most successful of all California wineries. The founder, lawyer and state senator Cullen Montgomery, was an early pioneer with an unquestionable love and commitment to California wine.

Senator Montgomery emigrated in the 1840s from Scotland and attended Harvard Law School. Following graduation, he pursued an opportunity to practice law in San Francisco. Leading a wagon train west in 1852, he met his wife, Kitherina MacKlenna from Lexington, Kentucky…

"*What?*" Meredith threw up her arms, and the papers scattered around the plane. "Kitherina MacKlenna? You've got to be kidding." Meredith unbuckled her seat belt, bent over, and collected the papers, which were now out of order. "Not that one." She tossed pages aside. "Not that one. Not that one. Where the hell is page one?"

She glanced around the floor and spotted the edge of a piece of paper under the sofa. Hands shaking with anticipation, she snatched it off the floor and continued reading, her heart thumping in her chest.

> *After arriving in San Francisco, Montgomery hired John Barrett, a farmer who had traveled west with Montgomery. He also hired vintner Giuseppe Raimondo from Italy, who had come west following the forty-niners in search of gold in the hills of Northern California. Montgomery ultimately settled in Sonoma, where he founded Montgomery Winery in 1854. The winery is California's oldest commercial winery and the oldest continuously run family winery.*
>
> *Montgomery sent Raimondo on several trips to Europe to import cuttings from the greatest European vineyards, which were then planted all over Northern California. At his wife's behest, Montgomery had extensive caves dug out for cellaring, which are still used today. He also promoted hillside planting. The rocky soils of Montgomery Winery currently produce some of the best California grapes on the market. The winemakers draw a rich palette of aromas to create wines of exceptional complexity.*
>
> *It was rumored that Mrs. Montgomery had unusual gifts and was able to predict the phenomenal growth of the wine industry. The winery currently has 10,545 acres throughout the cool California coastal regions.*
>
> *The Montgomerys had four children. Their only son, Thomas, continued the family business. The winery not only endured but prospered, and now celebrates 160 years of continuous wine-making in the valley.*

Meredith fanned herself with the papers. "Were there other

MacKlennas in Lexington? Or was Kitherina James MacKlenna's daughter or granddaughter?" If she was from that branch of the family, then the ghost mystery was solved.

Meredith leaned back against the headrest, closed her eyes, and tried to put the dots together, but gaps existed. Why would a young, single woman travel west in the mid-eighteen hundreds?

Who at MacKlenna Farm would know the family history? Maybe the old journals in the library that Elliott mentioned would have information. Now that she knew what she was looking for, the search might be easier.

She put the file back into her briefcase and pulled out the other file. Several pages were paper-clipped together. The copies she had made for Elliott at the registry house were placed on top. Gregory had read those, too, and highlighted paragraphs. One paragraph in particular had red and yellow underlining. She read the paragraph, then read it again. Stunned and speechless.

If MacKlenna Farm files for bankruptcy, this will make a difference.

After a long moment, she had to laugh. Surely Elliott would see the humor. "Who's the last MacKlenna now?" She put the file away, closed her eyes, and quickly fell asleep, dreaming of Kitherina MacKlenna Montgomery and a little boy from the Highlands born on the wrong side of the sheets.

Chapter Seventy-One

MacKlenna Farm – February 13

MEREDITH'S PLANE LANDED at Bluegrass Airport at ten o'clock that evening. The cabin door swung open, and she found David waiting at the bottom of the steps. Her body slumped with disappointment. Although Elliott had sent a text at eight saying he was still in a meeting, she held out hope that it would adjourn in time for him to meet her plane. She had amazing news to tell him.

A brisk wind whipped around her, and she shivered. "It's cold." She crossed her arms and held them close to her body. Thank goodness Napa wasn't like this. No one would come to the launch. "Any idea how much longer the meeting will last?" she asked David.

He shook his head. "Could be over by the time we get back or it could last 'til midnight."

"No hand signals among the participants," Meredith asked, teasingly.

"I wasn't asked to sit in."

"I can't tell whether you're relieved or disappointed."

"It makes me less effective when I'm out of the loop."

David had left the engine running, and the car's interior was toasty warm. "Doesn't he tell you everything that happens in meetings?" Meredith asked.

"I miss the innuendo and body language. That's often more telling than words." David closed her door and went back to the plane for her luggage.

Five minutes later, they were off the airport property and on their way back to the farm. "Do ye need to stop for anything?" he asked.

"Oh, thanks for reminding me. I need a drug store, Walmart, or Target. I went off without shampoo."

"There're several bottles in Kit's bathroom," David said.

"Good. I'm sure whatever's there will work. She won't mind, will she?"

"Not even a wee bit."

In the last few weeks, she'd seen a side of David she would never have thought possible. The man she met the first night she went to dinner with Elliott seemed entirely too serious, almost dangerous. But the man she now knew was both devoted and loving, and she trusted him explicitly.

Thirty minutes later, they pulled into the garage at MacKlenna Mansion. She climbed out of the car. David reached for her computer bag. "Let me carry that," he said.

"I'm not an invalid."

David gazed at her with his Superman stare. She assumed his eyes could see straight through her. A few weeks ago, she'd have stepped back out of his way. Now she knew that underneath his special agent facade, he was nothing more than a pussycat.

"If I'm around, ye carry nothing."

She didn't hesitate letting go of the straps.

"I'll take yer bags to Kit's room."

When she entered the house, she was met with an eerie silence. Her hands instinctively cradled her belly. The welcome home feeling, as if she'd stepped into a tub of warm water, had disappeared. The mansion seemed scrubbed clean of all that had defined it, leaving it cold and musty and just plain old.

Feeling out of sorts and confused, she dropped into a chair in the hallway and glanced around the foyer. The room, decorated in vivid greens and golds with polished antiques in pristine condition, was as beautiful as ever, but the house no longer breathed with life and certainty. Someone had sucked out its soul, or the house had given up, believing there was nothing in the future that held the splendor of the past.

Tears slid down Meredith's cheeks. *You're dying.* Whoever had killed the horses had killed the mansion, too. The tall windows and Doric columns—the venerable old soldiers standing guard on the portico—had opened the door to the enemy.

Meow.

"Hi, Tabor." The cat jumped into her lap. "You feel it, too, don't you?" Meredith rubbed her fingers through his thick fur.

Meow.

"Where's Tate?"

"That spoiled dog is probably at the stallion complex. That's where they're meeting," David said.

The smell of lemon polish made her stomach queasy. It rumbled with an embarrassing roar. Tabor jumped off her lap, and Meredith ran for the steps, gagging.

David ran after her. "What's wrong?"

Kit's bathroom was the closest. She dashed into the room. David switched on the light in time for her to throw up in the toilet. He wet a washcloth in the sink. "Here."

She lowered the lid and sat, leaning forward between her legs with her elbows on her knees and her hands pressing the cloth against her forehead. "I'm so frigging tired of being sick."

"Morning sickness passes after a few weeks," he said.

"If I have chemo, I'll be just as sick or sicker."

David took the washcloth and freshened it. "Do ye want a 7 Up? That helps settle the stomach."

She nodded.

"I'll be right back."

"Don't tell Elliott," she said. "It'll upset him."

David dimmed the lights in the room and turned up the heat. "I don't keep secrets from him, but he doesn't need to know ye threw up."

She forced a smile. "Would you bring me some crackers, too?"

"Sit tight. I'll be right back."

Meredith remained seated until David returned. She felt a bit weak and wanted him close by in case she wobbled when she walked.

He stood in the doorway holding a can of 7 Up and a box of crackers. "Do ye want these in here or in the bedroom?"

Meredith grabbed the towel bar and pulled herself to her feet. "Put them by the bed. I want to brush my teeth." A couple of minutes later, she sat on the bed and put her feet up.

David popped the top of the can. "Drink up."

With the soft drink in one hand and cracker in the other, she sipped and nibbled. After a few minutes, she began to feel better. "You don't have to babysit me."

Tabor jumped up on the bed and stretched out, purring. Meredith once again ran her fingers through his long, dense fur, and he purred even louder. "You're spoiled rotten, too, aren't you?"

Tate bounded into the room and jumped up on the bed.

"*Tate, get down*," David said.

The dog didn't listen. Instead, he plopped next to Tabor and stretched out alongside the cat.

"They need to spend time with Annabella. She'd teach them manners," David said.

"Annabella *is* well behaved," Meredith said.

Tate's ears perked forward.

Meredith scratched his belly. "Yes, you'd like Annabella. I bet she doesn't sleep on the bed."

David chuckled. "Annabella has to have her feet cleaned when she comes in the house. She'll stand in the kitchen and wait."

"If Elliott taught her that, why can't he teach these two?"

"Tate grew up going on long treks in a covered wagon with Sean, Mary, and Kit and learned to run wild."

"Really? Where'd they go?"

"Wyoming, Idaho, Oregon. They were pioneer reenactors."

"That is so weird. I just found out that my great-great-great-grandmother, Kitherina Montgomery, was a MacKlenna from

Lexington, Kentucky, and that she traveled west in 1852. Do you know if there are other MacKlennas in town?"

David rubbed the back of his neck. "Don't know."

"I'll ask Elliott."

"Now that ye've got two bodyguards, I'm going over to the complex and see how the meeting is getting on," David said.

Tabor got up, stretched, then climbed into Meredith's lap. "Go on," she said to David. "I'll be right here waiting."

"Don't leave, and don't let anyone in the house."

"I'm not twelve. I'll be fine. Go." She leaned against the headboard and drifted off. Tate woke her, jiggling his dog tags. "What's the matter, boy?"

He jumped to the floor and ran to the door barking.

"You want to go out?" Meredith asked, yawning.

He barked again.

She slipped on her boots and grabbed her coat. "Let's go." As soon as she opened the door in the kitchen, the dog ran off. "*Tate*, come back." She didn't know whether to let him go or go after him. It was eleven fifteen. Was he even allowed out alone at night? She didn't know, but she wasn't about to let anything happen to Elliott's dog. The night air was cool and crisp. A short walk would make her feel better.

The snow-covered ground crunched with each step. The lighted path circled around to the side of the house that faced the stallion complex. "Tate. Come here, Tate." No dog in sight. The path ended a few yards away where it intersected with the interior asphalt road that meandered through the two-thousand-acre farm.

Twinkling stars and a full moon illuminated the multi-barn stallion complex that dotted the landscape with dozens of yellow lights. Tate would either go looking for critters or people. The sociable dog would go looking for people first. Meredith hadn't seen Stormy since the day he went to the hospital, so she decided to start the search in his barn.

The door was open a crack, which surprised her. Surely, after all that had happened, the door would stay securely closed. Maybe security was making rounds. Night-lights lit the interior, providing enough light to see but not much else.

"Tate," she called in a quiet voice, not wanting to excite the horses. She crossed the open, brick-floored area. Stormy's stall was on the opposite side of the barn.

She stood in front of his door. "Hi, big boy. How're you feeling?"

Stormy pawed the padded floor.

"What's wrong?" She pushed her hand through the space between the bars, wishing she had a cube of sugar or an apple. He didn't move. Meredith opened the door and entered. "Come here." He still didn't move.

"What are you doing here?" a voice asked.

Meredith jumped, her heart racing. The deep James Earl Jones sounding voice belonged to Doc, but the tone held a hard, sinister edge.

"I *said* what are you doing here?"

She flinched. "Doc, you scared me." She licked her lips. "I…I was looking for Tate."

"He's not here."

There's nothing to be afraid of. It's just Doc. "Does he run loose at night?"

Doc remained hidden in the shadow. "That *damn* mutt does whatever he pleases. Elliott's ruined him."

Meredith gave a nervous laugh. "I heard Mary MacKlenna was responsible for that."

"Would have ruined Stormy, too, if I hadn't taken over the vet job." His heavy voice fueled her fear.

Stormy snorted loudly and fixed an intense stare.

"How's his leg?"

"Healing. It's late. You shouldn't be here."

She fisted her hands and took a step forward. Her foot rammed into something hard on the floor. She glanced down and recognized a vet's bag. Her heart went to her throat. "Something's wrong with him. That's why you're here." She patted Stormy's head. "Is he sick, or is it his leg?"

Doc stepped out of the shadowed corner, holding Stormy's halter with one hand. His other hand was hidden behind his back.

Adrenaline pumped faster through her veins in a pulse-raising moment. Her ability to sense danger was as well-defined as any other member of the human race. In the dark, in the quiet, danger was palpable. But why? Doc wouldn't hurt her.

"What's behind your back?" she asked.

He stepped closer, releasing his hold of the halter. "You shouldn't have come in here."

"I'll leave, then." She took a step backward. "You can get back to doing whatever you were doing."

He grabbed her in a headlock, rattlesnake fast.

"You're hurting my neck." The pinched nerve was going to start bothering her again. She twisted her body to get away from him. "*Stop.* You're hurting me."

He squeezed his arm around her throat.

She elbowed him in the gut, a linebacker-sized gut, solid as steel. Her punch was as ineffectual as a shout in a frenzied crowd.

This can't be happening. If she didn't stop him, he would kill her. He would kill her baby. The pain grew branding-iron hot. She couldn't breathe. She clawed at his arm, trying to break his hold before he choked off all her breath. The dim room grew darker. Light-headed, she fought with the same reserve that saw her through the last six miles of a marathon. She slammed her heel into the top of his foot.

"Bitch. Steel boots. Horses have tried harder."

His breath smelled of beer and garlic. She gagged. *You've got to fight. Don't give up.* She kicked and clawed. This was a man used to controlling thousand-pound horses. He held up his hand. Her eyes widened. He had a syringe with his thumb on the plunger. Beads of sweat coated her upper lip. Hope diminished with her breath. *Let go of me.* Tears filled her eyes. Her heart pounded jackhammer fast with enough force to bruise her.

"This will hurt that son of a bitch more than killing his damn horses."

"Why?" she asked in a barely audible voice.

"They cheated me. They got millions. I got nothing but horses shoving me against walls. Had more broken bones than a jockey. I should've had a share. I *deserved* it. They'll suffer for what they did to me." He pressed the needle against her neck.

"They'll catch you," she said, her knees jellying.

"I'm too smart for them."

Her heart rasped with her breath. Flashes of her life appeared before her eyes. Years flew by in a second. All the people who had been important to her emerged for a brief moment. Mother, father, grandparents, Elliott, and the baby in her womb, all intermingled with grapes and bottles of wine.

It can't all end. Not now. Not like this.

The needle punctured her skin.

Please, help me.

Stormy reared, screaming a loud roar of rage. The other stallions snorted and stomped, creating the thunderous sound of a stampeding herd. The walls shook. Stormy's hoof caught the side of Doc's head. He fell, pulling her with him. The needle dropped from his hand and scraped the side of her neck. Warm liquid dripped to her shoulder. She pushed away from his arm, rolled onto her side, and slowly pulled to her knees. Breathing took effort. She willed herself to her feet, but she couldn't breathe and fell backward. Everything blurred. She could see nothing. Hear nothing. Feel nothing.

Then she could see everything clearly.

She floated out of her physical body, finding she no longer had chest-caving pain or raw-knuckled fear. Doc lay motionless on the straw. Blood gushed from his head. His silver hair turned crimson.

Stormy stood calmly as she patted his nose. His big brown eyes no longer reflected her image.

She glanced up and smiled. "You're here."

"I was sent to protect ye," Cullen Montgomery said, sitting atop Stormy's back.

"You failed."

"Nay, lass, I didn't."

Chapter Seventy-Two

MacKlenna Farm Stallion Complex Conference Room – February 13

ELLIOTT SAT IN a leather swivel chair at the large, oval-shaped table in the conference room. His stomach churned with frustration. From the signals David had sent him, he knew Meredith was in bed entertaining Tate and Tabor. He should be with her, or at least send her another text that he'd be there soon. But when he was in meetings with the board of directors, he didn't check or send messages. The members received his full attention. Tonight, though, the brain-draining meeting had siphoned off about seventy-five percent of his full attention. The members rehashed the same points for the fourth time.

He went back many years with the men and women seated at the table. They were fair and honest. However, none had ever been in the position they now found themselves. Some grimaced with lowered chins; others had stiff postures and rushed speech. They were embarrassed and frustrated, and he didn't blame them. They were all gun-drawn serious about finding a solution and refused to believe there might not be one.

David signaled the time. The meeting had to end, but there was little shifting in that direction. Elliott had uneasiness about Meredith. He signaled David to go check on her. Before David could leave the room, a security guard opened the door and stuck his head around the doorjamb.

"I just heard a stallion scream," the guard said in a panic-laced voice.

Ten people jumped to their feet.

Bone-melting fear raced through Elliott's veins. "What barn?"

"I can't tell," the guard said.

"Notify Jake and Doc." Elliott's heart quickened as he left the room. "Get the paramedic on call, too." Lyles had put him back in a walking boot hours earlier and told him no fast walking. "Could be a fire," Elliott said, limping toward the exit.

Manning grabbed his coat and followed Elliott out of the conference room. "There's no alarm."

"If a fire was intentionally set, they could have cut the circuit. Damn it. If we lose another horse, there won't be anything left for the bankruptcy court to liquidate," Elliott said.

David already had the door open. He handed Elliott a cane. "Use this." He waved it away, but David shoved it into his hand.

Elliott accepted it with a growl. He pushed through the door and took a big whiff of cold air. No smoke. He breathed relief, but fear remained lodged in his throat. He cut across the crisp snow. Security guards driving converted golf carts painted MacKlenna Farm green drove up, and a half dozen guards spilled out.

"Spread out," Elliott ordered. "Check each barn. I'm going in number one. David and Jim, come with me." When they reached the door, they found it ajar. "This shouldn't be open."

David withdrew his sidearm. "Ye two stay here."

"The light switch is on the right side." Elliott leaned on the cane, glancing around. Lights had come on in all the barns. The kitchen light was on in the house. He couldn't see Kit's bedroom from where he stood. *Are you awake, Meredith?* His nerve endings bristled, warning him, but of what he didn't know. If Meredith would come to the door, the iron-grip intensity in his gut would slacken.

Kevin drove up in his truck and came to a screeching stop. He barely turned off the engine before he jumped out. "Nobody's at the security gate. What's going on?"

"A stallion screamed."

"Why?"

"We don't know," Jim said.

"Why don't you go inside?"

"Damn it, Kevin. Be quiet."

The lights came on inside the barn. Elliott waited with barely contained patience. A minute passed, then another. He'd give David thirty more seconds.

David shouted, "*Elliott.*"

He hurried through the door. "Where are ye?"

"Stormy's stall. Meredith's down. Doc's dead. Call 911." David's tone sounded in-the-trenches intense.

Blood-spiking fear enveloped Elliott. "Ye said she was in bed," Elliott said, hobbling toward the stall.

"She was."

Elliott held back his own scream. Getting to her any faster was impossible. In five years, he'd never wanted full use of his leg as much as he wanted it at that moment.

Kevin hurried ahead, making the 911 call as he ran. "Get the bus to barn one now."

Manning wrapped his arm around Elliott's shoulders. "Lean into me. We'll go together."

Chapter Seventy-Three

MacKlenna Farm Stallion Barn – February 13

FROM ABOVE, Meredith had watched the golf carts full of security personnel gather outside the barns. She had watched Elliott pace as he waited for David to finish the search. She had tried to tell Elliott that she loved him, but he couldn't hear her.

Kevin knelt next to her body. "Meredith, can you hear me?" He felt for a pulse. "She has a pulse, but she's not breathing." He tilted her head and lifted her chin to keep her airway open, pinching her nose and placing his mouth over hers.

Elliott limped into the stall and fell to his knees. "My God, what happened?"

"She has a puncture wound on her neck. Doc may have injected her," David said.

"With what?"

"Don't know," David said.

Elliott sat beside Meredith and held her hand. "I'll do that, Kevin."

"No," Kevin said, pausing between breaths to let the air flow out. Her chest didn't rise and fall. He retilted her head and tried again. "Check her pulse."

Elliott did. "Thready."

"Ambulance?" Kevin said before giving her more breaths.

"I see the lights," David said. "It's here. What do ye need?"

"Bag her now."

"Get Stormy out of here," Elliott said.

A groom rushed in and led the horse away. Cullen Montgomery stood beside Meredith, watching.

"Breathe, Meredith," Kevin said. "I won't let you die. Breathe."

You're too late, Kevin. Doc killed me, Meredith said.

The ghost pointed toward her lifeless body. *Ye need to go back.*

"Breathe, my wee sweetheart." Elliott lifted her hand to his lips and kissed her fingers. "Don't give up. Breathe."

It's not yer time, the ghost said.

If not now, then soon. I have cancer, Meredith said.

Elliott's waiting. So is yer son, the ghost said. *Go now.*

Meredith slipped back into her body. Elliott and Kevin faded into the distance. Their voices quieted. Then she heard nothing more.

Chapter Seventy-Four

MacKlenna Farm Stallion Barn – February 13

"THERE'S A SYRINGE over there," Elliott said, pointing.

David picked it up. "It's empty."

"Look in the vet bag. Find out what he used," Elliott said.

David grabbed a bottle out of the bag and read the label. "Pentobarbital."

Elliott and Kevin locked eyes. "Keep breathing for her," Elliott said.

"Looks like Stormy kicked Doc in the head. The horse probably saved her life," David said.

The ambulance drove into the barn and cut the engine.

"In here," David said, waving from inside Stormy's stall.

A paramedic entered. "What's the situation, Kevin?"

"One dead. One injected with pentobarbital. We need to bag her," Kevin said between breathing for Meredith.

The paramedic ran back to the ambulance and returned with a bag valve mask. "Do you want me to do it?"

Kevin shook his head. The paramedic gave him a pair of gloves. Kevin inserted the airway, the tube, and placed the mask over her nose. "Check her pulse."

The paramedic took her vitals. "Keep her breathing."

Kevin began ventilation. "Let's get her out of here."

Elliott remained at her side, chin and lips trembling, never letting go of her cold hand.

The paramedic and David got Meredith onto the gurney and into the ambulance while Kevin continued to intubate her.

"David, call the police. Stay here and talk to them. Then come to the hospital," Elliott said, climbing into the ambulance.

David squeezed Elliott's shoulder. "The lad got to her in time. She'll make it."

"The police are here," Manning said.

"I'll be right there," David said.

As soon as Kevin had Meredith stabilized, he said, "Let's roll."

Elliott had never prayed, but he did now, watching the woman he loved fight for her life. *God, help her. Please don't let her die. If Ye will, Lord, heal her. Anything Ye've ever done for anyone, at anytime, anywhere, Ye can do for my wee sweetheart. If Ye will, Lord, heal her.*

The paramedic started the bus, but before he drove off, David yelled, "Wait." He jogged up to the passenger's side. "Here's the bottle." He held it with a handkerchief. "I'll come to the hospital as soon as we wrap up here."

"Let the police tell his wife," Elliott said. "Find out if she knew what Doc was doing."

David looked through the window of the ambulance. His eyes watered. "I'll take care of it. Ye take care of Meredith."

Chapter Seventy-Five

University of Kentucky Medical Center – February 13

THE LIGHTS-AND-SIRENS RIDE to the University of Kentucky Medical Center took minutes, but to Elliott, sweating and sick to his stomach, it seemed like an entire day. Meredith was rushed into a cubicle where a team of physicians prepared to treat her. Elliott waited in the hallway. Several minutes passed before Kevin left the cubicle and joined him.

"They're putting her on a ventilator and have called in a high-risk ob-gyn."

Elliott's feet went out from under him. Kevin caught him before he collapsed to the ground.

"Get me a wheelchair," Kevin yelled.

A nurse's aide rushed over with a chair and helped Kevin get Elliott seated.

"Got an empty room?" Kevin asked.

The aide pointed to a cubicle on the end. "Take him in there. I'll get the supervisor."

Kevin wheeled Elliott into the room. "Let's get you up here and take your vitals."

Elliott couldn't move. He didn't care about himself. All he could think about was the woman he loved possibly dying in the other room. How could this have happened? If Doc's intention was to hurt him, this was the ultimate pain. He buried his head in his hands and sobbed, deep gut-wrenching tears. If Meredith died, there was no reason for him to live. He would have lost everything that was important to him.

"Elliott," Kevin said. He knelt in front of his boss and grasped his arms, shaking them gently. "Elliott. You've got to hang in there. We can't lose faith. She'll get through this."

Elliott heard him, but he couldn't stop sobbing.

A nurse entered. "Dr. Lyles prescribed a sedative for him."

Elliott shook his head. "No. I have to be alert in case decisions have to be made. Take that away." He sat straight in the wheelchair and wiped his face with his sleeve. "Go check on her, Kevin. I'll wait here. I have to know what's happening." He gazed at the nurse. "Where's Lyles?"

"He's finishing up with a patient. He'll be down shortly."

"How'd he know I was here?"

"He got a call."

Elliott sighed. David must have called him. "Thanks. I'm okay now." Elliott pushed himself over to the sink and washed his face. Then he sat quietly, calling upon the patience his grandfather had taught him years earlier.

Kevin returned. His lips turned up in a slight smile. "The obstetrician did an ultrasound. The baby's alive. That's all they can tell at this stage."

"What about—"

"She's on the ventilator. They're going to move her to ICU. Her heart never stopped. That's good. We'll just have to wait and see."

Elliott stood and walked toward the door. "I want to see her." He reached the hallway just as she was wheeled from the room. He gasped. "My God." She was surrounded by medical personnel and machines. Her face had no color. He stepped back out of the way. "I want to go with ye," he said to no one in particular.

"They'll notify us when we can go in to see her," Kevin said.

Elliott grabbed Kevin's arm. "Go with her. They'll let ye stay in the room."

"They won't let me this time, Boss."

Elliott returned to his cubicle and collapsed in the chair. Kevin came up behind him and pushed the chair into the hallway. "We're going to the coffee shop. You need coffee, and so do I."

They had finished one cup and were starting on the second when Lyles entered the shop. He sat down next to Elliott. "She blinked."

Kevin slapped the table. "Hot damn."

More tears rushed to Elliott's eyes. "She's going to make it, isn't she?"

"It's a good sign," Lyles said.

Elliott scrubbed his face with his hands. "When can I see her?"

"I'm the bearer of good news. You can see her now."

Elliott scooted up against Lyles in the bench seat. "Move yer ass. I've got a date."

"Boss, wait," Kevin said. "Don't go in there thinking she's going to talk to you. She can't. She's got a tube down her throat, and she's not fully awake."

"But she will be, and that's all that matters."

Several minutes later, Elliott stood at the foot of her bed. It hadn't been that long ago that she had stood at his. If she bitched at him when she woke, he'd take it like a man and be glad for the cussing out. She appeared so fragile. Never again would he put anything in front of her. She would be his top priority from this day forward. God had answered his prayer, and he wouldn't waste a day of the gift.

She blinked, or he thought she did. He took her cold hand and tried to warm it between his palms. "I'm here, sweetling. This is my fault. I'm so sorry." She squeezed his finger. It wasn't a big squeeze. Well, maybe it wasn't a squeeze at all. He just wanted to believe. He kissed her forehead, cool to the touch. "Wake up. We have plans to make." One of his tears dripped onto her face.

She blinked.

This time he knew he hadn't imagined it. "Meredith, if ye can hear me, blink again. Please, my wee sweetheart, blink."

She blinked.

A knot formed in his throat, and goose bumps popped out on his arms helter-skelter. "Kevin."

"What, Boss?" Kevin stood in the entrance to the ICU cubicle.

"She blinked." The words poured out in a flood of relief.

A nurse entered. "What'd you see, Dr. Fraser?"

"When I asked her to blink, eyelashes on both eyes fluttered."

The nurse wrote the time and his comment on her hand. "Let me know as soon as she opens her eyes. I'll call her doctor."

"How long will it take?" Elliott asked the nurse.

"It's up to her," the nurse said.

Elliott didn't take his eyes off Meredith's face. Minutes passed, but nothing happened.

"Want another cup of coffee, Boss?" Kevin asked.

Elliott nodded. Kevin was halfway out of the room when Elliott asked, "What do ye think? Will she be all right?"

Kevin stopped and chewed his lip for a moment. "I believe she's here by some grand design, and you probably won't like hearing this, but I bet Kit's ghost was responsible for what Stormy did. Think about it. There're too many coincidences. Stormy screamed, and we arrived in the nick of time."

"Ye think a see-through person saved her life?" Elliott asked.

"Probably."

"Stormy wouldn't have hurt Doc unless something provoked him," Elliott said.

"I think you've answered your own question, Boss. I'll be back in a few minutes."

Elliott sat in the recliner and closed his swollen eyes. Meredith moaned, and he popped up out of the chair, coming face-to-face with Cullen Montgomery's ghost. Elliott grabbed the railing. *I can see you.*

Ye've always been able to see me, but ye didn't believe.

Ye saved her life?

The ghost floated above the bed. *I did what I came to do.*

Will she be all right?

Be patient, Elliott. All that will be will happen in its own time. Meredith's ancestor brushed her cheek with his ghostly fingers, paused a moment, then disappeared.

From the deep recesses of his mind, Elliott heard his grandfather Fraser. "Patience, lad. Grow a wee bit of patience."

For the first time in hours, Elliott sat, and a thin smile crossed his face. He would wait patiently, because he now knew his wee sweetheart would come back to him. Not in his time, but in hers.

Chapter Seventy-Six

University of Kentucky Medical Center – February 14

ELLIOTT WOKE TO a metal-on-metal tapping sound. One, two, three, stop. One, two, three, stop. Pain, similar to a three-day drinking binge, sliced through his skull. *What day is it? And where the hell am I?*

The tapping continued. One, two, three, stop. One, two, three, stop.

Then obnoxious medicinal smells permeated his nasal membrane. The smell jerked him awake. *Hospital. Meredith.* He shot a glance at the bed. Her hand was wrapped around the metal side rail. The ring on her finger clinked against the railing.

He came up out of the chair, catching sight of the most beautiful blue eyes he'd ever seen. He went stun-gun still. He willed away the shock so he wouldn't alarm her. "Trying to get my attention, huh?"

Meredith smiled around the tube in her mouth. She placed her hand at her mouth and furrowed her brow.

Hooked to a machine, Meredith appeared helpless, and it was the most heart-wrenching sight he'd ever seen. His body shook with fear and exhaustion. "I don't know when they'll remove the ventilator. Soon, I hope."

She slid her hand down her body and pressed her fingers against her belly.

Elliott kissed her cheek then whispered in her ear, "Our wee son is fine, and ye'll be, too."

Tears rolled off her face and into her hairline. She tapped his watch.

It was after eight o'clock in the morning. "Ye've been out almost nine hours."

She moved her hand in a writing motion.

"Ye want to write something down?"

She nodded.

He didn't have paper or pen with him. "I'll go get some paper."

She grabbed his arm, pointed at him, then pointed at her mouth.

"Ye want me to kiss ye?"

She shook her head.

"Damn." He thought a minute. What would he want to know if he couldn't speak? "Do ye want me to tell ye what happened?"

She nodded.

He took a deep breath to control his anger. There would be plenty of time later to rant about Doc's cowardly actions. "Doc injected ye with pentobarbital."

She grimaced.

"The drug stopped yer breathing. Not yer heart. Kevin was able to breathe for ye until he had equipment to intubate. We rushed ye here, and they put ye on the ventilator."

She pressed her fingers against her belly again.

"The doctor did an ultrasound. The baby's heart is beating. That's all they can tell at this stage of his development."

Elliott was conflicted about whether or not to tell her about the ghost. He didn't want to stress her, so he decided to wait until later.

A doctor and nurse entered the room. "I'm Doctor Thomas. We're glad to see you're awake. In a few hours, we'll start weaning you from the ventilator."

Meredith pinched her lips, and her blue eyes stared intently at the doctor. Elliott knew her well enough to know that she was planning an escape if the doctor didn't release her in time for the event at the winery.

"She *has* to be back in California in two days," Elliott said.

She raised her hand in a fist.

"She'll fight her way out of here if she has to."

The doctor tugged on his chin. "We'll see how the trials go later today. If you have good lung function, weaning won't take long."

Meredith punched her palm with her index finger.

"Ye can't call anyone," Elliott said.

She pointed at him.

"Kevin's already talked to Cate. I'm sure he's given her an update by now."

Kevin entered the room on cue. "She sends her love and said to tell you not to worry about anything. It's all under control. There was one more thing, but in all the excitement I forgot what it was." He scrolled through his iPhone. "*Oh.* Your dress arrived, and it's hanging in the closet."

Meredith's lips curled up slightly.

"How about we get out of here and let you rest?" Kevin said to Meredith. "I'll have Elliott back after he showers and gets something to eat."

She reached for Elliott, and he kissed her again before whispering in her ear, "Maybe when I come back, ye'll make room for me in yer bed."

A wee bit of color returned to her face.

Chapter Seventy-Seven

MacKlenna Farm – February 14

AFTER A NAP and a shower, Elliott went looking for Kevin and David.

"They're not here," Mrs. Collins said. "Come eat. I have chili and pimento cheese sandwiches."

"Any word from the hospital?" Elliott asked.

She picked up a piece of paper off the kitchen counter and handed it to him. "Kevin left this for you."

Talked to Meredith's nurse at ten. She's doing great. I'll be at the hospital.

Elliott checked the time. It was twelve thirty. Damn. He shouldn't have slept so long. "I've got to go back to the hospital."

"Sit. Eat. That gal doing's fine. Kevin's there. He'll call if you're needed."

"Have ye seen David?"

Mrs. Collins threw up her hands. "Lordy. He's here. He's not. Even when he is here, you don't see him. He's a quiet one, that's for sure. Now eat. I fixed chili and sandwiches 'cause they're your favorites. Got to keep nourishment in you while you're healing. And you got to take care of the missy, now that she's gonna have your baby."

Elliott rolled his eyes. News traveled around the farm by an invisible telegraph. There were no secrets. "What are people saying about Doc?"

"I don't know nothing about it. I don't spread gossip, and I don't listen to it either."

Elliott almost gagged on his sandwich.

Mrs. Collins slipped on her coat. "I'm off to the store. I figure Miss Meredith will want some of those fancy eggs when she comes home tomorrow."

He cocked his head, his mouth full of pimento cheese. The woman said the damnedest things. He swallowed the food in his mouth. "What makes ye think she's coming home tomorrow?"

"When she decides to go for something, she goes all out. By my calendar, she's got a big shindig in California in a couple of days. No doctor can keep her where she don't plan to be." Mrs. Collins put on her hat and walked to the door. "No way will Miss Meredith stay in the hospital one minute longer than she has to."

The door closed, leaving Elliott alone with his thoughts. In six weeks, he'd had three surgeries, met the most incredible woman, lost the farm, and almost lost the love of his life. His priorities had shifted, and he'd stopped drinking. If he could pack up and leave today, he would. He'd take Meredith, the lads, Tate, Tabor, and Stormy off to Fraser House and never look back.

Chapter Seventy-Eight

University of Kentucky Medical Center – February 14

AN HOUR LATER, Elliott entered Meredith's cubicle and swallowed hard. There was no hissing ventilator, and the monitor screen was blank. His heart fell to his stomach. He grabbed the bed rail. "The machine's off."

From the darkened corner, David said, "They're weaning her."

Startled, Elliott said, "I didn't know ye were here."

"I drove up as soon as ye went to sleep. I didn't want her to be alone."

"Ye're a good lad." Elliott's heart made its way back to its rightful place. He walked around to the side of the bed and kissed Meredith's forehead. "I'm surprised they're weaning her so soon."

"They didn't want her on the machine longer than she has to be. She's healthy. She's breathing on her own."

"Has she been asleep all this time?" Elliott asked.

"She was awake for a couple of hours. Made notes on her iPad." David pointed to the device lying on the bed close to her hand.

Elliott picked it up and switched it on. "How the hell did it get here?"

"I had it sent over."

The screen came up asking for the password. Elliott turned the iPad around for David to see. "Do ye know it?"

"No."

"Did ye see what she wrote?"

"No."

Elliott put the device down where he found it. "How long has she been asleep?"

"About an hour."

"Did she say anything?"

David scowled.

"Okay, that was a dumb question."

David stood and put on his jacket. "I didn't ask her what happened either. The doctor told me to keep her calm."

"She's been through a lot in the last few weeks," Elliott said.

"Ever since she met ye."

"Thanks. Ye know how to hurt a guy."

David patted Meredith's hand then headed toward the door. "Truth always hurts."

"Where're ye going?"

"Chuck and I are meeting at the police station to go over the investigation and what happened last night. I'll fill ye in later."

Elliott sat in the recliner David vacated. "Stay in touch." Elliott then closed his eyes and drifted off to sleep.

The doctor stopped by to see Meredith at two o'clock and decided to remove the ventilator tube.

She woke as they were pulling it out.

"I know you're glad to be rid of that," the doctor said.

Meredith held her throat. "Very glad," she said in a raspy voice.

"We'll move you to a regular room as soon as one is available," the doctor said while making notes on her chart.

"I'd rather go home," she said.

"Let's see how you do today. I know you want to leave town. We'll try to get you out of here."

"Great news," Elliott said, stepping over to the bed.

"I didn't see you," Meredith said. "I thought David was there."

Elliott slapped his chest with both hands, feeling crushed. "That sounds like ye'd rather have him here."

"He has a gun," she said.

Her words were a knife to his gut. He'd been so relieved that she'd survived that he hadn't thought through how traumatized she would be from the attempt on her life. David had understood that, and that's why he hadn't left her alone. Elliott vowed he wouldn't either.

After the doctor left, Elliott said, "Do ye want to talk about what happened?"

"Let's not talk about Doc or the cancer or the baby until I'm out of the hospital, please."

"Deal," he said, then he kissed her.

Chapter Seventy-Nine

MacKlenna Corporate Jet – February 15

MEREDITH CHECKED OUT of the hospital the next morning and, after meeting with the police, David drove her and Elliott to the airport. Kevin was already on the MacKlenna jet going through his preflight checklist. Thirty minutes after arriving, they were wheels up and on their way to Montgomery Winery for the celebration.

She and Elliott curled up on the sofa, holding each other. About an hour into the flight, she relaxed and started talking.

"I thought I was going to die. I've never been so scared in my life. Cancer scared me. Jonathan's stroke scared me. Daddy's heart attack scared me. But thinking I was going to die was the most horrible experience I've ever had. I felt cheated. I'd come through so much yet still had battles to fight, but nothing was more important than you and our baby. I wanted to live."

Elliott didn't say anything. He stroked her face, ran his fingers through her hair, and listened.

"When I found out I was pregnant, thoughts of the baby consumed me, and honestly, I thought more of the child than I did for my own life. I was willing to sacrifice myself to have this baby.

"It's not that I think less of the baby, but I want to live more than anything, and I'm willing to do whatever I have to do to survive. The only thing I won't do is have an abortion, but I'll have surgery, and if baby-safe chemo is recommended, I'll have it.

"I don't want to die. I know that now. I love you. I want to spend my life with you, and I'm ready to fight. No more surrendering."

His tears dropped on her cheek and mingled with hers.

"I know you don't like to talk about ghosts—"

"I feel differently about that now," he said with quiet, even words. "Cullen Montgomery came to the hospital."

Meredith sat up slightly. "You *saw* him?"

"And talked to him."

"Nooo," she said.

"Really," Elliott said. "He told me he did what he had come to do—protect ye. And he told me ye and the baby would be fine, and then he left."

"I talked to him, too, while I was in the barn. I died, but he told me I had to go back."

"He saved yer life. That's why he was here."

She seemed to think about that for a minute or two. Then she said, "In all the excitement, I forgot to tell you what I discovered. My great-great-great-great-grandmother's last name was MacKlenna. She was from Lexington. Do you know any other MacKlennas?"

"No, but maybe there's something in the journals in the library. We'll read them next time we're there."

"There's something else," she said. "I found the session record about your relative born on the wrong side of the sheets."

"Ye solved the mystery?"

She nodded. "Are you ready for this? It'll come as a shocker."

"I don't think there's anything ye can tell me that would surprise me."

"Try this out," she said, smiling. "James Thomas MacKlenna had an illegitimate son with the daughter of Gregory Fraser."

"Gregory Fraser lived in the late 1700s. He's my grandfather's grandfather," Elliott said. "Ye're telling me that I'm a direct descendant of Thomas MacKlenna?"

"If I've counted right," Meredith said, "he's your great-great-

great-great-great-grandfather, and the baby would have been the first Sean MacKlenna's half brother. That makes you the last male MacKlenna."

Elliott laughed a roll-on-the floor-in-tears laugh.

David stepped out of the flight deck. "What's so funny? Ye're shaking the damn plane."

Kevin hurried out of the galley. "What's up, Boss?"

Elliott continued to laugh. Finally, he stopped, but he couldn't contain himself and laughed some more. After several minutes, he said, "Well, lads. Ye're not going to believe this."

Chapter Eighty

Montgomery Winery – February 16 – The Gala

ELLIOTT STOOD IN front of the fireplace in the main room of the winery's welcome center. Above the mantel was a painting of a woman in her late sixties or early seventies. Hard to tell. Beautiful, with expressive green eyes with gold flakes. Everything about her from the tilt of her chin to her straight back and her petite hands folded in her lap spoke of her elegance. Although she had noticeable wrinkles around her eyes and mouth, she seemed timeless.

Meredith walked up behind him and snaked her arms through his. "She's beautiful, isn't she?"

Elliott squeezed her hand. "From what I've heard, ye're so much like her."

"I'll never have the guts she had." Meredith fingered the corner of the antique gilded frame, straightening it ever so slightly.

"Ah, my wee sweetheart," he said, shaking his head, "ye're filled to bustin' with guts."

"But to forge a path through the wilderness, that takes an extra special person."

Elliott checked the time. He had told the gang to be at the fireplace exactly at eight o'clock. They had one minute. "Ye've got yer own path to forge. Ye and the wee one."

Meredith opened her small purse and pulled out a mirror to

check her lipstick. She dabbed here and there. "Did you make the appointments?"

He caught his reflection in the glass covering the portrait and adjusted his bow tie. "Ye want to talk about it now?"

"Not particularly," she said, snapping her bag closed, "but I would like to know when surgery is scheduled."

"A week from Monday. Yer surgeon talked to the pulmonologist in Lexington. They thought ye should wait a week to ten days."

"You talked to the oncologist, too?"

He nodded.

"And the plastic surgeon and the obstetrician?"

"The entire team will be there."

"Thank you. I just…"

He kissed her. "I'm here. I'm not leaving ye. We'll do this together." But the next thing that had to be done required him to do it all by himself. His heart beat at an irregular rhythm.

"There ye are," Louise said, walking into the reception area. "Am I late?"

"No, we're gathering early so Elliott won't panic over missing the receiving line," Meredith said with a teasing lilt to her voice.

Elliott glowered at Louise.

"He told us to meet at the fireplace at eight." Kevin's voice echoed off the natural stone floor along the hallway in the winery's welcome center.

"Why are we meeting?" Lyles asked. "I'm ready to taste the wine."

Women's high heels and men's dress shoes clicked on the floor, announcing each step they took. "I don't know," Kevin said, "but we better not be late. You know how he gets."

David, Kevin, Evelyn, Dr. Lyles and his wife, Ted and Laurence, and Cate and Gregory rounded the corner.

"We're all here, Boss," Kevin said.

The photographer entered, following the group.

"Are we getting a picture of all of us? What a wonderful idea," Meredith said.

"Aye," Elliott said, "along with another picture that I hope brings a huge smile to yer face." He tapped his index finger twice against his leg.

David moved away from the group and extended his arm. "If everyone will step this way, we can get the photograph." David placed Louise and Evelyn on Elliott's left side, Cate and Gregory on Meredith's right side. Ted and Laurence stood next to the girls, and Dr. Lyles and his wife stood next to Cate and Gregory. David and Kevin stood at each end.

"Smile big," Louise said, giggling, her rings jingling.

"Damn rings. Remind me never to give her another one," Elliott said to Meredith under his breath.

She laughed. "Tonight, she can jingle every ring she has. Nothing will spoil this evening."

He pulled Meredith into his arms and kissed her to the tsking of everyone.

"Stop, Elliott. You'll mess up her makeup," Cate said.

Meredith patted at the corners of her lips and smiled.

After the photographer took several pictures, Elliott said, "Since we're all gathered, I thought I'd make this an even more special moment. Not to detract from *Cailean*'s debut, but to add to it." He turned and faced Meredith, knelt down on one knee, and took her hand in his.

An audible gasp went through the gathering.

"I have loved ye," Elliott said, "since the day I met ye. Today, I pledge to love and protect ye through sickness and in health as long as we both shall live. Will ye marry me?"

She went weak-kneed and dropped to the floor beside him. "Marry?"

"Me," he said.

She placed her hand on her belly. "Are you asking because of the baby?"

"I'm asking because ye are the love of my life, and I want to spend the rest of my days with ye." He slipped an Edwardian style, oval-cut, solitaire diamond ring on Meredith's finger.

"It's beautiful," she said.

He smiled. "It belonged to my mother."

Meredith started crying. "When I think of you, I'll always have a smile on my face. I love you."

"Is that a yes?" Elliott's voice was soft, hesitant, and he knew she could see fear in his eyes.

She cupped his cheek. "Aye, my wee sweetheart."

Chapter Eighty-One

Fraser House, the Highlands, Scotland – December 24

MEREDITH SAT CUDDLED up on the daybed in the master suite at Fraser House, reading the latest issue of *Wine Digest. Cailean* had been voted outstanding new wine of the year. According to the spreadsheets on her lap, sales had already surpassed Gregory's projections. Thinking back through the year, all her worries and fears had vanished in the arms of her Scotsman.

The gamble, adding a new wine to the portfolio, paid off tenfold. Her father would be proud of her. Elliott certainly was, but she couldn't take all the credit for the achievement. Gregory had done a masterful job with the marketing campaign, and as a result, she had promoted him to senior vice-president. Giving up control of a large portion of the business had been easier than she thought possible. She was even considering taking the company public.

Elliott entered the bedroom carrying their baby in his arms. "My wee son couldn't stay awake long enough to wrap yer Christmas gift, Mrs. Fraser."

"Did he burp? Did you change him?"

"Yes and yes, my wee sweetheart."

Anabelle and Tate trotted in behind Elliott, then stood guard at the sides of the bassinet. Tabor jumped up on the bed and watched from a perch created out of a stack of pillows.

Meredith laughed. "We should change her name to Queen Tabor."

"These two don't pay any attention to her," Elliott said. "She'd be queen of a realm of one."

When Elliott placed his son in the bassinet, the baby squeaked, making that special sleeping noise he'd made since birth. Both dogs' ears stood straight up. "Ah, ye wee laddie. Yer grandda would try to fix you with some oil."

Meredith stacked the magazine, documents, and Kit's journal on the table to make room for Elliott beside her. He picked a tie-back scarf up off the floor and kissed her head. "Put this on, hen. Ye'll catch a cold."

"It's hot and makes my head sweat. Being bald doesn't bother me." Months ago, the thought of losing her hair terrified her. But after it fell out, Elliott's constant reassurance of how beautiful she was convinced her that she didn't need hair to be loved or respected.

"I just worry about ye."

"It's eighty-five degrees in the room. I'm not going to get sick."

"Cullen lad needs to sleep in a warm room."

Meredith rolled her eyes. "He sleeps in a room with Jacobite ghosts. A cool temperature doesn't bother him." Thankfully, Elliott had a workout scheduled with Ted. As soon as he left the room, she'd lower the thermostat.

He handed her an envelope. "You have mail."

She flipped it over and read the return address. It was from her oncologist. She gave it back to him. "You read it."

"Are ye sure?"

"We already know the scan was clear. It's her recommendation for the next scan that I'm concerned about."

He ripped the envelope along its crease. The sharp sound of tearing paper fueled anxiety stirring in her belly. He withdrew a single sheet, unfolded it, then read silently.

For Meredith, time crawled in the room where only the sweet sound of her baby's breathing broke through the silence.

Then he said, "She recommends having another one in six months. If that one is clear, ye can wait twelve months for the next one."

"I was afraid she'd want me to come back in three. Now I feel comfortable scheduling the breast reconstruction."

"Ye don't have to have it."

"I know it doesn't matter to you, but it does to me." Many of the statements the girls had made about Elliott in those early days weren't true at all, but she had formed opinions of him that took time to correct.

He kissed her. "It's yer decision. I'm fine either way."

She wrapped her arms around his neck and kissed him back. "No woman could have asked for a more supportive and loving partner. You went above and beyond during the surgery, pregnancy, and chemo. I couldn't have gotten through it without you."

"It's all behind us now." He held up another letter. "This may tell us what's in our future."

She looked at the return address and gasped. "It's from the bankruptcy court. It's what you've been waiting for? Open it."

"Will ye be disappointed if the court doesn't approve the sale of the farm to me?"

"There's no reason the judge shouldn't approve it. You made a fair offer, and you are a MacKlenna."

He ripped open the envelope, pulled out a sheet of paper, and said, "Looks like we're breaking out another bottle of that expensive wine ye like. The sale's been approved." He tossed the letter up in the air.

"Shhh," Meredith said. "You'll wake the baby."

"James Cullen MacKlenna Fraser should wake up for this. MacKlenna Farm will be his inheritance one day."

"And I bet you already have mares lined up for Stormy."

Elliott's eyes sparkled. "He'll be our foundation sire."

"Kit would be thrilled, not only for Stormy's success but also for the winery's," Meredith said, glancing at the journal.

A knock on the bedroom door interrupted her.

"Come in," Elliott said.

Kevin stood in the doorway. "Hey, Boss. I thought I'd take

Cullen for a walk. It's a beautiful day. He needs fresh air."

"He just went down for a nap."

"Then I'll take him when he wakes up."

"Ted scheduled a yoga class for Meredith after my workout," Elliott said. "Ye can take him while I shower."

"I heard Ted registered you for a 10K in Edinburgh in the spring. I might have to run that one with you," Kevin said.

Elliott put his hands on his hips. "Why? Don't ye think I can do it?"

"Of course, you can. I just want to be there to watch."

"Ted signed me up for a fall marathon," Meredith said. "Will you run with me?"

"I'll do a half, not a full, but I'll do training runs with you," Kevin said.

Elliott slipped out of his trousers and into gym shorts. "Where's David? Have ye seen him?"

"Gone to meet his sister," Kevin said. "At least that's what he told Alice. She has a betting pool going that David's secretly meeting with an editor."

David had talked to Meredith about his book, and she had found an editor for him, but she wasn't going to tell Kevin or Elliott.

"Right. He told me that," Elliott said, "and I don't know anything about a book. If he's writing one, I hope I'm not in it. Have ye heard from Louise?"

"She and Evelyn will be here tomorrow," Kevin said. "And before you ask, the Mannings will be here tonight about seven o'clock. I told everyone you planned to entertain them at Christmas dinner with a story about a ruby brooch."

Meredith placed her hand on top of the journal, smiling. Kit had gone off to travel the world with her soul mate and live happily ever after. No one could ask for more.

Elliott stood and threw Meredith a kiss. "Since ye haven't mentioned Cate and Gregory, they either plan to surprise us or they aren't coming."

"Her doctor won't let her travel," Kevin said. "It's too close to her delivery date. I can't believe you didn't know that. You've got spies at Fraser House, MacKlenna Farm, and the winery. Nothing gets past you."

Elliott wiggled his eyebrows, and his eyes twinkled again. "The more things change, the more they stay the same." He grabbed his towel and sweatband. Before leaving the room, he gazed down one last time at his sleeping son.

"Merry Christmas, laddie. May God hold ye in the palm of His hand."

AUTHOR'S NOTES

After completion of *The Ruby Brooch,* I had intended to start writing *The Sapphire Brooch,* but a character in *The Ruby Brooch* demanded his story be told next. I am deeply indebted to the following people. Without them, *The Last MacKlenna* would have remained only an idea.

Special thanks to:

Horse experts: Dr. Frank Marcum, Robin Reed, Cathy Foster, J.M. Madden, and Lizbeth Selvig for answering dozens of questions about Thoroughbreds, medications, and injuries.

Members of Kentucky Romance Writers (Teresa Reasor, Amy Blackman Durham, and Kim Jacobs) who stayed up late one night and brainstormed the opening to this story.

Early readers: Amy Blakeman Durham, Angie Rueckert, Christoph Fischer, Deborah Taylor, Donna McDonald, Eryn LaPlant, Gail Morris, Joan Childs, Judith Natelli McLaughlin, Shirl Deems, Shirli de Saye, Theresa Snyder, Tahalia Newland, Maria Lenartowicz whose comments and suggestions were invaluable.

Mark Wilson of Edinburgh, Scotland, for keeping me supplied with Scottish words and for his videotaped reading of the first chapter so I could hear how the story sounded with a Scottish accent.

Kendall-Jackson personnel for an incredible afternoon at the winery and for answering dozens of questions about wine.

Paul Salvette with BB eBooks for formatting assistance.

My sisters-in-law Rhonda Jean McMillin Lowry, Donna Conley Lowry, and the late Sally Manning Lowry for sharing their breast cancer stories, and to my friends Sandy Hippe and Becky Hicks for sharing theirs.

My daughters Lorie Logan and Lynn Hicks whose belief in me is astounding, and my granddaughter, Charlotte, who proudly announced to a teacher that both of her grandmothers had run a marathon and published a book.

And finally, my special thanks to Ken Muse, M.D., for his medical advice, love, support, and taking me to Edinburgh this summer. This story couldn't have been finished without him.

My love and thanks to all for being a part of this three-year journey.

THE CELTIC BROOCH SERIES

THE RUBY BROOCH (Book 1)
Kitherina MacKlenna and Cullen Montgomery's love story

THE LAST MACKLENNA (Book 2 – not a time travel story)
Meredith Montgomery and Elliott Fraser's love story

THE SAPPHIRE BROOCH (Book 3)
Charlotte Mallory and Braham McCabe's love story

THE EMERALD BROOCH (Book 4)
Kenzie Wallis-Manning and David McBain's love story

THE BROKEN BROOCH (Book 5 – not a time travel story)
JL O'Grady and Kevin Allen's love story

THE THREE BROOCHES (Book 6)
A reunion with Kit and Cullen Montgomery

THE DIAMOND BROOCH (Book 7)
Jack Mallory and Amy Spalding's love story

THE AMBER BROOCH (Book 8)
Amber Kelly and Daniel Grant's love story
Olivia Kelly and Connor O'Grady's love story

THE PEARL BROOCH (Book 9)
Sophia Orsini and Pete Parrino's love story

THE TOPAZ BROOCH (Book 10)
Wilhelmina "Billie" Penelope Malone and Rick O'Grady's love story

THE SUNSTONE BROOCH (Book 11)
Ensley MacWilliam Andrews and Austin O'Grady

There are many more Brooch Books to come.
To read about the next few books, visit
www.katherinellogan.com/whats-next-2

ABOUT THE AUTHOR

Author Katherine Lowry Logan couples her psychology degree with lots of hands-on research when creating new settings and characters for her blockbuster Celtic Brooch series.

These cross-genre stories have elements of time travel, sci-fi, fantasy adventure, mystery, suspense, historical, and romance and focus on events in American history.

A few of her favorite research adventures include:

- attending the Battle of Cedar Creek reenactment and visiting Civil War sites in Richmond, Virginia (*Sapphire Brooch*),
- riding in a B-17 Flying Fortress bomber, and visiting Bletchley Park and the beaches at Normandy (*Emerald Brooch*),
- research in Paris, France, and Florence, Italy, with an art lesson in Florence (*Pearl Brooch*),
- a tour of New York's Yankee Stadium and several hours with their historian (*Diamond Brooch*),
- wine tours in Napa (*The Last MacKlenna*),
- and following the Oregon Trail for the first book in the series (*Ruby Brooch*).

Katherine is the mother of two daughters and grandmother of five—Charlotte, Lincoln, James Cullen, Henry, and Meredith. She is also a marathoner and lives in Lexington, Kentucky, with her fluffy Goldendoodle, Maddie the Marauder.

Website
www.katherinellogan.com

Facebook
facebook.com/katherine.l.logan

Twitter
twitter.com/KathyLLogan

I'm A Runner (Runner's World Magazine Interview)
www.runnersworld.com/celebrity-runners/im-a-runner-katherine-lowry-logan

If you would like to receive notification of future releases sign up today at KatherineLLogan.com or

send an email to KatherineLLogan@gmail.com and put "New Release" in the subject line. And if you are on Facebook, join the Celtic Brooch Series for ongoing book and character discussions.

* * *

Made in the USA
Monee, IL
09 December 2021